"EXPI… OUTRAGE, VAYLE."

"I could not begin to try. I have no idea how this female"—he glared so contemptuously at Angel that her soul seemed to shrivel—"got into my bed."

Dear God, could he be right? For the first time, Angel noticed that the bed hangings were beige tapestry, not the green silk of the bed she had gone to sleep in. Was she in *his* bed? Certainly she was not in her own.

His voice was ominous. "Come, my angel from Hell, why don't you tell me and our audience how you happen to be in my bed?"

"I do not know."

Praise for Marlene Suson's

THE LILY AND THE HAWK

"Glitters with wit and passion . . .
A sensual, fast-paced read."
Amanda Quick

"An enchanting tale"
Rendezvous

"Gentle, tender, witty . . .
Engaging and refreshing"
Romantic Times

Other Avon Romances by
Marlene Suson

THE LILY AND THE HAWK

Other **AVON ROMANCES**
THE HEART AND THE HEATHER *by Nancy Richards-Akers*
MY LADY PIRATE *by Danelle Harmon*
MIDNIGHT RAIN *by Elizabeth Turner*
NIGHT SONG *by Beverly Jenkins*
THE SAVAGE *by Nicole Jordan*
SWEET SPANISH BRIDE *by Donna Whitfield*
WILD FLOWER *by Donna Stephens*

Coming Soon
ANYTHING FOR LOVE *by Connie Brockway*
TEMPT A LADY *by Susan Weldon*

And Don't Miss These
ROMANTIC TREASURES
from Avon Books
RUNAWAY BRIDE *by Deborah Morgan*
LORD OF THUNDER *by Emma Merritt*
WITH ONE LOOK *by Jennifer Horsman*

AVON BOOKS NEW YORK

DEVIL'S ANGEL is an original publication of Avon Books. This work has never before appeared in book form. This work is a novel. Any similarity to actual persons or events is purely coincidental.

AVON BOOKS
A division of
The Hearst Corporation
1350 Avenue of the Americas
New York, New York 10019

Inside cover author photo by Debbi De Mont
Published by arrangement with the author
Library of Congress Catalog Card Number: 94-94078
ISBN: 0-380-77613-8

First Avon Books Printing: September 1994

AVON TRADEMARK REG. U.S. PAT. OFF. AND IN OTHER COUNTRIES, MARCA REGISTRADA. HECHO EN U.S.A.

Printed in the U.S.A.

RA 10 9 8 7 6 5 4 3 2 1

To Dick
For the humor, support, and love that sustain me.

Chapter 1

England, June 1690

He was being followed.

His instincts honed by years of danger on the battlefield and off, Lucian Sandford, the Earl of Vayle, hastily stepped off the narrow path that meandered through a woods thick with ash, oak, and hazel.

Grabbing the low branch of an oak, Lucian hauled himself up into the tree. From this vantage, he peered through the screen of green leaves. Some forty yards back along the narrow path, he sighted a woman walking purposefully toward him, the black of her gown standing out against the foliage. He could not make out her face, but she was alone.

A lady looking for a little amorous diversion perhaps? He was used to such unsolicited feminine interest. Nonetheless, he was startled that one of Viscount Bloomfield's female guests was so audacious she would seek Lucian out during the celebration of his betrothal to their host's daughter Kitty.

At another time and place, he might have welcomed the unknown woman's boldness.

But not today. He wanted to be alone to savor his betrothal. His marriage to Bloomfield's daughter would mark the ultimate triumph in his secret campaign. It had taken him fourteen years, but the vindication he had pursued for so long would, with his marriage, be his at last. He was not about to jeopardize it with the silly female who was following him.

Lucian knew just how to ensure his escape from her.

With a crafty smile, he dropped from the tree and strode rapidly down the slope until he reached a creek, swift and deep, that flowed through the wood.

No bridge spanned it, but near its edge a rope dangled from a sturdy branch of an oak.

Lucian seized the rope, ran up the slope, then turned, and took a running leap.

The rope swung out over the wild, tumbling water. He looked down and caught his breath. The furious torrent beneath him was a daunting sight even to a man who had performed such a maneuver many times.

Then the rope carried him over the opposite bank and he dropped onto terra firma.

Lucian concealed himself behind a wide hazel bush, where he could observe the lady's approach without her seeing him.

When she came into view, he frowned in surprise. God's oath, he had not even been introduced to the female, although he had overheard someone say that she was the sister of that scoundrel Horace Crowe.

Lucian knew Horace and his father, Sir Rupert Crowe, mostly by reputation. That was enough to discourage any desire to become better acquainted with them.

Or with any of their relatives.

Her black gown was hopelessly plain and unfashionable. Her hair was so well hidden beneath an unbecoming cap that he could not even ascertain its color. At this distance, she had the look of a timid, dried-up spinster.

Thank God he had outwitted her pursuit of him. He gleefully anticipated her frustration when she saw the churning creek with no bridge across it and realized that she was stymied.

But when she reached the water, she gathered up the skirts of her gown, revealing to Lucian's startled gaze one of the shapeliest pair of legs and trim ankles that he had ever been privileged to see. Who would have thought that such beauty could be hidden beneath that sorry dress.

He was so bemused by the charming sight that he paid no heed to what she was about until she began to run.

Only then did he realize that she had knotted her skirts

around her thighs and grabbed the rope suspended from the oak.

Lucian gasped. Surely she did not mean to cross the creek as he had!

Her feet lifted off the ground.

He could not believe that a female would dare to cross *any* creek in such a manner, but especially one that was a raging torrent as this was.

She was damned eager for his attention, Lucian thought wryly. This one would not be easily discouraged.

Yet he was forced to applaud her courage even as he cursed her foolhardiness. How wrong he'd been to think her timid.

She lacked the weight and speed he had had to propel the rope. For one terrifying moment, he thought that its momentum would not carry her to the opposite bank and she would be left dangling over the foaming silver water beneath her.

He was already stripping off his coat, preparing to leap into the stream to rescue the little fool should she panic and let go of the rope.

But she did not. Instead, to his astonishment, a trill of exhilarated laughter bubbled from her.

She was something else again, Lucian thought with grudging admiration.

The makeshift knot she had tied in her skirts came undone, and they fell about her ankles. The rope swung with heart-stopping slowness until she was finally over the bank, her feet dangling several inches above the ground. She was looking down so he could not see her face.

Lucian stepped from behind the hazel bush and grabbed her as she dropped from the rope. She squeaked in surprise, and her head bobbed up. She had a very ordinary nose and mouth.

Her eyes seemed huge in the delicate oval of her face. They were a rich, startling shade of blue as bright and clear as the English sky on a rare summer day when not a cloud marred it. Her dark brows and lashes, long and curling, offered a startling contrast to her complexion that was as fresh and fair as virgin snow.

"Are you out of your mind trying such a dangerous stunt as that?" he demanded as he set her on the ground.

She was petite, not even coming to his shoulder, but then he was an exceptionally tall man.

Clearly unchastened, she scoffed, "Oh, fie, it's not dangerous." Her voice had a lovely, musical cadence to it that he found most pleasing. "I've used that rope to cross the creek many times. It is great fun."

Suddenly she smiled at him. Lucian was amazed by the transformation it wrought in her. The smile embraced not merely her mouth but her entire face. Her eyes sparkled with vitality and laughter.

It was the most charming smile he had ever seen, and his body responded to it in a way that startled him.

A few wisps of hair, as dark as her brows, had escaped from her matronly cap and fluttered around her face. Despite the cap, she was much younger than he had thought. Perhaps seventeen or eighteen. Indeed, she looked to be such a young innocent that Lucian was suddenly certain his suspicion must have been wrong. He could not have been her quarry after all.

Nor did he believe that blackguard Rupert Crowe could possibly have fathered this delightful little elf.

Lucian was angry, though, that she had taken the risk she had over the treacherous stream.

"Why did you cross the creek like that?"

"I was following you," she confessed, her gaze meeting his without evasion or coyness, "because I wanted to approach you when no one else could observe us."

He could think of only one reason for wanting such privacy. That and her candor nonplussed him. Apparently he had been mistaken to judge her too young and innocent to be playing amorous games. Well, he thought with cynical amusement, if the bold chit wanted to play with him, who was he to argue with her.

"I am only too happy to oblige you," he told her sardonically, catching her face in his hands.

Lucian's mouth descended upon hers. He could not identify her perfume, but he found the fresh, clean scent that clung to her startlingly erotic. Her lips were warm and supple against his, and he was surprised at how much he liked the taste of them. Her mouth acquiesced to his, and he felt the tremor of response in her.

Aroused despite himself, he tried to deepen the kiss, but her lips instantly stiffened and remained tightly closed against his invasion.

Damn, but he despised teases who promised, then reneged! He would teach this green girl that she should not be playing a sophisticated woman's game. His mouth became hard and punishing.

Belatedly she grabbed at his wrists trying to free her face from his grip. When that failed, she delivered such a flurry of painful kicks to his shins that he let her go.

"You little hellcat," he growled with a glare that had never failed to reduce the officers and soldiers who had served under his command to abject terror.

Not only was she unfazed, but she actually seemed oblivious to it. Her pluck astonished him as much as her conduct did.

"How dare you kick me like that?" he demanded.

Blue fire blazed in her eyes. "How dare *you* kiss me like that?"

Lucian's lip curled contemptuously. "I assumed a girl as bold as you would prefer to get down immediately to the purpose of your following me."

She stared at him as though he were speaking in a foreign tongue. "I do not comprehend your meaning. Nor do I understand how you could kiss *me* when you are betrothed to Kitty!" Her voice quavered with indignation and reproach.

How could he indeed? "Because you wanted me to kiss you," he snapped. "Don't deny it."

She looked at him as though he were a bedlamite. "I do deny it!" she protested. "Why ever would you think that?"

Her ire was clearly not feigned. It belatedly occurred to him that she was indeed as innocent as he had first thought her, that her sudden resistance to his kiss sprang from that, not from any coquettish intent. He said softly, "You have never been kissed by a man before, have you?"

"Oh," she exclaimed in surprise, "how did you know?"

"You do not have the faintest idea how to do it."

"Is there a proper way?" she inquired naively.

Amused, he asked, "Shall I teach you?"

"No. I do not think I like your kiss."

"I did not mean for you to like it," he said brusquely. He had meant to teach her a lesson, so why did her answer disgruntle him?

She frowned. "I don't understand."

"I'm glad you don't." She looked so innocent and perplexed that Lucian felt like a cad. "Why the devil were you following me?"

"To warn you."

"About what? And why would you want to warn me about anything when you have never even met me?"

"Because you are Kitty's betrothed. You see I am—"

"I know who you are—Horace Crowe's sister," Lucian interrupted impatiently. "And I must tell you that he is no friend of mine. Indeed, I despise the little fop."

To his astonishment, she beamed at him. Once again his perverse anatomy reacted disconcertingly to her dazzling smile.

"I thought when I saw you that you would be a man of excellent judgment. Horace is a dreadful little weasel, is he not?"

It was such an apt description of him that Lucian nearly laughed aloud. He murmured dryly, "Your familial affection overwhelms me."

"Indeed, it is Horace that I have come to warn you about. He and Sir Rupert mean to do you and Kitty evil."

Lucian scarcely knew the Crowes, and he could conceive of no reason why they would want to do him evil. But from what he had heard of them, he would put nothing past them either.

Sir Rupert was cunning and corrupt. As a young man, he had squandered his large inheritance, then tried to recoup by abducting an unwilling young heiress and forcing her to marry him. Her money, too, was soon gone.

It was said that Rupert, who could exert considerable charm when it suited his purpose, had then turned to seducing rich, aging dowagers and relieving them of sizable portions of their wealth. Now he was rumored to be the owner of a London gambling hell that preyed upon halflings and rustics from the country.

Rupert was reputed to be as shrewd as he was unscrupulous, but Horace, his son by the unfortunate heiress, was said to lack even that advantage.

"Kitty is my dear friend," the girl said earnestly. "I cannot let the Crowes succeed."

"What evil do they intend to do us?"

"They mean to prevent you from marrying Kitty so that Horace may do so."

Chapter 2

Angel Winter stared up at the glowering giant before her. She could not blame the earl of Vayle for being furious at the Crowes' plot, but she was having difficulty comprehending what he was saying. In his anger, he had reverted to a language, full of odd-sounding words, that she had never heard before.

She wondered whether it could be Dutch.

After all, Lord Vayle had lived in Holland. That was one reason why he was reputed to be so close to England's new king, William of Orange, and Queen Mary.

Although Angel prided herself on not being a faintheart, Lord Vayle was an intimidating figure, scowling as though she were his enemy instead of trying to help him and Kitty.

He looked more savage than civilized. His face was strong and sharply etched with an aristocratic nose, a hard jaw, and a mouth that had a cynical curve to it. Light, piercing eyes, the color of hammered silver, contrasted sharply with his bronzed skin. His hair, which he wore in a queue, was thick and black. So were the flaring brows that gave a roguish cast to his face.

He looked more like a devil than an earl.

No wonder they called him Lord Lucifer behind his back.

No other man had ever raised the strange, fluttering unease in Angel that he did. Particularly when he touched her.

She had initially felt this odd response when he had grabbed her as she had dropped from the rope and she had seen his hard, silver eyes.

Then, when he had first kissed her, she had been positively shaken by the sensation curling within her. She ran her tongue over her lips, unconsciously savoring the lingering taste of him.

Angel had told him she did not think that she liked his kiss, but she had not been entirely truthful. She had liked it very much until, for some unfathomable reason, she seemed to have angered him, and his mouth had turned punishing.

Was it because she did not know the proper way to kiss?

Aye, she decided, that must have been it.

He finished his indecipherable tirade, and she inquired curiously, "Is that Dutch you are speaking?"

He looked at her as if *she* were the one who was speaking a foreign language. "What?" he asked blankly.

"I did not recognize the words you were using. I thought that they must be Dutch."

To her surprise, a dull flush spread across his cheeks. He opened his mouth, closed it, then finally said, "Aye, I frequently resort to—er, Dutch when I am angry."

He sounded very grave, but his lips were twitching as though he were amused by something.

"Now, tell me, young Mistress Crowe, how—"

"My name is Winter, not Crowe!" Angel interrupted vehemently. "That dreadful Sir Rupert is my stepfather, not my father."

"Ah-ha, I was right!" He smiled at her in a way that made the fluttering sensation return stronger than ever, even though he was not even touching her.

Angel was disconcerted to discover how sinfully handsome he looked when the hard, angry lines of his face relaxed in humor. "Right about what?"

"That Crowe could not have fathered you, Miss Winter."

Actually, she was Lady Angela Winter, but before she could correct him, he said with a grin that was so engaging her heart skipped, "I offer you my sincere condolences on your mother's unfortunate choice of a husband."

She laughed aloud at that. Suddenly she found herself liking him very much.

"You have a lovely laugh."

Normally Angel paid no heed to compliments, but for some reason his made her blush with pleasure. She sensed that he was not a man who often paid them.

"Whatever possessed your mama to marry Crowe?"

"I do not know." Angel could not conceive how any woman could desert a man as fine and good as her father and later marry a scoundrel like Sir Rupert. But then Angel had not seen her mother since she had run off with one of her lovers when her daughter was four.

"How do the Crowes plan to stop me from wedding Kitty?"

"Unfortunately, my lord, I do not know that. I only overheard part of their conversation. It is some sort of trap that Horace says will make the marriage impossible. They plan to spring it on you during this celebration of your betrothal. You must be on your guard."

"Can you tell me no more than that?" He was scowling at her again. He sounded so disappointed that Angel felt as though she had failed him.

"No, that is all I know. I am sorry."

The high-pitched trill of a goldcrest came from a nearby tree, and Angel turned toward the sound. She quickly located the bird's distinctive bright yellow crest bordered in black. The shadows were deepening, reminding her that it was growing late.

She smiled at Lord Vayle. "I pray that you will be able to outwit the Crowes. Now that I have warned you, I must go back before they miss me and begin asking questions I do not want to answer."

Angel reached for a rope dangling from an oak. It was a twin to the one across the stream that she had ridden over.

Her companion's hand caught hers. The fluttering sensation that had plagued her earlier began anew.

"Do not go back that way!"

"Why not?" The goldcrest took wing from its perch on the tree branch and soared upward. Angel, pulling her hand from Lord Vayle's, gestured toward the bird. "I feel as free as it when I fly over the water on the rope."

He frowned at her. "If God had meant man—or woman—to fly, he would have given us wings."

"Nonsense, God means us to devise our own way to fly," she retorted. "I am convinced that we are capable of it. Did you know that Leonardo da Vinci made models of craft that would enable man to do so?"

"But none of them actually succeeded, did they?"

"No, but Papa said that was only because the proper means of propulsion has not yet been invented."

Lord Vayle was staring at her with a strange expression. Angel pulled her hand from his grasp and reached again for the rope.

"Please don't," he said quietly. "It is too dangerous."

"Oh, fie," she exclaimed impatiently, but she was touched by his concern for her. No one had worried about her since Papa had died six months ago in a riding accident. "You intend to use this rope to go back, do you not?"

"Aye, but—"

"It is as safe for me as it is for you. I apprehend you are one of those stuffy men who think all females are helpless. Well, you are wrong! Why are you laughing?"

"I have been called a great many things by women, but stuffy was never among them." A teasing light danced in his silver eyes.

"Oh," she exclaimed, instantly interested, "what did they call you?"

His mouth curved in amusement. "I don't think you would understand."

When she started to protest, he said hastily, "Actually, some of them were in—er, Dutch."

"You could translate them for me," she suggested.

"I think not," he said dryly.

Angel reached for the rope again, and this time he did not try to stop her. She belatedly realized that she had forgotten to tie up her skirts, but modesty prohibited her from doing so while he was watching. "Please turn your back, my lord," she said primly.

His sudden, wicked grin sent a tremor of excitement through her. "Must I?"

"You are a gentleman, are you not?"

"Only occasionally." His grin widened. "Has no one warned you that my nickname is Lord Lucifer."

She blinked in surprise that he could smile about it. "Does it not bother you to be called that?"

He shrugged carelessly. "Why should it? It is even deserved at times."

Angel decided that he was merely trying to shock her, and she was determined not to let him know he had succeeded. She asked coolly, "Are you telling me that you refuse to turn your back?"

His grin reminded her of his nickname, but then he presented his broad back to her. "You shame me into it."

"You see, you are better than you thought," she retorted as she hastily tied up her skirts.

Then she grabbed the rope and executed her unorthodox departure.

As soon as the girl's feet left the ground, Lucian turned to watch her. He wanted to make certain she made it safely across the water, but he also welcomed the chance it offered him to see her lovely legs again.

When she landed on the other side of the creek and saw him watching her, she cried, "You broke your word!"

"I did not! You asked me to turn my back, and I did. You did not tell me how long I must keep it turned."

Lucian watched her until she disappeared into the wood, then seated himself on the stump of a felled oak. He would wait fifteen minutes before he crossed the creek, to make certain that she had plenty of time to return to the house.

If he followed her too quickly, it might arouse suspicion that they had been together. Rarely had he given much thought to a female's reputation, but she was such a delightful innocent that he was loath to cause the smallest blight on hers.

He wondered what plot her step-relatives had concocted. Lucian had been furious when she had told him. By God, no one, least of all conniving blackguards like the Crowes, were going to rob him of the triumph that his marriage to Bloomfield's daughter represented. Now that his temper had cooled, however, he was not overly concerned. He would outwit them.

Lucian admired the Winter girl's courage in warning him. If the Crowes were to learn she had done so, he shuddered to think what they might do to her. Yet the hoyden apparently feared them no more than she did flying across a raging creek on a rope.

She was a beguiling combination of innocence, bravery, and intelligence. He had never before met a female who was aware of Leonardo's models, and here was one who even believed human flight was feasible.

When Lucian returned to Lord Bloomfield's house, it was nearly time for him to go riding with his friend David Inge. Hurrying along the hall toward his room where he was to meet David, he noticed one of the doors was ajar. As he approached it, it opened suddenly, and a buxom female, her long black hair cascading about her shoulders, emerged.

Her hips swinging provocatively, she stepped toward him with a seductive smile on her full lips. There was no mistaking the invitation in her dark eyes and very little doubt that this encounter could be accidental.

It seemed to be his day for eager females, Lucian thought cynically.

Except, he reminded himself, Miss Winter had not been eager, merely naive.

Something this female clearly was not. No innocent walked as she did nor wore a red satinisco gown cut so low it barely confined her very large breasts.

Ignoring her silent invitation, Lucian went into his room and would have shut the door behind him had she not hastily thrust herself across the threshold.

"My lord," she began with the smile of a woman certain of her charms.

Angered by her confidence that she could captivate him, he pointed out coldly, "I did not invite you in."

Undeterred, she crooned, "But if you do, I shall make you very happy, if you take my meaning."

"I do, and I am not interested."

An angry gasp escaped her. Clearly, she was unused to

being refused. Lucian watched in amusement as she struggled to contain her temper. Finally she succeeded, then fixed a provocative smile on her lips. "You do not know what you are missing, my lord."

"Nor do I care to find out."

"But we'll have such a good time together. Maude here knows how to treat you like a king."

Her persistence in the face of his rude rejection puzzled him. "Whose room was that and what were you doing in it?" Lucian demanded suspiciously.

" 'Tis my lady's room," she cried, flushing indignantly at the implication of his words. "I am her maid."

Lucian had never known a lady to employ a maid who wore such a vulgar, revealing dress. The slut must pick up extra coin by servicing men at house parties her mistress attended.

"Perhaps I should come back later," David Inge said from the doorway.

"No," Lucian replied, thankful for his friend's appearance. "Maid Maude is just leaving."

She glared at both men, then swept from the room.

David, who had stepped back from the doorway to let her pass, came in. Sparely built, he walked with a slight limp, a permanent reminder of the severe wound that had ended his military career. Once, some years ago, he had saved Lucian's life in battle at great risk to his own, and Lucian had subsequently returned the favor twice.

"I fear your eyesight is failing, Lucian," David said wryly. "Maude is no maid."

"Not maid as in maiden; maid as in servant. God's oath, but she is the boldest, most determined female I have encountered in a long time."

"I find that hard to believe," David said with a grin.

Lucian was pleased to see the laughter in his friend's clear, gray eyes. David was normally the most amiable and amusing of companions, but lately he had been grave and quiet. Although Lucian had not pried, he wondered what was troubling him.

David said, "I recall that female you encountered only a fortnight ago outside Whitehall."

"Your memory is too good!" Lucian grumbled. "Let us go riding. I want to see Sommerstone."

Angel had taken refuge in Lord Bloomfield's deserted library, where she sat with a copy of *The Man in the Moone* open before her.

When she had returned to the house after seeing Lord Vayle, she had been loath to go to her room, fearing that Maude, the dreadful maid the Crowes had foisted on her, would be there.

Angel had objected strenuously to Maude accompanying her to Fernhill, Lord Bloomfield's country estate. She had argued that she had never had a maid before and did not need one now. The Crowes had insisted, however, that no lady would dream of attending a country house party without a maid in attendance.

Since Angel had never been to such a gathering before and had no idea what was customary, she could not argue with them.

The library was a small room, for her host was not a bookish man. His modest collection was a disappointment to Angel, used to her late papa's far superior library at Belle Haven.

The two men's country estates were adjacent to each other, and their daughters, as children, had been good friends. But sixteen months ago, Lord Bloomfield had suddenly decreed that Kitty and her mother must accompany him for a lengthy stay in London. Their departure had been particularly painful to Angel because it had come only three weeks after the death of Angel's brother Charles. Angel had not seen Kitty since then, and she had missed both her late brother and her friend dreadfully.

At first, Kitty had written often, but then her letters had become less and less frequent until they had stopped altogether. Two parallel themes had run through her final several letters: her increasing absorption with the London social whirl and her love for David Inge. In her final note five months ago, she confided that she planned to marry him. Her papa did not approve of the match, but Kitty was certain she could change his mind.

With each passing week, Angel had expected to hear that Kitty was officially betrothed, but no word came until a fortnight ago.

And then the betrothal was to the Earl of Vayle, not Mr. Inge. The announcement was accompanied by news that the Bloomfields were returning briefly to Fernhill for tonight's grand party celebrating the betrothal.

Timms, Fernhill's butler, whom Angel had known since she was a child, appeared at the door. "Lady Angela, Miss Kitty was looking for you. She is in her bedchamber."

Angel hurried up to Kitty's room, where she hardly recognized the vision of loveliness that greeted her. Kitty had left Fernhill a coltish girl and returned a beautiful young woman with soft, doe-shaped brown eyes and a full, pouting mouth. Golden blond hair in charming ringlets framed her heart-shaped face.

"Oh, Kitty, I am so glad to see you," Angel exclaimed, hugging her friend warmly. "I have missed you so."

When they drew apart, she looked admiringly at Kitty's russet silk gown with its open overskirt that revealed an elaborately embroidered and pleated cream underskirt. Angel suddenly felt hopelessly dowdy in her plain black dress that had been made over from one of her mother's long-ago castoffs.

"How pretty your gown is, Kitty."

"Not nearly as pretty as some of my other new ones. I'll show you." She led Angel into her dressing room, crowded with costly gowns in silk, velvet, and satin.

Angel's papa had ridiculed society's trappings, especially fashion, which he had mocked as the silly concern of idle, frivolous minds. He had raised his daughter to pay no heed to clothes, but Angel loved pretty things, and she could not help feeling a little envious as she looked at Kitty's finery.

Kitty said, "My papa has been so generous to me since my betrothal. He has not complained about a single one of my purchases."

Certainly she had given Lord Bloomfield much to complain about.

"Papa is so pleased and proud that I have captured

Vayle. You have no notion how many gorgeous females were dangling after him, even the Duke of Carlyle's daughter. They are all so envious of me." Kitty was clearly as proud of her achievement as her papa was. "My betrothed is one of the most powerful men in the realm."

"But do you love him?" Angel asked, thinking of Kitty's letters, in which she had professed to adore David Inge.

"What a silly question!" she responded in an unnaturally high tone. "Lord Vayle is the trusted confidant of King William and Queen Mary. As his wife, I shall be a member of the royal inner circle. And I shall be a countess after all."

The sudden triumph in Kitty's voice startled Angel as much as her words. "What do you mean 'after all'?"

Kitty's beautiful cheeks colored. "I . . . I have always dreamed of being a countess, like my sister Anne is."

She sounded as though being a countess with a powerful husband who moved in royal circles was all that she cared about.

"What of David Inge?" Angel asked. "You wrote me that you had agreed to marry him."

"That . . ." Kitty's voice faltered. For an instant she looked so unhappy that Angel thought she might burst into tears. Then her expression hardened in determination. "That was before I met Lord Vayle. Papa said I would have been wasting myself on David. And he is right," she added in a shrilly defensive voice. "It is my duty to myself and my family to make the best marriage I can."

She sounded as though she were trying to convince herself as well as Angel.

Recalling sadly the glowing things Kitty had written about David, Angel said, "I should like to have met Mr. Inge."

"You can," Kitty said unhappily. "He is here. Lord Vayle is his friend and insisted that he be invited. I could not believe he would come, but Mama says he has."

"I fear that you have two other guests that you did not expect," Angel said in embarrassment.

The Crowes had insisted upon bringing Angel, the only

one of them invited to the party celebrating Kitty's betrothal, to Fernhill. Upon their arrival, there had been a humiliating scene in which the Crowes had said that unless they were allowed to stay, Angel must leave too.

Lord Bloomfield would have ejected all three of them had his wife not interceded on Angel's behalf. Kind Lady Bloomfield had always been very fond of Angel, and she would not allow her to be turned away even though it meant putting up with the Crowes.

"Who are they?" Kitty asked.

"My stepfather, Rupert Crowe, and his son, Horace."

Kitty's pretty face twisted in revulsion. "Oh, no! Not that horrid little toad, Horace Crowe," she wailed. "I despise him. He has made such a nuisance of himself to me."

"Horace confided to me that he is madly in love with you." Something about the peculiar light in Horace's eyes when he had talked of Kitty had made Angel uneasy.

Kitty's lip curled scornfully. "As if I would have anything to do with him! I cannot tolerate him, but the more I try to discourage him, the more determined he seems to become. Please, do not talk about him to me. I cannot stand to hear his name."

Angel did not want to upset Kitty even more by telling her about the Crowes' plot. She had warned Lord Vayle, and surely he would be more than a match for the Crowes.

From high on a ridge overlooking Sommerstone, Lucian looked down at it in disappointment. This was the first time that he had actually seen the estate that he had worked for the past fourteen years to acquire. He reminded himself it was not Sommerstone itself but what it represented that was important.

Its house was smaller than he had expected, an undistinguished hodgepodge of Gothic, Tudor, and Dutch architectural styles. Lucian had anticipated something grander. Nor did he approve of where the house had been placed at the bottom of a small dale. He would have built it on the knoll opposite him.

David Inge asked, "What do you think of it?

"I confess I am not impressed."

"Bloomfield would be happy to keep it," David said. "Indeed, I am surprised he agreed to give it to you in the marriage settlement. I once heard him say he would never part with it."

"That was before he made the mistake of backing the wrong king, siding with James against William," Lucian said cynically. "Since James was deposed a year and a half ago, Bloomfield has been desperately trying to work his way into King William's good graces. He hopes I will be the key to his escaping the royal displeasure. He was so eager for me to wed Kitty that he agreed to everything I wanted in the marriage settlement."

"Your bride is as eager as her father." The sour, bitter edge to David's voice puzzled Lucian.

"I do not flatter myself that Kitty cares so much for me as she does for my power and connection with the king and queen," Lucian said. David was the one person on earth besides Selina to whom he would speak so bluntly.

"Does that not disturb you?"

"Why should it?" Lucian did not love Kitty, and he could hardly demand a higher standard of her than of himself.

He had no romantic illusions about marriage. Respect, deference, and, above all, obedience were what he required from his wife. Kitty would give him all three. She was awed and a little afraid of him.

"As you well know," Lucian said, "a man in my position does not marry for love but for a prestigious alliance, estates, and an heir of suitably impressive bloodlines. With Kitty, I will have all three."

Plus vindication, the most important reason of all, but Lucian would not tell even David that. Instead he confided, "I hear on good authority that Rupert and Horace Crowe hope to prevent my marriage to Kitty."

"Odd's fish, why?" David sounded as startled as Lucian had been.

"So Horace can wed her himself."

"That bloody little rascal!" David exploded with uncharacteristic ferocity. "If there is some devious, underhanded way of achieving that, the Crowes will do it. You cannot let that happen."

"I do not intend to," Lucian said calmly. "Why would Horace aspire to marry Kitty?"

"It is common knowledge that he is infatuated with her," David said. "He has been a terrible bother to her."

Lucian frowned. Kitty had said nothing to him about Horace.

"He is also desperate to win for himself the acceptance his father long ago forfeited in society," David continued. "Marriage to Kitty would help him do that. He fancies himself one of the beaux, aping their affectations of manner and dress, but I know of no one who likes him except his father. I doubt that Rupert ever cared for another human being in his life, but oddly he dotes on his son."

"Horace will not get what he wants this time," Lucian said. "Shall we ride back?"

"First, let me show you one of the handsomest houses in Berkshire. It was designed by Inigo Jones. There is an excellent view of it from that high point on the ridge."

David turned his horse in that direction, and Lucian followed him on his big bay.

When they reached the spot, Lucian's breath caught at the sight of the great house that graced the hilltop in the distance. Its elegant, classical facade, with a pillared portico and balustraded roof, was unified and symmetrical, uninterrupted by the confusion of turrets, towers, bays, and gables that in his view marred so much English architecture.

The house was set in a casual park that had none of the formal rigidity still prevalent in England.

His soldier's eye, so used to measuring defenses at a glance, automatically noted the estate's weaknesses. A high wall had been installed around the perimeter of the park, but it would be easy enough for an agile man to defeat it.

Although Lucian had never seen the house before except in a drawing, he said instantly, "It is Belle Haven, the earl of Ashcott's home, is it not?"

"*Was* his home. He is dead now, killed in a riding accident last winter."

Lucian frowned. "I knew he died, but he had a son. Did the boy not succeed to his father's title?"

"Charles died several months before his father. If he were still alive, you would not be marrying Kitty. He was Bloomfield's first choice for her husband."

"So instead of an old, prestigious title like Ashcott's," Lucian said cynically, "Bloomfield has to settle for my newly created one for his daughter. I gather Ashcott had no other son."

"No other male heir at all. The title reverted to the crown."

"What about Belle Haven. Who lives there now?"

David shrugged. "I believe Ashcott's daughter, Lady Angela."

Lucian wondered if the lady could be persuaded to sell it. It was a far handsomer property than Sommerstone, which he had labored so long to attain.

"How did you know it was Belle Haven?" David asked. "Have you seen it before?"

"No, I recognized it from a drawing in one of Ashcott's books, *Journal of Belle Haven.*" In it, the earl had chronicled his observations of nature at his country estate. Lucian confessed, "I have wanted to see Belle Haven ever since I read the *Journal.*"

Ashcott had been called "the scientific earl" for his work in advancing natural philosophy. His contributions lay less in the experiments he conducted in his "elaboratory" at Belle Haven than in his ability to grasp and explain new theories and discoveries in clear, felicitous prose that communicated his passion for his subject. Lucian had devoured all of Ashcott's books.

He told David, "I had the honor of meeting Ashcott once years ago in London. I count the three hours I spent in his company as among the most memorable of my life."

His friend grinned. "Considering the life you've led, that's no small compliment."

Ashcott had shared Lucian's interest in astronomy. Once Lucian had dreamed of devoting himself to its study, but that had been before his father, Viscount Wrexham, had consigned him to the army when he was sixteen and washed his hands of him.

The young Lucian had been bewildered and heartbroken by his father's rejection of him. Wrexham had always favored Fritz, his elder son, over his younger, but as Lucian approached manhood, his father's neglect of him had seemed to harden into hate.

The youth, who had tried so hard to please his sire, never knew why.

He still did not know.

Chapter 3

When Angel reached her bedchamber after leaving Kitty's, the voices of Horace and Rupert Crowe drifted through the door.

"It is a brilliant scheme," Horace was saying. "Not only will it prevent Vayle from marrying Kitty, but it will rid us of our other problem, too.

"Aye," his father agreed, "and far more cheaply than we could ever hope to do otherwise."

Had another guest not picked that moment to step into the hall, Angel would have listened longer. When she stepped into her room Horace, in a flowing blond wig, was standing near the window. Cascades of lace dripped from his sleeves and cravat, and he carried a long cane decorated with scarlet-and-gold ribbon loops. Sir Rupert was lounging in a damask-covered armchair with carved, barley twist arms. They immediately fell silent.

"What are you doing in my room?" she asked.

"Making certain you are comfortable," Sir Rupert replied smoothly, rising from the chair.

It was the first time that he had concerned himself with her comfort, and she looked at him skeptically. He was a muscularly built man who still retained some of the exceptional handsomeness that he had enjoyed as a young man, but dissipation had aged and coarsened his features. A hard cruelty lurked in his slate-colored eyes.

Horace had been cursed with his father's character but not blessed with his good looks. With a long sloping forehead, large nose, and receding chin, his profile—like his character—strongly reminded Angel of a weasel.

"If you wished me to be comfortable," she said, "you

would not have remained here where you were not invited nor wanted."

"The Bloomfields should have invited us, too," Horace complained. "We are their neighbors. It was rude of them not to."

"No, it was rude of you to force your company upon them," Angel retorted.

"Don't presume to tell us what is rude, you stupid little chit," her stepfather growled.

He stepped into the hall, and his son dutifully followed him.

They had been gone no more than three minutes when Kitty's mother appeared at the door. She was his lordship's second wife and fourteen years younger than he. It was from her that Kitty had inherited her beauty and her brown doe eyes.

She took Angel's hands in her own. "I only just learned about your father's missing will. I was never so shocked."

Lord Ashcott's last will and testament, in which he had bequeathed his daughter his considerable fortune, could not be found. That left in effect an old will that he had signed years ago, long before his wife had deserted him and their children. In that earlier document, he had left all he possessed to his son Charles; if Charles predeceased him, as he had, it went to his wife.

Lady Bloomfield said, "Your father must be turning over in his grave to have that woman whom he hated inheriting what should be yours."

"The worst is that when Mama married Rupert Crowe immediately after Papa died, control of her property passed to him. I hate what he is doing at Belle Haven. He raised the tenants' rents far above what they can possibly pay. And he turned away the older servants that Papa had promised to take care of for their lifetime." It was all Angel could do to keep from crying in anger and frustration over her stepfather's cruelty to people for whom she cared deeply. "I am fighting him, but it is hopeless unless I can discover the will."

Lady Bloomfield's lips tightened in disgust. "So Rupert

had an even more dishonorable motive than I thought when he married your mother."

"What did you think his motive was?"

"That he foolishly hoped marrying the Earl of Ashcott's widow would help him regain the position he long ago forfeited in society, but she is a greater pariah than he is. Rupert does not care for himself, but everyone knows how much that dreadful son of his yearns to be accepted."

Lady Bloomfield, still holding Angel's hands in her own, squeezed them tightly. "Why, dear child, did you not write to me in London about this dreadful situation with your papa's will?"

"You could have done nothing."

"Perhaps not, but I would have tried." Her ladyship relaxed her grip on Angel's hands. "Do you have no clue at all to where the missing will might be?"

"No," Angel said sadly. "Rupert maintains there never was another will, but I know there was. Papa showed it to Uncle John and me."

"But unfortunately your uncle is dead, too, and cannot help you," Lady Bloomfield said grimly. "Could the Crowes have found and destroyed the will?"

Angel, swallowing hard, admitted, "It is my worst fear."

Lucian's gaze roved over the scores of people crowded into Fernhill's long gallery to celebrate his engagement to Kitty.

"Searching for your betrothed?" Lord Randolf Oldfield asked at his elbow. "She is over there."

Lucian realized that he had not been looking for Kitty at all, but for the Winter girl.

He had caught a quick glimpse of her as the Crowes had escorted her into the long gallery. The distaste on the faces of the other guests at their entrance was no more than the Crowes deserved, but unfortunately Miss Winter, because she was with them, shared in the disapproval.

Lucian glanced in the direction that Lord Oldfield had indicated, but his gaze did not linger on his betrothed. Instead it moved on restlessly, still searching for the Winter lass. He did not understand why he was so eager to catch sight of the little hoyden again, but he was.

On a balcony at the end of the gallery, an orchestra, partially concealed behind a bank of flowers, began to play again.

Lucian noticed David Inge, who usually stood with military erectness, slouched against the far wall. What the devil was wrong with him? Initially David had refused to come to Fernhill, and now that Lucian had persuaded him to do so, he looked as though he were at a wake instead of a betrothal celebration.

Lucian finally located the Winter girl standing alone near a door to a small terrace. In another black gown that was as simple as it was unfashionable, she was a somber contrast to the other women in their elaborate, colorful silk, satin, and lace creations. Her dark hair had been pulled tightly up into an unbecoming knot. No one came near her, and Lucian's heart went out to her.

Even had she been as fashionably dressed as Kitty, her entrance on the Crowes' arms undoubtedly would have tainted her, and the other guests would have shunned her. While the Crowes deserved to be outcasts, she did not. She must be miserable, he thought sympathetically.

He would have gone to her, but Kitty came up to him. "Who are you watching so intently?"

"The girl by the door."

Kitty looked in that direction. "You mean Angel?"

Angel—so that was her given name. Lucian smothered a smile. From what he had seen of the little hoyden, she had been singularly misnamed.

"Why would you watch *her* when the cream of society is here tonight?" Kitty demanded incredulously. "Are you not delighted by all the important people who have come to fete us?"

Clearly Kitty was. She was as ambitious as her father.

Lucian had not wanted this elaborate celebration. He had intended to make a fast trip on horseback to see Ardmore, the estate in Hampshire that he had just purchased sight unseen. He could not be absent from London long because King William was in Ireland and Lucian was one of the Council of Nine that the king had appointed to help the queen rule in his absence. William had gone to Ireland to put down a rebellion led by the ousted king—his father-in-law—James II.

Bloomfield had not cared that Lucian could scarcely spare the time to stop at Fernhill and still travel to Ardmore but had insisted upon this party. His future father-in-law was determined to call maximum attention to his connection with a favorite of King William and Queen Mary.

"It is the most exciting night of our lives!" Kitty gushed.

Not of Lucian's. He would rather be at Ardmore, but he kept that thought to himself. Instead, he said lightly, "I would find it even more exciting if we danced."

Angel had never been to a ball nor any other society soiree before. She was far too excited by the splendid panorama before her to notice that she was being ignored by her fellow guests, virtually none of whom she knew anyhow.

She was dazzled by the opulent beauty of the clothes and jewels. The women's gowns of silk and satin had draped overskirts open at the front and looped at the sides to reveal wonderful petticoats with tiers of lace or fine pleating.

Angel had always heeded her papa's stricture against an interest in fashion, but it had been easier to do to in the seclusion of Belle Haven. Now, among this glittering crowd, she could not help wishing that her plain, dull gown was more like the other women's. Could it be that she had one of those idle, frivolous minds Papa had ridiculed?

Beautiful as the women's gowns were, they were often outshone by the male raiment. The men's magnificent coats and vests of brocade or velvet dropped to the knee. They were ornamented with gold braid, elaborate embroidery, and long rows of buttons.

But Angel was most staggered by the men's long, flowing wigs. She had never seen her papa in a wig, but then her father had dismissed all male fashion as foolish foppishness. In the case of wigs, she decided he was right. She did not find them attractive.

Yet all the males in the room, save one, wore wigs with masses of curls cascading over their shoulders.

The only exception, to Angel's delight, was Lord Vayle. His thick black hair, gleaming like polished jet in the candlelight, was tied back at the neck.

He and Kitty took the dance floor and glided gracefully through the intricate, stately pattern of a minuet.

Angel watched them admiringly. Papa had taught her to dance, but she had never done it anywhere except in the privacy of her home. Kitty's gown was one of the prettiest in the room. Its purple petticoat was decorated with row after row of lace while its tiered lavender overdress fell into a train behind her. Angel was proud of how beautiful her friend looked.

She could not help feeling dowdy in comparison, but Angel firmly reminded herself of her beloved papa's disgust for fashion.

It did not comfort her as much as it should have.

Lord Vayle was resplendent in a gold brocade coat. He was the tallest man in the room, yet he moved with an easy grace that was surprising for someone of his size.

As Angel watched him, she felt a little breathless. Warmth curled within her, and she wondered dreamily what it would be like to dance with him.

Not that she would ever know.

When the music ended, her gaze drifted over the crowd and fell on Kitty's former love, David Inge. Angel knew who he was because earlier she had overheard him being introduced to another man. Now he was leaning against the wall, watching Kitty with love in his eyes as Lord Vayle led her from the floor.

The gallery had grown very warm, and Angel slipped out to the coolness of the terrace. It was deserted except for one couple looking out over the balustrade toward the lawn, now swallowed in darkness. Angel made her way to a dark corner so quietly that the couple did not notice they were no longer alone.

"Did you see how Kitty is preening herself tonight," the

woman said waspishly. "She is so proud of capturing Lord Lucifer. Wait until she discovers she must share him with his mistress."

"She will demand that he give up Selina, but he won't," the man predicted. "Nor would I if I were in his place. Selina is worth ten of Kitty."

"Old Bloomfield is ecstatic over the match," the woman said.

"He should be. For a cunning, ambitious politician, he miscalculated badly in supporting King James so enthusiastically. Our new king has a long memory for such things, and Bloomfield is desperate. Having Vayle as his son-in-law is his chief hope of insinuating himself into Dutch William's good graces."

"What I do not understand is why Vayle would want to marry Bloomfield's daughter. He could have done better."

"Aye, but it was Vayle who proposed the match," the man said. "Old Bloomfield could scarcely believe his good fortune."

The pair fell silent for a moment, then began discussing an assassin who had attacked Lord Colefax, a leader in the intrigue that had replaced James on the throne with his daughter Mary and her Dutch husband.

The man said, "I suspect the killer was in James's pay."

"James is a fool to think he can regain his crown from William and Mary," the woman said.

"But James was always that. That is why he is no longer king. If the assassin is in his employ, Vayle better guard his back. Close as he is to Dutch William, he would be a likely target."

Angel smothered a horrified gasp. Although she had only met Vayle that day, the thought of him lying dead—his teasing silver eyes closed, his wicked smile erased—distressed her so much that she gripped the stone rail of the balustrade.

"It is growing cool," the woman said. "Let us go in."

From the shadows, Angel watched them return to the long gallery. She wondered what they had meant by Kitty sharing Vayle with his mistress. How did a wife share her husband with another woman? Did they all live in the same house?

Angel sighed. There was so much she did not know about the mysterious things that happened between men and women. Her dear papa, who had been eager to instruct her on subjects like astronomy and mathematics, had been silent and even hostile whenever she had raised this topic, telling her brusquely that she had no need to know.

He had actually gotten angry at her when she had asked him how babies were made. By then Angel had known how they were born—although for years she had thought that they were found under a cabbage leaf as her old nurse had said. But she had wanted to know how babies got into their mama's belly in the first place.

Papa had adamantly refused to discuss it with her. Angel surmised that it was connected to the secret thing a man and a woman did behind the bedroom door that people whispered and smirked about. Angel hated being ignorant about anything. As she stared up at the distant stars, glittering in the night sky, she wondered whom she could ask.

"Counting the stars?" a resonant male voice inquired behind her.

Whirling around, she discovered Lord Vayle so near her that she could smell his pleasant, spicy scent. The strange, uneasy quivering that had plagued her earlier in the woods began again, stronger than ever. Angel did not understand it at all.

She tried to step backward to put a little more space between them but discovered that she was trapped against the balustrade. When she spoke her voice was unexpectedly wobbly. "What . . . what are you doing here?"

"Turning the tables." The light that fell through the window beside him illuminated the strong planes of his smiling face. He was very handsome when he smiled, Angel thought. "This time I followed you. Fortunately, I did not require a rope to reach you."

Angel was startled by how thrilled she was that he had sought her out.

"Have you learned any more details of your stepbrother's plot?"

Her burst of happiness vanished as she realized his reason for wanting to talk to her. "Only that it apparently will also rid them of another problem very cheaply."

He frowned. "What other problem?"

"I cannot conceive what it could be."

His lordship rubbed his chin thoughtfully with his long tapering fingers, drawing Angel's attention to his mouth. The fluttering within her quickened, and she wondered what it would be like to kiss him "the right way"—whatever that was.

A happy thought struck her. Surely any man who volunteered to instruct her about kissing would also be willing to enlighten her on the other matters troubling her. She smiled warmly at him. "I have some questions that I would very much like answered. Would you help me?"

He grinned. "If I can. What is your first one?"

"How are babies made?"

His grin vanished. He looked as though she had poleaxed him.

For a minute he could not seem to speak at all, then he demanded in a strangled voice. "God's oath, why are you asking *me that?*"

"Since you were kind enough to offer to instruct me on the right way to kiss, I thought surely you would be willing to answer that, too."

"You thought wrong! Don't you know that a girl does not ask a man she scarcely knows—or any man at all—such a question?"

"Why not?"

"Because . . . because she does not."

"Oh, fie, that's no answer."

Lucian stared at her innocent face. She was by far the most naive young lady he had ever met—and the most entertaining. He said dryly, "I suggest we discuss another subject, like the stars. They seem remote enough to be safe."

She looked up at the heavens. "Did you know some Greek philosophers taught that the sky is a hollow globe surrounding the earth, and the stars are inlaid on the inner surface like jewels?"

Lucian was dumbfounded to hear a girl ignorant of the basic facts of life talking about the theories of Greek philosophers. "Do you believe that?" he inquired.

She gave him an indignant look. "Of course not! I know the earth is not the center of the universe but only one of several planets revolving around the sun. Have you ever studied the sky through a telescope?"

"Aye." Lucian had not lost his boyhood interest in astronomy, but he saw no reason to tell her that. "Have you?"

"Oh, yes, I love to do so."

Even in the pale moonlight, he could see that her eyes glowed with excitement. A light breeze had sprung up, and her clean, refreshing scent that he liked so well drifted over him.

"Your interest surprises me," he told her.

"Why?"

He smiled. "Because it is not a subject that would normally interest a female."

"I hope you are not one of those silly men who believe a woman's intellect is too frail to study natural philosophy."

Lucian replied smoothly, if evasively, "I am never silly."

Her huge eyes looked him over thoughtfully, then she asked abruptly. "Why do you not wear a wig like the other men do?"

God's oath, was there nothing that she would not ask him?

"I prefer my own hair."

"I much prefer it, too," Angel said.

He wished Kitty did. She had been irate at him for refusing to wear a wig tonight. He wondered self-mockingly whether he would have been so averse to wigs if nature had not provided him with a thick head of hair that showed no sign of thinning.

Angel said, "I cannot fathom why the other men wear wigs."

"Surely you must know that no aspiring gentleman dares appear at a formal ball wearing his own hair instead of someone else's."

From her surprised expression, she clearly had not known. Lucian was deeply puzzled that a girl informed on a subject like astronomy could be so ignorant of both common social conventions and elementary human biology.

"But you do not wear one," she protested, "and you are a gentleman."

He grinned. "As I told you earlier, only occasionally."

She studied him thoughtfully. "Other men wear them because they fear what people will think, but you do not care, do you?"

"No, I do not." There were very few men whose esteem he craved. He looked at Angel approvingly. For all her naïveté, she was astute.

He started to ask how she liked the ball, then realized that she could hardly be enjoying herself, ignored as she was by the other guests. He phrased his question more neutrally, "What do you think of the ball."

She turned and looked into the crowded gallery. "Oh, it is splendid!" she exclaimed. Her expression was full of wonder and unfeigned delight.

She reminded Lucian of a mischievous elf.

"This is my very first ball, and I had no idea how beautiful it would be! I have never seen such gorgeous clothes, and I love to watch the dancing."

Suddenly, Lucian felt bad for her. It was her first ball, and no one had even asked her to dance.

Smiling, he inquired, "Would you consent to dance with me?"

Her marvelous smile illuminated her face, telling him how much she wanted to do so. Feeling wonderfully warmed by it, he took her arm and led her into the long room.

Although a number of the female guests had hinted

broadly that they would like to stand up with him, until now he had danced only with his betrothed and her mother.

A collective gasp sounded as he led Angel to the dance floor, and every eye turned toward them. He was amused to see some of the best-bred members of English society actually gaping at his choice of dancing partner.

Angel suddenly looked very uneasy. "I have never danced in public before, nor with anyone but Papa. I hope I shall not embarrass you."

He was touched that she would worry about embarrassing him rather than herself. "You won't," he reassured her. "I will guide you. Only follow my lead."

As it turned out, she need not have been concerned. She was an excellent dancer, light and graceful on her feet, and instantly responsive to him as he guided her through the pattern of a country dance. He wished that Kitty danced as well.

When the music ended, he told Angel, "You are a delight to dance with."

She looked at him as though he were hoaxing her, then quickly looked away, a pretty blush reddening her cheeks.

As he led her from the floor, they passed David Inge, and she exclaimed, "Poor Mr. Inge looks so unhappy, but one cannot blame him. He is clearly still in love with Kitty."

Lucian stopped abruptly and his hard grip on Angel's arm forced her to do the same. "What are you talking about?"

She blinked at him in surprise. "Surely you know that Kitty once intended to marry him."

Lucian had had no inkling. When he had met Kitty, he had thought her interested in Lord Peck's son, Roger.

"Look at how Mr. Inge watches her with his heart in his eyes," Angel pointed out.

To his horror, Lucian saw that she was right. Bloody hell, so that was what was wrong with David!

"They were not formally betrothed," Angel explained, "but she had secretly promised him that she would wed him. Even though Kitty is my friend, I think she treated him most shabbily."

So did Lucian. Kitty had pledged herself to David, then jilted him when more impressive prospects—first Peck, then himself—came along. She was like her ambitious father, whose word could not be counted upon except when it benefited him. Lucian was suddenly furious at his fickle betrothed.

Kitty picked that unpropitious moment to sweep up to them. With only a curt nod to Angel, she said to him, "Darling, you recall the next dance is mine."

Lucian recalled nothing of the sort.

As Kitty linked her arm possessively in his, he was startled by the jealous glint in her eye. Was she afraid of losing her prize catch?

As he led Kitty away, she hissed angrily, "With all the lovely women here, why would you single *her* out?"

"But I understood Angel was your friend."

"She is no friend of mine," Kitty snapped.

"No, you have it backward," he retorted icily. "You are no friend of hers!"

His tone clearly unnerved his betrothed. "Please, do not look at me so," she begged uneasily, edging closer to him. "People will think we have quarreled."

Let them! he thought, still angry at her treatment of Angel.

As he led her toward the dance floor, he said, "I do not recall requesting this dance from you." Nor was he looking forward to it after having danced with Angel. Kitty, for all her beauty, was neither light nor especially graceful on her feet.

"If you prefer, we can sit it out," she said placatingly.

"Good," he said, leading her toward two chairs.

When they were seated, Kitty, as she always did when he was displeased with her, began to chatter nervously, as though her rush of words could erase his irritation.

She was a little afraid of him, and perhaps that was just as well. Lucian was determined to have an obedient wife, and Kitty would be that. She would not dare go against his wishes.

But other things began to bother him about her. He had never noticed how monotonous her voice was, and she had an irritatingly shrill laugh. He liked Angel's melodious voice much better.

When the dance ended, Lucian, still out of charity with Kitty, happily relinquished her to her next partner, Lord Bourn.

Lucian was heading toward the room where refreshments were being served when his future mother-in-law, Lady Bloomfield, stepped into his path.

"I am very grateful to you for dancing with Angel," she told Lucian with obvious sincerity.

Too bad her daughter did not share her sentiments. If only Kitty took more after her sweet, caring mother, instead of her wily, ambitious father. Lucian liked Lady Bloomfield far better than her husband.

She said sadly, "Angel is such a dear child, and everyone else is ignoring her."

"Certainly she has captured no male interest."

" 'Tis just as well!" Lady Bloomfield exclaimed.

Lucian raised a questioning eyebrow.

She explained, "Angel is so naive that an unprincipled man could take dreadful advantage of her. I doubt she even knows what happens between a man and a woman. Her late father was an eccentric recluse who eschewed society and fashion. He kept Angel totally ignorant about them and about men."

"Why would he do that?"

"He was obsessed with preventing her from becoming like her wanton mother. He had the nonsensical conviction that once Angel learned of passion she would follow in her mama's disastrous footsteps. She would not—the two are as different as night and day. A more flighty, frivolous, selfish, faithless creature than Angel's mother never lived. She cared only for clothes, jewels, and men's adulation."

Like most women, Lucian thought cynically.

"She ran away with one of her lovers when Angel was

four. Angel's father was so humiliated that he retired to the country to raise his two children in seclusion, away from what he considered the corrupting influence of London society. He even insisted on educating them himself." Lady Bloomfield's expression tightened in disapproval. "And a very strange education it was for Angel."

The orchestra began playing again, and Lord Bloomfield claimed his wife for a dance. Lucian was sorry to lose her company. He wanted to learn more about Angel and her odd upbringing.

When Angel went to bed that night, she began to sneeze as soon as her head touched her pillow, and she could not seem to stop. She had no idea what could be wrong. Never, except a few times when she had gotten her nose full of dust, had she ever sneezed like this.

Maude, who was sleeping on a cot in Angel's room, offered her some of a special elixir made from her grandmother's secret recipe.

"Never go anywhere without it," the maid confided. "Never seen anything like it for stopping a body from coughing and sneezing."

Angel decided to try it. Certainly it could not hurt her, and it might help.

Maude poured the thick, brownish liquid into a small glass until it was half-full, then handed it to Angel. "Best to drink it down all at once."

Angel obeyed. When she had emptied the glass's bitter contents, she gave a little shudder. "It tastes vile."

"But 'tis worth it, for it works," Maude said. "Here now, your pillow looks very flat to me. I saw another that looked better in the chest of drawers."

She pulled open the bottom drawer and produced a much plumper, fluffier pillow. As she replaced Angel's pillow with it, she said, "You will find this one more comfortable."

Angel was surprised by how solicitous Maude suddenly was of her. She thanked the maid and laid her head on the new pillow. It was much better than the other had been.

The elixir clearly worked, too, for Angel stopped sneezing.

And suddenly she was so sleepy that she could not keep her eyes open.

Chapter 4

"I am surprised, Lucian. Solitary drinking is not your style."

Lucian was sprawled in a chair in Bloomfield's small library, where he had been sampling his host's fine claret. He looked up from his glass at the sound of David Inge's voice at the door.

"Then join me." Lucian gestured toward the chair beside him. "You are just the man I want to see."

He would have poured David a glass of wine from the decanter on the table beside him, but his friend said, "None for me."

Lucian refilled his own glass instead, then asked bluntly, "Are you in love with Kitty?"

The sudden pain in David's eyes answered the question better than words could have.

Dismayed that he had unwittingly hurt his friend, Lucian said, "Believe me, I had no notion until tonight how you felt about her."

"I know that."

"Why the hell didn't you tell me?"

"Because you are not at fault!" Bitterness permeated David's voice. "Roger Peck was the villain. He condescended to dance attendance on her."

"Not for long, though." No woman held that handsome young peacock's interest for long. He was aided in his conquests by a face and physique that enticed women like flies to honey. If that were not ample attraction, he was the son and heir of Lord Peck, one of the richest men in the realm.

"No, Roger dropped her soon enough," David said.

"Fortunately, you appeared on the scene at that moment. She made it very clear to me how much she—and her damned father—preferred you to me."

"What they prefer are my power and rank," Lucian said grimly. "Yet you love her still?" In David's place, he would have despised the faithless chit. Maybe he was doing his friend a favor by marrying Kitty. David deserved so much better than that ambitious, fickle female.

"Stupid of me, is it not?" David said savagely. "I berate myself for being every kind of fool. But I blame Bloomfield more for what happened than I do Kitty. He kept telling her that she would be wasting herself on a younger son like me, that she could do so much better." David's mouth twisted in a sardonic smile. "And now she has."

"No, she has not," Lucian said softly.

David smiled bleakly at the compliment.

Long after his friend went up to bed, Lucian remained alone in Bloomfield's library, liberally partaking of his lordship's claret and brooding.

Poor David. Men made such fools of themselves for love. That would never happen to Lucian. Not since that miserable day his father had sent him away to the army had he let his heart rule his head. And he never would. No woman would ever do to him what Kitty had done to David. There was not a woman in the world he could not walk away from if he put his mind to it.

Lucian looked up at a portrait of a lovely young woman hanging over the fireplace. She was his host's eldest daughter, Anne, by his first wife. Years ago, when Bloomfield had been at the height of his considerable political power, he had rejected the suit of Lucian's older brother Fritz for Anne's hand because he did not consider the Sandford family good enough for a union with his own.

Now Lucian, the younger son whom his father hated, would marry into the family that had rejected his father's favorite.

That pleased Lucian enormously. So did the fact that he now outranked his father, Viscount Wrexham. When King

William had offered to make Lucian a viscount, he had declined the title and audaciously asked for an earldom instead. It was a measure of the king's esteem for Lucian that he had gotten it.

And very soon now, Lucian would own Sommerstone, the Sandfords' ancestral home. It had been in his family for more than a century until Lucian's grandfather had lost it at the gaming tables to a man who subsequently sold it to Bloomfield.

The most-cherished dream of Lucian's father had been to regain the estate. With marriage to Kitty, Lucian would succeed where his father had failed.

At last, he thought with intense satisfaction, he would prove to his father how badly he had misjudged and underestimated his hated younger son. At last, Lucian would have the vindication that had been his most-cherished goal for the past fourteen years.

Lucian wished that he could see his father's expression when he heard the news of his younger son's betrothal. Would Lucian's acquisition of Sommerstone bring Wrexham to his son to ask his forgiveness? No, his proud, stubborn father would never admit he had been wrong, but he might plead to visit Sommerstone.

What did it matter that Kitty bored Lucian with her endless, mindless chatter about gowns and social standing? He could bear to be bored when Sommerstone was his and he was married to one of Bloomfield's daughters.

And he would have Selina, whose beauty put Kitty in the shade. With her wit and quick intelligence, his mistress would provide him with the entertaining companionship that Kitty could not.

Although Lucian was fonder of Selina than he had ever been of another woman, he did not delude himself that he was in love with her. Nor did she love him. Her heart, like his, was encased in a protective barrier that could not be breached.

What had built the wall around Selina's heart, he did not know. She had rebuffed his effort to find out, saying tartly that she was entitled to her secrets as he was to his.

Although the initial blaze of passion that had brought

them together had cooled a little after nearly two years, they preferred each other's company to anyone else's.

Lucian had been surprised at how vehemently she had objected to his marrying Kitty, even though he had made it clear to Selina that his marriage would not change their relationship.

"It is not your marrying I object to," she had retorted scornfully. "It is your choice of bride. She will not make you the kind of wife you need."

"And what kind do I need?" he had teased.

Selina, usually so frank, had replied evasively, "Whatever it is, Kitty is not it."

Lucian drained the last of the wine from his glass. Fernhill was quiet now. Even the most stubborn revelers had gone to bed. Lucian rose from the chair to retire and discovered that he was somewhat unsteady from all the claret that he had consumed.

A candle was burning when he went into his room. He stopped abruptly at the sight of the voluptuous woman lying in an inviting position on his bed. A lace night rail had been carefully arranged to display enticingly her large breasts and other charms.

Lucian felt his body's instant, uncontrollable response to this flagrant provocation. He should not have drunk so much. It undermined his self-control and his will to resist.

Belatedly he recognized the maid, Maude, and his mouth hardened.

"Oh, my lord, you have kept me waiting so long," she whispered huskily.

"And you have wasted your time," he told her bluntly. "I do not pay for a woman. So be on your way."

He had thought that would discourage her, but instead she batted her eyes at him and cooed, "Oh, la, my lord, I want no money. Such a fine specimen as yourself is reward enough."

Lucian let his skepticism show on his face.

Maude hurried on. "It will be an honor for me to bed a great hero like the Earl of Vayle."

He had met more than a few females who were eager to

sleep with him for that reason. They wanted the legend, not the man.

She giggled. "Might say 'tis my patriotic duty."

He should send the bold baggage packing, but her wanton display of herself had had its intended effect on his body.

Since Maude was so eager to offer herself to him, why should he not take advantage of it? Lucian's body ached for relief, and his brain was dulled by too much claret.

He began to remove his clothes. As he dropped his brocade coat across a chair and started to unbutton his long matching vest, she protested, "No, no, let me do that."

Rising seductively from the bed, she moved close to him. His nose discovered that she had made liberal use of civet in trying to enhance her charms. It had been a mistake. Lucian wistfully recalled the sweet, refreshing scent that had clung to Angel Winter.

Maude finished undressing him, taking advantage of every opportunity it offered to excite his body.

As she divested him of the last of his clothing, he noticed that her hand shook a little. Seizing it in his own, he observed, "How nervous you are."

It trembled more violently. "Aye, I am," she agreed. " 'Tis the honor of bedding a great man like you. I declare I need a bit of claret to steady my nerves."

Maude went to a table near the bed. Lucian noticed for the first time that it held two glasses of wine and an empty bottle. From the rich, ruby shade of the liquor, it looked to be of excellent quality.

Raising his eyebrow, he inquired coldly, "Prigging our host's claret?"

"Nay, 'tis none of his!"

Lucian gave her a skeptical look.

She said hurriedly, " 'Tis my mistress's. Brings it with her, she does. Likes it before she goes to sleep, if you take my meaning. Calls it her sleeping medicine." Maude held one of the glasses out to him. "Let us drink a toast to our night together."

He wanted no more to drink. When he declined the glass, she cried angrily, "So, fine gentleman that you are,

I am not good enough to drink a toast with, only good enough to bed!"

God's oath, Lucian thought wearily, he did not want a noisy scene of wounded feminine sensibility. All he wanted was to satisfy the urgent need of his body in hers. Irritably, he took the glass from her. He'd already had so much to drink that one more glass hardly mattered.

He raised it to her and said, "To a pleasurable night."

Lucian drained the glass in three gulps. The claret was not as good as it had looked to be. It left a bitter, unpleasant aftertaste in his mouth.

She took the empty glass from him, replaced it on the tray, then took a dainty sip from her own glass. "You must forgive me, but I cannot drink it as quickly as you do."

"Don't bother to drink it at all," he growled impatiently, sinking down on the bed. "You have had your toast; now let us make it come true."

"Only a few sips, my lord, to quiet my nerves."

He felt a prickling along his own nerves. It was the intuitive warning of danger that had more than once saved his life, but Lucian was suddenly so sleepy that he could not isolate what it was that bothered him about Maude.

He must order her out of his room. Lucian opened his mouth to do so, but his tongue would not work properly. He fell back on the pillows, unable to keep his eyes open any longer.

Angel turned over in her sleep and bumped against something very warm and very hard in her bed.

She was having a dream, she decided, more asleep than awake. It was not the first strange dream she had had that night. In an earlier one, she had been picked up and carried in a man's arms.

This latest dream, however, was much more pleasant. The object in her bed was as warm as a hot brick and far nicer to snuggle against.

Suddenly, the object shifted, and she found herself pulled tightly against it. A sudden heat, delicious and thrilling, permeated to the very marrow of her bones. Angel wanted to stay next to this wonderful, comforting warmth forever.

Slowly it penetrated her sleep-fogged brain that somewhere in the distance, a great commotion was going on. It sounded as though a hunt were in progress.

Then much nearer, not more than two inches above her head, she heard a sigh. A male voice, deep and thick with sleep, muttered, "So sweet. Smell nice, too."

Angel's eyes flew open. A man's chest, thick with dark curling hair, was pressed against her. She realized that it was his arms that were holding her—and so closely that she could not see his face.

For a moment, Angel was too stunned to move. Then she tried to wriggle from his embrace, but his arms tightened around her so fiercely that she complained, "You're hurting me."

His grip instantly relaxed. "Don't go," he mumbled, clearly still asleep. One of his hands lightly caressed her hair. The sensations that his touch sent coursing through her made her forget all about trying to squirm away from him.

She was so bemused by the feelings he aroused in her that she hardly noticed that the distant furor she had been hearing was much closer now.

The door to her room burst open. The bed curtains had not been closed, and suddenly the faces of Lord Bloomfield, her stepfather, and several of the guests appeared hovering over the bed. They stared down in shocked horror at her.

The noise apparently penetrated her companion's sleep deadened senses. He stirred and loosened his grip on her.

Angel hastily scooted away from him. For the first time, she was able to see his face.

Lord Vayle! What on earth was he doing in her bed?

He looked dazed and terribly groggy, as though he were in the grip of a sleep so strong that he could not seem to shake himself awake.

Angel sympathized with him, for she felt terribly dull and lethargic, too, and her head ached dreadfully.

More people, both men and women, many in nightclothes, were crowding into the room. There were at least a score now.

"What is the meaning of this?" Sir Rupert roared, yanking away the bedcovers from Angel and her companion.

She was mortified for she was clad only in her thin, lawn night rail, but that was better than Lord Vayle.

He wore nothing at all.

Angel stared in helpless admiration at the powerful muscles of his bronzed shoulders, arms, and chest. Then she looked lower. She had never before seen a nude man, and she was startled by the differences between his anatomy and hers.

He did not appear in the least embarrassed by his nakedness. Indeed, he did not even seem to notice it. Instead he looked as furious as she had ever seen a man look.

"Bloody hell!" he exploded, thrusting himself into a sitting position. "Damned, sarding whoresons!"

Angel sat up, too, wondering why he was so angry. Violent words continued to spew from his mouth. Unfortunately, he seemed to have reverted to Dutch again, and she could not understand what he was saying.

"Hold your tongue!" Bloomfield ordered, looking as incensed as Vayle. "There are ladies present."

"And quite an eyeful they are getting, too!" Vayle said scornfully. "Surely you ought to be as anxious to spare their eyes as their ears from this travesty."

Angel realized to her acute shame that her night rail was twisted up about her thighs, leaving her bare legs exposed. She started to pull the material down, but Sir Rupert's hand shot out and seized her wrist in an iron grip.

"Only look at that, the bastard!" He was pointing at something on the skirt of her night rail. Horrified gasps escaped the staring onlookers gathered around the bed.

Looking down, Angel was startled to see bloodstains on the skirt of her garment.

"Where did that come from?" she wondered aloud. "I did not cut myself."

Lord Vayle gave her a look so full of fury that she shivered.

Before she could ask him what was wrong, Sir Rupert

blustered, "I will not let you get away with this outrage, Vayle. Explain—"

"Explain this farce?" the earl snapped. "I could not begin to try. But you could, damn you! I have no idea how this female"—he glared so contemptuously at Angel that her soul seemed to shrivel—"got into my bed."

Dear God, could he be right? For the first time, Angel noticed that the bed hangings were of beige tapestry, not the green silk that had been on the bed she had gone to sleep in. Was she in *his* bed? Certainly she was not in her own. Yet her wrapper was lying at the foot of the bed.

He turned on her. His silver eyes were as hard and piercing as a sword's point, and his voice was ominous. "Come, my angel from hell, why don't you tell me and our audience how you happen to be in my bed?"

"I do not know," she admitted. "I—"

Sir Rupert drowned out her answer by shouting at Vayle. "Do not try to turn attention from your own despicable behavior."

It was almost as though her stepfather were declaiming on the stage of a large theater and wanted everyone in it to hear him.

Angel asked him, "Why are you yelling at Lord Vayle when he is no more than two feet from you?"

Rupert ignored her. So did the people gathered around the bed. They were too busy staring down at the tangled skirt of her night rail.

Terribly embarrassed by her state of undress, Angel tried to tug the covers back up around her, but Rupert held them so that she could not.

"Let me cover myself," she cried angrily.

Suddenly Lord Vayle, a ferocious look in his eye, yanked the blankets out of her stepfather's hands and pulled them up about both her and himself. "Damn you, Crowe! At least allow her a little belated modesty now that she has done your dirty work for you."

"What dirty work?" Angel asked, baffled.

Vayle whirled on her. Angel was not easily frightened, but the savagery of his expression did so now. How apt his nickname was. Never had she seen a man who looked more like Lucifer.

"As if you didn't know," he growled, "you damned little whore!"

Angel blanched. She knew that she was plain, but she truly did not think that she was so ugly that she could be called a *horror*. It was terribly unkind of Lord Vayle, and she objected indignantly, "I am not a horror!"

"No?" His eyes raked her with contempt and derision.

"Of course, you are not a whore, my dear, sweet innocent," her stepfather assured her soothingly.

Lord Vayle demanded, "How does it happen that your dear, sweet innocent is the one who has come to *my* room and *my* bed?"

"Because you seduced her into doing so," Rupert shouted. "We all saw how you singled her out for your attention at the ball."

An angry hiss echoed among those crowded into the room.

A perplexed Angel frowned. "What does seduced—"

"Damn you, Vayle," Rupert interrupted, "you lured her away from the watchful eye of her maid, who would have immediately warned me of what you were about. My Angel has lived a secluded life. The poor girl knew nothing about evil, debauching men like you, who would use her for their amusement, ruin her, and then abandon her."

"Laying it on rather too thick, aren't you Crowe?" Vayle inquired scornfully. "But then the role of defender of lost innocence is such a novel one for you."

Rupert flushed but was not silenced. "Angel is my responsibility and, by God, you will marry her!"

Lord Vayle did not seem in the least surprised at her stepfather's astonishing statement, but Angel was stunned. Why would Rupert think his lordship should marry her when he was betrothed to Kitty.

"But I do not want to marry him!" she protested loudly.

Vayle eyed her with sharp suspicion.

"Shut up," Rupert ordered her.

But Angel ignored him. "Lord Vayle is Kitty's betrothed. Even if he wasn't, I scarcely know the man."

"You know him in the most intimate way a woman can know a man," Rupert shot back.

Angel had no idea what her stepfather was talking about. "I think you are mad," she said with conviction. "And I will not marry him."

"Nor will I marry her," Lord Vayle said flatly.

A rumble of anger and hostility toward him rippled through the room. Someone hissed, "Lucifer." By now Angel was certain that every guest at the house party must have crowded into this room. She caught sight of Lady Bloomfield's shocked face.

"You will marry Angel, Vayle," Sir Rupert cried. "Honor requires it."

"Honor?" Lord Vayle scoffed. "What an odd word to hear on your lips. Am I to gather you will call me out if I do not marry her? I shall be delighted to oblige you."

Sir Rupert suddenly looked very uneasy. "I am certain you would be happy to take on an old man like me."

"Old!" Lord Vayle exclaimed derisively. "You are no more than five-and-forty. If you consider that too decrepit to fight for your daughter's *alleged* honor, there is always your son to do it for you. He is some years younger than I." The earl's grim smile was full of menace. "I am convinced that I shall derive even more pleasure from running through that little snake than I would from doing the same to you."

Angel glanced at Horace, standing near his father. His face was ashen with fear.

Lady Bloomfield worked her way to Angel's side and squeezed her shoulder comfortingly.

Rupert shouted, "You cannot deny, Vayle, that my precious Angel was as pure as new-fallen snow until you touched her. The proof of her innocence is on her gown."

Now it was Sir Rupert who made absolutely no sense to Angel. What did he mean by innocence, and how did a woman prove it?

She was certain of one thing, however, and she voiced it again, loudly and vehemently. "I tell you I will not marry Lord Vayle. Nothing will induce me to do so."

Lady Bloomfield took Angel's hand in her own. "You must, my dear. You may be with child."

"Not with my child, she isn't!" Vayle interjected savagely. "That would be a bloody impossibility."

Angel was utterly confused. "How could I be with child?"

Lady Bloomfield said very gently, "You have lain with a man."

Angel's eyes widened in astonishment. Was that all it took? She had only to lie down beside a man and his child began growing inside her.

"I never dreamed that making babies was so easy," she said in wonder. How silly of Lord Vayle to have refused to tell her something that simple when she had asked him. She turned to him and in a voice laced with reproach said, "You should have told me."

Vayle looked at her with murder in his silver eyes.

But Angel hardly noticed; she was so disappointed to learn that lying beside each other was all there was to the mysterious thing that a man and woman did behind the bedroom door. She was surprised that so much whispering and snickering went on about such a simple, insignificant act.

"If she is pregnant," Lord Vayle snapped, "it is not my bastard she is carrying."

Lady Bloomfield gave him a scathing look. "She has never lain with another man. As her stepfather says, the proof is on her gown. You must marry her."

Chapter 5

Lucian glared at Lady Bloomfield. After this very public scene, he knew that she was right about his having to marry Angel, but he would be damned if he would concede defeat so easily. He would go down fighting every step of the way.

He silently cursed the Crowes, Angel, and himself, too. Lucian had made the fatal mistake that he had always been so careful never to make on the battlefield.

He had underestimated his enemy.

How could he have been so bloody stupid?

Even more stupidly, he had not suspected that Angel was in league with her step-relatives in their plot against him.

Fool that he was, Lucian had thought her a delightful innocent who had kindly tried to warn him of her evil relatives' plot against him. All the while she had been telling him with such seeming candor about it, she had known full well that she was its linchpin.

The duplicitous little witch had let them drug him and then had willingly crawled into bed beside him until the Crowes could snap the trap shut on him.

Everything that he had worked and sweated and sacrificed for during the past fourteen long years had been lost because of her treachery. Never had he been so duped by a female.

Lucian longed to strangle her with his bare hands.

Angel, clutching the covers up to her chin, met his searing gaze of contempt and hatred with a look of hurt puzzlement.

Even now that she had betrayed both him and her "dear

friend" Kitty, Angel managed to look so damned sweet and innocent, just like her name. God's oath, had there ever been a more misnamed female?

Her huge blue eyes gave no hint of her perfidy but managed to look terribly confused and wounded. This was the first time he had seen her hair down. Long and thick, it was the color of rich chocolate, and it hung about her shoulders in tangled waves.

Lucian treated the gaping, censorious faces surrounding the bed to the savage scowl that had helped win him the appellation Lord Lucifer.

In that voice of command that had propelled frightened, reluctant men into battle, he ordered the onlookers out of the room. They proved no more willing to disobey him than the soldiers under his command had. Slowly they filed into the hall. Only Lord and Lady Bloomfield and the Crowes remained behind.

A dull throb tormented Lucian's head, no doubt from the drug in the wine that Maude had insisted he drink.

The thought of the buxom maid made him grind his teeth in fury. How could he have been such a bloody idiot? He should have suspected her. She was so forward in seeking his attention, but then so were a good many other women who were not trying to give him a Judas kiss.

The hall quickly filled with a crescendo of excited voices. This would be one of the most delicious, talked-about scandals of the year—or even the decade.

Bloomfield closed the door, shutting out the hubbub.

Lucian looked at the Bloomfields and said in a voice that defied them to challenge him, "I am betrothed to your daughter, and I intend to marry her."

Kitty's mother seemed to swell with indignation. "You dare to say that after revealing yourself to be so debauched that you would seduce a sweet, innocent child like Angel!"

"My dear," her husband said placatingly, "perhaps you are being too hasty in your judgment of Vayle."

Bloomfield was desperate not to lose his golden ticket into the king's good graces, Lucian thought in disgust. The wily, ambitious viscount would do anything, make any concession, if it would further himself.

"I would hear Vayle's explanation," Bloomfield continued. "We owe it to him and our daughter to listen to it."

Her ladyship turned an indignant eye on her spouse. "We owe him nothing but our contempt! This man seduced our daughter's innocent friend in our own home! And he did so on the very night that we and our friends were celebrating Kitty's betrothal."

Even though Lucian was innocent of her charge, he much preferred Lady Bloomfield and her honest anger to her husband's hypocritical stance.

The lady continued, "We all saw how Vayle singled Angel out last night for special attention at the ball."

Aye, he had, Lucian thought, cursing himself. Angel had been the only woman other than his betrothed and her mother with whom he had danced. Now his kindly action would be taken as further proof that he had been intent on seducing her.

One more nail in the coffin of his dead dream of achieving vindication in his father's eyes.

"Vayle has humiliated our daughter and us," Lady Bloomfield angrily told her husband, "and he has ruined Angel!"

"I did not ruin her."

Her ladyship regarded Lucian scornfully. "The evidence is incontrovertible."

"To the contrary, it must be controvertible since I did not touch her!"

No one would believe that, though. Nor did Lucian expect them to. Not with those damned bloodstains on her night rail.

He turned to Angel on the bed beside him. "How very kind of you to warn me of the Crowes' plot against me." He spoke in a voice so low that only she could hear, but it oozed with scorn and sarcasm. "Did you think that if you warned me of the plot, it would go easier for you after I was forced to marry you?"

She looked at him with such wide-eyed innocence that had he not known better, he might have believed her blameless. He marveled at what a fine actress she was.

He ground his teeth in fury. Well, by God, he'd give her something to think about—and to fear.

"Did you think I would not beat you after we were married?" He gave her a hard, cruel smile. "Well, you were wrong."

She recoiled as though he had already struck her. Then anger sparked in her eyes, and she cried, "You are very, very wrong to think that I would marry you!"

Not for an instant did Lucian believe her.

"What nonsense is this, girl," her stepfather blustered. "Of course you will marry him."

Angel's chin rose to an obstinate angle and her brilliant blue eyes radiated defiance. "No, I shall not! He is betrothed to Kitty."

Her stepfather gave her an ugly look. "You should have thought of that before you sought out his bed, you little slut!"

Lucian's eyes narrowed. Now that Sir Rupert's rapt, scandalized audience was gone from the room, his dear, sweet innocent had suddenly become a slut.

She was also clearly deviating from her stepfather's script for her. Was it because Lucian's threat to beat her had frightened her? She did not look fearful, though, only stubbornly defiant.

"I will not marry you," she repeated even more emphatically.

He wished to hell she had shown a bit of the backbone she was displaying now when Crowe had sought her aid in his plot against Lucian.

"If you think I will marry my best friend's betrothed, you are mad," Angel cried. "I would never do such a terrible thing to Kitty."

Sir Rupert, his face thunderous, snarled, "You will do as I say!"

"No, I will not!" Angel cried, undeterred by the anger in his expression that boded ill for her.

The door to the hall that Lady Bloomfield had closed was flung open with such force that it banged against the wall. Kitty, in a violet silk wrapper, her hair a cloud of spun gold drifting about her shoulders, flew into the room.

Bloody hell, Lucian thought. This farce needed only her to be complete.

At the sight of her betrothed in bed with her friend, Kitty let out a most unladylike screech of pure fury. "I heard that . . . I could not believe it . . . but now that I see it with my own eyes . . ."

To Lucian's surprise, Kitty scarcely seemed to notice him. All her attention and her wrath were directed at her friend. "How could you do this to me, Angel Winter?" she shrieked. "How could you humiliate me like this!"

Angel, her face a study in horrified disbelief, cried, "Kitty, I would never knowingly do anything to hurt you. You must believe me."

"As if I would believe anything that you told me! I regarded you as my friend, fool that I was. And you have repaid my kindness by seducing my betrothed in my own home."

Kitty regarded Angel with abhorrence. "You have always been so jealous of me! This is your way of getting even, is it not? Well, you have succeeded, you dreadful creature."

Angel stared at her friend with such an agonized, heartbroken gaze that Lucian actually felt a tinge of sympathy for her despite his own anger at her.

Kitty screamed, "You are evil, heartless, conniving . . . !" Suddenly she lashed out with her hand and would have slapped Angel had not Lucian, with the lightning reflexes that had several times saved his life in battle, grabbed her wrist and held it.

She gave him a terrible look. He dropped her wrist, belatedly realizing that by instinctively protecting the little witch who had betrayed and trapped him, he had further damned himself in his betrothed's eyes.

Kitty turned and ran from the room, slamming the door hard behind her. Horace Crowe hurried after her.

Lucian turned to Angel. Tears ran unheeded down her cheeks. She looked so confused and vulnerable and forlorn that Lucian felt a sudden, irrational impulse to comfort her.

You damned fool, he told himself furiously. *Look at what the conniving jezebel has done to you!*

It had taken her only a few minutes to render for naught fourteen long years of struggle and sacrifice on his part to prove to his father that he had wrongly judged his younger son.

She was so damned good an actress that she ought to go on the stage with the other whores!

Angel croaked brokenly to Lady Bloomfield, "I did not . . ." Her voice failed, and she could not continue.

Lady Bloomfield grabbed Angel's cotton wrapper from the foot of the bed and held out her hand to the girl. "Come with me to my apartment."

"No!" Rupert Crowe protested, stepping forward. "I will not permit you—"

Her ladyship cut him off. "You will not presume to tell me what I may do in my own home," she said, giving him a look of such loathing that it seemed to freeze his tongue. "Now get out of my sight before I have you ejected from my house."

Crowe, apparently unwilling to put her threat to the test, departed.

When he was gone, Lady Bloomfield again held out her hand to Angel. As she obediently slipped out of Lucian's bed, the sheer lawn of her night rail clung to her like a second skin, revealing her full, firm breasts, tiny waist, and the shapely legs that he had admired when she had swung across the creek. For such a petite girl, her body was exquisitely proportioned.

Lucian felt his own body's response. Had he lost his mind? How could he possibly feel desire for a girl who had ground his most cherished goal into dust?

Lady Bloomfield helped Angel into the wrapper, then led her toward the door.

The girl looked so miserable that Lucian wondered whether the Crowes had somehow forced her to go along with their plot.

A flicker of hope sputtered within him. Angel was a brave little thing. He remembered how she had laughed as she had swung, suspended from a rope, across the roaring creek. Perhaps now that the Crowes were gone, she might summon up the courage to tell Kitty's mother what had really happened.

Lucian called, "Lady Bloomfield, get her to tell you the truth of what occurred in this room. I swear that nothing happened between us."

Frowning, Lady Bloomfield paused and asked Angel gently, "Is Lord Vayle's claim that he did not, er, lie with you the truth?"

Angel looked perplexed by Lady Bloomfield's question.

Lucian held his breath. After fourteen years, it all came down to this. His fate lay in her hands.

Angel hesitated, but when she spoke it was with ringing firmness. "Of course, it is not true! How can you even ask me? You have seen with your own eyes that he lay with me."

The nascent sympathy that had been budding in Lucian for her died an instant death.

The damned, unprincipled liar! He would make her regret her perjuries.

She would soon rue this day as much as he did.

Chapter 6

"Now that we are alone, Angel, there is something that I must ask you," Lady Bloomfield said, her face grave.

She had brought Angel to her own large bedchamber, sent a servant to bring them tea, then settled her on a comfortable settee by the windows that looked out over Fernhill's formal garden, with its topiary and parterres.

"How did you come to be in Lord Vayle's bed?"

"I do not know," Angel replied, embarrassed by how foolish her answer sounded.

"Tell me the truth, child. Did Vayle coax you into it?"

"No. I don't know how I got there." Angel stared down at her tightly clasped hands in mortification. "When I went to sleep I was in the bed with the green silk hangings in the room you always gave me. But when I awoke I was in his room and his bed."

Lady Bloomfield's frown deepened. "How is that possible?"

Angel wished she knew. She had the uneasy feeling that what had happened might somehow have been her fault. Clearly, Lord Vayle thought it was. Could she blame him for that when it was she who had been in his bed?

"Have you ever walked in your sleep, child?"

"Not to my knowledge. Oh, dear heaven, do you think that I could somehow have walked into his room in my sleep and got into bed with him?" Angel blushed with shame.

"No, it seems quite impossible to me."

A footman arrived with a silver tea service and blue-

and-white porcelain cups. He placed the tray on a small walnut table in front of the settee and quietly departed.

Lady Bloomfield poured tea into one of the cups and gave it to Angel. She took it gratefully, hoping that it would help relieve the odd, throbbing headache that had plagued her since she had awakened.

As Lady Bloomfield poured tea for herself, she asked, "When you awakened in Lord Vayle's bed, was he, er—touching you?"

"Aye," Angel could feel her face growing hot at the memory of the delicious pleasure she had felt lying in his arms. "He was hugging me very tightly to him."

"Dear God! Did you attempt to get away from him?"

Angel remembered how she had tried to do so only to have Lord Vayle's arms tighten around her. "Aye, but I could not. He was too strong."

Lady Bloomfield looked aghast. "Dear heaven, and because he was too strong, were you then forced to, er—lie with him?"

Angel was surprised that her hostess would ask such a foolish question. It was perfectly obvious that if she awakened beside Lord Vayle in his bed that she was lying with him.

She set her cup down on the walnut table. "Aye," she replied, although saying that she had been *forced* to lie with him was not entirely accurate. After all, he had been asleep, too.

Angel was about to explain this when Lady Bloomfield seized her hands in her own.

"You poor, dear child," she said pityingly. "He must have hurt you terribly."

Angel, thinking of how he had tightened his grasp painfully when she had tried to wiggle away, answered truthfully, "No, only a little and then only for a moment."

Tendrils of excitement curled in her at the memory of how pleasant it had been lying in his arms. "After that, I enjoyed it very much," she confessed with an embarrassed little smile.

Lady Bloomfield looked astonished. "You did? Oh, my poor sweet child, I am glad for that. Often when a woman lies with a man for the first time, the experience is agonizing for her, especially if he does not love her. At least Vayle was not such a monster that he . . ." Her mouth hardened in a thin, determined line. "However, the sooner he marries you the better."

"But he will not marry me. You heard him say he would not."

"Do not let that trouble you. Whether he likes it or not, he *will* marry you."

"I do not want that," Angel protested. From the recesses of her memory, she recalled her father's repeated admonition: "Never marry a man who does not want and love you, my precious Angel, for he will make you miserable. You deserve better than that. You deserve a man who will cherish you."

Not a man who called her a *"horror"* to her face.

She shivered as she recalled the rage and loathing with which Lord Vayle had regarded her. She would never marry a man who felt that way about her, and especially not when he was betrothed to the girl who had been her closest friend. Her heart still ached at the memory of Kitty's outburst when she had seen Angel in Vayle's bed.

"I will not marry him," Angel said firmly. "He belongs to Kitty."

"He forfeited any right to her when he slept with you under our very roof." Lady Bloomfield took a slow sip of tea from the blue and white porcelain cup. Then, as though fortified by it, she said, "I will be blunt with you, child. I preferred Kitty to marry David Inge, but my husband would not hear of it."

"Why Mr. Inge?"

"Because he loved Kitty."

"But surely Lord Vayle must have lost his heart to her, too, or he would not—"

Lady Bloomfield interrupted her with a snort. "I strongly doubt that Vayle has a heart to lose."

"But everyone has a heart," Angel protested, much shocked.

"Not Vayle! On the other hand, David Inge would make Kitty a kind and loving husband." Her mother sighed.

"But she is still too young and fickle to appreciate how important that is."

"Papa thought it was very important, too."

"Nobody knew better than your father the price of marrying a spouse who did not love him. Poor man."

Lady Bloomfield absently traced the abstract pattern on her teacup with her index finger. "What is saddest is that Kitty truly cared for David, but then Roger Peck, Lord Peck's son and heir, deigned to pay her heed. He is disgustingly rich as well as handsome and charming. Women throw themselves at his feet."

"Did Kitty?"

"No, but he swept her off hers. Kitty was so proud that she had captured him—or thought she had. Roger quickly lost interest in her, as he does in every woman. I had warned her he would do so, but she would not listen. Then Vayle, who was considered a great marital catch, appeared, salving Kitty's pride."

But now, Angel thought mournfully, it had been savaged again by the scene this morning in Lord Vayle's bedroom. "Poor Kitty, I have unwittingly hurt her, and I would not have done so for the world."

"In truth, this morning's incident could prove salutary if it helps her realize the worth of a man like Inge, who loves her." Lady Bloomfield poured more tea into Angel's cup and then into her own. "Not that I want you to marry Vayle either. I had hoped for a kinder, gentler man than Lord Lucifer for you, but there is no help for it now."

"Why not?"

"Because he has ruined you. That unfortunate scene in his bedroom this morning destroyed your reputation beyond repair. You may be certain our guests will tell the story everywhere, and then no man would dream of marrying you."

Angel, who knew nothing of the conventions of society, stammered, "I don't understand why I am ruined."

"Dear child, if an unmarried girl sleeps with a man, no other man will have her as his wife. She must never have lain with a man until she goes to her husband on her wedding night. Did your father never explain that to you?"

No, he had not. How terribly unjust, Angel thought, to be ruined simply because she had lain on a bed beside Lord Vayle. It had been very pleasant to snuggle against his warm strength, but not *that* pleasant.

"Poor child, Vayle has callously robbed you of your honor."

Angel did know how important honor was. Her papa had emphasized over and over to her and her brother Charles that honor was a man—or woman's—most priceless possession.

Papa had told them that honor involved many things. They must always do what was right and be honest and fair in their dealings with others. They must always be kind to everyone, generous to those less fortunate than themselves, and responsible for those dependent upon them. But most important, they must never allow anyone to cast aspersions on their character.

"If any man does so," Papa had told Charles, "you must call him out. That is why it is so important that you learn to fence well, for that is how you defend your honor. You must never permit a man to challenge your honor without demanding redress."

When Angel had learned that her father did not intend for her to learn to fence too, she had been indignant.

"But, Papa," she had asked, "is not a woman's honor as important to her as a man's is to him?"

"More important," her father had said, a caustic edge to his voice, "but a woman has a different way of protecting her honor than a man does."

"What is that, Papa?"

"She will have nothing to do with any man who cannot or will not offer her marriage. She knows that such a man is a scoundrel and intends to rob her of her honor."

"And how will he do that?" Angel had asked in puzzlement.

"By whispering sweet lies in your ears."

"What kind of lies?"

"He will shower you with compliments and blandishments that are as false as he is, and then he will ruin you. Know him for what he is, a man with no honor."

Now Angel was confused. Lady Bloomfield said Lord Vayle had stolen her honor, yet he had not whispered sweet compliments to her. None at all. Instead he had called her a horror.

She was baffled as to what she should do. Had Lord Vayle cast aspersions on her integrity, she would have known immediately she must call him out and defend her honor.

Her father, always loath to deny her instruction on any subject her brother was taught, had given in to Angel's pleadings and permitted her fencing lessons. She had proven to be far more skillful than Charlie, who had been clumsy on his feet.

Lady Bloomfield studied Angel over the rim of her teacup. "Are you certain, child, that you have no notion how you got into Vayle's bed?"

"None at all."

"Tell me everything you remember before you went to sleep."

"Maude and I had both gone to bed and—"

"Who is Maude?"

"The maid Sir Rupert insisted I must bring with me."

"If she was with you, she must know how you got out of your room," Lady Bloomfield exclaimed, ringing a bell for a servant.

Of course, she must. Angel should have thought of that herself, but the dull throbbing in her head seemed to have made her exceptionally dull-witted this morning.

When a footman answered her ladyship's summons, she told him, "Find Lady Angela's maid, Maude, and bring her to me at once."

"Aye, m'lady," he said, rushing off.

"Perhaps I won't have to marry Lord Vayle after all," Angel said hopefully.

"If you do not marry him, Angel, you will be condemned to a life of lonely spinsterhood, without husband or children of your own."

"But . . . but you said earlier that I might already be with child," Angel said in confusion.

"That is true. Whenever you lie with a man as you did with Vayle, you can become pregnant."

"I did not know that." Angel wondered again why Lord Vayle had refused to tell her how babies were made. He should have told her instead of getting upset.

Angel smiled happily at the thought that she might be going to have a baby of her own. She adored children. She loved playing with them, and she loved teaching them. She had set up a classroom at Belle Haven to teach the offspring of its dependents to read and write. Her most cherished dream was to have children of her own to love and raise.

"Oh, I hope I am going to have a baby!" she burst out with a sunny smile.

"Then you had better hope, too, that Vayle will marry you."

"Why?"

"If he will not, you cannot keep your baby. It will be sent away."

Angel was horrified. She jumped to her feet, too agitated to sit. "No one will ever take my baby away from me!" She had never been so determined about anything in her life. "Never, never, never!"

Her own mother, even before she had deserted her family, had paid her daughter no heed. All Angel's life, she had longed for the mother's love that she had never known. She would never permit any child of hers to suffer that fate.

"Then," Lady Bloomfield said quietly, "you will have to marry Vayle."

Angel was aghast at the choice she faced. She would never give up a baby of her flesh, but neither did she want to marry a man who felt the hatred and contempt for her that Lord Vayle did.

Lucian knocked on the door of the room that he had seen Maude come out of the previous day.

No one answered.

He knocked again, but still there was no response.

Lucian gently tried the door. The knob turned easily. He

checked to make certain the room was empty, then slipped inside, and shut the door behind him.

It was small but elegantly outfitted. The drapes and the bed hangings were of green silk. Both the bed and the cot beside it were unmade. A large oak wardrobe and a chest of drawers stood side by side against the wall.

He tried the chest of drawers first, going through it quickly. The first drawer held a pair of boy's breeches. Lucian frowned, wondering what breeches were doing in a room supposedly being used by females.

The second drawer was empty. The bottom one contained a dirty old pillow that should have been thrown out long ago. It was so covered with dust that it looked as though it had been rolled through a dustheap. How odd that anyone would have bothered to save it, Lucian thought as he shut the drawer.

The wardrobe contained a boy's white shirt, ruffled down the front, and two black garments, which Lucian recognized as those he had seen Angel wearing yesterday. It did not surprise him this was her room. Maude had obviously been in the Crowes' employ. After the maid had drugged him, she must have fetched Angel to come to his bed.

Lucian examined the shabby clothes in the wardrobe with distaste. Both dresses were clearly hand-me-downs that had once belonged to a larger woman. He wondered whether Angel had a single presentable gown to her name. If she had, she surely would have worn it to the ball last night.

He had thought that her father must have been a rich merchant who had made his money in trade, then died unexpectedly, leaving his foolish wife a rich widow and the prey of an unscrupulous man like Rupert Crowe. But Angel's sorry wardrobe indicated her family had little or no money.

Lucian massaged his head with his fingertips. It still ached from the drug that had been in the wine.

A pretty young chambermaid came into the room. "Beg pardon, sir, I am to make the bed. Would you be wishing me to come back later?"

"No, do it now. Can you tell me where I would find the maid who came with the guest staying in this room. The maid's name is Maude."

The girl's eyes widened in dismay. "Oh, sir, did she prig something of yours?"

Only his honor and his most cherished dream! "Why do you ask me that?"

"Because Rosie, one of the other maids, saw her sneaking away at dawn's first light, carrying a small bag. Then Rosie thought she heard the sound of a horse galloping off, and Maude, she ne'er came back. Rosie told Mr. Timms, the butler, and he was afeared she prigged some of the guests' jewelry. No one's complained of anything gone missing. But why else, I ask you, would she sneak away like that?"

So I cannot wring a confession out of her as to how Angel really came to be in my bed. Lucian remembered how nervous Maude had been while she was trying to seduce him. She just might prove to be the weakest link in the Crowes' scheme. With a little persuasion, financial or otherwise, she might be induced to betray what they had done.

Lucian had to find her.

It would do him no good, though, to look for her now. Dawn had been hours ago. By now, she would be many miles from Fernhill, and he had no idea in which direction she had gone. Furthermore, she had undoubtedly been instructed to remain in hiding for several weeks.

But Lucian would locate her if it took him the rest of his life. And when he did, one way or another, he would get the truth out of her.

He went back to his own room, where he discovered David Inge waiting for him.

Without preamble, David demanded angrily, "How could you hurt and humiliate poor Kitty like this?"

Lucian wearily rubbed his aching temples. He was tired of being regarded as the villain in this piece when, in fact, he was the victim. "I did nothing!" he snapped.

"Damn you, Lucian, how can you say that when you have broken Kitty's heart!"

"As she broke your heart when she jilted you!"

"But at least we were not formally betrothed. You publicly humiliated Kitty. How could you seduce another woman on the very night you were celebrating your betrothal to Kitty?"

"You will not believe this, but I have no notion how that girl came to be in my bed."

"You are right, I do not believe it. It is not like you to act like that, Lucian. Were you foxed?"

"No, I was duped and drugged!"

"You?" David was incredulous. "You are too clever for that."

"As it turns out, I am not as clever as you think. Damned fool that I am, I underestimated the Crowes. I told you they meant to prevent my marrying Kitty, and now they have succeeded."

Murderously angry as it made Lucian, he knew that he must wed Angel. The repercussions of not doing so made his head ache even worse than it already did.

He told David how he had found Maude in his room and had acquiesced to her wish to drink a toast.

"The claret was clearly drugged. I passed out immediately afterward. When I came to, my bedroom was crowded with shocked onlookers, and Crowe's stepdaughter was in bed beside me."

Lucian looked with revulsion at the unmade bed where his dream of vindication—and fourteen years of striving—had died.

He strode angrily past the rumpled bed to the windows that overlooked the front entrance to Fernhill and stared grimly out. Dark, threatening clouds blotted out the sun, matching his own mood. Already a few drops of rain were spattering against the leaded glass panes.

Below him, guests were leaving. The gala celebration that had brought them here had come to an abrupt, untimely end—and one very different than anyone could have imagined.

Lucian watched the cream of society being helped into their carriages, undoubtedly rushing off in the hope of being the first back to London to spread the deliciously scandalous tale.

Although Lucian was innocent of despoiling Angel, no one would believe that after the very public scene her stepfather had staged.

Especially not when the damned little liar kept insisting that he had slept with her.

David asked, "What does the stepdaughter say?"

Lucian's jaw clenched as he remembered Angel's words to Lady Bloomfield in the hall. "The perfidious little witch insists I slept with her. I give you my oath I did not—even though the skirt of her night rail was liberally stained with blood. I also stand unjustly convicted of stealing her virginity."

"Odd's fish," David exclaimed. "You will have to marry her or you will be ostracized by society."

"Aye," Lucian agreed. "I knew that the moment I saw the blood on her night rail. I must marry her, not because I ruined her, but because the world erroneously thinks I have. And under the most scandalous and public of circumstances."

If Lucian did not marry her, he would most likely lose his royal patronage. The king would be furious with Lucian when he heard the story, and the queen, a pious woman, would be even more unhappy and disgusted with him. If he did not wed Angel, he would be even more unwelcome at court than Bloomfield was.

Both the Crown and polite society would brand him a dishonorable cad unworthy of their notice.

Much as it infuriated him to be forced to marry such an unconscionable liar, he had worked too hard to achieve his present position of eminence to throw it away now.

Behind him, David said, "That bastard Crowe made certain you had a large audience. He woke everyone on the pretext he was looking for his stepdaughter. He claimed her maid had just come to him after awaking and discovering that the girl was missing from her bed."

"The maid who has conveniently disappeared." Lucian turned away from the window to face his friend. "I trust that you will comfort Kitty for my loss. The only good to come out of this day's disaster is that you will be free to court her again." The corner of Lucian's lip curled up in a grim half-smile. "You ought to be well pleased by what has happened."

"I am not!" David cried. "I do not want to see you tricked into marriage when you did nothing wrong."

"But society perceives I have, and in society perceptions are everything."

Lucian cast a revolted glance at the tumbled bed that had been the downfall of his ambition. "What irony! Only yesterday I told you how a man in my position marries for rich estates, an alliance with a prestigious family, and impressive bloodlines for his heir. Now I am trapped in a wasted marriage that will bring no benefit: no estate, no dowry, no powerful alliance, and a bride of very dubious bloodlines."

"What do you know about the girl's parentage?" David asked.

"According to Lady Bloomfield, Angel's father was an eccentric recluse and her mother a notorious wanton who was as selfish as she was faithless."

"Clearly she must be stupid, too, or she would never have married Rupert Crowe," David observed. "He has made himself so notorious that no intelligent woman would consort with him."

And this was the wretched family, Lucian thought angrily, that he was being forced to marry into.

But the most agonizing realization was what Lucian's father, Lord Wrexham, would think when he heard of this day's events. His lips hardened in a thin line. It would reassure his father that his judgment of his younger son had been justified.

Lucian still remembered the shattering day his father had disowned him and sent him away to the army.

Penniless and hard put to live on an officer's inadequate pay, Lucian had turned to gambling to support himself. He excelled at games that involved skill as well as chance.

Rather than squandering his winnings, he had shrewdly invested them in building, shipping, joint stock companies, and other speculations that in time had made him a very rich man.

Although the military was not the career Lucian had wanted, he distinguished himself on the battlefield with his courage and the tactical brilliance that stood him in such good stead at the gaming tables, and he had quickly risen to high rank.

He had also endured years of mud and dust and wretched rations, of blood and gore on the battlefield and tedium off of it. He had come to hate the stench, waste, and carnage of war.

Through it all, the one thing that had kept him going, that had driven him to excel, had been his determination that someday he would force his father to admit to him that he had been terribly wrong in his judgment of his younger son.

And now, just as his goal was within his grasp, all those years and the sacrifices he had made were for naught.

Sommerstone would never be his. Instead of it again belonging to a Sandford, it would remain in Bloomfield's hands.

Any hope of marrying into the family that had rejected his older brother as beneath it was now dead.

And this day's fiasco would reenforce Wrexham's contempt and hatred for his younger son.

Lucian longed to smash his fist through the wall in his fury and frustration at what the Crowes and that devil's spawn misnamed Angel had cost him.

Lucian might have underestimated the Crowes, but they had underestimated him even more. He would not be able to escape the marital trap they had set for him, but in the end he would have his vengeance. He was not nicknamed Lord Lucifer for nothing.

He told David, "Tell Rupert Crowe that I will marry his wretched stepdaughter. I do not trust myself to see him without killing him."

"Knowing Crowe, he will demand a marriage settlement," David warned.

"Tell him the only thing I will settle on his accurst stepdaughter is my name. Nothing else." Lucian's hand settled ominously on the hilt of his sword. "Except perhaps my sword through his body."

David nodded, then asked softly, "How do you feel toward the girl?"

"How do you think I feel toward her? I loathe her!"

"Not a sentiment conducive to a long, happy marriage."

"The marriage will be neither long nor happy," Lucian said savagely.

"What do you mean?"

"I will marry her because I must, but as soon as I have done so, I will take her to Ardmore and leave her there to repent her sins against me in lonely isolation. Once she is there, I intend never to set eyes on her again."

He would still make the trip to his Hampshire estate that he had planned, but now he would take his unwanted bride with him and dump her there.

"Angel will be my wife in name only and not even that for very long if I have my way," Lucian told David. "I intend to find Maid Maude, and one way or another I will get a full confession out of her about how I was tricked into this situation."

"Then what will you do?"

"Have the marriage annulled on grounds of fraud."

Chapter 7

No more than fifteen minutes after David left Lucian to see Rupert Crowe, he was back.

"The wedding will be this afternoon in the drawing room," David told Lucian. "As I predicted, Crowe wanted a marriage settlement, but he knew better than to press his luck."

David took his leave of Lucian a second time. A half hour later Lady Bloomfield came to his door.

Lucian had not seen her since she had led Angel from his bedroom. He liked Kitty's mother, and he was determined that she should hear the truth about what had happened, even though she would not believe it.

"I swear to you that I did not seduce Angel Winter. Nor did I rob her of her virginity."

Lady Bloomfield looked outraged. "You dare to claim she was not an innocent when you took her? You will never make me believe that!"

"I have no notion whether she is an innocent or not. I swear, though, that no matter how strong the evidence against me appears—and I am the first to admit how damning it is—I did not take her at all."

"She says that you did," Lady Bloomfield said coldly. "Angel is the most honest person I know. She would not lie about it."

But she was lying about it, damn her! Choking down his rage at her perfidy, Lucian forced himself to say calmly, "I do not wish to debate her character with you, but I am telling you the truth."

"I do not believe you."

He could feel the leash on his temper slipping. "If you

were a man, I would call you out for daring to challenge my veracity."

"And if I were a man, I would accept for what you have done to Angel."

"God's oath, I have done *nothing* to her!

"She told me that you did lie with her."

"She is the only one who is lying!"

"If it were anyone but Angel, I might believe you," Lady Bloomfield confessed. "I have never known you to be a liar. But even if you are telling the truth, you have ruined her in the eyes of the world. And that is what counts."

"I know. That is why I agreed to marry her."

"Sir Rupert said you had. He has already sent for the rector at Bourton. You will be married as soon as he arrives, provided, my lord, you can convince Angel to wed you."

"What?" Lucian could not believe he had heard her right.

"That is why I have come. Angel refuses to marry you. She knows you do not want her, and she has told her stepfather that nothing can force the vows from her lips."

"That's wonderful," Lucian exclaimed, feeling the marital noose the Crowes had flung about his neck loosen. Honor required that he offer for her and he had done so. But if she refused him, he would be released from his obligation to marry her.

He wondered why, after trapping him like that, Angel was suddenly willing to let him go. She must have lost her nerve when she realized that, after the damning lies she had told about him, he would make her life miserable.

"No, it is not wonderful," Lady Bloomfield snapped. "No other man will look at her now. You must change her mind. You must persuade her to marry you."

"I must?" He stared at her in openmouthed astonishment, then exploded, "God's oath, woman, I want to marry her even less than she wants to marry me! And now you tell me that you expect me to convince her to go through with a wedding that is the last thing on earth I want. You are mad!"

"No, I am desperately concerned about Angel's future. I want her out of Rupert Crowe's control. She is like a second daughter to me. I love her dearly."

"Apparently even more than your own flesh and blood," he said scornfully. "Don't you care that Kitty is the one who will be most hurt if I marry Angel."

"It will hurt Kitty's pride far more than her heart," her mother said bluntly. "I will be candid with you, my lord. I preferred her to marry David Inge, although my husband strongly opposed the match. David is a good and honorable man."

"The best," Lucian seconded.

"He is also in love with Kitty, something you are not. In fact, I have often wondered why you offered for her."

"The usual reasons a man of my position offers for a wife."

"Ah, yes," Lady Bloomfield said coolly, "a prestigious alliance, property, and good bloodlines."

"And Angel will bring me none of them."

"To the contrary, she would bring you all three if you help her recover the inheritance her stepfather has stolen from her."

"You consider marriage to the daughter of some eccentric recluse and the stepdaughter of that blackguard Rupert Crowe a *prestigious* alliance?" he scoffed.

"There is not an aristocrat in the land who can look upon marriage to Lady Angela Winter as beneath him, and that includes you, my lord."

"She is a lady? I don't believe it! Who the devil was her father?"

"The Earl of Ashcott."

Bloody hell! Ashcott. The scientific earl. Belle Haven's late owner.

He remembered the dedication of the earl's *Journal of Belle Haven:* "To my precious Angel."

Lucian wondered bitterly what the scientific earl would think of his precious Angel if he could see the lying jade now.

Nevertheless, Lucian felt the marital noose tightening around his neck again. To appear to have publicly ruined an earl's daughter and then not marry her would put him beyond the pale. Nor could he do that to Ashcott's daughter.

Much as it galled him, he would have to convince her to marry him.

"Very well, I will talk to her," he said wearily. "In return, I ask a favor of you. Please find her something that is not black and ugly to wear for our wedding. She has abysmal taste in clothes." At first, he had thought it was because she had no money, but her father had been very rich.

"It is not Angel's fault," Lady Bloomfield said. "Her father ignored fashion and ridiculed it to her as silly and frivolous. The dear child has no notion of how to dress. Quite frankly, I suspect that he wanted her to look shabby and dowdy in the hope that she would attract no man's eye. I think he hoped to keep her with him as his companion in his seclusion."

"Will you see what you can find for her for our wedding?"

"Aye, but there will not be one unless you can change her mind about marrying you."

Lucian said grimly, "There will be a wedding."

He found Angel huddled on a settee in Fernhill's small library, where he had been drinking in the early hours of that morning.

She was wearing the shabby black gown that he had first seen her in. Once again her lustrous chocolate hair had been caught up in an unbecoming knot atop her head. A few wisps had escaped the fastening and curled about her face.

A book was open in her lap, but she was not reading it. Instead she was rubbing her temples as though she had a headache and staring unhappily out the window at the green lawns still wet from the rainstorm that had been intense but brief.

Lucian quietly shut the library door to give them privacy. He silently crossed the room to the settee. Angel was so lost in her thoughts that she did not notice him until he said her name.

She started in surprise. When she looked up at him, he forgot his anger, so stunned was he by the change in her. Her eyes were no longer brilliant but dull and unhappy. All trace of the vitality that he found so winsome was erased. She looked pitifully young and small, defenseless and woebegone huddled there. Lucian had an irrational urge to comfort her.

Bloody hell, was he going daft?

He reminded himself of what she had done to him, of what she had cost him, and his heart hardened against her.

Lucian saw a quick flash of unease in her huge blue eyes before she managed to hide it. Then her face tightened in determination, and she met his gaze defiantly.

Despite his anger at her, he could not help admiring her courage. Many men he knew would have quailed before the look he had given her.

"I will not marry you," she told him firmly.

Taken aback by the intractable note in her voice, he said, "I do not want to marry you either, but unfortunately we must—"

"No! I shall not! I am a woman of honor—"

"You certainly fooled me on that point," he interjected sardonically.

"Well, I am!" Her eyes, the color of the sky on a summer day, blazed with indignation. "And a woman of pride, too. I will not marry a man who does not want me!"

"You should have thought of that before you sneaked into my bed, and left us with no choice in the matter."

There was no mistaking the resolve in her expression. Her delicate chin tilted proudly, stubbornly. "Papa said a person always has a choice when it comes to his honor."

Lucian was astonished that after what she had done to him, she could still have the audacity to prattle about honor. "What an odd sense of honor you have in light of that very public performance you staged this morning." The memory of it made him grind his teeth. "You should have told our very interested audience the truth—that I did not sleep with you."

"But you did! Everyone saw you."

Lucian was baffled why, now that Angel seemed determined not to marry him, she would continue to lie about his having slept with her.

"Everyone saw what you and your evil stepfather wanted them to think they saw, and you know it," he exploded. "If you were half so concerned about your precious honor as you profess to be, you would confess what really happened in my bedroom!"

Angel's expression was so troubled and mortified that he wondered whether the reprehensible Crowes had forced her to help them against her will. Was she trying to atone for it now by refusing to marry him?

"Why won't you tell the truth?" he pressed. "Are you afraid of what your stepfather and brother will do to you?"

He sat down on the settee beside her and took her hands in his own. They were as cold as two chunks of ice. "If that is what it is, Angel, I swear that if you tell the true story about this morning, I will protect you from the Crowes' wrath." He gave her an encouraging smile. "Did they force you into my bed."

Her troubled eyes met his without evasion. "No."

He dropped her icy hands as though they had stung him. His sympathy for her vanished. He wanted to throttle the little liar.

"Then why did you come to my bed like that?"

"But I did not."

"Well, I surely didn't coax you there, as you well know!"

She looked horribly embarrassed and her gaze fell away from his. "The truth is I do not know how I got in your bed."

"God's oath, what you will try to tell me next—that the world is flat?"

"Please, I know it sounds impossible"—her mouth and chin were trembling—"but I swear that when I went to sleep I was in my own bed, and when I awoke I was in yours." She looked at him with those wide blue eyes that seemed incapable of guile. "Do you think I could have been sleepwalking?"

"No, I do not," he said sharply. She managed to look so damned innocent that she would have had Lucian believing anything she said if he had not heard her lie so convincingly to Lady Bloomfield about his having taken her. He could only marvel at what a superb actress she was.

Suddenly, her face crumbled, "I know I must be at fault in what happened, for I am the one who was in your bed."

"How kind of you to admit that much," he said sarcastically.

Angel rubbed her temples again as she had done when he had first come into the library.

"Do you have a headache?" Lucian asked.

"Aye, I do not understand it. I have never had one before, but ever since I awoke this morning I have had this dull, throbbing pain."

So did Lucian from the drug in the wine.

Bloody hell, could Angel have been drugged, too?

He grabbed her arms. "Tell me everything you did last night between the time you left the ball and you fell asleep."

She blinked at him, clearly surprised by the sudden urgency in his voice. "I went directly to my room and went to bed."

"Did you talk to anyone?"

"Only the maid the Crowes insisted I must bring with me."

"Maude?" Lucian asked, releasing Angel's arms.

Her eyes widened in surprise. "How did you know her name?"

"I met her yesterday."

"I did not like her at first," Angel confided, "but she was very kind to me last night."

"How?" Lucian asked, certain that Maude would not have been kind except for some nefarious reason.

"When I got into bed, I started to sneeze terribly. I could not seem to stop. I don't know what was wrong with me. I have never sneezed like that before except when I got a nose full of dust."

Lucian's hands tightened into fists as he remembered

the dust-covered pillow hidden in the chest of drawers. It would have made anyone sneeze.

"Maude gave me some of her grandmama's special elixir to stop my sneezing, and it worked wonderfully because I stopped sneezing almost immediately and went sound to sleep."

"Angel, when Maude gave you the elixir, did she by chance also do anything with your pillow?"

"Why, yes, she did. How did you know?" Angel asked in innocent surprise. "She said my pillow did not look very comfortable, and she was right. She brought me a new one that was much better."

Maude and the Crowes had drugged Angel, too. An inexplicable surge of joy and relief washed over Lucian at the realization that she was as innocent as she claimed. She had not been a willing participant in the Crowes' trap after all.

After drugging her, they had dumped her in his bed. The naive girl had awakened to all those staring faces and been utterly mystified as to how she had gotten there. He at least had known immediately that the Crowes were responsible and what their reason was.

Lucian wanted to snatch her up in his arms and hug her.

Then his elation faded. If she was innocent, why the hell did she keep insisting he had slept with her when he had not?

An ugly suspicion seized him. "Angel, have you been sleeping with another man?"

"No, only you."

"God's oath, why do you continue to insist that I slept with you when you know it is a lie," he growled. "I ought to beat the truth out of you."

"But I am not lying!" she cried, clearly distressed.

"You may be able to convince everyone else of that, but I know better. I was there, remember? I know that I did not sleep with you!"

Angel looked at him in bewilderment. "But you did."

"God's oath, why do you persist in that fiction?" he ground out through rigid jaw. "I have already agreed to marry you."

Her eyes glittered with defiant anger. "I told you I will not marry you."

"And I told you that we have no choice."

"Why? Because of the baby?"

He looked at her blankly. "What baby?"

"The one we may have made when we lay together." Her eyes were suddenly bright and hopeful again. "Well, you need not worry about it. I want the baby very much, and I promise you that I shall take very good care of it. I will never let anyone take it away from me."

"Angel," Lucian said through clenched teeth, "I have not given you a baby."

"Lady Bloomfield said you might deny responsibility for it. She said men often do."

Lucian prayed for patience. "Angel, I am not denying responsibility. I am telling you for a fact that you are not carrying my baby. It is an impossibility."

Angel frowned in confusion. "But Lady Bloomfield says there is no sure way to prevent a baby."

"She is wrong. There is one absolutely foolproof way of doing so, and I used it."

"What is it?"

"Abstinence."

"I don't understand . . ."

"Lady Bloomfield is under the mistaken impression that I slept with you."

"But you did. Do you deny that I was in your bed with you when you awakened!"

"Aye, you were in my bed, but I did not sleep with you."

"You are making no sense! How can you admit that I was in your bed, and then say I did not sleep with you?" She looked up at him with huge blue eyes full of reproach. "Why did you not tell me when I asked that it is so easy to make a baby? I had no idea I had only to lie on a bed beside you and your baby would begin to grow inside me."

Lucian's jaw dropped in astonishment. Surely, she must be hoaxing him. No one could be *that* innocent.

Then he recalled Lady Bloomfield's words: *"Angel is so*

naive . . . I doubt she even knows what happens between a man and a woman."

Bloody hell, she did not know! His anger at her dissolved in relief, followed by the unhappy realization that he was now more securely trapped than ever. When he had believed her a willing participant in the plot against him, he had not cared what happened to her. He had intended to dump her at Ardmore until he could obtain an annulment, but now that he knew she was blameless, he could not even do that.

She was as much the Crowes' innocent victim as he was, and she deserved better than a husband who would abandon her to solitary confinement at a remote estate.

His anger that his long struggle to redeem himself in his father's eyes has gone for naught—fourteen wasted years—had not abated, but now it was directed at the proper target, the Crowes. It was not Angel's fault that he had been robbed of his chance to prove himself to his father.

But it was the Crowes' doing. And he swore that he would have a full measure of vengeance against them. His eyes narrowed assessingly as he recalled something his hostess had told him.

"Angel, Lady Bloomfield said that the Crowes stole your inheritance from you. How did they do that?"

She told him how her father's will was missing. "The only one that can be found was made many years ago before my mother deserted Papa and leaves everything to her."

Lucian frowned. Ashcott had been a very rich man. By marrying Angel's mother, Rupert Crowe had gained legal control of the great fortune she had inherited from her first husband—the fortune that should have gone to Angel.

His mouth tightened as he thought of the girl's shabby, made-over clothes. Clearly that bastard, Rupert Crowe, did not intend for her to have a pence of what was rightfully hers.

"Are you certain there was a later will?" Lucian asked.

Angel nodded. "At least two, but neither can be found. The first one Papa executed after my mother left him so that she would inherit nothing. Then after my brother Charlie died, he made one that left everything to me."

"Did you actually see that second will with your own eyes."

"Aye, Papa showed it to me and to my uncle."

Now Lucian knew how he would achieve his revenge on the Crowes.

And fittingly, Angel would be his instrument.

He would find her father's later will, and then he would have the pleasure of legally taking Ashcott's fortune away from the Crowes.

They would curse the day that they had decided to make him their victim.

Eager to launch his scheme, he asked Angel, "Where can I find your uncle who saw the will?"

"In the graveyard. He is dead, too."

Lucian bit back a curse.

Angel, her voice weighted with frustration, said, "My worst fear is that the Crowes may already have found the will and destroyed it."

If they had, Angel would not have a prayer of recovering what was rightfully hers.

She patted her stomach and said wistfully, "I want our baby to inherit Belle Haven someday."

"Angel, there is no baby," Lucian said in exasperation. "Making one is not quite as easy as you think."

"It is not?" She looked so surprised and perplexed that he had to smother a sudden urge to simultaneously laugh and hug her. A fierce desire to protect her suddenly gripped him.

"No, little one," he said gently, "a man must do more than merely lie on a bed beside a woman to give her a baby."

"What must he do?"

"He must make love to her."

Her dark brows knit in puzzlement. "How does he do that?"

"He takes her in his arms—"

"But you did that to me."

"He also touches her in special places that I did not."

"What special places?"

Angel looked so fascinated and delectable that Lucian was seized by an overwhelming desire to show her instead of tell her.

And why should he not? Before the day was done, she would be his wife.

He touched the tip of her breast and caressed it lightly with his finger. "There."

From her amazed look, he knew that no man had ever touched her like that before. Through the thin, black material of her gown, he felt her nipple harden, and she gave a little moan. She was so responsive to his touch that he was certain she would be a wildly passionate little creature in bed.

His own body reacted with embarrassing fierceness to her innocent provocation. God's oath, but she was so sweet.

Lucian knew just as surely as he knew that his manhood was swelling to unusual size that he was playing with fire, but he could not help himself any more than he could prevent his erection. Smiling at her, his hand dipped lower.

His fingers lightly teased her belly. "And there."

Chapter 8

Angel gasped, her face flushing hotly with the sheer pleasure of Lucian's touch. It unleashed wild sensations, simultaneously exciting and aching, deep within her.

"Then," he said, his eyes so intense and hot that she was reminded of molten silver, "if I wanted to give you a baby, I would caress you in an even more private place."

He gestured vaguely toward the apex of her legs that suddenly seemed to be bathed in an aching heat. She found herself yearning for him to touch her there.

"Would that give me a baby?"

"No, to do that I must unite my body with yours and plant my seed in you."

Angel stared at him uncomprehendingly. He sounded like a farmer cultivating his crop.

"You see," he continued softly, "when people say a man and a woman have lain or slept together, they do not mean that they have merely reclined on a bed together. They mean that they have joined their bodies."

Angel's brows knit in puzzlement. "How could our bodies be joined? You mean by wrapping your arms around me."

He paused as though he were searching for the right words.

"Tell me," she prodded.

A faint flush crept into his face. "I would, er, insert part of me inside you."

Her eyes widened in amazement. "Truly?

"Truly?"

"What part of you?"

He glanced downward. Angel followed suit.

At the sight of the bulge that strained against his tight breeches, she gave another gasp, this time of shock and fear instead of pleasure.

Angel could not believe her eyes. Surely *that* would never fit in her! It was huge.

When he had been naked this morning, she had noted the curious difference in his anatomy there, but then it had been small and flaccid. It could not possibly have swelled into this giant appendage, could it?

But even as she watched, the bulge seemed to grow larger.

She gulped, then stammered, "That . . . that is the part you are talking about?"

"Aye."

Dear, merciful heaven, it seemed even larger now. She trembled at the thought of having that giant thing thrust into her.

He took her face gently between his hands and raised it toward his own. "I am sorry. I do not mean to frighten you, but I am helpless to do anything about it."

Angel jerked her face from his grasp, looked down again. and blurted, "No wonder Lady Bloomfield said it was agonizing for a woman the first time she slept with a man."

Lord Vayle looked positively chagrined. "That is not necessarily true," he said sharply.

"Why? Are some men smaller than you?"

"Aye, but that is not the reason."

"Surely you do not expect me to believe *that* would not hurt!"

"With the right man, only briefly."

"I definitely do not think you are the right man for me," she said nervously. "We cannot possibly be married. You are much too large!"

His fingertips gently stroked her face. It was so pleasant that for a moment Angel almost forgot her fear.

Almost.

"I promise you, little one,"—his deep, rich voice was as caressing as his fingers—"that I would see that you would like it very much."

"No, I do not think that would be possible," she said with conviction. "I am quite certain that I would not like it at all. In fact, I do not think I would like any man making love to me."

He smiled ruefully. "That is not what your soon-to-be husband wants to hear."

"But there is no reason for you to marry me! Don't you see, you have done nothing!"

"I have seen that from the beginning," he said dryly.

She remembered the certitude with which she had assured Lady Bloomfield that she had slept with him.

"Dear heaven, what have I done to you," Angel wailed. "I did not understand. I have unintentionally misled everyone."

"Aye," he said without rancor.

"You did not sleep with me. You did nothing to me!"

"No," he agreed, "nothing."

"No wonder you were livid with me. I wonder that you did not throttle me."

"I thought of it."

"I must tell everyone that I made a terrible mistake. Then you will not have to marry me."

"Save your breath, little one. It will do no good. After that scene in my bedroom this morning, no one will believe you if you belatedly tell them the truth now."

"Not believe me! Why not?"

"Among other things, the bloodstains on your night rail."

She frowned. "I cannot understand how they got there. I did not hurt myself."

"Undoubtedly your stepfather put the blood there, but no one will believe that either. They are all convinced that I robbed you of your virginity."

It was a word Angel had not heard before. "What is that?"

He rolled his eyes heavenward. For a moment she thought that he did not mean to answer her, but then he said patiently, "A girl is a virgin until a man makes love to her the first time. When he does, he breaks her virginal barrier and she bleeds. It is how a husband knows that his wife has slept with no other man before him. If a girl gives her virginity to a man who is not her husband, she is considered a fallen woman."

"Fallen?" Angel inquired uncertainly.

"Dishonored."

"Oh!" She had thought of honor differently, in terms of honesty and integrity and courage. "So that is what Lady Bloomfield meant when she said you had robbed me of my honor."

"Aye, everyone is convinced that I did so."

There was no anger in his voice or his expression. His silver eyes were oddly tender, making the sensations he always seemed to stir within her stronger than ever.

"But you did nothing," she protested.

Now that the sharply carved planes of his face were relaxed, Angel thought him one of the handsomest men she had ever seen.

"Nor did you."

He caught her face gently in his hands. When he rubbed her cheeks lightly with his thumbs, she felt as though she would melt.

"You are as much your stepfather's victim as I am. He has made the world believe that I have ruined you, even though I have not. I cannot abandon you to face the world's scorn alone."

Angel perceived that beneath Lord Vayle's veneer of cynicism, he lived by his own rigid code of honor, and it required him to marry her even though that was the last thing he wanted.

"Listen to me, Angel. No other man will marry you."

"Therefore, you must do so!" Her gaze met his stubbornly. "I do not care! Do you not see it would be wrong to marry you when you have done nothing." *Especially when you do not want me.*

He studied her assessingly for a moment, then said sternly, "You will do me far more damage if you refuse to marry me."

"Why?" she demanded in surprise.

"Because my honor would be destroyed as well as yours. I would be regarded as an unspeakable blackguard for apparently ruining you so publicly, then not marrying you." He gave her a calculating look. "Perhaps you do not care about your honor, but I—"

"I care very much!" she interjected hotly.

"As I do about mine. That is why I beg you not to dishonor me by refusing my suit."

Angel frowned in consternation. "Are you saying that I must marry you to save *your* honor?"

"Aye," he answered gravely, "that is precisely what you must do."

Questions of honor could be more perplexing than Angel had ever imagined. The choice she must make dismayed her. She could not deliberately cost a man his honor. Yet neither could she disregard her father's warnings against marrying a man who did not want and love her. There was also Kitty to think of.

"But you want to marry Kitty."

He shrugged. "It is too late for that now. After that scene in my bedroom this morning, her parents would not permit it, and she would not want it."

No doubt he was right, Angel thought glumly. She knew that Lady Bloomfield was opposed.

Angel dropped her gaze and caught sight again of the bulge in his breeches. Unnerved, she blurted, "I could not possibly marry such a large man."

A sound escaped Lord Vayle that was part groan, part laugh. His silver eyes suddenly gleamed. An irresistible grin softened his hard, dark features, making him look boyishly mischievous and deliciously handsome. He took her face in his hands again, and his mouth claimed hers in a kiss that was at first gentle, then grew bolder and more demanding.

It made Angel tingle all the way to her toes. She never wanted him to stop.

He might not want to marry her, but she realized in that instant that she wanted to marry him.

Wanted it more than she had ever wanted anything.

When the long kiss ended, he grinned down at her as though he were fully aware of the effect it had on her. "Any other objections?"

Sanity was slowly returning to her, and she mentally catalogued them in order of importance. She would save the most important—that he could not love her—for last.

"I cannot marry a man who thinks I am so appallingly ugly that he calls me a *horror*. I know that I am very plain, but I truly do not think I am a horror."

To her surprise and indignation, he started to laugh.

"Oh, little one, you are priceless." He hugged her to him, smoothing her hair gently with his hand. "I think you are very pretty, especially when you smile. Even when I was angriest at you, I never thought you were that kind of horror."

She was perplexed. "What other kind is there?"

"The one I was talking about is spelled w-h-o-r-e."

"What does that mean?"

"A, ah, fallen woman, but I know now you are not that kind either." He drew back a little and grinned down at her. "Have we taken care of your objections to marrying me?"

Angel wished he would not smile at her like that. Not only did it affect her heartbeat, but it made refusing his offer all the harder. But she must stand firm, she reminded herself. He neither wanted nor loved her.

"I cannot marry a man who will beat me daily."

His grin faded, and he looked insulted. "I will not beat you, Angel."

"That is not what you said this morning."

"That was when I thought you were in league with the Crowes to trap me into marrying you."

"What?" she cried, grievously offended. "How could you think that when I was the one who warned you of their plot?"

"What else was I to think when I awoke and discovered you in my bed beside me."

Angel was appalled and outraged. "How could you think me such a despicable person?"

A sardonic smile tugged at his lips. "It was quite easy, actually."

Belatedly Angel understood what he had been saying to her stepfather that morning. "So that is what you meant by my doing Sir Rupert's dirty work for him! I would never, never stoop to anything so low." Her indignation was rising like a river at flood stage. She had never been so insulted in her life.

Her father's exhortation to her brother flashed through her mind: *"Never allow anyone to cast aspersions on your character. If any man does so, you must call him out . . . You must never permit a man to challenge your honor without demanding redress."*

She glared up at Vayle. "My lord, you have insulted my honor and I must have satisfaction. I challenge you to meet me on the field of honor."

For a moment, he merely looked flabbergasted. Then he laughed uproariously at her, as though she had told him some particularly funny joke.

Thoroughly incensed now and determined to make him take her seriously, she cried, "I have no glove, so I must use my hand."

She would have slapped his face then had he not caught her wrist before her hand could impact on his cheek.

"God's oath," he exclaimed, "you are serious!"

"I have never been more serious in my life," she informed him frostily.

"You are also out of your bloody mind?" he thundered. "You cannot challenge me."

"Why not?"

Lucian uttered a succinct expletive. "Because a woman cannot challenge a man to a duel."

Angel tilted her head proudly. "Well, I can. And I am doing so now. Papa said one must not let a slur upon one's honor go unavenged."

"Angel, don't be a fool. You cannot hope to defeat me." Lucian was not bragging, but merely stating a fact. His reputation with a sword caused most men to go to great lengths to avoid dueling him. "I am an expert swordsman."

"So am I."

Lucian admired Angel's pride and determination and courage, but the thought of a green girl thinking herself in his league with a sword was so laughable he had to rub his hand over his mouth to hide his smile.

He teased, "Are you not afraid that I will run you through."

Angel held her head proudly. "It is you who should be afraid!"

The more Lucian tried to talk Angel out of dueling him, the more stubbornly insistent she became. It soon became clear to him that she would not be dissuaded from defending her honor.

Then he saw a way to use her challenge to get what he wanted from her with no further argument.

"Very well, Angel, I will accept your challenge on one condition. You must promise me that when I—er, *if* I win," he corrected himself hastily, "you will marry me immediately without further protest. Do you swear to me that you will do that."

"I swear," she said gravely, "but you must promise that if I win, you will marry Kitty."

If she won! Lucian had to bite his tongue to keep from laughing aloud. It was a moment before he could manage to say with a straight face, "I promise. Now I will find you a sword. Meet me in the long gallery in ten minutes."

Chapter 9

"David, I require your sword," Lucian told Inge when he answered the knock on his door.

"Why?" David gestured toward the weapon at Lucian's side. "You have one of your own."

"But my opponent does not."

"Odd's fish, have you gotten yourself involved in a duel? That will only make the scandal that much worse."

"I do not intend anyone but you, me, and my opponent to ever know of it."

"I see. Does that mean I am charged with secretly disposing of your opponent's body afterward?"

"It will not come to that."

"You should not have challenged—"

"I did not. I tried very hard to avoid this meeting, but my opponent was adamant."

"I own I am amazed," David said as crossed over to the chest of drawers where he had laid his sword. "I did not think that either of the Crowes would have the courage to challenge you."

"You are absolutely right about that," Lucian assured him.

David drew his weapon from its scabbard and handed it over to Lucian. It was beautifully balanced, with a fine silver hilt.

"However, my opponent is not one of the Crowes."

David frowned. "Who is he? Surely not Bloomfield!"

"No, nor is my opponent a he. *She* is Angel Winter."

"You are joking."

"I wish I were," Lucian said fervently.

"Great God in heaven, I cannot believe it!"

Lucian nodded. "My sentiments exactly."

* * *

When Lucian reached the long gallery, it was, to his intense relief, unoccupied. He wanted no witnesses to this ridiculous caprice of Angel's.

Who the devil ever heard of a man dueling his bride on their wedding day?

Or, for that matter, of dueling any female? Women were to be coddled and protected, for God's sake. The only kind of match he wanted with a female was in bed, not on the field of honor.

But Angel had been so insulted and so determined. He smiled to himself at the memory. He would, however, put a quick end to her notion that she could duel him. He would disarm her within fifteen seconds.

No, that would be a mistake. It would hurt her pride terribly if he were to do that.

Remembering how stubbornly determined she had been to defend her honor, he smiled tolerantly to himself. Instead of vanquishing her immediately, he would indulge her for a few minutes in a little harmless swordplay and let her think that she really could duel him. Then he would disarm her, and they would proceed to their wedding.

He looked around the gallery. In the harsh light of day, empty of the elegantly dressed crowds of people swirling about in satins and brocades and glittering jewels, it seemed cold and cavernous. Lucian's footsteps echoed on the polished floor.

The servants had already cleaned away all evidence of the previous night's ball. The oak floor had been repolished, the burned-down candles in the chandeliers and wall sconces had been replaced with fresh ones, and the gilt chairs had been lined neatly against the wall.

Through the long windows, all trace of the earlier storm had vanished, leaving the sky blue with an occasional puffy white cloud.

Angel came into the gallery. She had changed into the ruffled white shirt and black breeches that he had seen in her room.

Lucian's breath caught at the enticing sight that she made. Her breasts were high and full, and a jolt of desire shot through him at the memory of how her nipple had responded to his touch. Her waist was so tiny he could easily span it with his hands, and her derriere looked delectable in those tight breeches.

He felt his own body harden at such charming provocation.

Her long, curly chocolate hair had been pulled back from her face and tied at the neck with a white riband. He had an overwhelming impulse to untie it and run his hands through her thick, glossy locks.

She looked so small and weak and defenseless that the idea of his dueling her was preposterous. God's oath, what if he accidentally hurt her? He would never forgive himself.

"Please, forget this nonsense," he begged. "Withdraw your challenge."

Her brilliant blue eyes, the shade of the sky beyond the windows, widened. "Why? Are you afraid of me?"

"No, but someone could get hurt." He tactfully refrained from saying that someone would be her.

"I must defend my honor," she said stubbornly.

Lucian thought sourly that it was just such obstinate, misplaced faith that right would win out over might that had cost many an innocent young idealist his life when he was pitted against a older, wilier, more ruthless opponent, who was guilty as hell.

Although Lucian had fought more than his share of duels and won them, he had never considered them a just way of settling disputes or of defending one's honor. It was only one more excuse for might to masquerade as right.

He also knew it would accomplish nothing for him to tell his innocent, naive Angel that.

Lucian looked down at her face glowing with excitement. The vitality that had been drained from her earlier was replenished now. A few wisps of hair has escaped from the riband she had used to tie back the shimmering waves, and they curled beguilingly about her innocent face. Her hair, like Angel herself, seemed to have a mind of its own.

He could not help smiling at her. She was such a delightful little elf. It was all he could do to keep from kissing her sweet, inviting little mouth.

Bloody hell, the only sword he wanted to use on her was making a very large nuisance of itself at this very moment. It was, he thought wryly, the very first time he had ever had an erection for his opponent on the field of honor.

Angel, looking at David's sword that Lucian was carrying, held out her hand for it, and he gave it to her.

She admired its silver hilt, then tested its edge and balance. To his surprise, she appeared to know exactly what she was doing.

"A fine sword," she said approvingly.

After they removed their shoes and were in their stocking feet, they saluted.

"On guard."

Lucian allowed Angel the first thrust, quickly parrying it. She seized the offensive, and he let her.

Blade clanged against blade as she attacked and he parried.

She feinted in seconde, then thrust in tierce, penetrating his guard, but he recovered with a *coup d'arrêt*.

Seldom had Lucian seen such intense concentration in an opponent as he did now in Angel. As his renown as a swordsman had grown, so had the nervousness of his opponents. But Angel, who clearly had no idea of his reputation with a sword, suffered from neither nerves nor fear.

It was not as easy as he had thought it would be to frustrate her offensive. This match that he had expected to be child's play was demanding far more skill and effort than he had anticipated. He found himself retreating along the polished floor of the gallery.

Angel was remarkably quick on her feet. So fast, in fact, that Lucian soon found himself sweating profusely.

No lazy match with a sadly inferior opponent was this.

Suddenly she lunged, and he had barely time to parry. She immediately riposted. He parried again, then counterriposted, thinking to catch her off-balance, but she danced away from him.

Bloody hell, it was like trying to fence with a whirling dervish.

His breath was coming hard now.

It was time to end this nonsense by disarming her, but Lucian quickly discovered this was not nearly so easy as he had thought it would be.

He had the advantage of strength, but he could not remember a quicker, more agile opponent.

Lucian realized in amazement and chagrin that she was as good as any man he had ever faced.

Angel dived forward in a flèche, her blade so low that it threatened to unman him. He managed to twist sideways and leap aside as the sword's blade whistled a mere fraction of an inch from a highly prized part of his anatomy.

"God's oath," he exploded, "you damned near rendered our marriage meaningless with that maneuver."

She blinked up at him in surprise and confusion.

He took advantage of her momentary hesitation to launch an attack of his own. Caught off guard, she tried to parry, but he used his superior strength to deliver, forte on forte, a numbing blow against her sword that sent it flying from her hand.

It crashed loudly to the floor. Hastily Lucian snatched it up before Angel could recover it.

"I have disarmed you, and that makes me the winner," he said, unable to take any pride in it. There had been no finesse in his final blow, merely brute strength.

He looked down at her flushed face. Like him, she was panting from her exertion. More wayward chocolate curls had escaped from the white riband and curled damply about her face.

He could not help admiring her spirit and reckless courage. Nor could he remember when he had last had a male opponent who had been as daring and skilled.

Lucian looked at Angel as though seeing her for the first time. God's oath, she was magnificent.

Her eyes blinked hard and rapidly. He realized that she was fighting back tears. He wondered in consternation whether he had hurt her without realizing it? "What is it, Angel?"

Swallowing hard, she wailed, "I failed to defend my honor. Now, you will always believe that I was in league with my horrid step-relatives."

He was so relieved that she was not hurt that he said more sharply than he intended, "I believe nothing of the sort."

She looked at him skeptically.

"I was very wrong to think that you would have any truck with those scoundrels."

Her face brightened.

He pulled her close to him and stroked the damp curls away from her face. "I apologize sincerely for doubting you. I think you are the most honorable woman I have ever met, Angel."

And that was the truth.

The idea of having her as his wife was no longer repugnant to Lucian. He smiled to himself. Whatever else marriage to Angel would be, it would not be dull. Surely he must be the only man on earth who had ever had to duel his own bride for her hand in matrimony.

Still holding her to him with one arm, he used his other hand to tilt her face toward his. "Now, it is time to pay the piper, Angel. We will be married shortly."

Her expression dissolved into panic. "No!"

"You agreed that if I won our duel, you would marry me," he reminded her.

"But—"

"Your honor is at stake," he told her solemnly, knowing that as important as her honor was to her, this would settle the issue. "Furthermore, you promised that you would marry me without further objection."

At this reminder, she ceased arguing, but she looked so miserable that Lucian was insulted.

"God's oath, do you find me that repulsive?"

She stammered. "Well, you are . . . very . . . large."

He remembered how huge and frightened Angel's eyes had been when she caught sight of his erection. He knew that it had terrified her. How the devil could he make marriage to him more palatable to her?

"Little one, what do you want most in the world? If I

had the power to give you whatever you wanted, what would you ask me for?"

"Belle Haven," she said without hesitation.

He caught her face between his hands. "Then you shall have it. If you get nothing else from this marriage, you will get Belle Haven. I swear to you that I will recover it for you."

Somehow Lucian would find a way to keep this vow. If he could not locate the missing will, he would find another way to restore the estate to her.

His promise elicited such a glowing smile from her that his breath caught, but then the smile faded and she looked dejected.

"What is it, Angel? Is there something more that you want from me?"

"Aye," she said forlornly, "your love."

For a moment, he was too surprised to speak. He should have known she would be a silly little romantic who believed in such nonsense. Well, he did not! Nor was he going to lie to her about it.

"Angel, now you are asking me for more than I can give you," he said gently. "I cannot force myself to love you—that is beyond my control. But what I will give you is my care and protection. I promise you, little one, that I will take very, very good care of you."

She looked as though he had struck her. "But that is not enough!"

"It will be enough, Angel." It would have to be.

Her expression was anguished. "Do you not care whether your wife loves you? Is that not important to you?"

"No, it is not," he said sharply, his patience fraying. "What is important to me is obedience. I want a wife who will obey me and be faithful to me."

"But Papa said one should only marry a person he loves and respects."

Lucian was incredulous. "The scientific earl said that? I cannot credit it!"

"Why not?"

"Because love has nothing to do with marriage." Lucian

decided to put a quick end to this discussion, and he knew just how to do it: appeal to her honor. It worked every time.

"What is most important to me is a wife who is honorable enough to keep her promises. And you promised if I won our duel, you would marry me. Do you mean to break it?"

Angel bowed her head in defeat. "No."

Chapter 10

Angel had just finished changing out of her breeches when Lady Bloomfield came to her door, her arms piled with clothes.

"Lord Vayle told me that you have relented and agreed to marry him. I am glad. Under the circumstances you can do nothing else."

She dropped the garments she was carrying on the green silk coverlet of the bed.

"I have been searching frantically for something suitable for you to wear for your wedding," Lady Bloomfield said, holding up one of the garments.

It was a frilly white confection of ruffles and lace that Kitty had worn when she was about twelve. At the time, Angel had secretly coveted it, thinking it the prettiest dress she had ever seen.

"This is the best I could come up with," Kitty's mother said apologetically. "You are about the same size that Kitty was when she wore this. I found it in a trunk in the attic. Try it on."

Kitty's mother laid the gown back on the bed and began to help Angel out of her shabby black dress.

"We must hurry," Lady Bloomfield said. "Vicar Thompson of St. Stephen's in Bourton is already here. Your stepfather wasted no time in getting him here to marry you to Vayle."

"But I want the Reverend Throckmorton to marry me. He is such a dear man. Papa and I were both very fond of him."

Angel refrained from adding that neither she nor her father had liked Thompson very much. He was always so obsequious that Angel was uncomfortable with him. Papa had said it was because he, as earl, controlled the living Thompson held. But Papa had also controlled Throckmorton's, and that gentle, kind man had never toadied to her father and her as Thompson did.

"It is too late now. Vicar Thompson is already here," Lady Bloomfield said.

Angel pulled on the gown of ruffles and lace. "I wonder why Sir Rupert sent to Bourton when Lower Hocking, where the Reverend Throckmorton lives, is much closer?"

"Now that Crowe controls your father's estate, he also controls the livings. He can be certain that Thompson will go along with whatever he wants rather than jeopardize his position," Lady Bloomfield said bluntly. Her nimble fingers were already at work fastening Kitty's old gown. "The Reverend Throckmorton would not be so accommodating, particularly if he thought you were not willingly marrying Vayle."

No, the Reverend Throckmorton would not. He had even had the courage to remonstrate with the Crowes over their sorry treatment of Belle Haven's dependents.

Lady Bloomfield stepped away from Angel. "Let me see how the gown looks." After a moment's scrutiny, she said dubiously, "It fits tolerably well."

Angel went over to a long looking glass by the door to examine herself. When she saw her image, she had to struggle to hide her disappointment. The gown did fit her petite figure, except that it was too tight across the chest. It was as pretty as she remembered it, but it was a dress a child would wear. She looked like a little girl instead of a bride on her wedding day.

Lady Bloomfield pointed toward the pile of clothes that she had left on the bed. "I found some other things in the attic that Kitty has outgrown, and I brought them for you."

Angel, who realized now how shabby her wardrobe was, thanked her hostess for her thoughtfulness and generosity.

Lady Bloomfield pulled a filmy garment from the pile on the bed. "I brought you this, too, for your wedding night." She held up a pale pink night rail of sheerest silk, embroidered with delicate roses.

Angel had never had such a pretty nightgown. Unfortunately, however, it reminded her of the night ahead of her—and of that bulge in Lord Vayle's breeches. *"Often when a woman lies with a man for the first time, the experience is agonizing for her."* Angel swallowed hard, her apprehension rising.

"What is it, dear child? Why are you suddenly so pale?"

Angel said frankly, "I am afraid of tonight when I must sleep with Lord Vayle."

Lady Bloomfield patted her arm comfortingly. "But you already experienced the worst this morning."

"No, I did not," Angel confessed. "You see nothing happened between Lord Vayle and me this morning."

Lady Bloomfield looked dazed. "But you told me—"

"I was wrong."

"Wrong! How could you have been wrong about *that?"*

"I did not understood what you were asking me. When you wanted to know whether I lay with him, I thought you meant had I lain down on the same bed with him, which is all that I did."

"Dear God," her hostess breathed.

"Lord Vayle kindly explained to me what more must happen for me to lie with him in the way you meant, and I swear to you that it did not happen." Angel paused, then in a small, desolate voice, cried, "I have made such a mull of things. Poor Lord Vayle is more victim than I am. He is convinced that Maude helped Sir Rupert drug both him and me and that is why neither of us knew how I got into his bed."

"That would explain why she disappeared!"

"The Crowes were plotting to prevent Lord Vayle from wedding Kitty so that Horace could marry her instead. You know that he is obsessed with her."

"That little snake will never marry my daughter! I will not permit it. Nor will her father. Not that Kitty would have him. She despises him as much as I do." She frowned. "Are you saying that what happened in Vayle's bedroom this morning was nothing more than a snare set by the Crowes?"

Angel nodded. "But Lord Vayle says no one will believe that now."

"Unfortunately, he is right." Lady Bloomfield's face tightened into grim lines. "No wonder Vayle was beside himself with rage! I cannot blame him. Under the circumstances I am astonished he has agreed to marry you. It is surely the last thing that he wants."

Her hostess's assessment, undoubtedly a correct one, only increased Angel's anxiety. "I do not want to marry a man who neither wants nor loves me!"

"As Vayle says, you have no choice."

Angel swallowed hard, then gave voice to a forlorn hope. "Do you think that I could somehow win Lord Vayle's heart?"

Lady Bloomfield looked at her in alarm. "Do not, whatever you do, fall in love with him, child. If you do, he will break your heart. That is the way it is with a man who has none of his own."

Angel's fragile hope evaporated.

Lady Bloomfield held out her hand to Angel. "Come, child, we must go to the drawing room for your wedding.

To be followed by her wedding night, Angel thought nervously as she took her hostess's hand. "Do . . . do a bride and groom always sleep together on the night they are married?"

"Always."

"Even if the groom does not want the bride?"

Lady Bloomfield snorted. "Every man wants his wedding night. I doubt there has ever been a groom in the history of mankind who despised his wife so much that he failed to claim his rights to her on it. I only pray that Vayle does not vent his anger on you during it."

"What do you mean?" Angel asked in alarm.

Lady Bloomfield frowned. "Sometimes when a man must wed a woman against his will, he is not as gentle and patient as he should be with her on their wedding night." She muttered more to herself than Angel. "Lord knows, it is painful enough under the best of circumstances."

Angel struggled to conceal her fright. She despised cowards, and she would not allow herself to be one now. She followed her hostess into the hall with all the joy of a condemned woman being led to the hangman's noose.

They met Lord Vayle, accompanied by David Inge, in the hall outside the drawing room. His lordship might not have wanted this wedding, but he had dressed impressively for the occasion in a midnight blue velvet coat, ornamented with gold braid, over a matching waistcoat and breeches. He looked so handsome that Angel's heartbeat quickened.

When he saw her, he remarked dryly, "An unusual wedding gown."

"You do not like it," Angel said unhappily. Why did it suddenly seemed so important to her that he should find favor with what she wore? "You do not think it is pretty?"

He touched her arm comfortingly. "It is pretty enough, little one, but it makes me feel as though I am robbing the cradle. At least, it is not black. I take solace in that."

The Crowes were waiting outside the closed door of the drawing room.

Vayle told them coldly that he and Angel would be leaving immediately after the ceremony. "We will stop by Belle Haven so that Angel can collect her belongings."

"No, you will not," Sir Rupert Crowe snapped. "After the way Angel has humiliated us and the rest of her family by her scandalous, wanton behavior this day, she has forfeited all right to set foot in Belle Haven again. I will not permit her to do so. The gates will be barred against her."

Angel was so shocked that she could not even find her voice to protest. Never to be allowed at Belle Haven again. It was unthinkable!

Lucian demanded scornfully of Crowe, "Are you *that* afraid she might find her father's missing will?"

Rupert's eyes narrowed. "What lies has she been telling you? There is no missing will. Ashcott's own attorney swears to the fact that the will entered for probate is the only one Ashcott ever made."

"I saw a later will with my own eyes," Angel cried.

Rupert sneered at her. "Amazing, is it not, that you, the one person who would benefit from it, are the only one to have seen it."

"You cannot bar me from Belle Haven. It is my home!"

"No longer! In a few moments you will be this man's wife and his home will be yours." He turned to Lucian. "After the indecent spectacle the pair of you have made of yourself, she will come to you with only the clothes on her back, nothing else. She deserves nothing more."

"What do you mean, 'nothing more'?" Angel cried. "What of Fairleigh?"

"What is Fairleigh?" Lord Vayle asked.

"A small estate in Bedfordshire that, under the terms of my parents' marriage settlement, was to be my portion when I married."

"The settlement very clearly stipulated that it would come to you only if you married with the approval of your guardian, and you do not have that," Rupert said. "While I was forced to permit this ceremony after the scandal you made of yourself with this man, I do not *approve* of the match."

"So you mean to steal even that from her," Vayle said contemptuously.

Angel, remembering the conversation she had overheard between the Crowes, cried furiously, "So that is what you meant by being rid of your other problem—and more cheaply than you could ever have hoped to do otherwise. *I* was your other problem."

Her stepfather smirked.

Lucian said scornfully, "It is not enough that you have robbed Angel of her inheritance, ruined her reputation, and tricked her into marrying a stranger. Now you must rob her even of her dowry."

Sir Rupert gave him a look of malevolent triumph. "And you can do nothing about it."

"You bastard!" Vayle growled. "The lowest circle of hell is too good for you."

Angel turned anguished eyes to Lucian. "I must go back to Belle Haven."

He took her little hand in his large one and squeezed it consolingly. "Do not worry, little one, I will buy you a new and better wardrobe."

"It is not my clothes I care about," she cried. "I want something of Papa's to remember him by. I have nothing!"

The drawing room door opened, and the Reverend Thompson bustled out, carrying a very large leatherbound book beneath his arm. He fixed his attention on the elder Crowe, ignoring everyone else.

"I see the bride is here. Are we ready to begin the ceremony?" he asked Angel's stepfather as though only his pleasure mattered.

"Aye, and keep it short. I want it over as quickly as possible."

"Certainly, Sir Rupert," the rector said with servile alacrity. "It shall be just as you wish."

He turned to Vayle. "As soon as the ceremony is finished, you and your bride must sign the parish register." He nodded down at the large book he carried.

"You are to be commended for thinking of everything," Vayle said sardonically, "even the parish register."

"I confess the credit for that must go to Sir Rupert," the rector said fawningly. "I might not have thought of it had he not reminded me yesterday when he told me my services would be needed."

"Yesterday!" Lady Bloomfield cried. "Sir Rupert summoned you *yesterday?"*

"Why yes, my lady."

"Prescient of Crowe, was it not?" Lucian observed dryly.

Lady Bloomfield turned on the Crowes in fury. "You evil, despicable blackguards! Get out of my house at once."

"I will see my stepdaughter married," Crowe said stonily. "It is my duty."

"Your duty!" her ladyship cried in derision. "Get out or I will have my servants throw you out."

She glared at the younger Crowe, "As for you, you sniveling little rodent, I will never permit Kitty to marry you! Not that she would have you."

"Like it or not, she will have Horace, I promise you that," the elder Crowe said, his expression so evil and menacing that Angel suddenly feared for Kitty. "It is what I want, and I get what I want."

"Not this time," Lord Vayle said.

Angel, seeing his determined, scowling countenance, understood more clearly than ever how he had gotten the nickname Lord Lucifer.

Even her stepfather seemed shaken.

"I promise you, Crowe," Vayle said in a voice made all the more menacing by its calm resolve, "that for your work this day, I will destroy both you and your son."

Angel stared glumly through the window of Lord Vayle's coach as it hurtled through the gates of Fernhill.

Her new husband lounged on the seat beside her.

The ceremony uniting them in wedlock had been over much too quickly for the bride's peace of mind. The only witnesses to it, besides the principals and the rector, were Lady Bloomfield and David Inge. The Crowes, facing forcible ejection, had left. Lord Bloomfield and Kitty had flatly refused to be present.

Angel asked her bridegroom politely, "Where are we going?"

"Ardmore, my estate in Hampshire."

Her heart sank at the thought of leaving Belle Haven and the people she loved.

Who would fight on behalf of the estate's servants and dependents, now at the cruel mercy of the Crowes?

Who would tend the graves of her father and brother, lying side by side, beneath the great chestnut tree Ashcott had planted as a boy of eight?

Angel said sadly, "I do not want to leave Belle Haven."

"Your stepfather left you no choice," Lord Vayle reminded her.

"I cannot believe he would not permit me to return."

"You should be delighted that he would not. It undoubtedly means that he has not succeeded in finding and destroying your father's missing will. There is still hope that we can discover it before he does."

"Not if we are barred from Belle Haven," Angel pointed out.

Lord Vayle gave her an odd, enigmatic smile. "Perhaps your father did not hide it there."

"He had to have. It was there that he showed it to me and my uncle, and he did not leave the estate after that."

"Have you no idea at all where he might have hidden it?"

"I thought of many places, but it was in none of them. I cannot think of another spot where it might be."

"Where did you look first for it?" he asked casually.

"In my father's library and bedroom."

"Does you father have an excellent view from his library?"

Angel, startled by this strange change in subject, said, "Why, yes, he does. It is the southwest corner of the house, overlooking the park."

"What kind of view did he have from his bedroom?"

"The same," she replied, baffled by her new husband's sudden interest in views. "It is directly above the library. Papa even had a private staircase installed to connect the two."

It was inconceivable to Angel that she might never again be permitted inside that house she loved so much, and she said in a choked voice, "I am going to miss Belle Haven so much."

Her husband's large, warm hand touched hers. "I promised you that I would get it back for you, and I am a man who keeps his word in all things."

She gave him a grateful smile. "You are very kind after what I have cost you."

It was as though she had touched a raw nerve. He withdrew his hand, and his silver eyes were suddenly cold. "You have no idea what you have cost me, no idea at all."

He must have loved Kitty after all, Angel thought, and she blurted, "I cost you the woman to whom you lost your heart."

"No," he said scornfully. "I have no heart to lose."

Angel was profoundly shocked. She had not believed Lady Bloomfield when she had said much the same thing, but now he himself was confirming it.

Dear heaven, what manner of man had she married?

Lord Lucifer.

He said more gently, "Do not look so stricken, little one, I told you before that love has nothing to do with marriage."

"Certainly not with our marriage," she retorted, turning away from him to watch through the coach window as her beloved Berkshire rolled past.

They rode in silence for several minutes before Angel asked, "How far will we travel today?"

"We will spend the night at the White Horse Inn outside Lower Hocking."

"But that is only a short distance. Why are we stopping so soon?" Angel wondered uneasily whether it was because he was impatient to claim his wedding night. *"Often when a woman lies with a man for the first time, the experience is agonizing for her, especially if he does not love her."*

And her husband had made it resoundingly clear that not only did he not love her, he never would.

Lord Vayle shrugged carelessly. "I understand it is a passable establishment, and we will be quite comfortable there."

Angel cast a nervous, involuntary glance toward the apex of his thighs. Much as she hated to leave Berkshire, she would happily ride in this carriage all night if it would postpone her wedding night. Angel was not usually a faintheart, but Lady Bloomfield's remarks had made her apprehensive, even a little frightened.

In a shaky voice, she said, "I am surprised that you do not wish to go farther, Lord Vayle."

"Lucian," he said.

She raised her gaze to his face and blinked. "What?"

His ominous expression had vanished. His eyes were alight with amusement, and he was grinning at her in a way that made her heart skip a beat. "Call me Lucian. We are married now, remember."

How could she forget?

"We are stopping so soon because you have had a long, dreadful day, little one. The least I can do is allow you some rest."

Angel stole another nervous look at his thighs, then stared out the window of the coach. It was accompanied by two armed outriders and a beautiful bay saddle horse.

"Why the horse?" Angel asked.

"I had originally intended to ride to Ardmore on horseback, but now that I have acquired a wife, I must take the coach, too."

"Is Hampshire so dangerous that we require outriders?"

"I should not think so. Kitty insisted upon them on the journey to Fernhill." His disgust with his former betrothed's timidness was clear in his voice. "She refused to leave London without them."

The coach hit a series of hard bumps, bouncing them both. Lord Vayle put his arm protectively around her, and her breath quickened as he drew her against his warm, hard body.

He asked casually, "If Crowe had permitted you to take one memento of your father from Belle Haven, what would it have been?"

"His telescope," Angel answered without hesitation. "It was Papa's most prized possession. It was so precious to him that he would let no one else touch it. You see, it was made especially for him by Isaac Newton."

"Isaac Newton himself?"

"You know of him?" Angel inquired.

"Of course. His *Mathematical Principles of Natural Philosophy* is a work of exceptional genius," Lord Vayle exclaimed, his face lighting up much as her papa's had when he had discussed the same book. "Nothing has ever been done like it. He has integrated for the first time the laws of motion for both celestial and terrestrial bodies. Why, it has changed the way we regard the universe."

"Aye, it has," Angel agreed. "Papa was very excited about it."

Although the road was smoother now, Lord Vayle was still holding her in the protective circle of his arm. She decided he must have forgotten he was doing so. It felt so good that she hoped he did not remember. His closeness, though, seemed to play havoc with her heartbeat.

He said, "Tell me about the telescope Newton made for your father."

"It was his special design in which he used a mirror in place of a lens. It is called a reflecting telescope, and Papa said it is better than any other he had used."

"Where did your papa keep this valuable object?"

"In his library, on the desk where he did all his writing."

"Did he keep more than one telescope there?" Vayle sounded bored, as though he were merely making conversation to pass the time, but something about his silver eyes told Angel that he had a very definite purpose in mind.

"No, only that one. Why do you ask?"

He shrugged. "Curiosity. I was a great admirer of your father's."

"You were?" she cried in surprise. It was hard for Angel to believe that this hard, unyielding man of action would have taken any notice of a man whose mind was most comfortable with the abstractions of natural philosophy.

"Aye, I read everything he published. My favorite was the *Journal of Belle Haven*. I hoped that someday he would write a sequel to it."

"That is what he was working on when he was killed." Angel's face clouded at the memory. "If only I could make sense out of what happened."

"I thought your father was killed in a riding accident."

"He was, but . . ." Her voice trailed off and she looked out the coach window as they passed a stout woman in a gray linsey-woolsey gown walking toward Lower Hocking. She carried a creel on her back.

"But what?" her husband asked. "What bothers you about it?"

"Where it occurred, for one thing."

"Where was that?"

"On the path to the haunted cottage."

"Haunted cottage?" Lucian raised one of his flaring eyebrows questioningly. "Don't tell me the scientific earl's daughter believes in ghosts."

"No, but many of the people in the neighborhood do, and that is what they call it. They won't go near the place."

"Why did your father go there the day he died?"

"No one knows! That is what is so strange. It is the only time I ever knew of him going there—not that he believed it was haunted. He simply had no reason to go there."

"What did he tell you when he left?"

"I was not at home. It was a Tuesday. That's the day I always go to visit my old nurse, Mrs. Beard, who lives in a cottage that Papa gave her on the edge of Belle Haven."

He withdrew his arm from around her, and Angel felt suddenly deprived.

"Near the haunted house?" her husband asked.

"No, it lies in the opposite direction. When I left that day, Papa was in his library working on his sequel to the *Journal of Belle Haven,* and he told me he planned to spend the rest of the day there."

"Do you have any idea why he changed his mind."

She nodded. "A note was delivered to him about three hours after I left. Jepson, our butler, said it upset him terribly. Papa did not say what was wrong but he ordered up the fastest horse in the stables. Then he set off at a gallop in the direction of the haunted cottage."

Lucian frowned. "How odd."

"Aye, it was," Angel agreed, a catch in her voice. "It was not like Papa to act like that. An hour later the horse was back at the stable without a rider. By that time I was home, and I immediately organized a search for him. He was lying on the path twenty yards from the haunted cottage. His horse had thrown him, and he had hit his head so hard that it killed him."

"Do you think your father was going to the haunted cottage?"

"He must have been, for it is very isolated and the path he was on leads only to it." She chewed at her upper lip. "But I cannot understand why he would go there."

"Any indication of what caused his horse to throw him?"

"It was storming that afternoon, with much lightning and thunder. The horse he was riding was always skittish in bad weather."

"Tell me about the cottage. Why do people think it is haunted?"

She looked out the window with unseeing eyes. "It was once occupied by a young woodsman and his wife who were expecting their first child. Shortly before the baby was due, he was killed by a poacher who mistook him for a deer. His wife found his body and the shock brought on the child. She died giving birth to the babe and the babe with her. 'Tis said she still haunts the cottage."

"What about the note to your father? Did you ever discover who it was from or what it said?"

Angel looked up at her husband. "No, we did not find it on either his body or at Belle Haven."

Lucian's face darkened into a scowl. "How *very* odd."

She scarcely heard him, so lost was she in memories of that dreadful day. "If only I had been home when the note came," she burst out. "I would have been, had the tree not delayed me."

"What tree?"

"When I started home from Mrs. Beard's, the road was blocked by a large beech tree that had come crashing down during the storm."

"So you had to wait for it to be cut up and cleared away."

"No, I did not wait because I could see that it would take hours to do so. Instead I took the long way around through Lower Hocking, but I was still three hours late in getting home."

She swallowed hard, fighting back the tears that threatened at the memory. "If it not been for that tree, I would have been home long before he left." Her voice cracked. "As it was, I never saw him alive again."

Chapter 11

At the White Horse Inn, Lucian quietly requested a room with two beds. He had noted Angel's repeated, nervous glances toward his groin and knew that she was frightened about what this night held for her.

She was also exhausted. Her weary eyes and the dark smudges beneath them told him that. She needed a good night's sleep. It had been an awful day for her. First, she had awakened to the shock of finding herself in bed with a stranger whom she had met only the day before. Then she had been insulted and manipulated and forced to marry a man who did not want her. The only home she had ever known was denied to her, and she was leaving all she loved to go with a husband she barely knew.

Yet she had borne it all with courage and fortitude. Lucian was proud of her.

After all she had been through that day, the least he could do was let her sleep undisturbed by husbandly demands that clearly terrified her. He could not give her love, but he could at least be considerate.

The delay would also give her a little more time to get to know him. By the time they reached Ardmore tomorrow night, she would feel less like she was going to bed with a stranger.

His solicitude was not entirely unselfish. He would also be less likely to awaken her when he slipped out tonight for a secret foray to Belle Haven. This visit was the principal reason why he had stopped at the White Horse Inn, only a mile from the estate where he intended to search for Ashcott's missing will.

He would also obtain, as a wedding present for Angel, her father's telescope, which she wanted so much.

Lucian did not condone burglary, but he assuaged his conscience by reminding himself that Angel was the rightful owner of Belle Haven and everything in it. He was merely stealing the telescope back from the thief who had robbed her of it.

When the inn's proprietor learned that his guests were Lord and Lady Vayle, he was eager to comply with any wish they might have.

Lucian ordered dinner served in their room.

"I am not hungry," Angel protested. "Truly, I do not think that I could eat a bite."

Ignoring that, Lucian ordered enough food to ensure a substantial repast for both of them.

Their room was spacious, with two wide beds boasting clean white linen, a large cupboard, and an oak-framed privacy screen in one corner.

Angel, looking nervously at the beds, jumped at the sound of the door closing behind the departing innkeeper.

Lucian, who was standing behind her, put his hands lightly on her arms.

She jumped again and whirled to face him.

He decided to put her mind at ease immediately. "Take whichever bed you prefer, little one. I will use the other one. I am not going to touch you tonight."

"You are not!" she exclaimed in surprise.

Lucian thought sourly that she did not have to look quite so damned happy and relieved.

"Perhaps I will eat after all," Angel said. "I suddenly feel famished."

After the inn's servants had cleared away the remains of dinner, Lucian suggested that Angel retire immediately and get a good night's sleep. The sooner she fell asleep, the sooner he could leave for Belle Haven. He would pretend to go to bed, too, so as not to arouse her suspicions.

She had been noticeably less apprehensive after his promise not to touch her. He congratulated himself on his strategy in forgoing his marital rights for one night.

He had devoted himself during dinner to telling her amusing stories, with the express purpose of getting her to relax even more with him, and he had succeeded.

As Angel disappeared behind the screen in the corner to change into her night rail, it reminded him of the difference in their sizes. The screen would only have come up to his neck, but she was so petite that it hid even the top of her head.

Lucian took this opportunity out of her sight to strip out of his own clothes. He did not want to do anything now that might rekindle her tension.

"I will leave a candle burning on the table between our beds," he told her as he slid beneath the covers of his. "That way if you awaken in the night, you will know where you are."

It would also help him to make his way noiselessly out of the room when the time came for him to visit Belle Haven.

"How thoughtful of you," Angel said approvingly amid the rustling of her clothing being discarded.

An unbidden image of her shapely legs as she swung across the creek flashed through Lucian's mind, followed by the hazy memory of her sweet softness as he had held her against his naked body that morning in his bed.

He began to regret his decision about not touching her.

Then she stepped out from behind the screen's protective shield. Her pale pink night rail was so sheer it was transparent, and it revealed her delectably sinuous body beneath more erotically than if she had been naked. The sight of her breasts jutting against the diaphanous fabric goaded his body into instant, magnificent response.

She moved languidly toward her bed, innocently unconscious of the sensual sway of her breasts and hips that left him panting with desire.

Lucian was astonished by how much he wanted her. It took all of his willpower not to pull her down beside him and make love to her.

Even after her provocative body was hidden beneath the covers of her bed, he ached to join her there.

What the hell was wrong with him, he wondered in disgust. He was no randy youth, but a mature, disciplined man who had long ago learned to control himself.

He had promised her that he would not touch her tonight, and he would keep his word if it killed him.

Which it just might, he thought ruefully as he contemplated the size of the impromptu tent that had arisen in the middle of his bed.

Lucian lay listening to Angel's breathing and tried not to think about how much he wanted her.

He failed.

It amazed him how rapidly he had become reconciled to this marriage he had not wanted. Lucian no longer intended to seek an annulment. He would not even bother to track down Maude and wring the truth from her.

Seeking to justify his change of heart, he told himself that marriage to Angel did have its practical advantages. A union with the Earl of Ashcott's daughter was far more prestigious than with an offspring of a viscount in strong royal disfavor. Even Lucian's father would have to be impressed by the connection.

True, it would not bring Lucian Sommerstone, but it might bring him Belle Haven. He had coveted the estate the moment he had seen it. Sommerstone, despite its connection to his family, had disappointed him.

He smiled at the irony of finding himself trapped in a marriage that socially, dynastically, and even financially—if he could recover Angel's inheritance—was more advantageous than the one he had sought.

Angel's breathing had settled into the deep, steady rhythm of sleep.

From the room on the other side of the wall came the grunts, groans, and muffled cries of a man and woman coupling.

Lucian, realizing how thin the inn's walls were, was glad, despite the ache in his groin, that he had not made love to Angel tonight, when other guests could hear them.

She was so nervous and frightened about his taking her. He would do everything he could to be gentle, but her fear guaranteed her initiation to lovemaking would be painful for her. He had heard of incidents where innocent young brides had dissolved in screams and hysterical sobbing. His mouth tightened. He would not care to have the other guests think he was savaging her.

He promised himself that he would not take his bride until he could do so in privacy, beneath his own roof. What was one night to him?

He could last that long.

The sounds from the room next door gave way to noisy snoring.

It was time for Lucian to leave for Belle Haven. Silently, he got up, dressed, and tiptoed toward the door.

"Where are you going?"

Angel's voice so startled Lucian that he nearly tripped over a chair. "For a ride."

"In the middle of the night?" she exclaimed in surprise.

"Keep your voice down. You'll wake up the other guests." The last thing Lucian wanted was for someone to notice him sneaking out of the inn.

He turned to face Angel. She was sitting upright in bed, looking puzzled. "Where will you ride?" she whispered.

"Nowhere," he lied. "I merely feel like a ride."

In the pale candlelight, her eyes suddenly sparkled with excitement. "I know! You are going to Belle Haven!"

Angel might be naive, but she was too damned intuitive. "Why would you think such a ridiculous thing?" he parried.

She jumped out of bed. "I will go with you."

"No, you will not."

She came up to him, and Lucian was very careful to keep his gaze fixed on her face. One glance downward at her body in that damned, revealing night rail would be more provocation than his body could stand.

Angel protested, "But you need me."

"I said *no!*" Lucian was accustomed to commanding men and having them obey him with alacrity. He knew what was best for them. His ability to lead them through battles with minimum loss had made him one of the most popular commanders in the army. It was laughable that this slip of a girl could think he would require her assistance on a burgling expedition.

"But I know the way," she said. "You need me to guide you."

"I need no guide. I was a soldier, and I am used to stealing through strange terrain that was far more difficult and dangerous than this is."

"But I can show the house to you."

Lucian was affronted that she could think he required her help. He had never needed a female in his life—except in bed. "I told you I do not need you," he thundered, forgetting his own admonition about raising one's voice.

She looked so wounded that he felt like a cad. Putting his hands lightly on her arms, he said softly, "Angel, I cannot take you with me. I will not expose you to danger!"

Her eyes glowed in the candlelight. "But I like danger."

God's oath, she was as foolhardy as any eager, untried young soldier on the eve of his first battle.

She also looked so delicious in the candlelight with her bright, excited eyes and shining waves of hair tumbling wildly about her shoulders that he felt his desire for her rising again.

He muttered a curse, then said in a tone that had caused battle-hardened soldiers to quail, "You are not coming with me and that is final. My most important requirement for a wife is that she obey me. I will not tolerate a woman who does not."

Instead of looking properly subdued, her eyes glinted with a mixture of curiosity and defiance. "And what will you do if I do not obey? Beat me?"

That stopped him. What the hell would he do?

Certainly not beat her. He had never mistreated a woman in his life, and the thought of touching her in violence sickened him.

She was frowning. "You said you would not beat me, but I gather you only told me that to get me to agree to marry you."

The reproach in Angel's voice made him want to grind his teeth. "I told you that because it is the truth. But I will not have a wife who defies me. Do I make myself clear?"

"Very, but a wife should not blindly obey her husband when he is wrong!"

"I am not wrong," he sputtered.

"I know you believe that," she said soothingly, "but you are wrong."

"God's oath, you stretch my patience to the breaking point. You will stay here and that is the end of it. I will not have a wife of mine arrested for burglary."

"Since you would be with me," she pointed out, "we would be arrested together."

Lucian hit upon another tact. "Do you want your father's telescope."

"Aye! More than anything except Belle Haven itself."

"I will get it for you, but *only* if you obey me. Either you stay in this room or I do not go to Belle Haven. Which will it be?"

Her jaw clenched angrily, and she pointedly turned her back on him. "Very well, *my lord.*"

Let her sulk until he got back, Lucian thought as he left. At least, she would be safe.

It took him longer to reach Belle Haven than he thought it would. He had taken a wrong turn in the dark and gone a quarter mile before realizing his mistake and retracing his steps.

Lucian remembered from his ride with David Inge that Belle Haven had looked vulnerable to intruders, and he hoped now that he had been right. Rather than approach the estate by the road to the entrance gate, he went at it from the opposite direction.

When he reached the perimeter wall at the back of the park, he left his horse concealed in a small copse. He climbed a beech tree growing adjacent to the wall, slid out along one of its sturdy branches, and dropped down inside the grounds.

He set off with rapid stride toward the mansion. At the foot of the hill on which it was built, he discovered a gravel path leading up to it.

The night was clear, and the stars and a quarter-moon illuminated the mansion. It was long past midnight, and no light shone from any of the windows. All of Belle Haven's occupants appeared to be abed. The only sound was the chirp of crickets.

The moon and stars were casting more illumination for Lucian than he wanted. Although it made it easier to find his way over the unfamiliar terrain, it also made him more visible to anyone who might chance to glance out a darkened window in his direction.

Halfway up the hill he left the path and cut toward the southwest corner of Belle Haven, where Angel had said her father's library and bedroom were located. By asking about the views from these rooms, he had easily elicited their location from his unsuspecting wife.

As he passed a majestic horse chestnut tree in full flower, a large, murky figure stepped into Lucian's path. The shadows cast by the chestnut's heavy boughs concealed the man's facial features from Lucian, but he had no difficulty identifying the pistol that was pointed at his heart.

Chapter 12

Lucian stared down at the pistol aimed at his chest. Bloody hell, the Crowes must have posted guards, and he had walked right into one!

Although he could not make out the man's face, he was able to ascertain that he wore the utilitarian garb of a groom or other menial.

All Lucian could do was bluff in the hope that he could catch the man off guard and disarm him. That would be difficult to do, however, without making noise that would awaken the sleeping household. Especially when the man was damn near as big as Lucian himself.

In his most freezing tone, Lucian demanded, "What the devil do you think you're doing?"

"Seems to me that ought to be my question to you," the man responded in amusement.

Lucian was relieved to hear both the humor and the calm intelligence in the man's voice. At least he was not confronted by some jittery fool who might accidentally shoot him out of sheer nervousness.

"You Lady Angela's husband?" the man asked.

Startled, Lucian debated whether it would be wiser to confirm or deny it and decided to evade until he could learn whether the man was Angel's friend or foe, "Why would you ask that?"

"I guess that means you are, otherwise you'd say no," the man deduced. "Can't say as I like a man that isn't proud to claim Lady Angela as his wife."

Stung by the scorn in the man's voice, Lucian retorted, "I am very proud to claim her."

"Then you see that you take good care of her."

Lucian was torn between amusement and exasperation at this bizarre encounter in which a servant was presuming to instruct him on how to treat his own wife. "I intend to!"

"Well," the man replied skeptically, "you're not doing such a good job of it so far."

Lucian, much nettled to have his performance as a husband despairingly assessed by a servant and a stranger, demanded, "Who the hell are you? And why are you holding a gun on me?"

"Name's Orin. As for the gun, Sir Rupert has ordered trespassers shot."

"Sir Rupert would not consider his stepdaughter's husband a trespasser," Lucian lied.

Orin laughed humorlessly. "Methinks you're the one he specifically had in mind. He ordered the gates barred against both you and her."

"Are you going to shoot me?" Lucian inquired, sounding as though it was a matter of supreme indifference to him.

"Only if you treat your wife badly."

"I told you I intend to take very good care of Angel."

"If you mean that, you'll get her away from here before what happened to her father happens to her."

Alarm rippled through Lucian. "God's oath, what are you talking about?"

"Things weren't right about the earl's death."

Having heard Angel's account of it, Lucian agreed.

"Haven't said anything to Lady Angela because it would only have upset her more, and I was afraid she would do something rash that would put her in danger, too."

A wise man was Orin.

"What things weren't right?" Lucian asked tersely.

"For one thing, the earl had not planned to go out that day until some mysterious note was delivered to him. Then he wanted the fastest horse in the stable saddled up at once. I never saw him in such a frenzy as when he rode out of here that day."

"Did Lord Ashcott say anything to you about what was in the note?"

"No, but he was clearly beside himself that Lady Angela had not returned from visiting her old nurse. She should have been back an hour or more earlier. I thought perhaps he meant to look for her, but he did not go in that direction."

"I understand the note he received was never found."

"No, but he may have had it with him. I was one of those who found him, and it looked to me as though his pockets had been rifled. The pouch was missing, too."

"What pouch?"

"When Lord Ashcott left here, he was carrying a leather pouch that looked to contain coin. I saw him put it in his coat pocket before he mounted his horse."

"But it was gone when you found him?"

"Aye."

So a pouch of money, the note that had sent Ashcott to his death, and his will that left everything to Angel were all missing. Not for a moment did Lucian believe all this could be mere coincidence.

He asked, "Does no one have any idea who sent the note to the earl?"

"A woman, a stranger."

"How do you know that?"

"I tracked down the lad who delivered it. He lives in Lower Hocking. A woman he'd never seen before offered him five shillings to bring it here."

Sudden suspicion flashed in Lucian's mind. "Did he describe her to you?"

"Aye, he did. She was black-haired, dark-eyed, buxom, and I gather from what he said, certain of her charms."

Maude!

"Orin, do you think that Ashcott was headed for the haunted cottage?"

"Aye. No one who took the path he did could have been going anywhere else."

"How did you find him?"

"Lying facedown on the path as it wound through a dense patch of woods a dozen yards from the cottage."

"Do you think his death was an accident?"

"The doctor said it was."

"I want to know what you think."

Orin hesitated for a long moment, as though trying to decide whether he trusted Lucian enough to answer him candidly.

"If a man is thrown from his horse on his face, he doesn't hurt the back of his head as the earl did."

"God's oath, you are talking murder!" Were the Crowes guilty of a far more serious crime than cheating Angel out of her inheritance? "Have you told anyone else what you have told me?"

"I pointed it out to the constable, who warned me that if I spread malicious falsehoods like that, I'd be in a peck of trouble."

"Did you try to tell anyone else?"

"Who was there to tell that would have believed me, other than Lady Angela?" Orin asked, his voice limned with frustration. "And I was afraid of what she might do if I told her."

A reasonable fear in light of Angel's impetuousness.

Orin stepped away from the tree and the moonlight fell on his face, allowing Lucian to see his features for the first time. They were wide and blunt beneath thick, unruly hair. Lucian judged him to be in his late twenties.

"Lady Angela says you promised to get Belle Haven back for her," Orin said.

God's oath, who could Angel have been talking to that this had already become common knowledge in the neighborhood?

Lucian studied Orin's handsome face, strong and open. He was clearly highly intelligent, and his speech was that of an educated man, not a lowly stablehand. "You don't talk like a groom."

"No, but that is what I am now," he said bitterly.

Before Lucian could ask him what he had been before, Orin said, "You'd best not keep Lady Angela waiting any longer."

"My wife is fast asleep at the inn where we are staying. She will not miss me."

"She's not at any inn," Orin scoffed. "She's waiting for you in her father's library."

"She's what!" Lucian exploded in mingled consternation and anger. "Bloody hell, I don't believe it!"

"Sh-h-h," Orin cautioned him. "You'll wake up the Crowes."

Lucian forced himself to lower his voice even though he felt like bellowing in rage at Angel's blatant defiance of him. "I forbade her to come here tonight. It is too damned dangerous!"

"Aye, it is, but you won't get far forbidding Lady Angela." Orin gave Lucian a sympathetic grin. "She loves adventure, and she has a mind of her own."

"So I am discovering," Lucian said grimly, following Orin toward the corner of the mansion where one of the tall windows was slightly ajar.

Orin gestured toward it. "You can go in through there. You'll find Lady Angela inside. Get her to leave as quickly as possible."

"If I don't kill her first," Lucian muttered furiously.

Orin's face hardened. "Now, you treat her right, you hear. I don't care if you are an earl. If you hurt her, you'll answer to Orin. Don't care if they hang me for it."

Lucian regarded his companion with strong suspicion. "Orin, are you in love with my wife?"

"Everyone hereabout loves Lady Angela." In the moonlight, Orin's gaze met Lucian's belligerently. "Isn't anything the people of Belle Haven wouldn't do for her." He turned and stalked away.

A mock orange planted next to the casement window that Orin had pointed out perfumed the area with the sweet scent of its flowers. Lucian opened the window wider. Breathing deeply of the pleasant odor, he pulled off his boots, hid them behind the shrub, and stepped through the window opening into the darkness of Ashcott's library.

As Lucian pulled the window shut behind him, he reflected with amusement that he had often dreamed of visiting this room where the scientific earl had done his writing, but he had never expected to do so by stealing in through a window.

He caught sight of a flicker of light near the floor along the far wall of the large room. Between that flicker and the pale moonlight falling through the windows, Lucian had just enough illumination to thread his way carefully between the room's furniture without bumping into it.

The unsteady light was located between the back of a settee and a wall lined with books. Lucian, padding up on silent, stocking feet, looked over the back of the settee.

Angel, dressed in the breeches and ruffled white shirt in which she had dueled him, was sitting cross-legged on the floor, reading by the feeble light of a candle stub on the floor beside her. She was so absorbed in a book that she had pulled from one of the shelves that she did not notice him.

Lucian was used to unquestioning obedience, and it had never occurred to him that his wife would not be as compliant to his wishes as his troops, servants, and other hirelings. He could not remember the last time someone had dared to flaunt his wishes.

"What the devil are you doing here?" he hissed at her.

Angel started violently, then whispered, "Oh, Lucian, it is you at last. What took you so long? I have been dreadfully worried about you."

"You have been worried about me?" he echoed in an incredulous whisper. "Bloody hell, it's yourself, not me, that you ought to be worrying about."

"Why, because I disobeyed you?"

"Because it is very dangerous for you to be here!" Even more dangerous than Lucian had thought before he had heard Orin's sinister revelations.

Lucian wanted to lash her verbally for having disobeyed him, but this was not the place and he had not the time to do so. Instead he asked, "What the devil are you reading so intently?"

"My father's journal. He wrote in it every day of his adult life, and all the volumes are here." She gestured toward the bookshelves in front of her.

Lucian noticed for the first time more than two dozen thick, matching leatherbound volumes. Each had a different year stamped in gold on the spine. How he would like to have examined them, but there was no time.

"I need the candle," he told Angel. "I want to see if I

can find a secret compartment where your father might have hidden the missing will."

She handed the candle up to him, and he headed toward Ashcott's ornate walnut desk.

In the flickering light of the candle he caught sight of a steep, narrow staircase. "Is that the staircase your father had installed to his bedroom?

"Aye, he liked to work at odd hours, and he had it put in so that he could come down here to the library whenever he wanted without disturbing anyone."

Ashcott's desk was near the window through which Lucian had entered. It had seven visible drawers, three on each side and on top of them one larger drawer that extended the width of the desk. The broad top was bare except for a silver inkstand, a gold-framed miniature of Angel, and a small telescope.

Lucian, holding the candle close to the portrait, wondered how long ago it had been done. Not long, he suspected, for Angel looked much the same in it as she did now. The artist had perfectly caught the lively, mischievous gleam in her eyes.

Suddenly the muffled tread of footsteps sounded over his head.

Lucian froze. "Who is using your father's room?"

"Sir Rupert."

"Wonderful!"

"The footsteps stopped almost directly overhead.

Lucian let a long minute tick by. When no further sounds were heard from above, he gently, noiselessly eased out the wide top drawer of the desk.

Angel whispered, "I went through every paper in his desk three times, and Papa's will is not there."

Lucian pushed his hand into the recess that had held the drawer and felt carefully around the top, bottom, sides, and back. There was no sign of a secret compartment nor of a document attached to any of the interior surfaces.

He repeated the procedure with each of the side drawers. The last drawer that he pulled out, the bottom one on the right side, was four inches shorter from front to back than the others had been.

Angel noticed the difference in its size at once.

"You have found something," she said eagerly, forgetting to keep her voice as low as she should have. "How clever you are."

Once again the dull clump of footsteps was heard above them. This time, they were moving toward the narrow staircase.

Lucian swore silently and held his index finger vertically against his lips to signal Angel to remain absolutely silent.

The footsteps stopped at what Lucian judged must be the head of the staircase on the upper floor.

They waited as minute upon silent minute passed. Finally, the footsteps above them retreated slowly in the direction from which they had come.

When silence had reigned for another minute, Lucian turned his attention back to the desk, feeling carefully about in the recess where the shortened drawer had been.

Finally his fingers touched a small lever set in the frame. He pressed it, and the back of the recess dropped forward.

With rising excitement, he reached into the secret compartment. His fingers closed first on a leather bag that from the feel of it contained only a few coins. He pulled it out, then thrust his hand back in.

This time his fingers touched parchment. He slid the document out, praying that it was the missing will.

"You have found it," Angel whispered in elation.

Lucian unfolded the parchment, but it was a certificate for shares in a joint stock company.

Hastily he resumed his groping within the hidden compartment but it contained nothing else.

The intense disappointment on Angel's face was so heartrending that it was all he could do to keep from taking her in his arms to comfort her.

He put the leather bag back in the secret compartment, closed it, and replaced the drawer.

Each pier of the desk rested on four pawlike feet, leaving a space of two inches between the desk's bottom and the floor. Lucian slid his upturned hand into each of those cavities to make certain nothing had been attached to the underside of the piers.

Nothing had, but in the second cavity his fingers touched a ball of paper lying on the floor. Pulling it out, Lucian saw that it was merely a bit of cheap paper that had been crumpled up and discarded. Apparently it had rolled unnoticed beneath the desk.

Most likely it would prove to be nothing, but Lucian shoved it into his pocket to examine later, when he had more time and better light.

Rising to his feet, he asked, "Do you know of any other secret compartments your father might have had where he could have hidden his will?"

"No," Angel said, "but then I was not aware of the one in the desk."

He pointed at the telescope on the desk. "I assume that is the one you wanted."

Angel nodded.

"Good. I want to take a quick look around, and then we will be on our way with it."

Lucian picked up the candle and started around the room, looking for any sign of other secret hiding places, but he saw none. He motioned for Angel to stay by the desk, but instead she trailed along beside him.

When he reached the wall of books behind the settee, it occurred to him that Ashcott could have hidden the will in one of his books.

The thought was daunting.

Lucian stared in dismay at the row after row of volumes that lined the walls. It would take days to go through all of them.

"Did your father have a book that was very special to him, one that he might have concealed the will in?"

"I thought of that, and I went through all of his favorites after he died. I found several notes and old letters, but no will."

Lucian glanced down at the rows of leatherbound journals. "When did your father execute the will that is missing?"

"After my brother Charlie died."

"What was the date of his death?" Lucian asked impatiently.

"January 3, 1689."

"Do you know how soon after that your father made his new will."

"He went to London to do so two weeks after the funeral."

"Perhaps he left the new will in London."

"No, I told you, he brought it back here to Belle Haven, where he showed it to me and my uncle. That is how I know that in it he left everything to me."

Lucian reached down and plucked the volume stamped 1689 from the shelf.

Tucking it under his arm, he said, "I'll take this with us. Perhaps he wrote something in his journal that will give us a clue as to where he hid it."

Lucian resumed his circuit of the room.

As they rounded the settee, Angel brushed against a heavy book lying precariously on a small table.

He grabbed for it, but it fell to the floor with a crash that sounded as loud as a gunshot to his strained nerves.

It was followed almost immediately by the thud of feet hitting the floor in the room above them.

The footsteps moved hastily toward the staircase.

Lucian measured the distance across the big room to the windows and knew they had no hope of making it to them before Crowe descended the steps.

Snuffing the candle, Lucian grabbed Angel and pulled her down with him to the floor behind the settee. He pushed her as tightly against it as he could and threw his big body over hers. If Crowe discovered them and decided to shoot first, then ask questions, Angel would be protected by Lucian's body.

Although she made no sound, she squirmed a little beneath him, her soft curves teasing and tantalizing his body with their promise. He stifled a groan.

Rupert's footsteps trod heavily down the narrow staircase. When Angel's stepfather reached the library, he went first toward the windows. Lucian, lying silently over Angel, thanked God that he had closed the one by which he had entered.

Apparently finding nothing amiss by the windows, Lucian heard Rupert moving around the room. As he drew near to them, light from the candle he was carrying played over them as they lay huddled on the floor against the back of the settee.

The footsteps stopped in front of the settee.

Chapter 13

Lucian tensed, anticipating the sudden pain of a ball or blade in his back. Beneath him, Angel seemed to have stopped breathing.

For a long, long moment he waited. Then the footfalls retreated slowly, as though with each step Sir Rupert was stopping to look about him.

At last, the door to the hall opened with a creak. Gradually the footsteps faded away.

Lucian brought his mouth down to Angel's ear and cautioned in the lightest of whispers, "He may come back. Don't move, yet."

She didn't.

Lucian was acutely conscious of how heavy his big body must be over her delicate one, and he braced himself to take more of his weight off her.

Two minutes later, as Lucian had feared, the footsteps returned to the library. They stopped in the middle of the room for a breathless minute before tromping up the staircase.

Not until silence reigned once again on the floor above them did Lucian roll off Angel.

He did not attempt to relight the candle. Instead he motioned for her to follow him. They picked their way slowly across the dark room, taking care not to bump into any of the vague, blurred shapes in their path.

When they finally reached the windows without mishap, Lucian heard Angel expel a long breath of relief.

God's oath, but she was a brave little thing. Most females finding themselves in such a dangerous situation would have dissolved into hysterics.

But then most wives would have obeyed their husbands and not gotten themselves into such a perilous predicament. Lucian was torn between admiration for her courage and anger for placing herself in so much jeopardy.

He swung wide the casement window through which he had entered and signaled Angel to go through the opening.

When she had done so, he handed her the volume of her father's journal that he had taken, removed the telescope from the desk, gave that to her as well, then turned back for a final scrutiny of the library.

His eye fell on the gold-framed miniature of Angel on her father's desk. He swept it up and dropped it in his pocket, then followed Angel through the window.

At the bottom of the hill, Angel stopped and turned around to stare up at the mansion, white and ghostly in the light of the quarter-moon.

Lucian saw the devastated look on her face and the shimmer of tears in her eyes, and he forgot how furious he was at her for disobeying him.

"I love Belle Haven so much," she whispered shakily. "There are no words that can tell you how much it means to me. And now I will never be allowed inside it again. I may never even see it again! I am sure you do not understand, but I feel so bereft."

But Lucian did understand. He remembered what it had been like that day his father had banished him forever from Sandford Park, the country estate where he had grown up. Lucian had stopped outside its ornate iron gates and looked back in abject misery at the only home he had ever known. He had been filled with black despair and loss that he would never be permitted to walk through those gates again and that more than likely, given the uncertain future he faced in the army, he would not even live long enough to see them again.

Lucian gazed down at his wife's stricken face and wished for some way to erase her pain. So much had happened to her in the past few months, most of it bad, and none of it her fault. Her father had been killed, her home and inheritance stolen from her. Now she had been forced to marry a stranger who did not love nor want her.

Seeing how much she loved Belle Haven, Lucian was more determined than ever to get it back for her.

They sneaked silently up the backstairs of the White Horse Inn and tiptoed along the hall to their room.

As they entered it, Angel braced for the storm from her husband. She knew he was furious at her for disobeying him by going to Belle Haven. Although he had said nothing to her on the ride back, it was only because the need for quiet outweighed his desire to vent his wrath at her.

Lucian closed the door behind them. Without a word, he carried her father's diary and telescope to the scarred oak table between the beds. He laid them there and turned to face her.

"Angel, I ordered you to remain here tonight," he began in a low, stern tone. "When I tell you to do something, I expect you to do it."

"I know you do."

"Then why did you not do so?"

"I knew I could help you."

"Help me? You call knocking that book to the floor and nearly getting us caught *helping* me?"

"I am sorry about that, but it was an accident."

"An accident that would not have happened had you not disobeyed me! Your accident forced me to cut short my search for your father's missing will. I might have found it."

Angel doubted that he would have, but she said nothing. It would only exacerbate his anger.

"I will not tolerate a wife who disobeys me." He began unbuttoning his shirt. "Do I make myself clear?"

"Quite," Angel retorted, her own temper rising at his arrogance. "However, I do not see why a wife, even *yours,* my lord, should be expected to obey her husband when he is wrong."

His expression turned to irate disbelief. "Are you saying that I was wrong to try to keep you safe?"

"I am saying that you should have let me guide you to Belle Haven, my lord."

"Lucian," he corrected. "I told you to call me Lucian."

He stripped off his shirt and tossed it aside. Angel's breath shortened at the sight of his powerful bronze chest covered with swirling patterns of curly black hair. The sight of it made her want to call him several things besides Lucian.

Splendid and exciting came most readily to her mind. A delicious warmth crept through her at the memory of waking up that morning to find herself being held tightly against his muscled body.

She said, "Only see how much quicker you would have reached Belle Haven if you had taken me with you." Their return from the estate had taken considerably less time than his trip to it because she had used shortcuts.

His mouth tightened angrily. "May I remind you, Angel, that only a few hours ago, you vowed before God to obey me."

"And you vowed to love me, but you do not," she shot back.

"I also vowed to protect you, and that, damn it, is what I am trying to do." He sank down on his bed and yanked off his left boot. "As I told you before, Angel, I cannot force myself to love you—that is beyond my control."

Aye, he had told her that before. And it hurt her just as much this time as it had then.

"But it is within my control to protect you, and I intend to do so." His right boot hit the floor. "In return I expect, nay demand, your obedience. Do you understand me?"

"Aye, my lord." She understood him only too well, but she had no intention of becoming his obedient little handmaid. Nothing would be gained, however, by telling him that now. He would discover it soon enough.

He was unbuttoning his breeches as casually as though he did so before a woman every day of his life.

Her cheeks flaming, Angel snatched up her night rail from the bed and disappeared behind the screen in the corner to change into it.

She was removing her own breeches when she heard his bed creak beneath his weight as he settled on it.

Angel bit her lip at the sound. When she had arrived at the inn, she had been so apprehensive about sleeping with him for the first time that when he had told her he would not touch her tonight, she had been relieved enough to regain her appetite.

She had not known until dinner what an amusing man she had married. He had seemed intent on making her laugh with his funny anecdotes about incidents at court and life in Holland. He had served in that country for several years in command of an English regiment stationed there. That was how he had become so close to the new Dutch king who now sat on England's throne.

Lucian had patiently answered her questions about King William. It was true his majesty was short and unimpressive in stature, but her husband assured her that the king was a brilliant man and a good and just ruler.

As dinner progressed, Angel found herself increasingly fascinated by the man she had married. The odd excitement his presence always seemed to kindle in her blazed stronger than ever, accompanied by the strangest ache deep in her abdomen.

After the meal, when he helped her from the table, the most delicious shiver rippled through her at his touch.

And perversely, she found herself regretting his pledge that he would not touch her that night.

Why had he promised her that? Did he find her that unattractive? she wondered forlornly.

Now, changing into her night rail behind the screen, Lady Bloomfield's words came back to haunt her. *"Every man wants his wedding night. I doubt there has ever been a groom in the history of mankind who despised his wife so much that he failed to claim his rights to her on it."*

Well, there was one now.

The pain of this realization blindsided Angel, and she felt the sting of tears. It hurt her that her husband should despise her that much. Yet she could hardly blame him. He had wanted Kitty, not her. Lovely, charming Kitty, a beautiful rose in full bloom, while Angel was a plain, nondescript twig. He had been tricked into having to marry her, and he had done so only to save his honor.

So why should she be surprised that he despised her so

much he did not even want her on their wedding night. She fought to keep tears from trickling down her cheeks.

"Angel, who is Orin?" her husband asked.

She swiped at her tears and tried to compose her voice so that it would not betray her unhappiness.

"The son of Papa's former master of the horse, who died several years ago."

"Orin seems very well educated for a groom."

"Papa was so impressed by what an intelligent child he was that he had him educated. When Papa died, he was training Orin to become his agent-in-chief."

If Lord Vayle—Lucian—noticed the choked timbre of Angel's voice, he made no mention of it. "Then why is he working as a groom now?"

"He clashed immediately with my stepfather. Orin refused to oust elderly retainers from the homes Papa had given them for their lifetime or to raise the rents on the tenants to the levels Crowe wanted. Orin said the land would not support such increases, and he is right. But my stepfather's response was to reduce Orin to a groom and replace him with that odious, groveling Oliver Seiler."

Angel stepped from behind the screen. Lucian was in his bed, lying on his back and staring up at the ceiling. He did not so much as glance in her direction as she made her way to her bed and got in it.

His disinterest in her wounded her more than a tongue-lashing would have. Her gaze fell on her father's telescope, lying on the scarred oak surface.

It had been very kind of Lucian to go to such effort to get it for her, but why had he bothered in light of the way he felt about her?

She reached out and touched the instrument lovingly. It had been Papa's most cherished possession. That was why she had wanted it more than anything else.

"Angel, why does Orin not leave Belle Haven? Surely, he could find better employment elsewhere."

She looked over at her husband. He was still staring fixedly at the ceiling. She wished he would at least glance her way. "I told Orin the same thing, but he said he owed it to my father to remain and help me."

"What do you think of him?"

"He is the best friend I have had since Papa died."

Angel slid down in her bed and rolled over on her side, presenting her back to her husband. If he could not bear to look at her, she would not look at him. Suppressing a sob, she said, "I don't know what I would have done without Orin."

A puzzling rush of emotion hit Lucian at Angel's words and the quaver in her voice. He should have been grateful to Orin for helping her. Instead he had the irrational desire to hit the man.

Lucian turned his head and looked at the back of Angel's head. She was angry at him, he thought. Her unhappy face when he had told her that he could not love her haunted him. He had been rather hard on her, too, but she had to learn that he intended to be master in his own house. Angel would not be able to twist him to her will as she could some besotted rustic like Orin.

It was laughable that this slip of a girl could think she knew better than he. He had age and experience on his side.

Lucian tried to ignore the ache in his groin. He had not dared steal even a sidelong glance at Angel when she had emerged from behind the screen. The sight of her lovely body swaying beneath that damned sheer night rail would have forced him out into the night for an immersion in the cold creek that ran behind the inn.

Now his mind taunted him with memories of her as she had dueled him, her breeches revealing her tantalizing curves. He remembered, too, how soft and exciting those same curves had been when they were pressed against him as they had lain hidden behind the settee in her father's library.

Even in that moment of great danger, he had wanted her with an intensity that had shocked him.

It had been torment to lie there, his body sprawled protectively over hers, breathing deeply of her fresh, clean scent that reminded him of a field of wildflowers on a dewy morning.

She was young, but she possessed great vitality and courage. And passion, too—of that he was certain. He yearned to initiate her immediately to the joys of lovemaking.

He had the right to do so. It was his wedding night after all.

A damned strange one! As strange as the whole day had been.

He had awakened betrothed to one woman, then wed another. He had been forced to duel his bride to get her to marry him, and then he had spent much of his wedding night burgling her former home. Now, he was about to spend what was left of it alone in a separate bed.

But tomorrow night, he consoled himself, he would be at Ardmore in the privacy of his own home. He could wait until then to claim his bride.

Angel's breathing told Lucian she had fallen asleep. He quietly reached out for the breeches that he had dropped on the chair beside his bed. From the pocket, he extracted the crumpled ball of paper that he had found at Belle Haven.

Sitting up in bed, he carefully smoothed it out. The paper was cheap and thin and no bigger than four inches by four inches.

He picked up the pewter candlestick from the table between the beds and held it so that its light better illuminated the unusual slanting writing with curling flourishes to the letters.

LORD ASHCOTT:

We have your precious Angel. If you want to see her alive again, you will come immediately to the "Haunted Cottage" with a bag containing one hundred pounds. Leave the bag on the table there, and your daughter will be home by nightfall.

Come alone. Tell no one of this note. Do not bring anyone with you or your daughter will die.

Come at once.

The note was unsigned. Lucian turned the sheet over. Ashcott's name had been written across the back.

Clearly this was the missing note that had sent Angel's father from his house in a frenzy. And no wonder.

Lucian could picture Ashcott, already worried because his daughter was late in returning home, reading it, then in his fear for Angel's safety, mindlessly crumpling it up and dropping it on the floor.

Most likely he had accidentally pushed it beneath his desk with his toe as he worked to open the secret compartment.

"When Lord Ashcott left here, he was carrying a leather pouch that looked to contain coin."

Lucian suspected from the size of the bag that he had found in the secret compartment of the desk that it once had held considerably more money—perhaps another hundred pounds.

Yet Angel had not been abducted. She had merely been detained by a fallen tree, but whoever had written the note must have known that. Before Lucian left the area on the morrow he intended to have a look at the stump.

He studied the message again. Its diction, spelling, even the handwriting, betrayed that no roving member of the criminal underclass was responsible. A well-educated man had composed it.

Lucian was convinced now that the riding mishap that killed Angel's father had not been an accident, but murder, as Orin had suspected.

And he was equally certain that the Crowes were responsible for it.

But how could he prove it?

Again, Maude was the key. From the description given Orin, he was willing to wager that she was the woman who had delivered the note.

Lucian would have to find her after all and extract the truth from her.

But even if he tracked her down and she confessed, Angel would not be assured of recovering Belle Haven and the rest of her inheritance unless the missing will could be found.

He had little hope of locating it during another surreptitious, nocturnal visit like tonight's to Belle Haven.

Lucian would need days, not hours, to go through all the books in Ashcott's library. Besides, the most likely place to look for the document now was in the late earl's bedroom, but Sir Rupert's presence there made that impossible.

Lucian had no intention of telling Angel the truth about her father's death yet. Given her impulsive nature, God only knew what she might do.

Most likely challenge Rupert Crowe to a duel.

Chapter 14

The day had dawned cold, gray, and stormy. It matched Lucian's mood as he stalked across the drenched courtyard of the Wild Boar Inn toward his coach. The rain had stopped only minutes before, and he was anxious to be on his way to Ardmore.

"We'll make it there today," Tom, one of the outriders, assured him cheerfully.

"That's what you said yesterday," Lucian grumbled.

The journey to Ardmore that he had expected to take one day after leaving the White Horse Inn in Lower Hocking had already consumed two, and they still were not there.

"Should be there afore noon. Made it last night weren't for the rain turning the road to mud."

The trip was taking so much longer than Lucian had anticipated that he ought to abandon the idea of going to Ardmore and turn back toward London. The queen had very reluctantly given him permission to leave the capital, but only for a few days, and he dared not exceed the time she had allotted him.

Yet they were so close to Ardmore now. He could not force himself to forgo seeing the only estate he had ever owned, even though he would have time only for a quick inspection.

More than rain was to blame for their delay in reaching Ardmore. Lucian had wanted to see the remains of the tree that had blocked the road the day Angel's father had been killed. That isolated spot had been considerably out of their way and had cost them several hours.

His examination of the stump had shown him that no

lightning bolt had brought that beech down. It had been partially chopped through, then left to snap from the wind and its own weight.

Lucian started into his coach, then stopped as he realized that Angel was not in it. "Where is Lady Vayle?"

One of the outriders nodded his head toward the corner of the inn.

Angel was talking to a gaunt, young woman huddled beneath the inn's eaves with a whimpering baby in her arms.

Lucian hurried across the wet, slippery cobbles toward them. The woman's thin clothing was soaked through. So was the tattered blanket in which the baby was wrapped. The mother was shivering uncontrollably, and he recognized the baby's mewling from his war experiences as that of a starving infant.

The pair wrenched at Lucian's heart. Poor miserable creatures. He reached into his pocket for some coins.

His wife unfastened the red wool tippet that she was wearing and handed it to the woman.

Lucian would have been happy for the poor creature to have it had it not been the only cape of any sort in Angel's virtually nonexistent wardrobe. He took hold of the garment as it was changing hands and pushed it back at his wife.

"Keep it," he told her brusquely. "It is a cold, wet day, and you will need it yourself."

"Not as much as she and her baby do!" Angel cried defiantly. "Her husband died a month ago, and she has nothing. She came here seeking a job as a chambermaid, but the innkeeper would not hire her because she has a babe."

Angel tried to hand her cape back to the woman, but once again Lucian intercepted it.

"They need shelter and food more than your tippet," he said sharply. "Go to our coach. I will handle this."

She started to protest, but then she saw the coins in his hand. She gave him one of those brilliant, approving smiles of hers that embraced her entire face. It warmed Lucian like a blazing fire.

She left him with the woman. As his wife retreated quietly across the cobblestones, he wondered whether she had any idea how captivating that smile of hers was.

Lucian gave the money to the woman, then led her inside the inn, where he had a quiet talk with the proprietor.

When he emerged a few minutes later, he was alone. He quickly crossed the courtyard and climbed into his coach.

In answer to his wife's inquisitive look, he said gruffly, "The innkeeper has changed his mind about hiring her."

Lucian's coach lurched forward. He settled back on the leather seat beside Angel. Beneath the tippet, she was wearing the same plain black gown that he had first seen her in.

Before he could present his wife to London society, he must buy her a suitable wardrobe and hire someone to tutor her on how to behave. It was not that he was ashamed of her. Far from it. But he was determined to protect her from those wicked wits, cynical and debauched, who would delight in cutting such a sweet, naive innocent to shreds. He had never felt so protective of anyone as he did of Angel. He told himself that it was because he had given her his name. She was his responsibility now.

Lucian studied Angel critically as she looked out the window at the chalk downs. At his behest, she was wearing her long, chocolate hair down, caught with a ribbon at the back of her neck instead of in that dreadful knot. With the right wardrobe and hairstyle, his wife would be an eye-catching young lady.

The coach, traveling at a rapid pace, rounded a sharp curve, throwing Angel against him. He automatically braced himself with his feet and put his arm around her.

She had the most disconcerting effect on him, he thought, striving to control his body against its unwanted response to her nearness. He had only to catch her fresh scent or have her sweet little body slide into his, and he was as randy as a young strut.

Her proximity to him in the coach had been continuing torment.

It had been even worse at night at the inns where they had shared a room but not a bed.

Lucian had sworn to himself that he would not take Angel until he was beneath his own roof at Ardmore, and he was not a man who went back on his word, even to himself.

But when he had made that promise he had expected to reach Ardmore the next night. He had not counted on two miserable nights on the road.

Lucian hoped to hell that Tom was right about their reaching Ardmore this morning.

He could not stand another night of torture.

The delay had served one good purpose though. Angel was considerably more relaxed with him now. She no longer referred uneasily to his size nor cast nervous glances at his breeches.

He smiled down at his wife. Seemingly oblivious to the coach's uncomfortable jostling, she was looking intently out the window, her eyes eagerly searching the Hampshire hillside for some fresh discovery.

It was not long in coming.

"See the beautiful butterflies."

He looked in the direction she was pointing and caught a glimpse of a pair with purple wings and white markings.

Angel said, "I believe they are purple emperors, but I cannot be certain."

Lucian had expected the journey to Hampshire to be as tedious as his ride from London to Fernhill with Kitty had been, but instead Angel had kept him entertained with her commentary, curiosity, and enthusiasm.

Her fascination with new sights and people; her innocently astute, often humorous, observations; her discernment for even the smallest detail, whether it be a butterfly or a flower, delighted him. Nothing, not even the subtlest differences in the countryside or in the people's dress, eluded Angel's big, bright eyes.

She might be naive but she was remarkably observant. He thought of the observations her father had recorded in his *Journal of Belle Haven,* and smiled. She was definitely the scientific earl's daughter.

A few minutes later she turned to Lucian, her face again alight with curiosity.

"We are coming to an inn that has a most intriguing sign, my lord—"

"Lucian," he interjected automatically, as he did every time she addressed him formally in private.

He leaned toward her and rested his cheek against her soft, silken hair, seizing this small excuse to touch her. He had taken advantage of every opportunity to do so the past two days to accustom her to his touch.

The inn's sign, hanging from a tall iron post, was decorated with a picture of a many-branched tree. A crowned head peeked from among its foliage at two armor-clad soldiers marching beneath. The name, "Royal Oak Inn," was painted beneath the scene.

"What do you think the picture signifies?" Angel asked.

"I suspect it recalls an incident at the battle of Worcester when King Charles II escaped with his life by hiding in an oak."

"I knew you would know," she said admiringly.

After passing the inn, the coach hit a bone-jarring stretch of rough road, and Lucian's arm again went protectively around his bride. He was proud of her fortitude and pluck. Not once had she complained about the travails of the journey: the terrible roads, the awful food, and the discomfort of the wayside inn where they had been forced to stop last night.

What a nightmare it would have been with Kitty. He shuddered at the memory of the trip from London to Fernhill with his former betrothed.

Kitty had alternated between boasting interminably about the pedigrees of the people who would be attending the betrothal party and complaining about the dreadful hardship she was being forced to endure on the journey.

Lucian had been able to stand her for only three hours before he had abandoned the coach for the saddle horse that he had brought with him for the ride to Ardmore. The horse still accompanied them, but not for anything would he have traded the coach and Angel's lively company for it.

The vehicle's pace flagged, and Lucian frowned irritably. "Why the devil are we slowing down?"

"You are an impatient traveler," Angel remarked.

"I am," Lucian agreed. The coach rounded a curve, then picked up speed again. "I am used to traveling as a soldier on horseback. I find the slower pace of a coach irksome."

"Do you miss the army?"

"No, I am delighted to be done with it." The king had tried to talk him out of resigning, but Lucian had been adamant. "I hate war," he confessed.

"I would hate it, too, but it must have been exciting to visit foreign lands. You have seen so much."

Too much, Lucian thought wearily, remembering the horrific scenes of war. "I prefer England. When I landed at Torbay with William, I was delighted to be back on English soil again."

"So you accompanied the king when he came to claim the throne."

"Aye, I was with him on the march to London." Lucian longed to lower his head and kiss Angel's beguiling lips, but he held himself in check, fearing he would not be able to stop with a few kisses.

Angel said wistfully, "I have never even seen the sea."

"I have seen more of it than I wanted—especially when we were becalmed."

"You are so eager to reach Ardmore," Angel observed. "You must love it very much. What is it like?"

"I have no idea," Lucian replied. "I have never seen it."

"Never seen it," Angel echoed in surprise. "How long have you owned it?"

"Only a fortnight."

He had decided to acquire it as both an investment and as an alternative country home should he find the proximity of Sommerstone to Fernhill and Lord Bloomfield too tedious. Now that Sommerstone was lost to him, Lucian was glad he had at least one estate to call home.

"What possessed you to buy it when you had never seen it?"

"My parents visited there when I was about twelve. They returned with glowing stories about how lovely the estate and its house was." Lucian's father, who was not easily impressed, had confessed to envying its owner, Lord Ackleton, such a handsome property.

When it was offered to Lucian, who had never forgotten his father's fondness for it, he was delighted to snap up a property that his sire would have liked to own.

"Who owned Ardmore before you?"

"Lord Ackleton."

"Why did he sell it to you."

"He did not. Ackleton's dead. He was hanged five years ago after he had the bad judgment to join Monmouth's insurrection."

When King Charles II had died in 1685 without legitimate issue, his brother, James II, had ascended the throne. Charles's illegitimate son, the Duke of Monmouth, had led a rebellion against James to try to win the crown for himself.

It was soon crushed. Ackleton was hanged along with many others who had supported Monmouth, and his lordship's estate was seized.

Then a fortnight ago, King William, in recognition of Lucian's services to him, had offered him Ardmore cheap, and he had bought it.

Lucian's coach slowed as it passed a long train of packhorses plodding along single file. Each animal was loaded down with heavy baskets.

"I counted thirty horses altogether," Angel said as they left the train behind and the coach again picked up speed.

She fell silent for a moment, then she turned to Lucian and said with one of her sunny smiles, "Tell me about your family."

He stiffened. "I have none."

Her eyes widened. "You mean you have no living relatives, none at all?"

"No, I mean that my family is dead to me."

She looked perplexed. "I do not understand. Are your parents dead or are they not?"

"My mother is. She died fourteen years ago."

"And your father?"

"I do not talk about my father," he said in an Arctic voice.

"You sound as though you hate him!"

"I do," he said bluntly.

He saw the shock register on his wife's face. He realized that to Angel, who had adored her own father, his answer must seem inconceivable.

She burst out, "How can anyone hate his father?"

"In my case, he made it very easy."

"But you loved him once very much—I can tell."

How perceptive she was. "Aye," Lucian admitted, "when I was small, I worshiped him."

Then he had followed his adored father around, tagging at his heels like a small shadow.

"He favored my older brother, Fritz. I thought at first it was because Fritz was his heir that Papa concentrated his attention on him and had less and less time for me with each passing year."

As the two sons grew older, it was Fritz that their father questioned about his lessons. It was Fritz that their father took riding and hunting with him. By the time Lucian was fifteen, Wrexham paid his younger son no heed at all, no matter how hard the bewildered boy tried to win his approval.

Lucian's hands clenched unconsciously into fists, and he said hoarsely, "I finally had to concede what my father had been making abundantly clear to me for years—he hated me."

"Surely, he did not hate you!" Angel protested.

"But he did. He even told me he did."

"How terrible!" Angel looked as though she were about to cry for her husband. "How could he?"

Her small hands closed around his large one, squeezing it hard, in an instinctive gesture of sympathy and consolation that touched his heart as it had not been touched in years.

Lucian had never before told the story of his father to anyone, not even Selina, and he had never intended to tell it. He was amazed that he was confiding it now to Angel.

She was holding his hand hard with her own. Her expression was so full of compassion and commiseration for him that he suddenly felt as though a burden had been lifted from him.

"God knows I tried every way I knew to please my father, but the harder I tried, the more I seemed to alienate him."

"Did he never explain why?"

Lucian shook his head. "When I asked him, he told me only that I was not worthy of his love."

"Perhaps your father was incapable of love. I think my mother was."

"Oh, Wrexham was very capable of it." Bitterness edged Lucian's voice. "He loved Fritz."

"How do you feel about your brother?" Angel asked quietly.

Although Lucian had been jealous of his father's preference for Fritz, he could not dislike the brother, two years older than himself, who had inherited their mother's cheerful, amiable nature.

"I am very fond of him," Lucian admitted. "He lives with his family on a small estate in Hertfordshire that he manages for Wrexham."

By the time Lucian was nine, he had been the bigger of the two brothers. He had outstripped his older brother mentally as well, and it was Lucian who had helped the plodding Fritz with his lessons.

When Fritz heard that his father had disowned Lucian, he immediately wrote his brother to tell him how unhappy he was about it and asking him why their father had done it. Wrexham had told Fritz only that he had "the best reason in the world for doing so."

For several months after that, Fritz sent Lucian money saved from his own allowance to help him. The sums were small, for their father had kept his heir on a tight financial leash, but they been a godsend to the destitute Lucian. He had hated, however, being beholden to his father's favorite. As soon as Lucian made enough money from gambling to get by, he wrote Fritz that he no longer needed his help.

Their letters grew less frequent, mostly because Lucian

would let his brother's go unanswered for months at a time.

After Lucian came back to England with King William, Fritz wrote time and again begging his brother to visit him in Hertfordshire, but Lucian always found some excuse not to do so. He had never even seen his brother's wife or their two small children.

Angel inquired, "How did your father feel about your mother?"

"Wrexham adored her."

"Then why would he hate you, her son?"

"I have thought about that question for years, but I still do not know the answer." Lucian stared bleakly through the window at the passing countryside, then confessed, "I have never told anyone this story before."

"Why not?"

"I guess because I was ashamed," Lucian said with a candor that surprised himself. "I never understood why Wrexham hated me, but I felt that it had to be my fault."

"Did you ask your mother if she knew why he felt as he did?"

He had. Lucian still remembered with acute pain putting that question to his beautiful, loving, gentle mother. She had cried as though her heart were broken, and he had been the one who had ended up comforting her.

"She told me that the fault was my father's, not mine, but she would not say why he felt as he did. She insisted that it was nothing I had done. Nor could I do anything about it except pray to God to grant me the strength to bear this trial He had seen fit to impose upon me."

"Your mother should have told you why your father felt as he did, especially if it was nothing you had done," Angel said disapprovingly. "You had a right to know."

"She said I was too young yet, but she promised she would tell me when I turned eighteen."

"But she did not?"

"She died when I was barely sixteen," he replied, careful to keep his voice devoid of the emotion he still felt when he remembered that tumultuous, terrible year.

Two months after his mother was buried, his father had forced him into the army and washed his hands of him.

Nothing—not the laurels Lucian had won on the battlefield, not the fortune he had accumulated off it, not the rank and great power he had attained—had been able to erase the memory of that day fourteen years ago when his father had cast him off, telling him bluntly that he never wanted to see him again.

The young Lucian, still grieving for his newly dead mother, had stared at his father in agonized disbelief. "Papa, you act as though you hate me."

"I do," Lord Wrexham had said coldly.

"Why?" Lucian had whispered brokenly.

Instead of answering, Wrexham had turned on his heel and left his stunned son staring after the father he had once adored.

In that moment something had died within the boy. He saw that love was a weakness, a weapon that others used against him. He swore to himself that he would never be weak again, never trust again.

From that day forth, he had encircled his heart with a protective moat that could not be breached.

No one would ever hurt him as his father had done.

Lucian would never again allow anyone to wield that weapon called love against him.

Chapter 15

Angel pictured the young Lucian as he must have been when his father had rejected him: a baffled, bewildered halfling, still grieving for his mother, who had suddenly had the foundation of his world knocked from beneath him for no reason that he could discern.

She knew that terrible feeling all too well, for she had experienced it herself when her papa had been killed and the Crowes had seized her inheritance.

Her husband had turned his head and was staring out the window at the rugged countryside. She studied his dark, handsome profile with the hard-set jaw. He was as strong a man as she had ever met.

Yet she had seen for an instant, before he could hide it, the naked pain in Lucian's silver eyes as he had talked about his father's renunciation of him.

Angel decided that both he and Lady Bloomfield were wrong. He did have a heart. And not even after fourteen years had the wound that his father had inflicted on it truly healed.

She longed to put her arms around this enigmatic man who was her husband and comfort him, but she was afraid that he would rebuff her for presuming to think she could do so.

Men seemed to feel it imperative to present a strong facade to the world. Foolish creatures, they had to hide their feelings for fear they would be thought weak.

Besides, what consolation could she offer him when she was not the wife that he had wanted. He had not even been able to bring himself to bed her since their marriage. It gnawed painfully at her that he found her so repugnant.

He had wanted Kitty, not her, as his bride, even though he had not loved her friend either. That puzzled Angel, and she asked, "Why did you offer for Kitty when you did not love her?"

Lucian's mouth twisted in a cynical smile. "Oh, I wanted her, although not for the usual reason."

Angel wondered what "the usual reason" was.

Apparently sensing her puzzlement, he said, "There can be more than one reason for wanting a woman, little one, and none of them may have anything to do with loving her."

"What was your reason for wanting Kitty?"

"Two reasons," Lucian said bluntly. "I wanted to marry a daughter of Bloomfield's—any daughter of his would do—"

"Any daughter?" Angel echoed in shock. "Why?"

"Bloomfield rejected my brother Fritz's suit for his eldest daughter, Anne, because he did not believe a Sandford good enough to marry her."

Comprehension dawned on Angel. "And you were going to show your father that there was one Sandford who was good enough."

"Something like that," he admitted.

"What was your other reason for wanting to marry Kitty?"

"I wanted the Sommerstone estate, which the marriage settlement would have brought me."

"What significance does Sommerstone have to your father?"

Lucian chuckled. "You are remarkably quick, little one. It was the Sandford family estate until my grandfather lost it at the gaming tables. It was my father's fondest dream to return it to the family."

"And you wanted to succeed where your father had failed."

"I would have, too, had it not been for those damned Crowes." Suppressed fury vibrated in his deep, rich voice.

"And for me." Angel's voice caught. "Oh, Lucian, I am so sorry for what I have cost you."

He stroked her cheek gently. "It was not your fault, little one. You were as much the Crowes' victim as I was."

"You should have married Kitty anyhow."

He smiled wryly. "Abandoning you after apparently seducing and ruining you in that very public scene hardly seemed the way to convince my father he had misjudged me."

Angel's heart ached for her husband at the realization of how desperately he wanted to prove to his father that he had been terribly wrong in his cruel judgment of his younger son.

"Have you seen your father since he rejected you?"

"Twice."

"Did he cut you?"

"I did not give him the chance," Lucian snapped. "I cut him."

Angel swallowed hard. Lucian might profess to hate his father, but he still unconsciously craved his approval—something that he was not likely to admit even to himself.

Angel remembered her own father once describing Lord Wrexham as a man of honor and pride, but sometimes infuriatingly stubborn and wrongheaded.

What obstinate, unjust idea had caused him to spurn his own son? Angel vowed to herself that she would learn Wrexham's reason for treating Lucian as he had.

Perhaps there was another member of the family who could help her discover the secret. "Do you have other brothers or sisters besides Fritz?"

"I had two sisters, neither of whom survived childhood."

So there would be no help there, but Angel would ferret out what had caused Wrexham's animosity if she had to beard him herself.

Lucian had promised her that he would recover for her what she most wanted, Belle Haven, and now she swore to herself that she would find a way to attain for him what he most wanted, his father's esteem.

And somehow she would effect a reconciliation between the father and son.

The wind was rising, a thin, eerie wail, and the temperature was falling. Angel drew her red wool tippet more tightly around her, grateful now that Lucian had stopped her from giving it away.

She looked up at the sky. Wave after wave of thick gray clouds scuttled across it, blotting out the sun.

The coach was climbing a chalk hill devoid of trees. Ahead on its crest to the right of the road, a dark gibbet rose starkly against the bleak sky.

Angel shuddered involuntarily. "Why is that there?"

"Unless I miss my guess, it is the gibbet on which Lord Ackleton was hanged. I was told that it was raised on the highest hill in the area at the boundary of his estate. It would appear that we have at last reached Ardmore."

As the coach descended the hill, Angel saw spread out below a wide valley with a stream flowing through it.

"How pretty it looks," she observed.

"Aye," her husband agreed, a pleased smile on his lips.

As he studied the rich cultivated fields that were now his, Angel was touched by his expression of pride and satisfaction.

They passed two cottages with sagging thatched roofs that stood in sorry contrast to the fertile green fields surrounding them. The daub on the walls had fallen away in large chunks, exposing the wattle beneath. Lucian's smile faded into dismay.

In front of one of these hovels stood a woman and two young children, all as thin as sticks.

Angel waved, but they did not respond to her greeting, only watched the coach's passing with suspicious, hostile faces.

A little while later, the coach stopped at a fork in the road. No signpost indicated the way to Ardmore's house. Tom consulted with Lucian as to which path they should take, but he did not know either.

"Methinks I spotted a village ahead on the left fork." Tom said. "We can seek directions there."

There was indeed a village. Its houses were strung out along the road and as dilapidated as the earlier cottages the Vayles had seen. They had once been whitewashed, but now all that remained of it was an occasional patch. The only grass Angel saw was on a bowling green next to an inn, the sole building in town in excellent repair.

Its sign boasted an amateurishly painted lion and the words, "Golden Lion Inn."

A small group of villagers was gathered in front of it, apparently waiting for something. They were shabbily garbed in well-worn garments, most of which had been patched at least two or three times.

When Lucian's coach stopped at the inn, the throng turned to stare at the expensive equipage. Their faces mirrored the same suspicion and hostility that the woman and her children in front of the cottage had exhibited.

The coach had the opposite effect on the fat innkeeper, who was all smiles as he bustled out of his establishment to greet Lucian effusively in the hope of obtaining his business.

"What can I do for you?" He caught sight of the crest on the carriage door. Instantly, his manner became even more obsequious, and he bowed deeply. "Such an honor, my lord, to have you stop at my humble abode. Mr. Ratliff at your service. Only tell me how I can assist you?"

"You can tell me the way to Ardmore."

The innkeeper gestured toward the chalk scarp that rose steeply behind the village. " 'Tis atop that hill."

Angel craned her neck in an attempt to see her new home, but the roof of the coach prevented her from doing so.

Mr. Ratliff said, "Dare I ask, are you Lord Vayle?"

"You dare and I am," Lucian retorted sardonically.

An apprehensive murmur ran through the gathering of villagers at Lucian's acknowledgment of his identity. Their expressions turned sullen, and they fell back a little, as though eager to put a little more distance between him and them. Angel heard someone hiss, "Lord Lucifer."

She wondered why her husband was the object of such animosity when he had only owned Ardmore for a fortnight.

Mr. Ratliff said, "Your house is not far now, my lord, less than a third of a league. You have but to follow this road and turn off at the gate to your left."

"This must be the village of Lower Ardmore," Lucian said, "which is part of my estate."

"Aye, that it is. Could I offer your lordship—"

The remainder of the landlord's sentence was lost in a cacophonous din that seemed to be moving toward them.

Angel picked out a woman's screams, a man's shouts, another man's furious cursing, and a child's terrified wailing.

Lucian flung open the coach door and jumped down. Angel scrambled after him.

The clamor was coming from a carrier wagon lumbering up the street toward them with eight occupants. The driver, his face frantic, was crackling his whip over his horses, trying desperately to speed them up to little avail.

All along the street, doors flew open and people, drawn by the racket, poured out.

At last, the wagon reached the inn and stopped. The little group that had been waiting there surged forward, and Angel realized they had been waiting to meet the wagon.

A woman with bright, coppery hair lay half-across one of its plank seats, moaning. Despite the cool wind, sweat was pouring down her face. Two other women passengers were trying to comfort her.

A boy of about eight, his hair the color of carrots, was staring at the stricken woman with terrified eyes. Huddled in the corner of the wagon, unheeded by anyone, a little girl of no more than three, with the same bright hair as the suffering woman, sobbed in fright and woe.

Two adult male passengers looked as though they were trapped in the anteroom to hell. The instant the wagon stopped, they leapt over the side in their haste to escape.

"What is it?" Angel asked.

One of the women on the wagon shifted, and Angel saw that the half-prostrate female she was helping was huge with child.

"Oh, Christ," Lucian muttered.

" 'Ave to get 'er to bed," the sweating driver said.

All trace of obsequiousness and eagerness to please had

vanished from the landlord's mien. "Not in my inn," he snapped at the driver. "Take her elsewhere."

"There's no time," the man protested. "Would ye 'ave 'er babe born on the street?"

Angel turned to the staring crowd, which seemed to have been turned to stone by the scene, and cried, "Is there a midwife in the village?"

"Aye," someone cried.

"Fetch her at once," Angel ordered in the voice of authority that she used when she was running Belle Haven.

From the corner of her eye, she saw Lucian cast a startled glance at her.

"Aye," a young girl called in response to Angel's directive and ran off down the street.

"Don't bring her to my inn," Mr. Ratliff called after the girl.

Angel heard Lucian mutter, "Damned animal, to turn away a woman in childbirth."

Her husband was not as heartless as he would have her believe.

A long, agonizing, ear-piercing shriek rang out from the woman in the wagon.

The little red-haired boy, desperation and fear for his mother having washed all color from his face, planted himself in front of the fat innkeeper. "Me mum needs help," he said fiercely. "Her's hurting. Ye must help her."

Angel's heart went out to the terrified boy desperately trying to assume a man's role to help the mother he loved.

"Out of my sight, brat," Mr. Ratliff growled and raised his arm, clearly intending to shove the child away. "I won't have her here."

Lucian caught the innkeeper's arm before it could touch the boy and yanked it down so viciously the man gave a squeal of pain.

"You will have her," Lucian announced in a voice all the more ominous for its quietness.

Mr. Ratliff's face was a study in consternation. "But, my lord, she cannot pay," he protested.

"Damn your greed, I will pay."

"But, my lord, the blood, the mess, the noise. I cannot . . ." His voice faded into silence at the look in Lucian's eyes.

"I believe," Lucian said quietly, "that you lease this fine property from me, Mr. Ratliff?"

The innkeeper looked confused. "Aye, my lord."

"And that lease is about to fall in."

"Not for another . . ."

Lucian silenced him with a withering look. "As I said, the lease is about to fall in. Perhaps, however, I might be induced to continue it if you give this woman a *comfortable* room and make certain the midwife has everything she needs. Do you understand me?"

A low murmur of approval ran through the crowd.

For a moment Mr. Ratliff gaped at Lucian, then he seemed to shrivel before him. "Aye, my lord."

Angel, silently applauding her husband, was very proud of him.

He reached over the side of the wagon and scooped the moaning woman up into his arms. As he did so, Angel heard her murmur hoarsely, "My babe, 'tis early. Another month yet."

"They come when they want to," Lucian told her gently. "There's naught you can do about it."

Mr. Ratliff ran into his establishment, bellowing orders to his maids.

Lucian carried the woman inside. The boy with the carrot hair followed hard on his heels.

The crowd stared after them in collective amazement.

"Did ye see the look 'e gave old Ratliff?" Angel heard one man mutter to another. "Me can see why they call 'im Lord Lucifer. Me'd as soon tangle with the devil 'imself."

None of the spectators paid any heed to the terrified, sobbing little girl huddled in the corner of the wagon.

Angel climbed into it. Taking the child in her arms, Angel hugged her tightly to her and whispered reassuringly, "Don't cry, your mama is going to be fine now."

The child wore only a thin cotton dress. Her teeth were chattering, and she was trembling from shock and cold.

Hastily, Angel removed her red wool tippet and wrapped the girl in it, trying to warm her.

"Can I help, ma'am?" the wagon driver asked.

"Would you lift her down for me, and I'll take her into the inn, where it will be warmer."

He did as she asked. She took the little girl from him and carried her past the crowd, which had broken up into small groups that were whispering among themselves.

As Angel went into the inn, an elderly woman with iron gray hair, accompanied by a plump young female of about twenty-two, rushed up.

"Do ye know where they took Nellie?" the older woman asked. "Me's the midwife."

Angel caught sight of her husband disappearing with his burden into a room down the hall. The red-haired boy was still dogging his heels.

She nodded her head toward the boy. "There, into that room where her son is going."

The midwife and her companion hurried off in that direction.

Angel, still hugging the little girl to her, started to follow, then thought better of it. Kinder to keep the child at a distance so that she could not hear her mother's screams.

She hugged the little girl to her, stroking her bright coppery hair and whispering consolingly.

The midwife and the young woman vanished into the room that Lucian had entered.

No more than three minutes later Lucian emerged from the room. This time he was carrying the red-haired boy, who was fighting valiantly but vainly to free himself from the earl's powerful grip.

Lucian walked with long strides toward Angel. As he reached her, she heard him tell the child sternly, "Stop fighting me."

"But me mum . . ."

"We must leave your mum to the women now. She is in good hands. You have done all you can for her. Now it is women's work, and we men would only get in the way."

Pride touched the boy's face when Lucian referred to "we men." He stopped struggling.

Lucian lowered him to the floor, warily watching to make certain that he did not try to bolt back to the room they had just left.

When he did not, Lucian turned to Angel. He touched her red tippet that she had wrapped the little girl in, and his lips twitched. "I see that you are determined to give this away. Come, we must be on our way."

Angel knew how eager he was to get to Ardmore, but she looked down at the sobbing girl in her arms and said firmly, "No, my lord, we cannot desert these poor children now."

She nodded toward the boy who was staring down the hall toward the room where his mother was. He was trying hard to be manful about it, but he could not hide the terror in his eyes.

Angel saw her husband's hard silver eyes soften, and she knew that he, too, was touched by the boy's pluck.

She smiled up at Lucian and whispered, "Perhaps you could distract him from the situation. I saw a bowling green beside the inn."

He looked at her as though she were mad.

She gave him her most brilliant smile. "Please, Lucian."

For a moment, he only stared at her, an odd light in his eyes. Then he muttered, "That damned bewitching smile of yours."

He turned to the boy. "What is your name, son?"

"Michael."

"Mine is Vayle."

The boy looked puzzled. "Like what a woman wears?"

The earl's mouth curled in amusement. "More or less. Do you bowl?"

"I like to, but Papa says I'm not good enough to play with him."

"I am not very good either," Lucian said, reaching down and taking the boy's small hand in his own large one, "so perhaps you are good enough to play with me."

Angel smiled as she watched him lead the boy toward

the inn door. Her husband definitely was not as heartless as he thought himself.

Many of the villagers who had been attracted by the commotion in the wagon were thronged about the door, talking excitedly and waiting for some word on Nellie's condition.

When Lucian and the boy reached the door, the people around it hastily fell back, and a sudden silence fell over the gathering. Angel, watching through the inn's windows, saw the gaping crowd outside part and make way for them. It reminded her of Moses at the Red Sea.

Angel turned away from the windows and went into the common room, where she took a chair in a corner. Once seated, she turned her attention back to the little girl in her arms, reassuring her over and over that her mama would be all right.

Gradually both the child's shivering and her sobbing stopped, but she continued to cling to Angel, who held her close and rocked her.

Two middle-aged women with frantic faces rushed into the inn. "Where is my Nellie," one of them demanded of a chambermaid carrying a pot of water.

The maid told them to follow her, and all three females disappeared down the hall.

A few minutes later one of the women, plump and motherly, reappeared, looking about anxiously. Her hair was tucked beneath a white cap, and her warm brown eyes bespoke a kind nature.

When she saw the little girl in Angel's arms, peacefully sucking her thumb, her lined face relaxed into a smile.

She came over to them. "Little Lucy, here ye be."

"G'an'mum," the little girl exclaimed happily. Her face broke into a broad smile, but she continued to cling to Angel, showing no inclination to forsake her arms for those of her grandmother.

"Where's yer brother gone, Lucy?"

Angel answered for the child. "My husband took him to the bowling green to distract him from his mother's suffering that he can do nothing about. How is she?"

"The babe's making its way into the world. Lucy, me child, where did ye get that cape?"

"It's mine," Angel explained. "She was shaking so from cold and shock that I wrapped her in it."

" 'Twas most kind of ye." The woman held out her arms to Lucy, but she turned her face into Angel's dress, still sucking her thumb.

"She likes ye," her grandmother exclaimed in surprise. "She don't usually take to strangers."

"Is Nellie your daughter?"

"Nay, she's me son James's wife. Mary Ilton's me name."

Angel wondered why a woman so large with child as Nellie would have been traveling about the countryside, and she never scrupled to inquire when she was curious. "Where had Nellie been with Lucy and Michael?"

"Visiting James. Me told her not to go with the babe so near its time, but the poor girl, she misses him so. He works the fields on the far side of Lord Cardmon's estate, nearly four leagues from here, and they don't see each other but once every other month. This poor little 'un"—Mrs. Ilton gestured at Lucy—"scarcely remembers her father from one visit to another."

Angel, ever practical, asked, "Why do Nellie and their children not live with him there?"

"They'd not have a roof o'er their heads," Mrs. Ilton replied, her lined face tightening in bitterness. "His lordship, he don't worry none that his workers have no homes for their families nor how they'll feed them on the wages he pays. Two pounds a year is all me son gets."

Angel was shocked. She knew for a fact that workers at Belle Haven were paid considerably more than that because she had kept the estate books for her father since she was fourteen. He had tried to teach her brother to do it, but Charlie had had no head for figures.

Lord Cardmon sounded like one of those landowners whom Angel's father had contemptuously castigated as "bloodsucking leeches."

Ashcott had been of the school that held a man fortunate enough to be born to a great estate was responsible for the people on it and their well-being, and he had instilled that philosophy in his children.

Angel looked down at Lucy. Her eyes were growing sleepy. Still wrapped in Angel's red tippet, she nestled her head in the crook of her benefactor's arm, her copper curls bright against the black of Angel's sleeve.

"Me James was a groom in Lord Ackleton's stables like his father and grandfather afore him 'til Ackleton was hanged. All of us been asuffering ever since for his treason," Mrs. Ilton said. "In Ackleton's day, most all us in the village worked at Ardmore. Now there's no work to be had 'cepting with Lord Cardmon, who would get blood out of a stone if he could. Not that Ackleton was much better, but at least he gave us roofs o'er our heads."

Such as they were, Angel thought, remembering the sagging thatch she had seen.

"I gather you worked at Ardmore too, Mrs. Ilton?"

"Aye, me did. Me would have been housekeeper there by now if Ackleton hadn't gotten himself hanged."

She paused, her lined face turning bleak. "And now we're to have a new lord. They say he's the worst of the lot. The stories they tell about him's enough to curdle me blood," she confided, her apprehension for the future plain in her expression. "They say if we thought 'twas bad afore, we'll soon think it were paradise itself to what it'll be like under the new lord. Such a cruel, hard man, he is, that he's called Lord Lucifer. They say he be the devil himself."

Angel wanted to leap to her husband's defense but, in truth, she knew so little about the stranger to whom she was married that she could not say with certainty what kind of master he would make. Would he would treat his people with kindness and generosity as her father had or would he be a miserly tyrant like Lord Cardmon? Lucian professed to have no heart, but she had already discovered otherwise, and she did not think he would be like Cardmon.

She looked down at Lucy, who had fallen soundly asleep in her arms, her face tucked against Angel's breast. "Poor darling, she is worn out."

"Let me take her." Mrs. Ilton held out her arms and Angel relinquished her burden carefully, so as not to awaken the child.

" 'Twas kind of ye and yer husband to trouble yerselves with a stranger's children." Mrs. Ilton examined Angel with curious eyes. "Why are ye here?"

Angel, knowing that the woman would be terrified if she learned that she had been confiding her fears of Lord Lucifer to the devil's own wife, said noncommittally, "I came with Lord Vayle."

The woman took in Angel's shabby, wrinkled black dress and said, "So ye work for Lord Lucifer," she said, clearly mistaking her for a servant. "Is he as bad as 'tis said?"

"He has been very kind to me," Angel murmured uncomfortably, "and I am certain he will be to the people of Ardmore as well."

He would be if Angel had anything to say about it.

And she intended to have a great deal to say. She would not stand by and watch innocent people being abused and mistreated, not that she thought her husband would do so.

"What work does your husband do for Lord . . ." Mrs. Ilton's question died on her lips as the plump young woman who had accompanied the midwife hurried into the common room.

She told Mrs. Ilson, "Ye have a new grandson, Mary, a fine little lad. He's on the small side but it's to be expected, coming into the world early as he did."

"And Nellie," Mary Ilson asked.

"Weary, but fine."

Mary Ilton called to the villagers by the inn's door, "Nellie's had a son and all is well."

A cheer went up from the group. Clearly the Ilsons were popular members of the community. The excited voices outside the inn gained volume as they discussed the birth.

Then abruptly they fell silent. Angel looked toward the windows. Outside the crowd was parting hastily to make way for her husband.

Chapter 16

When Lucian strode into the inn with Michael at his side, Mrs. Ilton gaped at him. He did look elegant, Angel thought, in his perfectly tailored fawn coat decorated with gold braid and a long row of gold buttons down the front.

Michael's face lit up when he saw his grandmother, and he rushed up to her.

"Is mum all right?"

"Aye," Mrs. Ilton assured him, "and ye have a new brother."

"See, I told you she would be fine," Lucian said, coming up behind the boy. He held out his hand to Angel. "Now that you have relinquished the child, we can resume our journey."

Michael looked up at his new friend with a bright grin. "Me beat him, gran'mum," he cried proudly.

The hard lines of Lucian's sharply carved face had relaxed, and Angel caught her breath at how handsome he looked. He winked at his wife, then smiled indulgently at Michael, and she knew that he had deliberately let the boy defeat him.

She remembered her husband coming instantly to the aid of Michael's mother, of his generosity with the young widow at the Wild Boar Inn, of his obtaining for his wife the telescope she so wanted.

A wave of gratitude and pride washed over Angel for this man she had married. He was a man of integrity, generosity, and honor. She sensed that he would make her an excellent husband if only she could crack the protective shell in which he had encased his heart.

In that moment, Angel realized that she was falling in love with him. She remembered Lady Bloomfield's warning against doing so, but Angel was convinced that he had considerably more heart than either that good lady or he himself thought he did.

And Angel intended to win it.

She recalled Papa telling Charles, who had always been more timid than his sister, "You can do anything that you set your mind to."

Angel would follow Papa's advice. She would set her mind to making her husband fall in love with her.

Mrs. Ilton was staring at Lucian uncertainly, an unpleasant suspicion clearly gnawing at her.

"He's got an odd name, too, gran'mum," Michael confided. "Veil."

Mrs. Ilton turned horrified, accusatory eyes on Angel, now standing beside her husband. "Ye said Michael was with yer husband."

Lucian said quietly, "I am her husband."

Mary Ilton stared at him in stunned disbelief.

Lucian smiled wryly at Angel. "Apparently, you have not introduced yourself, Lady Vayle."

Poor Mrs. Ilton turned a deep shade of burgundy and looked as though she wished the earth would swallow her—or at least her tongue.

"Been discussing me with my wife, have you?" Vayle asked in amusement.

The poor woman looked so distraught that Angel was greatly relieved when Lucian told her with a sardonic smile, "Do not worry, Lord Lucifer won't hold it against you."

The front wheel of the coach dropped into a deep mud hole, sending up a spray of muck and flinging Angel against her husband.

As Lucian's arm tightened around her, a red brick mansion came into view on the hilltop ahead of them. Angel felt his body tense at the sight, and he craned his neck eagerly for a better look. It was a sprawling affair with three gables along the front boasting oriel windows.

The hard set of his face softened into pride and excitement as he had his first view of the only estate he had ever owned.

The coach suddenly jolted to a stop. Their way was blocked by an iron double gate supported by two stone piers covered with lichen. The left half of the gate was hanging askew, half-off its hinges.

A brass plaque attached to the pier on the right side of the gate was so badly in need of polishing that Angel could barely make out the single word on it: "Ardmore."

Lucian's frown deepened at the sight of this neglect.

Tom dragged the gate open, and the coach drove through, following what must have once been a handsome road winding up the hill. Now it was overgrown with weeds.

Turning to her husband, Angel saw that his face was dark and forbidding. His silver eyes were as cold and bleak as winter.

When they reached the hilltop, they were met by dead parterres that marked the withered remains of an elaborate formal garden.

The house itself, imposing at a distance, was less so viewed close up. It looked more derelict than welcoming.

The slate roof had gaps in it where tiles were missing. A quarter of the glass panes in the mullion windows were cracked or broken out. Those that were still intact were encrusted with what looked to be years of grime.

The massive oak front door, low arched and honey in color, stood ajar.

Lucian, his face by now as ominous as the sky before a storm, jumped out of the coach and rushed up to the door, leaving Tom to help Angel down.

As soon as her feet touched earth, she hurried after her husband, following him inside.

Angel found herself in a great hall devoid of furnishings. The charred remains of a long-dead fire lay in the blackened fireplace. Dried leaves and dirt had blown through the partially opened door and littered the stone floor around her feet. Giant cobwebs decorated every corner of the room.

Lucian shouted, "Is anyone here?"

His cry echoed unanswered through the silent hall.

Angel's heart went out to her husband as she saw the disillusionment, dismay, and anger in his eyes at the condition of his new estate.

He strode angrily toward one of the doors that led off the hall. She hurried after him, lifting the skirts of her gown to keep them out of the dirt that covered the floor.

The rooms off the great hall were as filthy as it had been. Unlike it, however, they had some furniture in them, although most of the pieces had been overturned or upended as though for sport.

Angel studied the dreary wall paneling, so dark it was almost black, that added to the interior gloom. Her gaze traveled up to the grime-encrusted plasterwork of flowers and wreaths on the ceilings. She could see that it had once been a very handsome mansion. With proper cleaning, restoration, and servants hired and trained to maintain it, it could be again.

They wandered into the kitchen, a large room with a long planked oak table, flanked by wooden stools. It also boasted several smaller tables and a large array of pots and other cooking utensils.

Everything from the pots to the stone floor was covered with dust so thick that it must have taken years to accumulate.

They inspected the pantry that held rows of neatly stacked dishes and glasses, coated with grime.

"I cannot believe this," Lucian muttered in disgust. "I was assured that the estate was in the hands of a most capable agent who was keeping it in good repair."

Beyond the kitchen, they discovered a back staircase and followed it up to the next floor.

Its finest chamber was a large bedroom furnished with an assortment of oak clothes presses, cupboards, chairs, and a massive oak bed with an intricately carved canopy, headboard, and footboard. It had been stripped of its hangings, but at least its mattress, beneath a dirty sheet, remained.

Seeing the look on Lucian's face, a mixture of disappointment, outrage, and revulsion, Angel's heart ached for him. She remembered the unconscious pride in his voice as he had talked about the first estate he had ever owned. And now to find it like this.

Her mouth tightened in determination. She would hire Mary Ilton and some of the other people from the village to help her clean and restore it. With their help, she would make it into a place of which her husband could be truly proud.

But first they must have a place to sleep tonight.

She set about searching for bedding in the cupboards.

"What are you looking for?" Lucian demanded.

"Clean linen for us to sleep on tonight," she said cheerfully.

He looked at her as though she had lost her mind. "You cannot think I would require you to stay here in this . . . this pigsty," he said in a voice of loathing. "We will not stay here tonight—or perhaps ever."

"What shall we do?"

"Stay at the Golden Lion Inn tonight and leave for London in the morning."

He lightly brushed back a curl that had fallen across her cheek. Warmth curled in her at his touch.

"I am sorry, little one. I had no inkling we would find it like this or I would not have brought you here."

" 'Tis not your fault." Angel gave him a bright, reassuring smile and said optimistically, "It is only dirt. Once the house is cleaned and set to rights, it will be every bit as handsome as it was in King Charles's day."

"You have more faith in its promise than I do. It would be a monumental, if not impossible, task to restore it to its former grandeur."

Desperate to lighten his gloom, Angel cried eagerly, "You will be proud of it, I promise you."

She might be an innocent when it came to men and marriage, but she knew how to manage a great house. She had been running Belle Haven to her father's exacting standards since she was fourteen. "If it is agreeable with you, Lucian, I will hire several women from the village to help clean it."

"Hire an army, if you wish. I will not quibble about the

expense, although I suspect it is throwing good money after bad."

Angel was determined to prove his suspicion wrong.

Lucian took her arm. "It is time to go back to the Golden Lion."

When he handed her into the coach, he did not climb in after her.

"Are you not coming with me?" she asked.

"No, I want to inspect the rest of my *great estate,*" he said with a contemptuous, sarcastic twist to his final words. "I will join you at the Golden Lion later. Tell Ratliff to give you his best bedchamber. If you are hungry, order food. Do not wait for me."

He pulled a leather pouch filled with money from his coat pocket and gave it to her. "Use this for whatever you might need."

Had Angel not been so eager to launch her scheme for restoring the house to its former glory, she would have asked to accompany her husband on his tour of his estate. Instead she accepted the pouch and, with uncharacteristic meekness, allowed herself to be driven off.

When she reached the inn, she did not bespeak a room. In fact, her requests were quite different from her husband's instructions.

Then she set out for Mary Ilton's cottage. She had liked and trusted the woman on sight and was certain that she could be an immense help in Angel's plans for Ardmore.

When Mary saw Angel at her door, she was so astounded that she was speechless.

"May I come in?" Angel asked.

"In here, m'lady?" the woman exclaimed incredulously. Recovering herself, she said, "Aye, m'lady. If that is what ye wish."

Angel stepped into a kitchen that also served as dining and living room. Two loaves of freshly baked bread were on the well-scrubbed plank table, sending up a delicious aroma that blended with that coming from a black iron pot boiling on the hearth. The savory smell reminded Angel how long it had been since she had eaten.

Mary was clearly nervous and uncomfortable at having

a countess beneath her roof, but Angel, who was used to putting Belle Haven's tenants at ease, disarmed her with questions about Lucy and Michael.

Then Angel told her bluntly, "I need your help."

"My help, m'lady?" Mary stammered in surprise.

"Ardmore is in dreadful condition. I want you to help me restore it to what it once was. I will employ as many people as it takes to do so. You know the villagers, who are good workers and who are not. I want you to tell me whom to hire. It will be hard work, but my husband will pay them well."

Angel intended to pay them very well. Lucian had said he would not quibble at the expense, and it would be a way of helping people who needed it badly but whom she suspected would be insulted were they offered charity.

"And I want them to start immediately," Angel said briskly.

Mary's expression grew wistful. " 'Twould be grand to see Ardmore as it used to be. Makes a body want to cry seeing it now. When Lord Ackleton was alive, it was full of servants and so clean it sparkled. Did ye know: the soldiers who seized his lordship chopped up the furniture in the great hall for firewood."

Angel smiled at her. "Will you help me?"

"Aye, m'lady. Could I refuse ye after what ye and yer husband did for Nellie and her little ones. All the village is talking about the way his lordship forced old Ratliff to give poor Nellie a room and then carried her to it himself. Never thought to see the day when a lord of Ardmore would help one o' us."

Clearly Ackleton had not been liked by his people. Angel said, "I think you will find my husband a better lord than Ackleton."

"He could be no worse," Mary said with conviction.

By the time Lucian reached the Golden Lion Inn a little after nine that night, he had ridden Ardmore from one end to the other.

He had stopped at the house of the agent, Mr. Goldman, who had failed so miserably in his job of keeping the estate in excellent repair. The dwelling had been abandoned, apparently in considerable haste since the molding remnants of a partially eaten meal lay on the table.

Lucian subsequently learned the man had last been seen a week ago.

At least the estate's fields were in considerably better condition than either its house or the tenants' cottages.

The disrepair of the latter bothered him as much as that of the big house did. His tenants clearly did not know how well-off they were. He had seen the accounting sent to the crown by Goldman, and the tenants' rents were laughably low in light of how productive their fields were. Yet, not a one of them was making any effort to keep his cottage from falling into ruin.

The tenants themselves were hostile and sullen toward him. He suspected that they feared he would raise their rents substantially, but even that would not fully explain the undisguised hatred and distrust in their eyes as they watched him.

His stomach rumbled, reminding him that he had not eaten since breakfast. He looked forward to dinner, a glass of claret and, most of all, to Angel's company.

Lucian had become accustomed to her delightful presence during their journey. He was surprised by how much he had missed her this afternoon—not merely her conversation but also her sweet body sliding against his own as the coach rounded curves. He felt himself growing hard at the memory.

He had promised himself that he would not make her his wife in fact as well as name until they were beneath his own roof. He had intended to bed her this very night, but now they were back at an inn.

That was one of the reasons he had been so angry when he had seen Ardmore's wretched condition. He had realized they could not stay there and once again he would have to postpone bedding her. His body ached at the thought of another night of abstinence.

Ached so much that he seriously considered forgetting his promise to himself and making love to her at the Golden Lion.

Then he caught himself. God's oath, what was wrong with him? He was acting like a besotted fool instead of the man who could honestly boast that there had never been a woman he could not walk away from.

Yet, as he went through the door of the Golden Lion Inn, he unconsciously lengthened his stride in anticipation of seeing Angel.

He had been proud of her reaction to Ardmore. Lucian would have thought that no woman could be induced to spend a night there in its appalling condition, but she had been quite willing to do so. Had it been Kitty with him, she would have run screaming from the house, refusing ever to set foot in it again.

He was, he realized, growing quite satisfied with his unwanted bride.

A minute later, Lucian's satisfaction dissolved into anger.

"What the hell do you mean my wife is not here?" he demanded of Mr. Ratliff.

"She . . . she said that if you came here to tell you that she was awaiting you at Ardmore," the hapless innkeeper explained nervously.

Damn it, Lucian would not tolerate a disobedient wife. He stalked out of the inn, furious at Angel.

What could she have been thinking of to go back to Ardmore without him?

Then a more unnerving thought struck him. Would she be safe in the crumbling, deserted mansion? He remembered the sullen hatred on the faces of the tenants. His heart seemed to freeze, and he urged his horse to a gallop.

When he reached Ardmore, lights were glowing in several of the windows. He ran toward the front door, which opened at his approach.

A nervous youth in rough homespun bowed him in.

"Who the hell are you?"

"T-T-Tim, your new footman, my lord," stammered the young stranger uneasily. "Y-y-your wife hired me."

"And where the hell is she?"

"In the lord's bedchamber. She says you'll know which one it is."

Lucian ran up the broad staircase off the great hall three steps at a time. He hurried to the bedroom that he and Angel had been in earlier that day.

Stalking inside, Lucian checked himself at the sight of his wife sitting on an ornately carved chair studying a page in a large leatherbound book by the light of a triple-branched candelabra on a small table beside her.

When she heard him, she hastily shut the book. Jumping up, she laid it on the table next to the candelabra and glided gracefully toward him.

She had changed out of her black gown into one of Kitty's childish dresses that Lady Bloomfield had found in Fernhill's attic. Its red silk bodice was a too tight for Angel, stretching tautly across her full breasts, but the rest of the garment fit well, accentuating her slender waist and nicely rounded hips.

A bolt of desire shot through Lucian at the tantalizing sight.

Angel had washed her hair and left it loose. Almost dry now, it cascaded in thick, lustrous waves about her shoulders. Lucian yearned to bury his hands and his face in its luxurious richness.

She greeted him with one of her brilliant smiles that embraced her entire face.

It almost made him forget how annoyed he was with her.

Almost, but not quite.

"Why the devil did you not stay at the Golden Lion as I told you to?"

Her face puckered at his harsh tone. "I thought we would be more comfortable here."

"Here? God's oath, have you taken leave of your senses?" He was famished, not having eaten since breakfast, and he was exhausted. He wanted food and comfort. He demanded irritably, "What do you propose we eat?"

She looked toward a table that he had not noticed by the windows. Covered with a white linen cloth and lit by two candles in tall silver sticks, it held an array of covered dishes and a bottle of claret.

"Surely that repast did not come from that kitchen below stairs."

"No," Angel admitted, "I brought it from the inn."

When Lucian had entered the room, his attention had been so fixed on his wife that he had not noticed the changes to it. Now, as he looked around, he was dumbfounded.

The thick layers of dust were gone from the furniture, and its wood shone from vigorous waxing. The floor had been swept clean and scrubbed. The bed now boasted both clean linen and curtains embroidered with colorful flowers—pink roses, blue cornflowers, yellow daffodils.

"What have you done here?" Lucian asked, dazed by the change.

"It only needed cleaning. It will look even better when it is painted."

He frowned.

The glow immediately faded from Angel's smile. "What is it?" she asked anxiously. "Do you not like it?"

"How did you manage it?"

"I hired several people from the village to clean. You said I could."

"You did not waste any time about it," he remarked, startled and pleased by her initiative and energy.

But he was, he reminded himself, still annoyed with her for failing to obey him. "Angel," he said sternly, "while I applaud what you have done here, I am displeased that you did not follow my instructions and remain at the inn."

Her smile disappeared entirely.

Lucian felt a sudden coolness, as though the sun had just vanished behind a cloud. Bloody hell, he didn't want to chastise her, he wanted to make love to her.

But an important principle was at stake. He would be master in his own home.

"But I thought you would prefer to be beneath your own roof." Angel seemed to droop like a wounded blossom. "Is it not better here?"

"That is beside the point. I—"

"No, it is not! It is very much to the point." Her hurt expression was replaced by anger. "Why should I obey you when you are wrong? Only a fool does that. And you, my lord, have not married a fool."

No, he had not. Naive, but no fool. He would readily concede that.

"Angel, I have told you before that I will not have a wife who sets herself against me."

"I am not setting myself against you! I am trying to make things better for you."

Bloody hell, but she made him feel like an ungrateful churl. Her lips curled rebelliously, calling his attention to her lovely little mouth.

Lucian was beset by an overwhelming desire to kiss it. He struggled briefly to resist the temptation, then succumbed to it.

As his lips came down on hers, his arms went round her. She stiffened against him, but he would not allow her to escape.

After a moment, he felt the anger and resistance go out of her. He gentled his kiss. His mouth courted hers tenderly, coaxingly. She felt so good in his arms.

He hugged her more tightly to him. She hugged him back, and his body instantly responded. God's oath, but he wanted her.

And tonight, thanks to her insistence on staying at Ardmore, he could have her.

Lucian promptly forgot his annoyance at her for failing to obey him.

Chapter 17

Lucian deepened his kiss. When he felt the tremor of response that ran through Angel, he wanted to snatch her up in his arms and carry her to the bed.

Then he remembered her innocence and her fear of his size. He was not going to frighten her by acting like a rutting boar.

Reluctantly he forced himself to lift his mouth from hers.

She looked terribly disappointed. "I am sorry, Lucian, that I do not know the right way to kiss."

He realized in astonishment that she thought that was why he had ended the kiss. She had not cast a single nervous glance toward his breeches.

Which was good, in light of his present state of arousal.

Her eyes entreated him. "Please teach me to kiss."

"It will be my pleasure," he said, smiling broadly. And hers as well. He intended to teach her a good deal more than how to kiss this night.

"Have you eaten yet, little one?" he asked, hoping that she had. His hunger for food was nothing compared to his hunger for her.

"No, I waited for you."

He smothered his impatience. "Then let us eat first." He was determined to treat her with the forbearance that her sweet innocence deserved. After waiting days for her, what would another hour matter. "Then I will give you a lesson in kissing."

When they were seated at the table, Lucian poured claret into her goblet to relax her a little when he made love to her. After filling his own goblet, Lucian raised it in a toast. "To us, little one."

She looked surprised, then her bright smile returned, and her vivid blue eyes sparkled with delight. "Aye," she whispered happily, lifting her goblet. "To us."

Reluctantly, he dragged his gaze from her face. She was beautiful. How could he have once thought her plain?

Lucian turned his attention to the food spread before him: roast sirloin of beef, breast of capon, asparagus, freshly baked bread and butter and cherries for dessert.

"What a busy afternoon you must have had," he remarked as he helped himself to the asparagus. "How many people did you hire?"

Angel looked up from the bread she was buttering. "A dozen."

Even though she had taken only a few sips from her wine goblet, Lucian unobtrusively refilled it.

"I will have to find a housekeeper," he remarked.

"I have already hired Michael's and Lucy's grandmother, Mary Ilton, for the position."

"What?" he exclaimed, irritated that Angel would have dared to employ the household's most important female retainer without so much as consulting him. What did his innocent child-wife know of hiring housekeepers?

"Do you not think you should have asked my opinion first?"

Angel was clearly surprised. "I did not think you would want to be bothered. Papa never did at Belle Haven."

"I am not Papa," he said sharply, cutting himself off a bite of sirloin. "Are you certain she is qualified."

"Aye, Mary will make an excellent housekeeper."

He frowned. "How can you be so certain?"

"I can tell. Papa always said I was an excellent judge of character."

Much as Lucian respected the scientific earl, he was not willing to accept his judgment in this instance. But he did not tell Angel that. He had no intention of antagonizing her when all he wanted at the moment was to bed her.

Instead he turned his attention back to dispatching his food as quickly as possible, so he could move on to the dish he most craved.

Whenever Angel drank from her wine goblet, he quietly

refilled it so that she always seemed to be drinking from a full goblet. Not that she was in any danger of getting drunk. She drank so little that she would at most become pleasantly relaxed.

She asked, "How was your ride?"

Lucian, his mind preoccupied with thoughts of another kind of ride, looked at her guiltily. "My ride?"

"The one you took this afternoon."

"Oh, that one. The fields are in far better condition than the house, but the tenants seem to hate me with alarming virulence."

"That is not surprising."

"Is it not? I confess it was to me."

"Only because you did not know that the most shocking stories about you have been circulating through the countryside." She gave a little shudder, then smiled trustingly up at him. "I assure you I do not believe a word of them."

"Thank you," he said dryly. Then, unable to resist teasing her, he inquired, "Why not? The tales could be true."

"No." She shook her head emphatically. "They make you out to be cruel and dishonorable—and I know you are neither."

Her faith in him touched him deeply. "Do you have any idea, little one, where these stories came from?"

Angel looked up from the capon breast that she was cutting. "I tried to discover that, but it was difficult. From what I did learn, though, I believe that they were spread by Lord Cardmon's steward. His lordship is your neighbor to the west."

Much startled, Lucian exclaimed, "I do not even know Cardmon or his steward. Why would the man tell lies about me?"

"I think to make the people of Ardmore hate and fear their new lord." She pushed a bit of capon breast about her plate absently, then added thoughtfully, "Though he could have done that with less effort than he expended."

Lucian frowned. "What are you talking about?"

"The people would be inclined to distrust and dislike any lord after Ackleton. He exploited his servants and tenants dreadfully. They hated him, and no wonder. He paid his servants only a third of what we paid ours at Belle Haven." She gave her husband a defiant, challenging look. "I insist upon paying them here what we did at Belle Haven."

He could not resist teasing her, "By all means, throw *my* money away as you please!"

"It is a fair wage," she said defensively.

He grinned at her. "I am teasing you. I have no objection to paying good wages for good work."

Her beaming approval so warmed him that he would happily have doubled the servants' wages yet again if it would enable him to continue to bask in it.

Remembering Ardmore's low rents, Lucian asked in puzzlement, "How did Ackleton exploit the tenants?"

"He took so much from them as his due that they scarcely had enough left to feed their families. Since his death, the Crown has continued to do so."

"But that is not true. The tenants paid very little."

"They paid extortionate amounts!" Angel cried. "I have seen the ledger." She gestured toward the large leatherbound book that she had been reading when her husband had arrived. "I was shocked."

"I saw the accounting that Goldman—" Lucian broke off. "Bloody hell, could that be why he disappeared?"

He jumped up from the table, snatched the ledger from the table where Angel had left it, and studied the amounts recorded there. They were triple the figures that the agent had submitted to London.

Shutting the ledger, Lucian said, "You are right. Goldman was collecting extortionate rent from the tenants and keeping two-thirds of it for himself."

That was why the agent had disappeared so hastily a week ago. He had gotten the new owner's message that he would be paying Ardmore a visit.

Lucian laid the ledger back down on the table and contemplated his wife in amazement. She had learned more about Ardmore's people and problems in a few hours than he would have in a week. "How did you discover the people's complaints?"

"Mary Ilton and the other women told me."

"I am astonished they would have dared to do so." The

lower orders generally guarded their tongues most carefully around the quality.

"Papa used to say I have a knack for getting people to confide in me."

Lucian, remembering how he had told Angel about his own father, decided that at least on this point the scientific earl was right.

"From what I learned about Lord Cardmon," Angel said with a frown, "he is much like Ackleton in his treatment of his servants and tenants."

"But what does that have to do with his steward spreading lies about me?" Lucian went back to the table. Instead of sitting down, he refilled their wine goblets, then picked up his own and, still standing, drank from it.

"Don't you see?" Angel asked. "Between them, they owned almost all the land in the area. Their people could not escape the tyranny of one by seeking employment from the other, for each was equally bad."

Belatedly, Lucian grasped her point. "But if another landlord, one less greedy, were to appear, there would be somewhere else to go."

"Unless they were too afraid of the newcomer to do so."

Lucian studied his young wife over the rim of his wine goblet. He was startled by her acuteness—and very grateful for it. Without her, he would not have discovered the reasons for his tenants' hatred and hostility so quickly.

Nor Goldman's treachery.

They would not be able to leave for London in the morning as Lucian had planned. He would have to discover the extent of Goldman's fraud. King William did not tolerate thieves, and he would demand an exact accounting of what the agent had stolen. Furthermore, Lucian needed to set things to right with the tenants and let them know what he expected of them.

When he told Angel their departure would be delayed, she was delighted. "I was hoping that you would grant me more time to work with the people I have hired."

Angel had finished the food on her plate and was eyeing the cherries. She took a sip of wine, then unconsciously ran the tip of her tongue tantalizingly over her upper lip, sending desire coursing through Lucian.

He set his goblet down on the table and held out his hand to her.

She looked puzzled, but she took it and let him help her up.

He slipped behind her and sank down on her chair, pulling her sideways onto his lap. She threw him a startled glance but did not protest.

" 'Tis time for your first lesson in kissing," he explained.

He settled her against him so that her head nestled on his shoulder. She was so small and delicate in his arms, like a frail china teacup. He felt himself a clumsy giant, fearful of his own strength, fearful of unwittingly hurting the fragile treasure that he cradled.

Lowering his chin, he brushed it lightly back and forth across the top of her head. Her hair was as soft as sable against his skin. He buried his face in it and breathed deeply of her unique scent, a field of wildflowers on a dewy morning.

God, but she was sweet. As sweet as the spirit for which she was named—Angel. His Angel. And after tonight she would be truly his.

He brought his hand up and threaded his fingers slowly through the burnished chocolate waves, loving the silken texture and feel.

A contented sigh escaped her lips. She relaxed against him, as trusting as a child. The provocative curves that pressed against his body, however, were not those of a child, but of an enticing woman.

"You were going to teach me to kiss," Angel reminded him.

"But first you must be comfortable, little one. Are you?" he asked softly.

"Aye."

"Good. It is very important that you be so for your first lesson."

He held her quietly for another minute, his fingers still playing with her hair. Then he turned her face toward him and bent his head to touch his lips tenderly to her temples, her eyelids, her cheeks, her chin. Finally, his mouth brushed hers as lightly as a feather's touch. Then his tongue lightly traced her closed lips. He heard her sharp intake of breath.

His hand slipped from her hair and stroked lightly, as though by accident, the red silk that hid the crest of her breast.

She shivered.

He kissed her again, gently at first, his lips teasing hers lightly. Then his mouth became more demanding, surprising a little gasp from her.

His hand slipped slyly beneath the hem of her gown and glided over her ankle and calf, up and down, in the same slow, seductive rhythm with which his tongue explored her mouth. Her muffled moan echoed into the warmth of his mouth.

He yearned to move higher still and explore the center of her desire, but he reminded himself that she was an innocent virgin. It was too soon.

Much as he wanted her, the thought of hurting her was so repugnant to him that he regarded their first mating with almost as much unease as she did. He knew that he was swelling to an uncommon size, and he could do nothing about it.

But neither could he bear having her stiffen and cry out in pain when he took her.

He would have to be very, very careful. And very, very patient.

Lucian forced his reluctant hand to retreat from beneath her skirt.

Her head slipped back a little, breaking the contact between their lips. She looked up at him, her eyes filled with wonder and awakening passion. "So that is the proper way to kiss. You were right. I did not have the faintest notion of how to do it."

He smiled down at her. "But I have only begun to teach you."

"There is more?"

"Oh, yes, my sweet, much, much more. Let me show you."

His mouth returned to pleasuring hers, and she was oblivious to his fingers as they stealthily worked at the lacings of her bodice.

He longed to make this night perfect for her. He did not ask himself why he should feel so strongly about this. He was too intent on how he could make that happen to wonder why he should want to do so. He only knew that he was determined to give her a night to remember with wonder and joy for all the rest of her days.

Lucian's slow, sensual exploration of Angel's mouth was so enthralling that she was unaware that he had unlaced her bodice until his hand slid beneath the red silk.

Angel gasped and shuddered at the luscious feeling of his big, warm hand tenderly cupping her breast. His thumb lightly rubbed the rosy peak, ignoring her brief feeble effort to repulse him. It felt so good. She had never realized how sensitive she was there.

Lucian lifted his mouth from hers and parted the silk of her bodice. He slid both her stomacher and her shift down, baring her breasts to his eyes, now as hot and liquid as molten silver.

For a moment, he silently drank in the sight. She knew that she should be embarrassed, but the wine had made her languid and bold and relaxed. His expression thrilled her.

"Exquisite," he murmured.

The way he said it made her feel beautiful.

Her body ached for his mouth, for his touch.

Lucian gave her a lazy grin, as though he knew exactly the stunning effect he was having on her.

His mouth moved down her neck in a series of hot, sucking kisses, then dipped to her breast. His tongue began to circle her nipple as though he were licking some particularly delicious sweet. She trembled in pleasure.

When he lifted his head, she gave an involuntary moan of protest.

"A man kisses a woman with his fingers as well as his lips." Lucian's voice was low and husky. "I will show you."

His hand moved beneath her skirts again, and his head dipped to her other breast, drawing its tip into his mouth. His hand was caressing her ankles, her legs, then her thighs.

Awash in sensation beyond her imagining, Angel could not comprehend what was happening to her. Just above the apex of her thighs, a throbbing ache was building within her. She could not imagine where the embarrassing wetness that flooded her there had come from.

Despite that mortifying moisture, she pined to have his hand stroke her there, instinctively sensing that it would relieve the painful tension.

But he did not touch her there.

She must be utterly shameless to want him to.

But she was past caring.

Then his hand glided past that spot and his fingers began to caress her belly. His touch was as light and soft as swansdown. She writhed beneath it, yearning for something, for some relief that she sensed only he could give her.

Then suddenly his mouth and his hand were withdrawn. She was bereft. He surged to his feet with her in his arms and carried her to the bed.

He set her on her feet beside it and swept back the bedcovers. Then his mouth recaptured hers and held her in such thrall with its sensual rhythm that she paid no heed to what his busy hands were about until her gown, petticoat, and shift all fell about her ankles.

Her startled exclamation was not quite lost in the warmth of his mouth.

At last he broke the kiss and swept her off her feet, laying her on the bed. He pulled the covers over her, bent down, and kissed her eyelids shut.

"Promise me you won't open your eyes until I tell you to." His mouth was so close to her face that his warm breath teased her cheek.

It remained there until she promised him. Then it was gone, and she sensed he had moved away from her. She missed his mouth, his hands.

After a long minute had passed, she asked impatiently, "Can I open my eyes now?"

"Not quite yet."

The seconds ticked by. The bed groaned beneath an added weight. Her eyes flew open. He was lying beside her, the covers pulled up to the middle of his muscled, bronzed chest.

He raised himself on one elbow and gave her that wicked, devilish grin of his. His hand pushed the blanket to her waist as his head dipped, and he laid a blazing trail of kisses along the column of her neck and down to the crest of one breast.

His fingers began to trace abstract patterns on her belly, and he drew her nipple into his mouth, suckling her as a babe might at his mother's breast.

But what Angel felt had naught to do with an innocent babe. She gasped with shock and pleasure at the sensations that coursed through her.

"Sh-h-h, little one. It is my hand's turn to kiss your body."

At last his fingers buried themselves in the curls where she had been aching for him to touch her.

As though he understood the storm that was engulfing her, his finger suddenly found the very spot that was driving her wild, and she groaned aloud at the bliss she felt. She hoped he would never stop.

In time, he did, but only to slip that magic finger of his deep within her, where she was drenched by some rich, mysterious dew.

She gasped at his invasion, then gasped again as he moved his finger provocatively within her.

"So small, so tight, so sweet," he muttered thickly.

After awhile he withdrew his finger. She was dismayed. She wanted to protest, and she would have, too, had he not replaced the one with two that moved tormentingly within her, teasing, probing, stretching, while his mouth toyed with her breast until she could not catch her breath, let alone cry out.

She was panting and thrashing now and past caring about anything except the riot of sensations he was unleashing in her body. A secret spring seemed to be gushing about his maddening fingers. She had forgotten his size, her fear, everything. She was riding a crescendo of passion to the edge of some momentous discovery.

Suddenly, Lucian's fingers deserted her and he was lifting himself over her, bracing his big body to keep its weight off her. She felt a large object pressing where his fingers had been, but the moisture from her secret spring eased its passage.

She opened her eyes. Her husband was watching her face intently. To her surprise he was sweating profusely and his face was clenched as though he were in agony.

"What is it," she cried in alarm.

He groaned. "Don't ask. Am I hurting you, little one?"

She felt uncomfortable, but she could not call it pain. He looked as though he were in more distress than she was.

Angel gave him a tentative smile.

He exhaled a harsh sigh and began to move slowly, shallowly within her.

He whispered, "I have kissed you with my mouth and my hands. Now, my sweet, I am going to kiss you with my body."

His mouth swooped down and took hers just as he thrust himself deep within her. The warm recesses of his mouth swallowed up her sharp ejaculation of pain, but he groaned as though he shared it with her. He lifted his mouth a hairbreadth from hers and murmured, "I am sorry, so very sorry, little one, but there is no other way, and I will not hurt you again."

He was holding himself very still within her, as though giving her body time to adjust to his invasion, bracing himself on his arms, holding his weight off her. He crooned soft, wordless sounds of comfort and reassurance.

Then his mouth was busy dropping light feathery kisses on her brow, her cheeks, and her eyelids.

He began to move within her, and her pain was slowly assuaged by the eternal rhythm of love. The excitement and tension built unbearably within her. It was a moment before she realized that the moans she was hearing were her own.

Then her body convulsed around his in spasms of exquisite pleasure more intense, more all-consuming than anything she had ever thought possible.

His own body stiffened and jerked, once, twice, three times, and he gave an exultant shout.

For a moment after the storm had passed he lay still joined with her, and she savored a lingering elation and swelling serenity.

Now she understood why people smirked and whispered about what a man and a woman did behind the bedroom door.

She wanted to cry in protest when he lifted himself away from her. She loved the warmth of Lucian's body against her own. He lay on his side and pulled her into his embrace. Then he drew his head back a little and grinned at her in a way that robbed her of breath. He looked proud and delighted. "I think, little one, that we fit very well together."

She blushed as she remembered her fear of his size. "It seemed impossible that you . . . I . . ." She trailed off.

He was looking at her as though she were some rare, remarkable creature. She blurted, "Do you no longer despise me quite so much?"

"*What?*" He stared at her in astonishment. "What the devil are you talking about?"

"You could not bear to bed me on our wedding night." Seeing his blank look, she hurried to explain. "You see, Lady Bloomfield told me that there had never been a man who despised his wife so much he did not claim her on their wedding night. You must have been the first."

"Bloody hell! Is that what you thought?" He began to laugh uproariously.

"Why are you laughing?" Angel demanded. "Tell me the truth, Lucian. Promise me that you will always be honest with me."

He smiled at her. "I promise if you will give me the same promise."

"I do."

He stroked her face gently with his hand, his eyes alight with amusement. "The truth is that I wanted you very much on our wedding night."

"You did?" She was skeptical. "Really?"

"Hell, yes, I wanted you to distraction."

Happiness exploded within her at this confession. "Oh, Lucian, you do love me!"

He stilled. His smile vanished, and he withdrew his hand from her face.

"What is it?" she cried. "You promised me you would be honest with me."

"I did," he said gently, "but I do not think you want to hear my answer."

"Tell me!"

"Do not expect love from me, Angel. It is a foolish weakness to which I will never succumb. Do not ask me for more than I can give you."

He was right. She did not want to hear his answer. Angel's lip quavered. She half wished that she had not asked for honesty. "But . . . but you said that you wanted me to distraction."

"Aye, and that was the truth, but that has nothing to do with love. A man can lust for a woman's body to the point of madness but it does not mean that he loves her."

"Lust? Is that what you meant by 'the usual reason' a man wants a woman?"

"Aye.

Fighting back her tears, she asked, "Then what can you give me?"

"Pleasure in bed. My care and my protection." He gently pushed her tangled hair away from her face. "You will be safe with me, little one, and you will want for nothing."

Except his love.

Angel turned away from him, afraid that he would see the unshed tears smarting in her eyes. He had built a wall around his heart that he would never willingly let anyone breach.

Lucian waited until Angel was asleep before he slipped out of bed and snuffed the guttering stubs in the candelabra. He went over to the table, poured more claret into his goblet, and took a long draught from it. After snuffing one of the candles on the table, he picked up the other. With his goblet in one hand and the candlestick in the other, he walked back to the bed and stared down at his sleeping wife. She looked so small and vulnerable lying there with her shining hair tumbled across the pillow. He felt like a damned scoundrel.

He had hurt her, not only with his body, which was unavoidable, but with his tongue. Lucian flinched as he remembered the raw pain in her eyes when he had told her that he could not love her. He took a gulp of claret, trying to wash away the memory.

Lucian had always been contemptuous of a rake's lies. He prided himself that he had never found it necessary to employ such expedients to bed a female. Women came too easily to him, drawn by his strength, his skill at giving pleasure, and the dark challenge of conquering Lord Lucifer's unconquerable heart.

He took another swallow of claret, still watching his sleeping wife. He had suspected that she would be capable of great passion and tonight she had proved him right beyond his wildest expectation. The magnitude of her first powerful climax had thrilled and stunned him as much as it had her.

She delighted him in bed as well as out. As he watched her sweet face, a wave of tenderness swept over him for her.

He could not love her, but he would make her happy.

He would keep her in luxury, and he would give her ecstasy.

He would protect her, and he would recover Belle Haven for her.
Angel would have to learn that his love was not necessary. What he could give her would be enough.
It would have to be.

Chapter 18

Lucian stopped in the doorway of Ardmore's great hall and watched his wife directing the people she had hired to reclaim the house from years of grime and neglect.

The stone floor had been scrubbed to enviable cleanliness. The soot and cobwebs were gone from the ceiling, revealing plasterwork scrolls and wreaths. The dark, dreary paneling on the walls was now several shades lighter and gleamed from vigorous polishing.

The hall was no longer bare of furniture. Angel had found some pieces in the attic and had them brought down. Two matching Gothic oak coffers, their carved panels separated by ornamental balusters, had been placed against opposite walls. In the center of the room was a long oak table. Large bowls of colorful, artfully arranged wildflowers, Angel's handiwork, brightened the table and the coffers.

When Lucian had first seen the house two days ago, he had scoffed at her assurance it could be restored. Now he was willing to concede that she would succeed.

In fact, he was beginning to think that Angel could accomplish anything she set her mind to.

She might have been a total innocent about sex, but she could run a household and handle servants with a facility that a woman twice her years might well envy. Angel had confessed to him that she had been running Belle Haven since her aunt, her father's maiden sister, had died when she was fourteen.

Lucian was proud of his wife. With her ability to organize, she would have made a fine military commander.

She also had a way of getting people to do willingly, even eagerly, what she wanted.

He envied her the easy rapport she had with the people she had hired. Her energy and enthusiasm and generosity seemed to be contagious, and they all tried to outdo each other in pleasing her.

But they still gave her husband a wide, nervous berth.

Angel, catching sight of him in the doorway, hurried over to him, asking eagerly, "How did your meeting with the tenants go?"

Not at all as Lucian had expected it would. None of them had reacted as men might reasonably be expected to when they were told that their rents were being cut in half.

Their faces had remained as hostile and suspicious after that announcement as before. Lucian had faced enemy troops who had hated him less than Ardmore's tenants clearly did.

Even if they could not muster up any gratitude to him, he would have expected them at least to show relief that the intolerable burden they were now bearing was about to be lifted. But not even that was visible on their faces, only sullen distrust.

Lucian regretted that he had not taken Angel with him. She would have won them over if anyone could.

When he told her of the unenthusiastic response to his announcement, she said, "I suspect they did not believe you. After Lord Ackleton's treatment of them, their trust will not come easily."

Maybe she was right. He hoped so.

"It is crucial," she was saying, "that you hire an honest, capable, trustworthy agent to run the estate in your absence."

He had come to the same conclusion. "What would you say to my hiring Orin from Belle Haven. He is wasted there as a groom."

"Oh, yes!" she agreed. "He would be perfect."

"He can run Ardmore until I can pry Belle Haven away from the Crowes."

"If you can," Angel said sadly.

He caught her chin in his hand. "What little faith you

have in your husband. Do not worry; I will get it back for you. And when I do, Orin can go back there if that is what he wants."

Lucian looked around the hall, so changed since he had first seen it two days ago. "You have done an amazing job with the house, Angel."

She blushed with pleasure and her wonderful smile spread across her face, warming him like sunshine. He had to fight back the urge to hustle her off to bed then and there.

It was going to be damned hard to tear himself away from her tomorrow for the journey back to London. He should have departed for the capital well before now, but it might be months before he would be able to return to Ardmore again, and he wanted to set things right before he left.

The queen had given him until tomorrow night at the very latest to be back in London, although she had wanted him to return much sooner than that. Lucian was courting disaster by cutting it so close. He was certain, though, that if he started at dawn tomorrow and rode as hard as he could, changing horses frequently, he could make it to the capital in time.

If, however, a mount went lame or some other accident delayed him, he would be in deep trouble. When the queen was angered, she could be as stubborn and unforgiving as her father, the former king.

Lucian had not yet broken the news to Angel that he would be riding ahead of her to London on horseback. It would be a grueling trip, and he could not subject her to it. She would have to follow in his slower-moving coach. She would be safe enough with the armed outriders accompanying her. Still Lucian worried about her.

And he hated being separated from her. To think that he had initially planned to leave her here at Ardmore and never set eyes on her again. Now he chafed at being apart from her even for the journey to London. He told himself sternly that it was because she was so young and naive and needed his protection. It was because she was his wife, and he guarded what was his.

Angel lay beside her husband on the big bed, content and satiated. He had left a candle burning on the bedside table because he said he liked to watch her when he made love to her.

She liked to look at him all the time. Angel turned to do so now. He lay on his side facing her. His eyes, fringed with long, thick, black lashes under those flaring jet brows, were closed. His dark face in repose, its harsh lines relaxed, looked sinfully handsome.

As if sensing her scrutiny, his eyes opened, silver framed in black. He smiled at her, a slow sensual smile that made her toes curl. Surely any man who looked at her like that and made love to her with the ardor and tenderness that he did must care for her at least a little.

She was convinced that she was making some progress in her campaign to penetrate the protective wall he had erected around his heart. Angel was determined to win his trust and his love—as he had won hers. She did not fool herself that it would be easy to do, but she would succeed.

Their stay at Ardmore had been so happy for her that she said wistfully, "I wish that we could stay here longer instead of having to go back to London. What time do we leave tomorrow."

"I must leave at dawn. You may depart whenever you are ready."

Angel gulped in dismay. "Am I not to go with you?"

"No, I go on horseback, and you will follow me in the coach. I cannot spare the time to accompany you in it."

Cannot spare the time! Those were not the words of a man who was coming to care for his wife. Angel's happiness shattered like a china plate dropped on stone. And to think she had just told herself that she was making headway with him.

"Why not?" she asked, her mouth suddenly dry.

"I must be in London by tomorrow night. I have important affairs to attend to there."

Angel wondered dismally what affairs could be so important that he must desert her for them, but he did not seem disposed to enlighten her. "Please," she pleaded, "let me go with you on horseback."

His face took on that stern paternal expression she was coming to hate. "No, you cannot. I will be traveling at breakneck speed. You could not possibly keep up with me."

"I could," she protested. "I am an excellent rider."

"Angel—"

"I do not want to be separated from you, Lucian." It apparently did not bother him in the least to be parted from her. "Please, let me come with you."

"I said no, Angel." He was clearly annoyed by her persistence. "I am going alone. I do not want to hear another word about your coming with me."

She turned her face away from him and puzzled why he was suddenly so eager to get back to London. She recalled the conversation she had overheard on the terrace of Fernhill.

"Only wait until she discovers she must share Vayle with his mistress."

"She will demand that he give up Selina, but he won't. Nor would I if I were in his shoes. Selina is worth ten of Kitty."

And probably twenty of herself, Angel thought miserably.

Was that why he was so anxious to return to London? He wanted to get back to his mistress, whatever that was.

"Stop sulking," Lucian growled.

"I am not," she replied, her voice shaky.

Suddenly he rolled her onto her back, and his face hovered over hers. His lips descended on hers in a hot, possessive kiss. She was helpless to resist it, and soon she was responding passionately.

When at last he ended the kiss, he gazed down at her with a smug, satisfied smile.

Angel looked up at him. "Lucian, what is a mistress?"

His smile vanished. He looked the way he had when she had asked him how babies were made.

He studied her warily. "Why are you asking me that?"

"Because I want to know, and who better to ask than my husband."

"Who worse?" he muttered, looking distinctly uncomfortable.

He pushed himself into a sitting position against the pillows, and Angel followed suit.

"How does a wife share her husband with a mistress?" she asked.

"I can see this is going to be another one of our unique conversations," he said sourly, looking heavenward as though he were praying for patience.

"Does a man's mistress live with him and his wife?"

Lucian's expression defied her analysis. He said in an oddly strangled voice, "No, little one."

"Then I do not understand how they share him."

His lips compressed. "They share him in bed."

Her face bloomed crimson with hot embarrassment and dismay. "You mean all three sleep in the same bed together?" she exclaimed, aghast. "I am sorry, but I would not like that at all."

"Nor would I," Lucian retorted, looking rather red himself. "And that is not what I meant."

"What did you mean?"

Lucian groaned. "Bloody hell, why did I allow myself to be dragged into this conversation? I mean that he sleeps at different times with both women, but certainly not under the same roof where his wife resides. Not unless he is a cad."

"Why would that make him a cad?"

"Because it would hurt his wife."

"So does his taking a mistress," Angel pointed out.

"Not if his wife does not know about her. If a man is discreet, she need never find out. It is the way of society."

"No wonder Papa had no use for society," Angel said with conviction. "I do not understand why, if a man has a wife, he also wants a mistress."

"Sometimes a man finds himself married to a woman he does not—er, want in bed." Lucian looked as though he were picking his way through hot coals. "So he takes as his mistress a woman whom he does want that way, a woman he enjoys making love to."

Angel decided that she did not like the idea of sharing her husband that way at all. "You mean," she blurted, "he loves his mistress but not his wife."

"Not necessarily. He might love neither. Just because a man has affairs with other women does not mean he loves them."

"Affairs?"

"That is what the relationship between lovers is called."

His earlier words echoed through Angel's mind. *"I must be in London by tomorrow night. I have important affairs I must attend to there."*

So that was why he was rushing back to London. He could not wait to see Selina again. Angel felt as though a knife had been plunged through her heart. *"She will demand that he give up Selina, but he won't."*

Lucian's hand touched her cheek gently. "Why do you suddenly look so upset?"

She ignored his question in favor of one of her own. "If a man has a mistress, it means he does not want his wife in bed?"

"Not always. He may want both women."

Angel longed to ask Lucian whether he wanted both her and Selina in bed or only his mistress. For once in her life, however, her courage failed her. Lucian had promised her honesty, and she was not certain that she could bear to hear it.

Instead she asked, "What if a wife does find out about her husband's mistress?"

"Angel, it is time to discuss another subject. Did you—"

"I want to know what a wife should do if she learns her husband has a mistress," Angel insisted stubbornly. She must know how she was expected to act.

"If she is a lady, she ignores the liaison. She does not mention it to her husband, and she pretends that she knows nothing about it."

Angel swallowed hard. "I see. And does she take a master?"

"A what?"

"If a wife finds she does not like her husband in bed, should she not take a master—since he takes a mistress?"

"She takes a lover, not a master. Her husband is her master!" Lucian suddenly looked murderous. "And a good wife is never unfaithful to her husband! A good wife does not take a lover."

"Why not?"

"Why not?" he repeated as though he could not believe she could ask such a foolish question. "Because when she married her husband, she took a vow before God to be faithful to him."

"But he took the same vow," Angel pointed out. "If he does not keep it, why should she?"

"Because it is different for a man than a woman."

"Why is it different?"

Lucian looked harassed. "Because it is!"

"Oh, fie, that is no answer. And you need not shout at me."

He leaned over her, snuffed the candle on the bedside table. "Damn it, Angel, go to sleep."

Chapter 19

The London office of Thaddeus Wedge was in a dreary brick building on a crooked lane off Fleet Street.

Lucian was certain he would learn nothing about Lord Ashcott's missing will from the late earl's solicitor, but he wanted to take the man's measure.

Wedge bowed Lucian into his office, assuring him effusively what a great honor it was to have his lordship call upon him. The room was dominated by a large oak desk, its top so cluttered with papers that Wedge's visitor wondered how he ever found anything on it.

When Lucian was seated across the desk from Wedge, he wasted no time in getting to the point of his visit. "I am informed that you were the late Earl of Ashcott's solicitor."

"Aye, I had that honor." Wedge was a ruddy-faced man of perhaps five-and-forty with small, shifty gray eyes. His gray wig looked as though it had seen better days.

Lucian instantly disliked and distrusted the man.

"Have you a claim against his estate, my lord?" Wedge asked.

"In a matter of speaking. Perhaps you are unaware that his only surviving child is my wife."

Wedge started visibly at that. The news clearly did not please him. "No, my lord, I was not aware. Allow me to felicitate you."

"Ashcott had a will drawn up shortly after the death of his son in which he left everything he had to his daughter, my wife."

"No, my lord, that is not true," Wedge said emphatically, his gaze meeting Lucian's. "There is no such will."

"Will you swear to that?"

"Aye, I will give you my oath on the Bible that I never drew up such a will for him."

Bloody hell, the man was not lying. Lucian was certain of it.

"But my wife saw the will."

"Your wife who would be the sole beneficiary of such a will had it existed," Wedge pointed out. "No offense, my lord, but—"

"I am offended," Lucian snapped. "My wife is no liar. Furthermore, her uncle also saw it."

"Her uncle who is also dead."

"What about the earlier will that Ashcott executed after he and his wife were separated in which he specifically disinherited her?"

"I do not know what you are talking about," Wedge averred, but this time his eyes momentarily failed to meet Lucian's.

He was lying about this will, but not about the later one.

"My Lord, the last will that was executed by Ashcott is the one that was presented for probate."

"You are lying, Wedge," Lucian said bluntly.

For an instant, fear darted in Wedge's eyes, then recovering himself, he blustered, "How dare you—"

"I always dare to speak the truth." Lucian stood up. "Rest assured I will not permit my wife to be robbed of her inheritance by the likes of you and the Crowes."

Lucian, sitting down that night to a solitary dinner in his London house, was pleased with what he had accomplished on his first day back in town.

He had arrived last night, having made the journey from Hampshire in one long, exhausting day, taking shortcuts through fields and over heaths that were accessible only to a man on horseback.

Lucian had made it back by the queen's stipulated hour, but barely. He had immediately presented himself at Whitehall, where the queen had made it clear that she was very displeased with him for not having returned much sooner.

He returned to Whitehall this morning for a three-hour meeting of the Council of Nine. Before leaving for the palace, he had sent a messenger to Orin at Belle Haven with his offer to make him his agent at Ardmore.

After the council meeting, Lucian had gone to see Thaddeus Wedge, then had hired Joseph Pardy, reputed to be the very best in the business of tracking down men and women who did not want to be found. He told Pardy bluntly why he wanted Maude located and of what he suspected the Crowes.

Pardy had assured Lucian that, although it might take him a few months, he and his people would eventually find Maude.

Lucian had spent the remainder of the afternoon surrounded by sketches and fabrics with London's most fashionable dressmaker, Madame de la Roche, selecting clothes for his bride.

He had never before undertaken such a task for a woman, but he had a very clear image in his mind of how he wanted Angel to look. He was certain his selections would flatter her. She could choose additional gowns after she got to London, but given the pathetic, virtually nonexistent state of her wardrobe, he wanted to get her a few things immediately.

Lucian told Madame to have her minions make up his selections as quickly as possible and to bring them to his house when they were ready for fitting. He did not want Angel coming to her shop. Were any of the great ladies who patronized Madame's to see his wife in that sorry black gown or one of Kitty's castoffs, they were certain to make unkind comments. He intended to protect his wife from that.

Lucian must also engage a woman who would prepare Angel for her debut in society. It would be a delicate task, and no candidate came to mind.

He took a sip of the excellent burgundy that Reeves, his butler, had poured for him. Lucian had installed Reeves, who had served under him in the army, as his major domo, not because he was skilled in that line of work, but because he could find no man who would be more loyal to him. Reeves would make certain that Lucian's best interests were served.

With the exception of Reeves, the rest of the staff had come with this house when he had acquired it from its previous owner, Lord Dorton, three months ago. Lucian had decided to buy it less for the house itself than for its location on a large plot of land along the Thames with private steps to the river.

Lucian turned his attention to the roast lamb and pheasant that had been prepared for him. As he ate, Lucian was surprised to discover how much he missed Angel's presence and her lively conversation.

Although he had not confessed it to her, he had hated their traveling separately to London as much as she had. He should have told her about the queen's order that he must be back in London by last night, but he was unused to having to explain himself. It was a wife's duty to accept her husband's decisions unquestioningly. His mother always had his father's.

"Will you be going out tonight, my lord?" Reeves inquired as he refilled Lucian's glass with claret.

"I have not yet decided."

Without Angel to enliven the evening, it stretched long and lonely before Lucian. He should call on Lady Selina Brompton, whose husband was away for the month visiting his estate in Derbyshire. Lucian's brows knit at the thought of his beautiful, witty mistress, a sophisticated leader of society.

Lucian liked her better than any woman he had ever met.

Until Angel.

The realization staggered him, but it was true.

Selina and Angel were the only two women he knew that did not bore him.

He did not love Selina, but he was exceedingly fond of her. She was more than his mistress. She was a good friend, and that counted for more with him than being his bed companion. Best of all, she was a realist and that rare woman who preferred honesty to flattery.

At the start of their relationship, she had told him bluntly, "I want to hear no words from your lips that you do not mean."

Lucian had never given her any.

She had shown him the same courtesy.

There was no pretense between them. He could be himself with her.

He wondered what Selina would think of his bride. He could count upon her to give him her frank opinion. She certainly had made no secret of her dislike for Kitty and her disapproval of his betrothal.

"I do not understand why you are marrying her," Selina had said. "You can do much better."

Although Selina was the nearest thing to a confidante that he had ever had, he had not confessed even to her the reason why the union with Kitty was so important to him.

Instead he had teased, "Jealous of the bride, my dear?"

"Not at all," she had retorted.

Nor had she any reason to be.

"From my point of view," Selina continued, "Kitty is an excellent match for you."

"Why do you say that?"

"Because she is no threat to our relationship," Selina had said with her customary bluntness. "Kitty is too young for you. The silly chit will bore you silly within a month of your marriage."

It had not taken that long. By the time he had reached Fernhill with Kitty, he had known Selina had been right.

She had never confided to him why she and her husband, Lord Brompton, had gone their separate ways, and Lucian had not pried. But he was certain his lordship had been at fault. Selina was not the kind of woman who would cuckold her husband unless he had given her good reason to. Brompton was a damned fool.

Lucian wondered whether Selina had heard of his broken betrothal and hasty marriage.

If she had not approved of the lovely Kitty for his wife, she most certainly would not approve of Angel. *And*

Selina had the power to destroy Angel if she put her mind to it. The thought sent a chill through Lucian. He would make it clear to Selina that he would not tolerate that.

He should do so tonight. Before Lucian had left for Fernhill, he had told Selina that he would come to her as soon as he returned to London.

But she would expect him to make love to her, and fond as he was of her, he had no desire to do so tonight. He wanted no woman but Angel in his bed. The realization astonished him.

How the devil was he to explain it to Selina when he could not explain it to himself.

She was too astute to be fooled by anything less than the truth. And he himself was confounded as to what that was.

No, he decided, he could not call on Selina tonight.

Nor did he have any desire to attend any of the several glittering social affairs to which he had been invited. Instead he decided to spend a quiet night at home.

When he told Reeves that, the butler asked in alarm, "Are you feeling unwell, my lord?"

Only then did he realize how novel this choice was for him.

Lucian went up to his bedchamber, where he had left the volume of Lord Ashcott's journal that he'd lifted from Belle Haven's library. He had carried it back to London with him in one of his saddlebags.

The miniature of Angel, which he had also purloined from Belle Haven, was next to the journal on the table beside his bed. Lucian picked it up and studied the likeness of his wife's lively countenance.

A rueful chuckle escaped his lips as he remembered her naive questions about how a wife shared her husband with his mistress. Lucian could laugh now, but he had been damned uncomfortable at the time. He had feared that she would ask him if he had a mistress.

Having promised her honesty, he would have been compelled to tell her the truth. Yet he did not want to hurt her, and he had been enormously relieved that she had not asked.

Settling in a chair by the bed, Lucian opened Ashcott's journal, turned to the entries after the death of Angel's brother, and began to read.

Here, in these pages of his private journal, Ashcott had written frankly of his distrust of Thaddeus Wedge, which had been growing over a number of years, and of his decision to consult a different London attorney.

"A sorry thing," the scientific earl had written, "for both Wedge's father and his grandfather served the earls of Ashcott, but I dare not trust him with so important a document as my new will. Angel's future depends upon it. I must protect her. Nothing could be more terrible than for my estate to fall into the hands of her dreadful mother.

"What a consummate fool I was to marry a woman who did not want me and could never love me. But I was young and unwise, and I did not yet realize the importance of mutual love and respect in a marriage."

Lucian frowned. *Mutual love and respect.* He would not have expected such sentimental nonsense from the scientific earl.

He quickly skimmed the next pages of the diary. In them, Ashcott chronicled his trip to the city to have his new will drawn up by a "most reputable and recommended" attorney, whom he referred to as "Mr. K."

On Jan. 21, 1689, Angel's father recorded that he had executed his new will, "lifting a great burden from my mind."

The journal left no doubt that the missing will had existed and that Ashcott had hidden it at Belle Haven. On his return from London, Angel's father had noted: "My will is safely home with me. After showing it to my daughter and my brother, I took care to conceal it where no mischievous hands can find it. Only Angel will know how to locate it."

Lucian frowned at that entry. Why had Ashcott neglected to tell his daughter? It did not make sense that the scientific earl would have overlooked or forgotten something that important.

Lucian sat up until the small hours of the morning, reading the rest of that year's journal carefully, but nowhere in the volume did Ashcott identify the attorney who had drawn up the will except as Mr. K. Nor could Lucian find any clue in it to what Ashcott had done with the will.

The next day, Lucian went to Whitehall for a meeting of the Council of Nine.

Then he initiated inquiries aimed at finding out who the Mr. K in Ashcott's diary might be.

He did not call on Selina. Nor did he go out that night either. Although realistically he did not expect Angel to reach London before the next night at the earliest, he told himself that there was a remote chance she might arrive early and he wanted to be there to greet her.

She did not come, but Orin did. He was eager to serve as Ardmore's agent provided he could return to Belle Haven when it belonged to Angel. Lucian readily agreed, then filled him in on the situation at the Hampshire estate and what he expected of Orin there. The new agent promised to leave for Ardmore at dawn.

The following day Lucian, assailed by guilt for his unwarranted neglect of Lady Selina, decided he must pay her a visit.

When Reeves inquired whether Lucian wished his coach or his barge readied, he replied, "No, I am only going to Lady Selina's." The Brompton mansion was also on the Thames, not far from Lucian's. "I prefer to walk."

" 'Tis a fine day for that," Reeves agreed. "I intend to take one myself while you are gone."

Lucian set out at a brisk pace for Selina's. Nearing it, his pace slackened as he wondered what the hell he was going to say to her.

How did a man explain to a mistress he still cared about that he had suddenly developed a reluctance to bed her? If she could understand it, she would be doing better than he was.

Absorbed by this quandary, he failed to notice the stunningly lovely blonde, tall and statuesque, with unusual lavender eyes descending from an elegant coach ahead of him.

She noticed him, however, and headed toward him.

He was so lost in thought that she was upon him before he recognized her.

She said softly, "Remember me?"

"Selina!" he exclaimed, stopping abruptly. He was flustered and embarrassed that he had nearly passed her by.

"How glad you are to see me, Lucian," she observed mockingly.

"But I am," he said, kissing her bejeweled hand.

"And the sun sets in the east," she retorted, her remarkable lavender eyes frosty.

"I was on my way to call upon you."

"Were you now?" Selina sounded skeptical. "When did you return to London, Lucian?"

He would not lie to her. "Three nights ago." He could offer her no real excuse for his failure to call on her sooner, and he did not try.

Her pretty mouth quirked wryly. "One of the things I most like about you, Lucian, is your honesty. I heard you were back in London." Her voice took on a sharper note. "Why have you not been to see me?"

She was annoyed with him, and she had every right to be.

"I have been busy," he offered weakly. Busy trying to understand himself.

"So I have heard. Very busy at Madame de la Roche's buying gowns for your new wife." Selina lifted her exquisite, arched eyebrow. "How unlike you, Lucian, to take an interest in a female's wardrobe."

"It is," he conceded. "You have heard about my marriage?"

"Everyone in London has. It is the talk of the town. I own I can scarcely credit the stories." Her gaze was suddenly intense. "Nor the unflattering descriptions of your bride."

His mouth tightened angrily at that. Angel might not be a beauty in the conventional sense, but her spirit and vitality more than compensated for that.

Selina said thoughtfully, "It was never in your style,

Lucian, to seduce innocent, young virgins, even pretty ones."

"I did not seduce her," he said through suddenly clenched jaw.

Selina frowned, "I hardly see how you can deny it under the circumstances."

"Circumstances are sometimes deceiving."

"But you married her."

"Aye."

"You have suddenly become a man of very few words, Lucian." Her lavender eyes were studying him intently. "When you left London, it was to celebrate your betrothal to another woman."

"Considering your strong dislike for Kitty, I should think you would be relieved that connection ended short of the altar."

"Will I like your new wife better?"

What would the sophisticated Selina's reaction be to a naive innocent like Angel? Would she be even more contemptuous of his wife than she had been of Kitty? "I do not know."

"When will you introduce her to those of us who missed that most entertaining party at Fernhill?"

He scowled at that. "She is country bred and not ready for London society. I must find a woman to prepare her for it. Perhaps you can recommend someone." The words were out of his mouth before he realized how ill-advised they were.

Selina's lovely arched brows soared upward. "I shall give it some thought," she said noncommittally. "You seem quite concerned about this wife you were forced to take."

His scowl deepened. "I am," he said brusquely.

There was a moment's awkward silence. Then Selina said on a challenging note, "You told me that I would likely see more of you, rather than less, after your marriage."

"I did," he agreed, his brow furrowing in confusion.

"But now you have married a different wife, and you have not come to call on me."

"Aye," he agreed again, not knowing what else to say.

Another awkward silence ensued until Selina said coolly, "It is not like you to lose your heart to a female like that."

"I did not lose my heart," he retorted, affronted that she could think such a thing. She, better than anyone, knew his scorn for that foolish weakness called love.

"Then why did you marry her?"

"I was caught in a trap, and honor required that I do so."

Selina looked as though she were trying very hard to understand but could not. "What is your wife like?"

"She is . . . ah . . . ah . . ." He floundered around searching for some word that would adequately describe her ". . . unique."

Aye, that was it, he thought, grinning at the memory of Angel dueling him.

Unique.

"I look forward to meeting her," Selina said, an odd glint in her lavender eyes. "Good day, Lucian."

He started to protest her abrupt dismissal of him, then decided against it.

Chapter 20

Lucian's mud-spattered coach, accompanied by its two outriders, pulled up in front of his London home no more than three minutes after he had left for Selina's.

As Angel descended from it, she could hardly wait to see her husband, yet she was uneasy about the reception she would receive from him. She had been crushed by how easily he had left her at Ardmore. Apparently their nights together had meant nothing to him. She schooled herself for the awful possibility that he would not even be at home to greet her but with his mistress.

Angel was acutely dissatisfied with her own appearance. Her quick eye had not missed how attractively and richly dressed were the London women whom she saw being helped in and out of coaches, and she felt woefully plain and drab in comparison.

A young footman opened the door to her. Discovering she was his new mistress, he said, "Oh, my lady, you have only just missed your husband. He left no more than two or three minutes ago." The servant clearly did not know what to do with her, and he blurted uncomfortable, "Unfortunately, Reeves stepped out, too."

Angel swallowed her disappointment that Lucian was not here to greet her. She had no idea who Reeves was nor why his stepping out should be unfortunate.

The footman was rescued from his dilemma by the appearance of a stout gray-haired woman. "I will show my lady to her quarters," she said.

She turned to Angel. "I am Mrs. McNally, the housekeeper. If you will follow me, my lady."

As the woman led her upstairs, Angel asked, "Do you

know where Lord Vayle went and how long he will be gone?"

"I overheard him tell Reeves that he was going to call on Lady Selina Brompton." The woman cast her a pitying, sidelong glance. "I do not expect him back soon."

All Angel's excitement and eagerness to see Lucian again drained away. Her most painful fear had been realized. Instead of being here to greet her he was with his mistress, where he had undoubtedly spent the past three nights.

Angel had never felt so alone in her life, not even after Papa had died, for then she had at least had Belle Haven. Now she was in a strange city where she knew no one.

Mrs. McNally led her into a large bedchamber. It was a pretty, comfortable room, painted yellow, with frilly embroidered curtains on the big tester bed and the windows, but Angel knew immediately that this was not Lucian's room. With its embroidery and frills, it was far too feminine.

Her heart sank. She had assumed that she would share his room here, just as they had shared the lord's chamber at Ardmore. "Where is my husband's bedchamber?" Angel asked, trying to hide her dismay and disappointment.

"Next door. This is my lady's chamber," the housekeeper said with such firmness that Angel assumed Lucian had ordered her put here.

She was devastated. Now that Lucian was in London with his mistress, he no longer wished to share a bedchamber with her. Angel felt tears prickling at her eyes, but then her pride came to her rescue. She would not let Mrs. McNally, nor Lucian himself, know how hurt she was. Angel would pretend that she was delighted with this room, preferring it to his.

Reeves greeted Lucian with the news that Angel had arrived in his absence.

"God's oath, I have only been gone for twenty minutes," he exclaimed. "Where is she? In my bedchamber?"

Reeves winced. "I was not here when she arrived, and Mrs. McNally installed her in the lady's bedchamber next to yours. I had not thought to tell her differently since I expected to be here when Lady Vayle arrived."

Lucian muttered a curse. He had given Reeves explicit orders that Angel was to be put in Lucian's own room.

In his rush to see his wife again, he took the steps two at a time and opened the door to her room without bothering to knock. He checked himself at the sight of Angel in her lace-trimmed holland chemise.

"Oh," she exclaimed, instinctively trying to cover herself with her arms.

"It is only me, little one," Lucian reassured her, quickly shutting the door after him. "You need not hide from me."

But, as he moved toward her, he saw that she was suddenly shy with him.

"I—I did not expect you back so soon," she stammered, blushing rosily. "They said you had just left. I—I am sorry I am not dressed to greet you."

"I am not sorry." He grinned at her, and his voice was suddenly husky. "You can greet me like this anytime."

He crushed her to him, and his mouth came down upon hers in a long, hard kiss. She seemed to hesitate for a moment, then she returned it with equal ardor.

When at last he released her, she looked up at him and smiled shyly. "I believe you are glad to see me, my lord."

"Aye," he admitted. Then, unwilling to have her suspect just how glad he was, he said brusquely, "I was worried about your making the journey without me."

Her smile drooped, and she looked away at the frilly bed curtains. A moment later, she said in an oddly strained and subdued voice, "Thank you for giving me this lovely room."

Dismayed at the possibility she might prefer it to sharing his own chamber, he asked sharply, "Do you like it?"

"Aye, I love it. It is so bright and cheerful. Yellow is my favorite color."

He frowned, thinking of his own darker, masculine bedchamber done in burgundy and furnished with heavy, ornately carved pieces. Undoubtedly it would not appeal to a woman nearly so much as this one, but he wanted her there beside him.

Tactfully he asked, "Would you choose this one—"

She interrupted him before he could say "over my bedchamber?"

"Aye," she said. "My room at Belle Haven was done in yellow, and this reminds me of it."

Naturally, she would prefer a room that reminded her of her beloved home. Swallowing his hurt and disappointment, he asked gently, "Are you exhausted from your journey, little one?"

"Not at all."

"Good," he said. "Then we will go to bed."

She blinked at him. "But I said I am not sleepy."

"Did I say anything about sleeping?" He kissed her again hungrily. Then he untied the drawstring at the neck of her lace-trimmed chemise and pulled it wide. His mouth moved down to her breast, suckling it. She moaned and buried her hands in his hair. Her chemise fell about her ankles.

He lifted his head, and his eyes devoured her lovely, sinuous body. God's oath, but he was starving for her. He could not wait to have her.

The speed with which Lucian dispatched his clothes surprised Angel. Then as he pulled her down on the bed, she read the hunger in his eyes for her. Her heart leapt, and her own body answered him in kind.

With long, powerful strokes, he propelled them to a shattering mutual climax that seemed to turn her bones to water.

He rolled on to his side, taking her with him. They lay still joined together, their shuddering breathing slowly returning to normal. His hand stroked her cheek.

Angel opened her eyes and was instantly lost in the silver depths of his jet-framed eyes. He whispered tenderly, "I am sorry, little one, but I could not wait."

She was not in the least sorry, but rather very pleased at this evidence of how much he had wanted her. She smiled. "I am glad that you missed me so much."

The instant she said it, Angel knew that she had made

a mistake. His hands were suddenly still; the silver eyes, so warm a moment ago, were now cool and guarded.

"I told you I was worried about you," he said stiffly. "You are my wife. You and your safety are my responsibility."

The joy died in Angel. Could he not even admit that he had some affection for her? She said sadly, "You make me sound like a dreadful burden."

His face relaxed. "Not dreadful," he teased, running his hand possessively along the curve of her body. "Quite pleasant, in fact."

He pulled her more tightly against him, and they lay in silence. It was clear to Angel that, even if he would not admit it, he had missed her, and she took comfort in that.

She was more determined than ever to find a way to breach the barriers he had erected around his heart.

"Angel," he said suddenly, breaking the peaceful quiet, "are you certain your father never told you where he hid his will."

"Very certain," she said, startled by his choice of pillow talk. "If only he had!"

"But he must have. I have been reading his journal, and he made it clear in it that he would tell you where it was hidden."

"But he did not. Why would he have failed to do so?"

"I cannot imagine a man as precise about details as the scientific earl could have failed. Perhaps you forgot."

She was indignant he could think such a thing. "I would never have forgotten anything so important as that."

"Perhaps you did not grasp the importance of what he was telling you."

"Lucian, I am not a fool!" she cried, bitterly hurt.

The next morning, Lucian, eager to dress his wife as she deserved to be dressed, summoned Madame de la Roche and her minions to fit Angel with the first of the gowns he had ordered.

Her eyes glowed with delight when she saw what he had ordered for her. "They are all so beautiful!" she cried.

"May I try this one first?" She pointed to a rose silk overgown over a cream petticoat tiered with Mechlin lace.

Reeves scratched at the door. "My lord, a messenger is here from the queen. You must go to Whitehall immediately."

Lucian bit back a curse. He had been looking forward to watching Angel's fittings and passing judgment on each gown.

Reluctantly he left his bride and went to the palace, where he was ushered into Her Majesty's presence. Queen Mary II, who shared the throne of England jointly with her Dutch husband, was tall for a woman—five-foot-eleven—and fine-looking, with thick dark hair, large brown eyes, and milk white skin.

She held one of her Dutch pugs on her lap, and her fingers anxiously toyed with its hair. Clearly much agitated, she wasted no time in telling Lucian why he has been sent for.

"I must send a very private, very personal letter to my husband in Ireland. It is imperative that no eyes but his see it or his reply to me. You must carry it to him and bring me his answer."

It was the last thing that Lucian wanted to do, and he could not conceal his dismay.

"But, Your Majesty, surely someone else would—"

"No," she interrupted emphatically. "You are the only one I trust to carry the letter to him without looking at its contents."

Lucian knew that he should be honored that the queen trusted him so much.

He was miserable.

He would have to leave Angel alone in London, where she knew no one. He had not found a suitable woman to prepare her for her introduction to society; he had not even hired a maid for her.

Worse, he could be gone for weeks, depending on the king's pleasure and the winds needed to carry him across the Irish Sea and back again.

He opened his mouth to protest again, but the queen, anticipating what he could say, cut him off.

"If you were in my place, whom would you trust enough to send?"

The question stopped him. The queen was surrounded by men locked in political intrigues and schemes to enhance their own power and futures. Were he in her place, he would trust no one, save himself.

When he failed to answer, she said wryly, "I see you appreciate my dilemma."

He did, and he felt very sorry for her. Not only was she surrounded by scheming, untrustworthy men, but she was terrified for her husband's safety in Ireland. Even more upsetting to the queen, the enemy the king was battling there was her own father. Lucian knew she prayed that both men's lives would be spared.

Mary picked up a sealed letter from the ornate inlaid table and handed it to him. "Guard this with your life, and allow no eyes but the king's to see it."

"I will be worthy of your trust, Your Majesty."

"Leave at once. One of the king's fastest horses awaits you downstairs."

"Please, Your Majesty, allow me to say farewell to my bride. She arrived only last evening in London, where she knows no one. I cannot leave her with no explanation."

"Will you give me your oath that you will be on the road to Holyhead in one hour's time?"

"You have it," Lucian agreed, knowing that this was the best he could hope for.

As he rode home from Whitehall, he wanted to slam his fist into his saddle in frustration. He must protect Angel from society's intense curiosity during his absence. Given the stories circulating about their marriage, the inquisitive would flock to his doorstep while he was gone, eager to inspect his new bride. He knew how cruel and unjust London society could be to those who did not measure up to its sophisticated standards. They loved nothing so much as ridiculing young innocents.

Lucian, determined to shelter Angel from their scorn, would instruct Reeves to permit no callers to see his wife.

When he reached home, Madame de la Roche was coming down the steps with her assistants. Their arms were loaded with Angel's gowns, which they were taking back for finishing.

"My lord," Madame said approvingly when she saw him, "you have a good eye for what will become your lady."

He found Angel in their bedroom, donning one of Kitty's castoffs.

She broke into a wide smile when she saw him. "The clothes are all so lovely, Lucian." She glanced down in disgust at the frilly, childish gown in her hands. "I confess it is difficult for me to put this on now. I am afraid Papa would be dreadfully ashamed of me."

"Why?"

"He mocked fashion as the silly concern of idle, frivolous minds. I fear I have become very frivolous."

Lucian laughed aloud at that. "Not at all, little one. You have merely become a woman, and every woman loves pretty clothes. You would be odd if you did not."

Angel looked so adorable in her shift that he wanted nothing so much as to take her to bed, but he had no time.

"The queen is sending me on a mission to King William in Ireland. I must leave at once, so listen to me carefully, Angel. You must do exactly as I tell you while I am gone. First, you cannot go outside the confines of this house."

Her face fell. "Why not?"

"You have no maid to accompany you."

"But I do not need—"

"Angel, you will do as I say," he interjected firmly. "In London, a lady—and I expect my wife to be no less—does not go outside her home unaccompanied by her maid. Unfortunately, I have no time to hire one for you before I leave."

Her face puckered unhappily. "But I was so looking forward to seeing London."

"And I was looking forward to showing it to you," Lucian admitted. "I promise you, little one, that I will do so as soon as I return."

"Can I not even go out walking?"

"No! If you wish to walk, you can do so in the walled

garden behind the house. It is very large and extends down to the Thames."

He bent his head and kissed Angel long and hard, then said, "I am very sorry to have to desert you, little one, but I cannot go against the queen's command."

He crushed Angel hard against for a final moment before he hurried from the house.

How long would it be before he would see her again?

Chapter 21

Lady Selina Brompton's carriage clattered to a stop in front of Lucian's house. She had no intention of departing until she had met his wife.

As her footman let down the carriage step, Selina's nerve failed her at the thought of how angry Lucian would be at her if he learned about this visit. She hesitated for a moment but then her curiosity to see his new bride won out, and she stepped out of the carriage.

No one had been permitted to see the new Lady Vayle since her arrival in London three days earlier. Society was agog with curiosity about her after all the wild stories circulating about her and her marriage to Vayle.

Callers, pretending to be unaware that Lucian had left for Ireland, flocked to his house ostensibly to call upon him and his new bride, but in reality to look her over. They were all politely but firmly turned away by Lucian's butler with word that her ladyship would be receiving no one until her lord returned to London.

The stories circulated about her by guests who had been at Fernhill for the ill-fated betrothal party had not piqued Selina's interest nearly so much as Vayle's behavior. It was clear to Selina, although she suspected that it might not be to Lucian yet, that since his marriage his passion for his mistress had faded.

And his wife could be the only reason for that.

Although Selina was exceedingly fond of Vayle, she had never had any illusions that he loved her any more than she did him. Each, for their own reasons, had encased their hearts in a protective shield that kept love out.

She sensed that he, like she, knew the terrible pain of

love cruelly rejected and that he, like she, was determined never to place his heart in such jeopardy again.

But he was a considerate and accomplished lover—the most accomplished she had had except for her very first.

Unlike that first love, who had broken her heart, Lucian had treated her as a princess in and out of bed. He was intelligent, amusing, easygoing company and, to her enormous relief, he did not subject her to tiresome displays of jealousy and possessiveness as other lovers had.

A pang of regret assailed her for what she was losing. Perhaps if she been able to . . . She ruthlessly cut off that train of thought. If Lucian had fallen wildly in love with her, Selina was quite certain he would no longer have been such a tolerant and accommodating lover. He would have asked a good deal more of her. And that would not have suited her at all.

She smiled. What a complex man he was. He was impatient with most people and they, in turn, thought that he deserved his sobriquet, Lord Lucifer. But those rare, select few whom he honored with his regard could ask for no truer friend.

And it was his friendship that Selina most valued. She could count on him in any difficulty, and she knew no other man of whom she could say that. Even if she lost him as a lover, which she suspected she already had, she very much wanted to keep his friendship.

So why was she risking it merely to satisfy her curiosity about his wife? Although all society was talking about what an unsuitable wife Lucian had married, in Selina's opinion, the girl could hardly be worse than Kitty.

Selina's mouth curled in disgust. Lucian needed a strong woman who would stand up to him. That was one of the reasons, although she knew he did not realize it, that he and she dealt so well together.

And Kitty was a simpering, spineless fool who had allowed her father to dissuade her from marrying David Inge, who would have made her an excellent husband. Lucian had never confided in Selina why he wanted to marry Kitty, but she knew it had nothing to do with either esteem or affection for her.

From all that Selina had heard about Vayle's bride, she had even less to recommend her than Kitty.

Yet Selina sensed from the confusion she had seen in Vayle's eyes during their brief meeting that he felt very differently about his wife than he had about Kitty.

That was particularly surprising since Lucian denied seducing the girl and indicated that he had been tricked into that infamous scene at Fernhill. Most likely the Crowes had helped the girl sneak into Lucian's bed while he was asleep, and he had awakened to find the trap sprung. The chit, of course, had denied that she was guilty of such despicable behavior.

What baffled Selina was how Lucian, who from the stories she had heard had at first flatly refused to marry the girl, had then been induced to go through with the wedding.

It also baffled Selina why Lord Ashcott's widow would have married Rupert Crowe, but then Lady Helen had always been an unmitigated fool. The daughter of the Marquess of Brockhurst and a remarkable beauty, her behavior had been a scandal long before she had deserted her husband and run off to the Continent with her lover, Lord Benton.

Selina recalled hearing that Lady Helen, no longer young or beautiful, had returned to England after Benton's death a year or so ago, but no one in society, including her sisters and brothers, would have anything to do with her.

When Reeves answered Selina's knock, she took advantage of his momentary shock at the sight of her to brush past him into the house.

Recovering himself, the butler said, "Lord Vayle is not at home."

"I know that. I have come to see Lady Vayle."

"His lordship left strict orders that no one is to be admitted to see his wife while he is in Ireland."

Reeves had always seemed so humorless to Selina that she could not resist teasing him a bit.

"But surely you can make an exception for me." Selina gave him a wicked smile. "After all, his lordship and I are such old and dear friends."

"And that, Lady Brompton, if you will pardon my say—"

"I wish to see my caller, Reeves."

The feminine voice behind Selina was pleasant and melodious, that of an assured woman used to commanding a household.

Turning to see Lucian's wife, Selina found a very young girl with huge blue eyes watching her from the drawing room door. Her face was rather plain except for those eyes. Her dark hair was pulled back carelessly, and she had on a dreadful dress that no female over the age of twelve should have been permitted to wear.

The girl's voice was at such odds with her appearance that Selina could not help staring.

The girl stared back, clearly as curious about her visitor as Lucian's mistress was about her.

Poor Reeves, usually the soul of imperturbability, looked as though he were suffering from a bout of extreme indigestion. "But, Lady Vayle, his lordship expressly—"

The girl said, "I am certain, Reeves, that my husband would not wish you to turn away such a *dear friend.*"

Selina experienced a moment's unease. Surely, the child could not possibly know who she was.

The girl said, "Please join me in the drawing room, Lady Brompton."

The butler protested, "But, my lady—"

My lady said firmly, "I assure you, Reeves, that it will be fine."

Reeves looked as though it would be anything but fine. However, he was clearly at a loss how to explain to his young mistress the reason she should not welcome her husband's "dear friend."

Selina went into the drawing room, thinking that Vayle's wife might look like a child, but she was no weak, simpering miss.

When the two women were seated across from each other, Selina said politely, although not entirely truthfully, "It is a pleasure to meet you, Lady Vayle."

"Please call me Angel," she said with an enchanting smile that made her rather plain face suddenly seem lovely. With the right coiffure and clothes for her petite figure, she could be very striking.

Selina observed, "You cannot be wearing one of the gowns that Lucian bought for you from Madame de la Roche." Lucian's taste was much better than that.

Angel's smile faded. "No, it seemed a waste to wear them when Lucian is not here to see them."

The wistfulness in her tone touched Selina's heart, and she said sympathetically, "You must be lonely without him."

"I am," Angel admitted. "I am glad you called on me, Lady Brompton. I have been very curious to meet you."

"I am surprised that you would know who I am. Do you?"

"Aye," Angel answered with another friendly smile. "You are my husband's mistress."

For a moment, Selina's voice failed her. Then she said weakly, "Surely Vayle did not tell you that."

"No. I had great difficulty even getting him to explain to me what a mistress is." Her guileless gaze met her visitor's. "You see, I did not know."

Conjecture swirled in Selina's mind, and she blurted, "My dear child, just what did Vayle tell you?"

"That a man sleeps with both his wife and mistress." Angel paused, then added hastily, "But not at the same time, which would be excessively uncomfortable."

"Excessively," Selina agreed dryly. Fascinated by these candid revelations, she could not resist asking gently, "And now that you do know what a mistress is, how do you feel about me?"

Angel's face puckered a little. "I confess that when I learned that it meant he made love to you as he does to me, I was very jealous of you."

Selina said softly, "I think it is I who am a little jealous of you, Angel."

"Oh, you should not be," the girl assured her kindly. "If you are Lucian's mistress, it means he chose you. He did not choose me." Her brilliant eyes clouded. "The truth is he did not want to marry me at all. He was tricked into it by my dreadful stepfather and his son."

That was the last thing Selina had expected Angel to disclose to her, but she seized the opening. "How did they manage that?"

"They drugged him and me, put me in his bed, then arranged for us to be discovered like that before we awoke."

"Dear God," Selina said with feeling. "How terrible for both you and Lucian."

"It was, but then I made the situation even worse," Angel confessed dolefully.

"How did you do that?"

"You will think me very stupid, but, you see, I did not understand how babies were made. I thought I had only to lie beside him and I would . . ."

"I do not think you in the least stupid, Angel, only very innocent." Selina was remembering another young girl who had been every bit as naive and guileless as Angel when she had married, years earlier at age sixteen, the man of her dreams.

And then he had cruelly shattered those dreams—and her heart.

Angel recalled, "It made Lucian very angry because he thought I was helping the Crowes in their plot, which I would never do. I was furious that he could think such a thing of me."

"I hope you told him so."

"I did. Then I challenged him to a duel."

Selina stared at her in shock. "Sweet heaven, why?"

"I had to defend my honor. Don't you see?"

"What I do not see is how, after that, you two ended up married."

"Lucian would not accept my challenge unless I agreed that if I lost, I would marry him."

"I gather you lost," Selina said, struggling valiantly to maintain the gravity of her expression.

"Aye, but he said I was one of the best opponents he had ever faced."

"What a unique courtship," Selina observed dryly.

Now she began to understand the bafflement that she had seen in Lucian's eyes before he had described his bride as unique. He was, she suspected, as nonplussed and enchanted by his innocent, unconventional bride as she was.

She also understood why he was so anxious to keep Angel hidden away while he was in Ireland. Selina shuddered to think what some of the more malicious gossips would do if Angel confided in them what she had just told her. Lucian had clearly recognized the danger and tried to protect her.

The dear innocent was not ready for London society with its cruel wit and vicious backbiting. Just as Selina had not been ready . . .

Her mind slipped back through time. She had been twelve when she had met the dashing, handsome Earl of Brompton, a friend of her father's youngest brother. She had promptly become hopelessly infatuated with him.

When, after four years of paying her no notice, his lordship had offered for her, Selina had thought herself the happiest female on the face of the earth. She had never been to London, had never even been beyond the boundaries of her father's estate. She had been raised, like Angel, as a protected innocent.

Selina had known nothing of society or its ways, had not even known that she was a great heiress with coveted family connections and a very rich marital prize for an ambitious, impoverished earl with an expensive mistress to maintain.

Selina had known no more than Angel when her new husband had initiated her to the secrets of love with superb expertise. On their honeymoon, he had been everything an adoring young wife could want.

Then they had come to London where she soon discovered that her naïveté embarrassed her husband. He had mocked her ignorance and branded her stupid for her candor. His mistress had spitefully embroidered the stories of the rustic little bride's gaucheries and broadcast them to the world.

Selina had never forgotten how her husband and his mistress had humiliated her. Nor how lost and alone and confused she had felt when she had first come to London.

Fortunately, her aunt, the duchess of Stratford, had taken

her in hand, and taught her the ways of society. Selina had been a quick study. In time her beauty and vivacity had made her the toast of London.

After she had dutifully borne her lord two sons, she had coldly informed him, to his shock, that he was no longer welcome in her bed. She replaced him there with men who appreciated her.

But she never again let a man touch her heart.

Lucian had come closer than any other man.

They had met when he had arrived with Dutch William when the new king had come to London to claim the throne after his father-in-law had fled. Selina and Lucian had quickly become lovers and friends.

She had sensed in him a kindred spirit whose own heart and pride had suffered a devastating blow, although he had never confided to her what it was, just as she had not told him about her mortifying experience at the hands of her husband and his mistress.

Now Selina was determined that Vayle's captivating bride would not suffer as she had.

Angel needed to be taught how to dress and trained in the ways of London society. For her own protection, her candor must be curbed a little, but only a little. Angel had to be taken in hand as the Duchess of Stratford had once taken her niece.

And no one could do that better than Selina.

Chapter 22

Lucian had ridden like a madman from the coast, stopping only to change horses and to catch a few hours sleep.

Between the contrary winds in the Irish Sea and the king's wish to keep him at his side in Ireland until after the Battle of Boyne, in which William had defeated James II's troops, Lucian's trip to Ireland had taken three weeks all told.

Now, reaching London, he went immediately to the queen to deliver the king's messages to her and to reassure her personally, at William's order, that her father had suffered no harm in his defeat.

As Lucian waited impatiently to be ushered into the queen's presence, he pulled, as he had so often during the past three weeks, the miniature of Angel from his pocket and studied her face. It would not be long now.

He had worried about her sitting all alone, friendless and bored, in his London house, awaiting his return, and his heart had gone out to her, knowing how miserable she must be.

Once Lucian had given Queen Mary the king's letters and assured her that both William and her father were in good health, he withdrew from the royal presence and left Whitehall at a pace that would have done justice to an entry in a Newcastle race.

When he reached his London house at last, he bounded up the stairs and inside.

Reeves met him in the hall. "My lord, we did not expect you."

For some reason, his butler looked less than pleased to see him.

"I had no time to send word."

Hearing footsteps at the top of the stairs, he looked up expectantly, thinking he would see his wife.

Instead a woman he had never laid eyes on before gave him a haughty perusal and retreated down the hall.

"Who the devil is that?" he demanded.

"Lady Vayle's maid."

"Where the hell did she come from?" Lucian demanded, nonplussed. "And where is my wife?"

Reeves nervously picked at an invisible piece of lint on his sleeve. "I fear she has gone out, my lord."

"Out! I told her she was not to set foot beyond the front door." Lucian was disappointed that even more time must pass before he could see his wife again. He was also outraged that she had blatantly disobeyed him and that Reeves had permitted it.

He growled, "This is not the kind of surprise I like."

"No, my lord," the butler said politely, then muttered something under his breath to the effect that it was not the only one his lordship was in for.

Lucian frowned. "I told you, did I not, Reeves, that you were not to let her go out."

"Aye, my lord," the butler agreed, "but I fear it is quite impossible to dissuade my lady when she has a mind to do something."

"If she has gone out, why is her maid not with her? How could you let her—"

Lucian broke off at the sound of the front door opening behind him and turned to discover a very pretty young woman with glossy, chocolate curls caught up in a fetching style. Both the perky hat atop her curls and her rose gown were in high fashion. He was so taken by her that he paid no heed to the woman behind her.

The young woman saw him, and his breath caught at the sudden, brilliant smile that enveloped her face. She launched herself at him, throwing her arms exuberantly around his neck. "Lucian, Lucian, you are back."

God's oath, it was Angel.

His astonishment at the change in his wife since he had last seen her was overridden by his delight in seeing her at last. His own arms went round her, and he returned her embrace. Their mouths met in a long, passionate kiss that made him forget all else, including his ingrained abhorrence of displaying emotion in front of others.

Lucian drank in the sweet scent of dewy wildflowers that was Angel's alone. When he lifted his lips from hers, he wanted to bury his face in her cascade of shining curls, but that damned, cute little hat defeated him.

He belatedly remembered that he was angry with her for disobeying him. "Angel, why are you going about London alone without your maid? Speaking of her, where the devil did she come from?"

"Angel was not going about alone, Lucian," a familiar, throaty voice said from the threshold.

His jaw dropped in consternation as he realized that the woman with his wife was Selina.

"I was with Angel," Selina said.

Bloody hell! This was definitely not the homecoming he had been anticipating.

"That should comfort me?" he asked acidly.

Selina ignored his question. "I also hired the maid for her."

"Selina has been the greatest help to me," Angel said happily. "You cannot imagine all that she has told me."

Lucian could, but he would rather not.

"She has become my very best friend," Angel assured him with one of her glowing smiles.

Lucian felt as though he had just stumbled into quicksand. Damn it, a man's wife and his mistress were not supposed to become best friends.

His gaze chanced to alight on Reeves. His normally wooden-faced butler appeared to be struggling manfully to keep from grinning.

Lucian did not see a damn thing funny. He hoped to hell that Angel had no inkling of his relationship to Selina. But, of course, she could not, he reassured himself. She would never embrace his mistress as her best friend.

The house was so quiet one could hear a silk handkerchief drop. Lucian suspected that every servant who could manage it was an interested, if hidden, eavesdropper.

"Ladies, I prefer to continue this edifying conversation in the privacy of my library."

Reeves looked acutely disappointed.

After Lucian had shepherded the two women into the library and closed the door behind them, he studied his fashionably dressed wife. "You have become quite a lady in my absence."

She glowed at his praise. "Selina has been so kind to me. She has taught me so much about how to dress and wear my hair and how I should act in society."

"I am glad she has been of such service to you," he said stiffly, wondering what the hell else his mistress had taught his wife.

Angel met her husband's gaze with her guileless eyes. "I must confess that I was very jealous of Selina at first, but she is so kind and lovely that I can see why you would want her for your mistress, Lucian. I like her excessively."

His smile vanished. He wanted to throttle Selina. Why in bloody hell had she told his wife about their relationship?

Angel said, "You have excellent judgment, my lord."

"Thank you—I think."

"I was very unhappy when you explained to me what sharing you with your mistress meant," Angel confided, "but now that I know Selina I do not mind."

"God's oath," he exclaimed, deeply chagrined and more than a little angry that she would not care. "Doesn't it even bother you."

"Well, yes," Angel, ever honest, admitted, "but I want you both to be happy and—"

"You are very generous, Angel," Selina broke in, "but I assure you that I am now Lucian's former mistress. I do not feel that I can be both your friend and his lover." She threw Lucian a mocking look. "And I prefer to be your friend."

All power of speech had deserted Lucian. No, not in his wildest dreams, could he possibly have imagined this homecoming.

Angel protested, "But Lucian will be so unhappy."

"No, I suspect he will be greatly relieved," Selina said with a smile.

She was right. Her perception was another one of the things that he had always liked about Selina.

"I have given Angel an intense course in how to act and deal with society, and she is ready to be launched," Selina said. "My aunt, the Duchess of Stratford, and I have managed to put an end to the worst of the stories that were circulating about Angel and your marriage."

"How?" Lucian asked.

"With the truth. Angel told me how the Crowes had stolen her inheritance and drugged you both to stage that scene at Fernhill. My aunt and I have whispered the story far and wide. Coming from us, everyone believed it." She smiled in satisfaction. "The Crowes can never hope to regain a position in society now."

"And I look like a damned simpleton who fell so easily into their trap," Lucian complained.

"No, I helped you out on that score by embroidering the truth a little," Selina confessed. "And I require your support in my fib."

"What can I do?" Lucian asked.

"You must pretend that you fell wildly in love with Angel the first time you met her. You see I put it about that you did, and—"

Lucian cut her off furiously, "Bloody hell, Selina, you know that I have no truck with such nonsense as romantic love, and I am not going to act a lie."

He was conscious of the stricken look his words brought to Angel's face, and he felt like a scoundrel.

Selina ignored his protest, continuing smoothly, "And that after your initial—and very understandable rage—at the Crowes' perfidy wore off, you were delighted to marry her." Selina smiled at him wickedly.

Lucian glared at her, then turned to his wife. "Angel, please allow me a moment alone with my *former* mistress."

"Certainly," she said with quiet dignity.

As soon as Lucian was alone with Selina, he said coldly, "So you have taught Angel a great many things, have you? I hope one of them was not how to cuckold a husband."

"Don't be a fool, Lucian. I deserve better than that."

"Do you? Then why the hell did you tell Angel that you are my mistress?"

"I did not! She told me."

He groaned. "God's oath, how did she know?

"She overheard someone talking at Fernhill."

So that was why Angel had not asked him at Ardmore whether he had a mistress. She had already known that he had.

"Your bride, in case you have not noticed, Lucian, is very quick, which is one of the reasons that I like her so much. I am trying very hard to salvage her reputation, and it is imperative that you help me by pretending to have fallen in love with her."

His mouth tightened in a hard disgusted line. "So I am supposed to make it look as though the Crowes have unwittingly done me a great favor."

"Have they not, Lucian?" Selina asked softly.

He stared at her for a long moment.

"We have always been honest with each other," she said. "Let us continue to be so. Neither one of us was willing to trust the other with our heart, and without that no passion can be sustained. We had become more important to each other as friends than as lovers. I want very much to continue as your friend as well as your wife's."

"You have been remarkably kind and understanding," he said with genuine gratitude.

Selina smiled. "It came as a great surprise to me to discover, My Lord Lucifer, that the devil married an Angel. I beg you treat her with care."

"I gather you disapprove of me as her husband?"

"She deserves better than you."

"Yes," he agreed soberly, "she does."

Selina smiled. "Perhaps, there is hope for you after all, Lucian."

Chapter 23

"Sarah, you must excuse Angel and me," Selina told the Countess of Marlborough. "I promised Lord St. Albans that I would introduce Angel to him tonight."

Angel was too thankful for this chance to escape their hostess to say anything to Selina, but once they were well out of her hearing, she whispered, "I have already met his lordship."

Selina's eyes twinkled. "I know that, but Sarah does not."

Angel grinned at her friend. "Thank you for rescuing me from her. She makes me uncomfortable."

"With good reason," Selina said tartly. "Sarah can be charming when she wants, but she has the tongue of a viper. I do not trust her nor her husband either. Their ambition is boundless, and her lord is jealous of Lucian's close ties to the king. You must guard what you say around her."

"I do not know what I would do without you," Angel said, filled with gratitude for all that her companion had taught her, not only about how to act and talk and dress, but more importantly about who could be trusted and who could not, including rakes like Lord Nevin. Until then, Angel had not known what a rake was.

In the month since Lucian had come home from Ireland and Angel had been launched in society, Selina had patiently—and very successfully—steered her protégé between the shoals that lurked to trap a novice in society's waters.

Angel smiled at her friend. "You have been so kind to me."

"It has been my pleasure," Selina said.

"Even giving up Lucian? I cannot understand how you could bear to—" She broke off, much flustered at what her wayward tongue had nearly said.

Selina laughed. "Had Lucian ever looked at me the way he looked at you that day he returned from Ireland, it would have been much more difficult." Her lavender eyes were suddenly dreamy. "You see, I want a man who will look at me like that. Perhaps it might have been different if . . . You see when Lucian and I met, we suited very well. Neither of us could give our love or trust."

And Lucian still cannot, Angel thought sadly.

Selina paused for a moment, her lovely mouth turned up in a pensive smile, then she said briskly, "No use pining over what might have been. Lucian is all yours now."

"You make it sound as though he loves me," Angel said wistfully, "and he does not, you know."

Selina patted her arm comfortingly. "He cares for you more than he is willing to admit, even to himself."

Angel fervently hoped that Selina was right. She looked around the large room, crowded with elegantly dressed men and women, wishing her husband would make his appearance.

"I hope he will not be too late," she fretted. She was never entirely happy at these affairs unless he was at her side. "He promised he would come as soon as the Council of Nine meeting ends, but he warned that it could go on for hours."

Angel would have preferred to stay home tonight with her husband, but she feared he would not want to forgo a glittering entertainment for a quiet night with a wife he did not love.

Selina asked Angel, "What did you do today?"

"Lucian took me to call on my mother again. She still refuses to see us."

Selina frowned. "That is the third time—or is it the fourth—she has turned you away. How can a mother do that to her own child?"

Angel shrugged. "She never paid Charlie or me any heed, even before she ran away."

"How long has it been since you have seen her?"

"I was four the last time."

Selina looked aghast. "Not since then? Not even after your father died?"

"No, she sent my stepfather to Belle Haven in her place. She always hated it there. Country life bored her."

"Not enough men to pay her court," Selina observed acidly. "What a fool she is! How I wish I could have been so fortunate as to have had a daughter like you. I have two sons, and I love them dearly, but I yearned for a daughter."

"What of your husband, Selina?"

The warmth went out of her lovely face. "What of him?"

"You have never once mentioned him to me. Nor have I ever seen you with him."

"I avoid him whenever possible." Selina's expressive voice was suddenly flat and frigid. "If I know that he is going to a party, I go to a different one. I give him complete freedom and a wide berth. My husband prefers other women in his bed, and I prefer other men."

Angel could not comprehend how Lord Brompton could be such a fool as to want a woman other than his wife. She had not met another female in London who could surpass Selina in beauty, wit, and kindness.

"Were you forced to marry him?"

"No, the truth is I wanted desperately to be his wife, fool that I was." She gave Angel a sad smile. "Beware what you wish for, you might get it."

"What happened."

"He broke my heart and turned my love for him to hate. Please, I cannot bear to talk about him."

Lord Jermain came up, reminding Selina that the next dance was the one that she had promised him earlier. He was one of a dozen different men, ranging from a duke to a very wealthy baronet, who were vying to become Lucian's successor in Selina's life.

The orchestra began playing again, and Jermain led her away.

Angel turned her attention to the other guests. Everyone who was anyone seemed to be here tonight, and she wondered whether Lucian's father was among the guests. She had heard that he was in London, and she had been trying to think of how to meet him. She was still determined to find a way to reconcile the two men.

Angel smiled at the sight of a trio of nubile young ladies trying desperately to hold Roger Peck's attention. From his expression of only half-suppressed boredom, Angel deduced that they were failing rather miserably.

She did not understand the great fascination that Peck seemed to hold for females under the age of thirty. True, nature had been bountiful in its gifts to him. Not only was he very rich and Lord Peck's heir, but he was widely considered to be the handsomest man in London.

Angel did not agree with this assessment of him. True, the cast of his face was perfection itself with its broad brow, wide-set blue eyes, straight nose, and strong jaw. In her opinion, that was its problem. It was too perfect. Too bland. It lacked the imperfections that gave a face character. She much preferred the dark, more harshly sculpted planes of her husband's face.

Nor did Angel care for the smooth charm and easy compliments that Peck dispensed so fluently. He was still young, no more than five-and-twenty, but he already had the manner of an accomplished rake.

Angel watched as Peck gracefully edged away from the trio of young ladies who had tried vainly to hold his interest. As he strode across the floor, he stopped a few feet from Angel to greet another pair of girls, who promptly became tongue-tied at his attention.

He quickly moved on to Angel. She should have guessed that she was his quarry. He had made it a point every night for the past week of seeking her out, and she was not happy about it. Even if Selina had not warned her about him, she recognized—and despised—the insincerity of his compliments.

"Tonight is my lucky night," he said, kissing Angel's hand with practiced ease. "I have you all to myself for a moment."

To her relief, it was only for a moment. Then, to Peck's undisguised annoyance, Lord St. Albans and the Duke of Ormonde joined them.

* * *

Lucian's gaze swept Lady Marlborough's long gallery, looking for his wife. He was less than pleased to find her surrounded, as usual, by male admirers.

It surprised him that society found Angel every bit as refreshing as he did. Thanks to her unconscious charm and candor and to Selina's wise instruction, she had been an instant hit with both women and men, and he was proud of her.

Although it had chafed him to do so, Lucian had followed Selina's instructions to act in public as though he had fallen in love with his wife. Between that and Selina's spreading the word about the Crowes' treachery, Angel was now regarded with sympathy instead of censure. Even better, her step-relatives were greater pariahs than before.

Watching his wife laughing with her admirers, Lucian wished sourly that she did not seem to like social affairs so much. If the truth be known, he would much prefer to spend his nights at home with her, but after the isolated life she had led at Belle Haven, he could not ask her to forgo parties that she clearly enjoyed so much.

In the month since his return from Ireland, he had managed only four nights at home with her, and his mouth curved into a pleased smile at the memory.

They had all followed a pattern: He and Angel had lingered over dinner discussing a variety of subjects, from astronomy to politics, generally thought to be too taxing for a woman's frail intellect. They clearly were not too taxing for Angel's, and she offered convincing arguments when she disagreed with her husband. She was the scientific earl's child, Lucian thought proudly.

Selina had been right. The Crowes had done him a great, albeit unwitting, favor.

As the musicians began playing again, Lucian was surprised to see David Inge making his way toward him.

"Why are you in London," Lucian asked. "You should be at Fernhill courting Kitty."

"It would do no good. Her father still refuses to hear of it." David gestured toward Angel. "Your little bud has bloomed into a lovely rose, Lucian."

"Aye, she has."

"You should be pleased, but you sound disgruntled."

Lucian was. He knew that he should have been delighted that his wife was such a hit, but instead it disturbed him to see her constantly surrounded by admiring men.

David looked amused. "Not jealous, are you?"

"Me?" Lucian scoffed, irritated that David could think such a thing. "I don't know the meaning of the word."

His eyes narrowed as he watched that insufferably handsome Roger Peck, who had cut a notorious swath through the ranks of society's loveliest young ladies, lead Angel out to dance.

Roger of the flowing golden wig, silver tongue, and seductive eyes had a sly way of looking at a female whose honor and reputation he was about to devour.

He was eyeing Angel that way now.

Lucian suddenly wanted to smash Roger's teeth down his throat.

Beside him, David said bitterly, "Even if you are not jealous, you would be wise to keep Angel away from Peck."

Lucian belatedly remembered that it was Roger who had come between Kitty and David.

Angel was wearing a sea blue satin gown that her husband had not seen before. It was not one of those he had selected for her, but she looked lovely in it.

Its low-cut bodice cried out for ornamentation at her throat. The thought came unbidden to him that his mother's pearl necklace would have been perfect for Angel. It had been the one thing of his mother's that he had coveted, mostly because she had wanted him to have it, but his father had denied him even that.

Lucian edged closer to the dance floor to watch his wife. She was a graceful dancer, rather like a swan gliding. As the steps of the minuet brought her close to him, he discovered just how low her gown was cut. It revealed far too much of her for his taste. His smile turned to a glower.

The naive innocent had no idea what such a display did to a man. He would see that she did not make that mistake again. He would insist that she consult him before buying her gowns.

As soon as the music stopped, he was at Angel's side to reclaim her from Peck. Lucian hustled her to a quiet corner.

"Where the devil did you get that gown?"

The delight that had enveloped Angel's face at the sight of her husband gave way to dismay. "Do you not like it, Lucian? It is the very latest fashion."

"No, I do not like it at all. It is cut too damn low."

"But it is no lower than the gowns of half the other women in the room."

Lucian realized she was right.

Except those other women were not his wife.

"Angel," Lucian asked over breakfast the following morning, "are you certain that your father never indicated to you where he hid his will?"

"Very certain," Angel replied carefully. This was at least the dozenth time since Lucian had returned from Ireland that he had asked her this question. It hurt and irritated her that he thought her such a fool that she would not remember something as important as that. "Have you had any luck in learning Mr. K's identity?"

"I continue to make inquiries," Lucian said blandly, then changed the subject. "I have accepted an invitation for us to attend the Devonshire masquerade tonight."

Angel nodded, suppressing a groan. She had hoped that they might spend the night at home. To hide her disappointment, she turned her head and stared out the window. It was a rare sunny day, and she exclaimed, "It is so nice out, Lucian, could we go for a ride in the park this afternoon."

"I have business to attend to, but it should not take me longer than an hour or two. We can go then."

"What business?" Angel asked.

"It would bore you."

Angel bit her lip. Lucian did not understand that she loved him and, therefore, everything that he did was of interest to her. She ached to be part of his life, to be able to discuss his affairs and concerns with him as she had discussed Papa's with him. A wife should be part of her husband's life, and Angel so often felt shut out of Lucian's.

She said quietly, "I would like to be bored."

Lucian ignored that and changed the subject again. "That gown is very becoming on you. It enhances the fairness of your skin."

Angel looked down at the rose tabinet gown, open at the front to reveal a dull silk petticoat in pale pink. "Thank you. It is one of those you selected for me."

"I thought so." His smile cooled a little. "I did not recognize the gown you were wearing at the Marlboroughs last night."

"No, that is one Selina and I chose." Selina had said that she needed at least one gown a little more daring than those Lucian had selected for her. Daring it seemed was the height of fashion these days, but Angel did not tell him that. Seeing his frown, she reminded him, "You told me I could order additional clothes to supplement the ones that you chose for me."

"So I did, but from now on ask my approval on the design before you order them."

Angel was so surprised that she could scarcely credit her ears. "Why?"

"Because I am your husband, and I want to be consulted on such matters."

Angel's temper flared. Lucian arbitrarily made decisions, accepted invitations, bought her things, and took her places without bothering to consult her. Yet she was expected to obtain his permission before she ordered a new gown for herself.

"Well, I am your wife, and I wish to be consulted, too, on whether we shall attend the Devonshire masquerade and other social affairs or whether I should like a new tapestry for my sitting room."

She was referring to a lovely tapestry depicting a field of colorful wildflowers that she had found hanging there the previous day. Lucian had explained that when he had seen it, he could not resist buying it because he had known it would brighten her rather dark sitting room.

"I bought it because I knew you would like it," he said stiffly. "And you told me yesterday that you did."

"I do like it, but the point is, my lord, that I should like to be consulted, too. It is my sitting room."

"And it is my house." His temper was rising.

"And you own everything in it including me! But since I must live in it with you, I should like my wishes to be taken into consideration, too."

"Angel, I—" He broke off abruptly as Reeves came into the room, carrying a small package.

"For you, my lady. A messenger just delivered it."

Angel, excited at this unexpected present, instantly forgot her disagreement with her husband. "Is it from you, Lucian?"

The dark look on his face told her that it was not.

"If it were, I would give it to you myself, not have it delivered. It must be from one of your ardent admirers—like Roger Peck."

"Do you not like Roger?" she asked.

"No, I do not. Furthermore, you imperil your reputation by letting him court you as he does. He is notorious for seducing every married woman he favors with his attentions."

An outraged gasp escaped Angel's lips. She was angry and deeply hurt that Lucian could think she would have anything to do with another man. "He will not seduce me."

Her husband said acidly, "You will be the first young wife who has managed to resist his charms."

"How little faith you have in me!"

He did not respond to that. Gesturing at the gift, he inquired, "Who is it from?"

There was no card with it. Angel tore away the wrapping to reveal a case. Inside it, lying on a bed of black velvet, she discovered a spectacular pearl necklace of remarkable luster.

Her gasp of delight was drowned out by Lucian's harsh exclamation of shock.

Startled, Angel looked up from the necklace. Her husband was staring at it as though it were a coiled snake lying there instead of the loveliest necklace of flawless matched pearls she had ever seen.

A note was tucked beneath the pearls. She slipped it out and read:

"A wedding present for my new daughter-in-law to welcome you into our family. This was my late wife's favorite. Perhaps it will become yours, too. I hope to have the pleasure of meeting you soon.

WREXHAM"

The note seemed to lighten a burden that Angel had not been conscious she was carrying. Lucian believed their marriage had cost him whatever hope he had of proving his worth to his father, but surely if the older man disapproved of their union, he would not have sent her these beautiful pearls.

Nor would he have sent them to the wife of a man he hated.

Suddenly, Angel's yearning to reconcile father and son did not seem so hopeless.

"Only see what your father has sent me." She handed the note to her husband.

As he read it, his frown darkened into a scowl.

She lifted the pearls out of the case and held them up, admiring their perfection. At a loss to understand Lucian's reaction, she said, "Only look at how beautiful they are."

Lucian reached out and touched the pearls lightly with his finger. His voice was melancholy. "How my mother loved them."

Seeing the look on her husband's face, Angel had to blink back the tears that suddenly ambushed her. She said softly, "I can understand why this necklace was her favorite."

Lucian's wistful face tightened into hard, bitter lines. "I thought Wrexham had given it to my brother's wife years ago."

"Why did you think that?"

"He told me that it would go to Fritz's wife when he

married. You see, this necklace was the one thing of my mother's that I wanted. She had told me on her deathbed that she wished me to have it, but after she died, Wrexham refused to give it to me. He said I was not worthy of it." Lucian's mouth twisted in a parody of a smile that tore at Angel's heart. "Congratulations. Clearly he thinks you are."

"I want to meet your father," Angel said. "Please take me to see him."

"No," he snapped. "Wrexham made it very clear that he wanted nothing more to do with me, and I will have nothing to do with him. Nor will you."

"But, Lucian, this is clearly a peace overture to you."

Her husband's face was as hard as Portland stone. "He sent the necklace to you, not me."

"He sent it to me only because I am *your* wife."

"Then send it back to him."

Angel stared at her husband in exasperation and frustration. Although he refused to have anything to do with his father, it was clear to her that he still longed for his approval.

Men and their stiff-backed pride! Even a man as wise as her papa had been the same way. He had hidden himself away at Belle Haven after her mother had run away because he was so humiliated.

"No, I will not send the necklace back." Angel was determined not to let Lucian throw away this opportunity to end the breach between him and his father. "You are being very foolish. If you will not take me to meet your papa, I shall go alone."

Angel recoiled at the pure fury on her husband's face. He half rose from his chair before regaining control of himself and sinking back down. "You will do no such thing! I forbid you to see him."

"You treat me as though I am a child, and I am not. I am your wife, and as such I should have an equal voice in our marriage. Papa said a man and wife should be partners in life."

"That is the most nonsensical idea I have ever heard," Lucian scoffed. "A man is king in his home, and you will do as I say. You will not visit my father. Have I made myself clear?"

Angel fought down the inclination to hurl at his head the porcelain plate with her half-eaten breakfast still on it.

Instead she rose from the table with all the dignity she could muster, and said coldly, "Very clear, my lord."

She had no intention of obeying his edict, but he would find that out soon enough.

Chapter 24

Lucian strode into the office of Paul Kennicott on the second floor of a handsome brick building off Aldersgate Street. He had Lord Ashcott's journal tucked under his arm.

He had told Angel the truth this morning when he said he continued to make inquiries as to the identity of "Mr. K." He had not told her that the most likely possibility was Kennicott, one of London's most able and respected solicitors, nor that he would be paying him a visit that very morning. Lucian had not wanted to raise her hopes in vain.

In the outer chamber, a young clerk with a pockmarked face was hard at work copying a parchment document.

When Lucian asked to see Kennicott, the clerk looked at him skeptically. " 'Ave you an appointment?" he asked in a tone that implied anyone who did not would wait until doomsday to see his employer.

Lucian ignored the question. "Tell Kennicott the earl of Vayle is here to see him."

The clerk's manner underwent an instant change. "Aye, m'lord," he said, jumping up, suddenly eager to please.

The clerk disappeared through a door and was back a moment later to usher Lucian through it.

Kennicott, a portly man with red hair fading to gray, rose from behind a walnut desk with papers neatly arranged upon it to greet his caller.

Behind the solicitor a window looked out on new St. Paul's Cathedral—or what was completed of it. The old cathedral had burned in the great fire of 1666. This replacement, designed by Sir Christopher Wren, had been under construction for fifteen years and was still far from finished.

Lucian wasted no time in getting immediately to the point of his visit. "I have reason to believe, Mr. Kennicott, that in January of last year you drew up a will for the earl of Ashcott."

"Of what concern is that to you, my lord?"

"I am married to Ashcott's daughter, Lady Angela.

"I was not aware that she had wed." Kennicott looked troubled. "Have you been married long?"

"Several weeks."

Kennicott's shrewd gray eyes narrowed a little. "My felicitations. Lord Ashcott said he intended to consult me on a marriage settlement for her should the need arise, but clearly when the time came, he did not see fit to do so."

"When the time came, he was dead. Apparently you are not aware that Ashcott died seven months ago."

"No!" Kennicott exclaimed. "I was not."

"And the will you drew up for him has vanished. Do you know where it might be?"

Kennicott looked genuinely shocked. "No, I have a copy of it, but the earl took the executed original with him. He would not trust it in anyone's hands but his own. He was deeply worried—I thought overly so—about the possibility that the will might disappear. His greatest fear was that his estranged wife might somehow inherit his estate."

"Which is precisely what has happened. The family solicitor, Thaddeus Wedge, insists the last will the earl made was one in 1673 that left everything to his wife."

Kennicott's face tightened angrily. "So Lord Ashcott's fears were well-founded after all. He came to me because he no longer trusted Wedge who, by the way, is lying. After Lady Ashcott ran off with her lover, her husband had Wedge draw up a will that specifically disinherited her and left everything to their son, with instructions that the boy was to provide for his sister. Even if Wedge did not know about the will that I drew up, he knew about the previous one."

Kennicott paused and leaned back in his chair, tenting

his fingers over his nose. "In fact, that was when his lordship first became suspicious of Wedge. He had kept the first will. When the earl asked for it back so that he could personally destroy it, Wedge discovered he had somehow 'misplaced' it."

Lucian said sourly, "But once Ashcott died, Wedge found it quick enough and 'misplaced' the later one he had drawn up."

"It is more sinister than that. Ashcott gave me a letter that Wedge subsequently wrote to him, telling him that he had found the first will and assuring him that he had destroyed it."

Lucian stared through the window at new St. Paul's abuilding. "What has Wedge to gain from this fraud?"

Kennicott shrugged. "His lordship believed that Wedge was infatuated with his countess. Apparently she was a great beauty—and very skilled at enthralling men when it suited her purpose."

"I hope she rewarded Wedge well for his duplicity," Lucian said sarcastically. "I understand the missing will you drew up left everything to my wife."

"It did," the solicitor confirmed. "It was a very short will. For some reason I could not fathom, it seemed very important to Lord Ashcott that the will be brief."

"Did Ashcott give you any clue as to where he intended to conceal it?"

"None. He said his daughter would know where to find it."

Lucian sighed. "But she does not. She knows of the will's existence because her father showed it to her and her uncle, but he did not tell her where he hid it."

"How did you discover that I drew it up, my lord?"

Lucian showed him the passage in Ashcott's journal. "I concluded from your reputation that you must be the Mr. K referred to. Do you still have the letter Wedge wrote saying he destroyed the older will?"

"Aye."

That was a stroke of luck Lucian had not anticipated. "Good. It seems to me that with it, your copy of Ashcott's final will, and the entries in his journal, we can successfully challenge the validity of the old will."

"Aye, we can prove that the last thing Ashcott wanted was his estranged wife inheriting his estate, that he had repudiated the earlier will, and that he had been assured by Wedge that it had been destroyed. I think the court can be persuaded to set such an impeached document aside."

Lucian smiled in satisfaction. The Crowes were already ruing the day that they had made him their victim. He was quietly driving Rupert's gambling hell out of business. Lucian had seen to it that the stories of men being ruthlessly fleeced there had a wide audience. He had also used his considerable power to make certain that Crowe's bribes no longer protected his establishment from the authorities' attention.

Now Lucian would see that Rupert was legally stripped of both Belle Haven and control of the fortune that was rightfully Angel's. He still hoped to prove that the Crowes killed Ashcott, but he would say nothing about that until he had better proof.

But when he got that, he would see them hanged.

Kennicott said, "If the court sets aside the earlier will, it will appoint a trustee to handle Ashcott's estate until the later will is found." The solicitor was frowning now. "I must warn you, my lord, that it will be far more difficult, if not impossible, to secure your wife's inheritance for her unless the missing will is found. Her mother and the Crowes will undoubtedly fight her claim, and the estate could be tied up in litigation for years."

When Lucian returned home, Angel was not waiting for him to take her riding. She had gone out with Selina instead. He was disappointed, for he had looked forward to a ride in the park with his wife.

She had been very angry with him when she had left the breakfast table, but she had to understand that he would have nothing to do with his father—nor would he permit his wife to. Lucian would never bend on that point.

He would remember in the future, though, to ask her wishes on what invitations to accept or whether she would like something. He was so used to answering to no one but himself that it had not even occurred to him to consult her. Angel was becoming increasingly precious to him, and her happiness was important to him.

Lucian had just stepped into his library when the door knocker sounded, and he heard Joseph Pardy asking to see him. Perhaps Lucian's luck was running, and he would locate both Mr. K and the missing Maude on the same day.

Lucian called to Reeves, "I will see Mr. Pardy in the library."

The butler, his face reflecting his disapproval of the shabby caller dressed in a worn suit of black broadcloth and darned cotton hose, escorted him into the library.

As soon as the door closed behind Reeves, Lucian eagerly asked Pardy, "Have you found Maude?"

"Not yet, m'lord." Pardy gave Lucian a crafty smile, revealing a set of dizzily crooked teeth. "But me's discovered much about 'er that'll help loosen 'er tongue when me does find 'er." His smile broadened. "I've enough against 'er to send 'er to prison for years if she don't help. She's an actress who's been Rupert Crowe's mistress these four years. She's in 'iding now, but one a these days Crowe will lead me to 'er."

Despite this assurance, Lucian chafed at the delay in locating Maude. She was the key to proving that the Crowes had murdered Ashcott.

"Crowe's a bad one," Pardy said. "Even piracy's not beneath him. Me learned he's the scum who financed One-eyed Jake."

The notorious pirate One-eyed Jake was a much feared scourge of merchant ships on the high seas.

Lucian observed sarcastically, "That must have rewarded Rupert well."

"Aye, it did."

As Pardy left the library, he turned in the doorway and, with another display of crooked teeth, assured Lucian, "We'll find Maude eventually, m'lord."

"Eventually isn't good enough. You must find Maude quickly."

The words had no sooner left Lucian's mouth than he

saw Angel standing in the hall, her eyes wide. Clearly, she had heard him.

As soon as Pardy left, she stepped into the library. "Why are you looking for Maude?"

Lucian suppressed a groan. He dared not tell his impetuous wife the true reason why he was searching for the woman. Instead he improvised, "I want Maude's confession of how she helped the Crowes drug us both and trap us into marriage even though we had done nothing wrong. I want the world to know for a certainty that we did not."

Angel frowned. "But, Lucian, thanks to Selina and her aunt, everyone already knows that. The gossip about our marriage has died away. Why risk rekindling it?"

Good question. And one to which Lucian had no ready answer. Anxious to drop the subject, he said more sharply than he intended, "I insist you defer to my better judgment on this. We will not discuss it further."

When he saw the hurt that clouded Angel's eyes, he hated himself for having been so curt.

"Aye, my lord and master," she said with acerbity. She turned on her heel with her chin at a proud, elevated angle.

He did not want her to leave him feeling wounded and angry, and he said in a gentler voice, "Come back and tell me about your afternoon."

She did not so much as look over her shoulder at him, but said coldly, "I have nothing to confide in you, my lord."

"Well, I have something to confide in you if you will come back."

That stopped her, and she turned eagerly. "What is it?"

"I have located Mr. K. He is a solicitor named Kennicott, and he confirms he drew up the missing will for your father."

Angel was jubilant. "That is wonderful. Now people will know I was not lying about it."

Lucian decided against telling her about the legal effort he was launching to have the earlier will set aside. He did not want to raise false hopes in case it failed. "Your father told him you would know where it is hidden."

Her smile faded. "But I have told you time and again that Papa did not tell me."

"He must have," Lucian exclaimed in frustration.

"He never brought up the will again after he showed it to me and my uncle. I am certain of it."

It was inconceivable to Lucian that a man as precise with details as Ashcott could have left something so important as that undone.

Angel was eyeing him with a suddenly troubled expression, and he asked, "Did you remember something?"

"Was seeing Mr. Kennicott the business you told me you must attend to this morning?"

Lucian nodded.

Unhappiness clouded her face. "Why did you not tell me what it was when I asked?" Her voice was heavy with reproach. "Why did you not take me with you? You always shut me out, Lucian."

Stung by the reproach in her voice, he said, "I was not certain that Kennicott was Mr. K. If he was not, I did not want you to be disappointed. Besides, such business is better handled between men."

Her expression turned stormy. "Why is that? Is it not my inheritance?"

"That has nothing to do with it."

"Pardon me, but that has everything to do with it."

He was unused to being called to account like this. And it especially irked him that it was his wife, of all people—his wife whom he was trying to help and protect.

"Angel," he growled, "I promised you I would get Belle Haven back for you, and that is what I am trying to do."

"But I want to help you do it."

He gave her an incredulous look, then said sharply, "The only help you can give me is to remember where your father hid his will."

"I cannot remember what I was never told!"

She turned and swept angrily out of the library.

As Angel dressed for the Devonshire masked ball, she was still disturbed by Lucian's refusal to tell her why he was searching for Maude. She did not believe the excuse he had given her. Yet what other reason could he have? It made no sense to his wife that he should be looking for the woman.

She was just rising from her dressing table when Lucian came through the connecting door between their bedchambers carrying a stack of cards.

He handed them to her. "These are the invitations we have received. When you have time, look them over, and tell me which ones you wish to attend." He turned back to his bedchamber. "I will be ready to leave in five minutes."

Angel recognized this concession for the peace offering it was. It was not all that she wanted, but it was a start, her first small victory in her campaign to have him recognize her as a partner in their marriage and not a disobedient child. It was also the nearest thing to an apology from her proud, stubborn husband that she was likely to get. "Thank you, Lucian," she called after him softly.

After his gesture, Angel felt a little guilty when she took out his mother's pearl necklace and put it on. Before she left her chamber, she donned her black satin mask and her velvet surtout, which hid the pearls.

They went by Lucian's private barge on the Thames, departing from the steps behind their house. As they glided along the wide, moonlit river, Lucian regaled his wife with amusing anecdotes about various mishaps at court. Her husband could be wickedly charming when he set his mind to it, and he had clearly set his mind to it tonight.

When they reached their destination, Angel held her breath as the butler took her surtout from her, exposing the pearl necklace around her neck.

If her husband noticed it, he did not comment. As they strode toward the doors of the long gallery, Lord Nottingham, another member of the Council of Nine, pulled Lucian aside and said to Angel. "Pardon me, Lady Vayle, but I must talk to your husband privately."

Angel nodded. As she walked on, she heard her husband ask, "How did you know it was me behind this mask?"

"You and your wife are a distinctive pair, she being so petite and you, so large. Besides you are the only man in the room not wearing a wig. Wish I had the nerve to leave mine off. Itches like the very devil."

Angel was quickly joined by three masked admirers, who apparently had no more difficulty recognizing her than Nottingham had. She, however, had a more perplexing time identifying them. Only one of them was easily recognizable: Roger Peck, with his long, curly golden wig and classic profile that his black velvet mask could not conceal.

Angel suppressed a groan. Everywhere she had gone recently, he had appeared at her side and stuck there like a fly in honey.

When others were about, he was mostly silent, listening to her as she told amusing anecdotes or exchanged repartee with one or another wit. When he had her to himself, he plied her with flowery, insincere compliments that she hated. Lucian rarely complimented her, but when he did, she knew that he meant it.

Angel wished that Roger would leave her alone, but the more she hinted this to him, the more tenacious he seemed to become. She could not understand why he bothered with her when every other young woman seemed bent on capturing him.

Tonight followed the same pattern. When the other two men went off to greet arriving friends, Roger was quick to tell her, "You are looking especially enchanting tonight, you most beautiful of creatures. Your eyes are as brilliant as sapphires. Your smile outdazzles the sun."

He was not even original. He had expressed the same sentiments in identical words to her on at least four previous occasions.

"Oh fie, Roger, you tell all females that," she scoffed.

He looked hurt. "I mean it sincerely."

"No, you don't," Angel retorted, "and I would like you better if you did not insist upon plying me with such egregiously untrue compliments."

His eyes behind the mask were baffled. "You are the only woman I have ever met who did not love compliments."

She grinned at him. "And one of the few who does not vie for your attention."

He had the grace to color slightly. "But I like you better than any other woman I have ever met."

"More likely you like the novelty of a female who does not fall at your feet," she said tartly.

His flush deepened around the edges of his mask. "I admit I find you a challenge. But it is more than that. I love to listen to your stories, especially about your father and Belle Haven. I can tell how much you loved him."

"I did. I was devastated when he died."

"I would be the same were anything to happen to my father," Roger said with a depth of feeling she had never suspected in him. "Thank God, he is in robust health and will live for many more years."

"I thought that my father would, too," she recalled sadly. "Tell me about yours."

Roger did, painting a word picture of a loving father who had cared as much about his son as Angel's own father had about his children. She liked Roger, the son, much better than Roger, the rake, and she told him so.

As Lucian floated home with Angel on his barge that night, it was clear to him that Roger Peck with his rake's tongue and irresistible looks had singled Angel out as his next conquest. He had hovered by her all night.

And Angel was so naive that she probably had no idea that he was attempting to seduce her. Lucian must warn her away from Peck, and he said bluntly, "Angel, from now on, I must insist you avoid Roger Peck."

"Why?" she challenged, a defiant note in her voice.

Too late, Lucian remembered how unwise it was to order Angel not to do something.

"He means to seduce you."

Lucian felt Angel stiffen angrily on the seat beside him. The last thing he wanted now was another quarrel with her.

"I only want to protect you, little one," he said gently. "It is my responsibility as your husband to do so."

When they reached home, Lucian escorted her up the stairs to her bedchamber.

"You looked lovely tonight, little one," Lucian said. She was also, to his annoyance, wearing his mother's pearls in defiance of his wishes, but he refrained from commenting on them.

Her sudden smile made him forget his irritation about the pearls and all else except his swelling desire to make love to her.

It had become a ritual when they returned home from whatever entertainment the night had offered for him to take her up to her bedchamber and for her to ask him whether he would join her there. Lucian was worried that tonight would be different, that her anger at him might stop her from asking him.

When they reached her room, she turned to him with a provocative smile, "Will you join me, my lord?"

Relief surged through him at her invitation.

He smiled at her. "With pleasure."

As soon as he closed the door behind them, his mouth came down on hers in a long, passionate kiss.

She returned it without reservation. He delighted in her hot response, and it dissipated a tiny current of apprehension that had been plaguing him. He knew that Angel had been distressed and angry with him. But, thank God, she was not one of those spoiled women who sulked endlessly when they did not get their own way and withheld their favors in bed. No, he thought happily, Angel was not manipulative.

And he intended to show his appreciation for that by making this a night she would never forget.

He knelt before her, removing first one, then the other rose satin slipper. His hands slid provocatively up her legs to remove her garters, then her silk hose. Tossing them aside, he rose and took her face between his hands.

As his tongue explored her mouth, his hands stole down to undo the laces of her overgown.

He slipped if off, then removed her undergown and chemise. She was standing naked before him now except for his mother's pearls. His breath caught at the sight of her lovely body, slender and graceful. The pearls against her skin brought out its creamy luster and theirs.

"The pearls become you," he conceded.

"You will allow me to keep them?"

"Aye, if you want them," he murmured as his hands cupped her breasts. He bent his head and his mouth traced her smooth white neck.

"I do," she said on a soft sigh as his lips reached her breast. His hands roamed over her tenderly—teasing, stroking, seducing.

After awhile, he lifted his head and eased her gently down on the bed. "It is time, little one, for an advanced lesson in kissing."

He did not start with her lips, but with her shoulder. He rained kisses on her as his mouth moved down her body until he reached the core of her. He had never kissed her there before. Her hands buried in his thick jet hair, and she gasped and writhed beneath him. Then he felt her body spasm in pleasure.

"I want you," she moaned. "Please, I want you with me."

He gave her her wish, lifting himself up and taking her in one swift, smooth stroke. Then he took his time, delighting in bringing her again and again to the brink of rapture.

At last the storm broke once more, and wave after wave of ecstasy convulsed her. Lucian shuddered with the force of his own release.

They lay quietly, still united, in the aftermath.

"Oh, Lucian," Angel murmured, her voice still husky with passion, "I love you. I love you so much."

He went very still. He did not believe in such nonsense. Yet the effect her words had on him was stunning. The surge of glorious happiness that washed over him at hearing her profess her love for him caught him unawares, like a giant breaker thundering unexpectedly in from the sea and knocking him from his feet.

He hugged Angel close to him, wishing that he could tell her that he loved her, but he had promised her honesty, and he would not reciprocate her gift of love by telling her a lie. Instead he kissed her deeply. "Good night, little one."

He continued to hold her tightly to him, delighting in her warmth, the provocative curves of her body against his, and the memory of her words.

Angel lay quietly in Lucian's arms, listening to his breathing as it deepened into sleep. She had hoped so much that he would respond to her declaration of love with one of his own.

But he had not. She had felt his body stiffen at her words, and for a moment she feared he would throw them back at her, ridiculing her.

At least he had not done that, but she began to despair that she would ever be able to free his heart from the prison in which it was encased.

Trust was the key to doing so. Of that, she was certain. After his father had inexplicably rejected him, Lucian had never again dared trust anyone with his heart. Somehow she had to win his trust, but she was beginning to wonder if even that was possible. Only today, she had seen that he did not trust her enough to confide in her, to share his plans and schemes with her, to make her part of his life. He shut her out as he had shut everyone out since his father had rejected him.

Angel had suffered her mother's rejection, but that had been different. Even before her mother had run away, she had been no more than a vague shadow in her children's lives. One does not love a shadow, but Lucian's father had not been a shadow, and the boy had loved his father every bit as much as Angel had hers.

If her father had acted as Wrexham had, she did not think she could have borne it. Perhaps she, too, would have built barriers around her heart as Lucian had around his.

His mother had said it was not the boy's fault, and Angel believed that. She also suspected that Wrexham himself had come to realize it and longed for a reconciliation with his son. That was why he had sent her the pearls.

Even if Angel had somehow misread Wrexham's intent—

and she was certain she had not—it was crucial that Lucian learn the reason why his father had rejected him.

Her husband would be livid if she disobeyed him and went to see Wrexham.

Yet she had to do so. She had to discover the secret of why Wrexham had hated his son so. Until Lucian could understand the reason, he would never escape the shackles of the past, would never be able to trust enough to love again.

Chapter 25

Angel, her spine stiff with determination, marched up the steps to Lord Wrexham's house and banged the knocker loudly.

Lucian would be furious when he learned she had deliberately disobeyed him, but he was wrong to forbid her to see his father. Papa had insisted that a person of honor always did what he believed was right, no matter how much trouble it caused him.

And this visit to her father-in-law was certain to cause Angel enormous trouble with her husband.

But it was also the right thing to do. Of that, she was certain. She only hoped that she could eventually convince Lucian of that.

Angel prayed that this visit of hers would help bring about a reconciliation between the two men. She was convinced that was what Wrexham wanted when he sent her the pearls. She was equally convinced that it was what Lucian, deep in his heart, also wanted. But unfortunately, he seemed to have frozen his heart in such a thick layer of ice that he was numb to what it wanted.

An elderly butler opened the door.

"Please tell Lord Wrexham that his daughter-in-law, Lady Vayle, wishes to see him."

A joyous smile spread across the old man's wrinkled face. "At once, my lady, at once. Come with me, if you please."

He ushered her into the drawing room.

"My lord will be with you directly," the butler said eagerly, then added apologetically, "although it might be a few minutes because he has only just arisen." He sounded worried, as though he feared that Angel would refuse to wait.

"I am in no hurry," Angel assured the servant. "His lordship may take his time."

After the butler hurried off, she looked around the room. It was dominated by three large-as-life portraits. One was of a beautiful, fragile woman with a milk-and-roses complexion, soft blue-green eyes, and golden blond hair.

The second delineated a slender youth whose face was a little too round to be handsome. He had fair skin, pale blue eyes, and hair the same shade as the woman's.

The third portrait depicted a sturdy, handsome boy of perhaps ten with a devilish glint in his arresting silver eyes. His jet black hair and bronzed skin was in sharp contrast to the fairness of the other two images.

Lucian as a child, Angel thought.

She was still studying his portrait a few minutes later, when a short, thin man with a head that seemed oversized for his body rushed into the room. His deeply lined face was round, like that of the blond boy's in the portrait, and his eyes were the same pale blue. He had not taken the time to don his wig, and his closely clipped hair was white.

"I am so happy you waited, Lady Vayle. I am Wrexham."

Angel was so taken aback that she blurted, "You are Lucian's father?"

The friendly smile left his face, and he said coldly, "Most emphatically I am."

She felt herself blushing. "I am sorry. That was very rude of me, but you took me by surprise." Indeed, he had. She had noticed Wrexham watching her at more than one party since she had been in London, but she had not had the slightest suspicion that he was her husband's father. "You do not look at all like Lucian."

"No, he favors his mother's side of the family."

Angel involuntarily glanced at the portrait of the woman. She had thought it must be of Lucian's mother.

As if reading her thoughts, Wrexham said, "Aye, that is my late wife. Although Lucian does not favor her either, he is the image of her brother."

Wrexham's eyes, filled with love and loss, remained fixed on her portrait. "I think I miss her more every year."

"You must have loved her very much," Angel observed quietly.

"I adored her. She was a wonderful woman. Much better than I deserved. How sad that we rarely appreciate what we have until we lose it." Wrexham, his chin trembling, was staring with misty eyes at the portrait of Lucian as a boy. After a moment, he gestured toward the picture. "And that is Lucian when he was nine."

The pride and love on the old man's face as he looked at his younger son were so intense that it took Angel's breath away.

He did not hate Lucian!

Wrexham gave her a penetrating look. "Do you love my son?"

"Very much."

His face brightened. Not only had Wrexham not taken the time to put on his wig, but Angel noticed that his cravat was untied, and his shirt beneath his wine vest and coat was only half-buttoned, attesting to the haste with which he must have come to greet her.

"I fear that I have called on you too early," Angel said.

"No, no, not at all. It is I who have been abed too late. There seems little reason to get up these days." His voice had taken on a morose note, but it brightened as he said, "I assure you that I am delighted to receive you any time you wish to call."

"You are very kind. I have come to thank you for the beautiful pearls. I can see why they were your wife's favorite."

"When Lucian was very small, he loved to climb up on his mama's lap and play with them."

"What was Lucian like as a child?" Angel remembered her husband telling her how his father had always favored Fritz.

Wrexham smiled proudly. "He was quite something. Brightest child I ever saw. Beat me at chess when he was nine. And so curious. My God, the questions that boy used to ask. And he could ride and shoot better than anyone in the neighborhood. Why I remember . . ."

Angel listened quietly as Wrexham told her story after story about Lucian's exploits as a boy. As they talked, her puzzlement grew. They were the stories of a father bursting with pride over a much-loved son. Why, then, had he told Lucian he hated him?

Finally, Wrexham caught himself. "I must be boring you with this ancient history. I had hoped perhaps your husband would see fit to introduce you to me." The old man's disappointment was palpable. "But at least he has permitted you to come. For that I am grateful. It is a start."

He sounded so hopeful that Angel hated to disillusion him, but she would be doing him no favors by sparing him the truth.

"I am afraid my husband does not know that I am here," she said gently. "He forbade me to come, and he will be very angry with me when he learns of this visit."

The naked pain in her father-in-law's eyes wrenched at Angel's heart. He seemed to age ten years before her eyes.

"I see. He still hates me. I suppose I deserve it."

"He thinks that you hate him. He says that you always favored his older brother, Fritz."

Wrexham groaned. "I can see why it might have seemed that way to Lucian, but that was not the case. As a child, it was Lucian who was my favorite."

"But you told him that you hated him."

"God forgive me, I did. But that was later—when he was sixteen."

"What did he do to make you say that?"

"Nothing. The fault was all mine. None of it was Lucian's. He was blameless. I was a proud, stubborn man, and a fool." His voice broke. "Such an incredible fool. It is the one great wrong I have done in my life, and I want desperately to correct it, but he will not let me. I wrote him repeatedly, but the letters came back unopened. Since he returned from Holland, I have tried to see him, but I have been turned away."

"If you would tell me why you told Lucian what you did, perhaps—"

He shook his head. Tears were trickling down his lined cheeks now. "I cannot. The story is for no one's ears but Lucian's. If only he would come to me, I would tell him the reason I acted as I did, and I would beg his forgiveness on my knees."

Lord Wrexham was so wretched that Angel impulsively hugged him.

He returned her embrace. "Sweet girl," he murmured. "My son is lucky to have you."

If only his son felt the same way.

Wrexham wiped at his tears. "If Lucian would hear me, even if he cannot forgive me, at least he would know the reason I acted as I did. But I fear I shall go to my grave with him still refusing to see me."

Angel said sadly, "Lucian has built a wall around his heart that I am beginning to despair anyone can penetrate."

"Even you."

Angel nodded.

"You must find a way. And I pray that I can sneak through the breach after you."

Lucian returned home from a Council of Nine meeting, eager to see his wife. He smiled as he remembered how she had shyly told him at breakfast this morning that after examining the invitations they had received for tonight, she would prefer to remain at home with her husband.

Her husband had been delighted.

In truth, he could not remember being so happy in his life as he had been since he had married Angel.

Lucian handed Reeves his hat and gloves. "Where is my wife?"

"My lady has gone out."

Lucian frowned, part in disappointment, part in puzzlement. "So early. Where was she going."

"She did not confide in me," Reeves said.

That was odd, too. Usually Angel was so open about where she was going. He thought of Roger Peck's attentions to her the previous night, and unease prickled at Lucian. Then he remembered Angel's confession of love for him, and he relaxed.

When Angel arrived home twenty minutes later, he went into the hall to greet her. She looked wildly excited, yet oddly nervous.

His eyes narrowed suspiciously. "Where have you been, Angel?"

"Please, could we talk in the library?"

He led her into that room, his alarm growing. As soon as the door was shut, he asked again where she had been.

"To see your father."

He was stunned that after he had expressly prohibited her to see his father, she would have flagrantly disobeyed him like this.

"Oh, Lucian, he does not hate you, he loves you, and he wants to see you so desperately." Her words tumbled over themselves in her rush to get them out, as though she feared he would shut her off before she could finish. "He says that you were blameless and that you did nothing to deserve what he did to you, and he regrets it terribly."

"If he does, it is because I am now a powerful man, and he sees me being of some use to him."

"Do not impugn his motives! He cares because he loves you."

"Loves me! What a jest that is!" The excruciating pain of that day fourteen years ago when his father had told him he hated him engulfed Lucian like a poisonous fog rolling back in from the sea.

"If only you could have seen him, Lucian, seen how much he cares for you, and how much he grieves for the breach between you."

"The breach is of his making," her husband reminded her angrily.

"He readily admits that." Angel caught Lucian's large hands in her small ones. "At least listen to what he has to say, I beg of you. Before you dismiss him out of hand, at least go see him."

"I will never set foot in his house."

"Then I will invite him here."

No one had ever dared defy Lucian the way Angel did. It made his temper boil. His own wife, for God's sake! "You will not. I forbid it."

Angel's face was mutinous.

Lucian would not tolerate such insubordination. He was so angry he scarcely knew what he was saying. "If you invite him here, he shall be turned away at the door. And so help me God, I will banish you to Ardmore. And you will remain there until you learn to be a dutiful wife."

She paled at that threat, but she did not give up. "My duty is to do what is best for my husband, and that is what I am trying to do."

"You dare to tell me that you know what is best for me?"

"Please, Lucian, only listen to your father's reason for acting as he did."

"What was his reason?"

"He would not tell me. He said it is for your ears alone."

"He would not tell you because he knows full well that nothing can justify what he did to me." Lucian's voice was hoarse with the bitterness that had eaten at his soul all these years.

"At least hear what he has to say. That is all I ask of you. Are you not even curious to learn his reason?"

"No!" But that was a lie. Lucian wanted very much to know, but not if it meant crawling back to the man who had so cruelly rejected him. He would never give Wrexham another opportunity to inflict such searing pain on him. "I will not see him. I never want to see him again."

"But you do! If only you would look in your heart, you would see it *is* what you want."

His silver eyes were as cold as the ocean in winter. "You presume to tell me what I want?"

"You are your father's son," Angel said wearily.

"What do you mean by that?"

"You are so unbelievably stubborn. Your father said that he was a stubborn fool, but at least he has the grace to admit it."

He snapped at her, "Your graceless husband has had enough of this conversation."

Lucian stalked out of the library and out of the house.

He did not return the rest of the day. Angel, mindful

that before their quarrel they had agreed to spend tonight at home alone, dressed in a gown that she knew was one of Lucian's favorites, and waited for him to come home.

She twice set the hour for supper back, to the consternation of the chef, and in the end she ate it alone at 9:00 P.M. in the dining room, which seemed cold and empty without her husband's presence.

At 1:00 A.M. Angel gave up her lonely vigil and went to bed. She lay awake for a long time after that wondering where Lucian was. Finally she heard his unsteady tread in the hall. She held her breath as it approached her door. He did not pause as he passed it, but continued on to his own room.

It was the first night since his return from Ireland that he had not slept with her.

The next day he was cold and distant toward her. When he was forced to address her, it was with freezing politeness. He made it very clear that he had not forgiven her for having called on his father.

At dinner he rebuffed her efforts to converse. By the time the strained, silent meal ended, Angel's stomach was churning, but she resolutely brought up the subject that lay like a wall between them. She refused to be cowed because his future happiness—and hers—was at stake. Angel was convinced that unless he could understand why his father had rejected him and forgive him for it, he would never trust anyone, including her, with his love again.

"Please, Lucian, talk to your father. At least, find out why he did what he did."

He gave her a look that would have frozen fire. "You are not to broach that subject again—*ever.*"

"Don't you want to find out the truth?"

His jaw was rigid. "Not if it requires me to go crawling to Wrexham."

"You will not be doing that. He invited you to come. He will come here if you want. He has tried to see you and been turned away."

"I will not see him."

"You are impossible!" Angel cried in frustration.

Lucian shoved his chair back from the table and stood

up. "And you are a grave disappointment as a wife!" He threw his napkin down on the table and stalked out.

After that, Angel treated him as coldly as he did her. Two could play this game as well as one. She could not bow to him now. She must convince him to talk to his father. It was the only way that he could free himself from the past.

Rather than subject herself again to the stress and indigestion her last meal with Lucian had caused her, she avoided the dining room and had her meals brought to her room.

The escalating tension between them affected the entire household. Angel had won the servants' hearts, and they left no doubt whose side they took in this quarrel. Lucian's morning toast was burned, his other food undercooked, and his bathwater tepid. He grew so short-tempered that even David Inge remarked to Angel on it.

At night, the lord and lady of the house went their separate ways. Angel rarely saw him at the social affairs she attended. Roger Peck, however, was never far from her side. Since her set-down of him, he had not once paid her false compliments. Instead he talked to her about himself with a candor and openness that dissolved her earlier dislike of him. He had told her admiringly, "You are the only woman I have ever known that I can talk to honestly, without pretense."

If only her husband could do the same.

Lucian paced the floor of the drawing room, looking at the bracket clock every second minute. It was nearly 3:00 A.M., and Angel was still not home. He was as anxious and nervous as a father waiting up for a truant daughter.

He had seen her from afar earlier that night at the Duchess of Carlyle's. She had been in a quiet corner, deep in conversation with Roger Peck, who was always at her side.

Suddenly she burst out laughing at something Peck said. As her eyes sparkled up at her companion, Lucian had felt jealousy curling within him like a poisonous snake.

And what rankled him even more was how much she seemed to enjoy the damned rake's company.

Lucian looked again at the bracket clock. Where in the hell was Angel? Was Roger Peck the reason she was so late? The thought made him murderous.

She might not be the obedient, acquiescent wife he demanded but, God's oath, he *wanted* her. He was sick of the icy wall that had been between them for four damned days now.

True, he had started it. He had wanted her to know how angry and displeased he was at her for having gone to his father after he had expressly forbidden her to do so. He had meant to show her that he would not tolerate such insubordination in a wife.

Except she had turned his weapon back on him. He missed her: missed her bright face and beautiful smile across the dining table from him, missed her astute observations that made him laugh, missed her soft delectable body entwined with his in bed.

The servants had all sided with her in this quarrel. By now he felt like an unwelcome intruder in his own home.

When at last Lucian heard Angel arriving home a few minutes past three, he pulled his frayed nerves together and schooled his face in a bland mask.

Not for anything would he let her guess that he had been concerned nor that he had cared in the least where she had been.

He politely helped her off with her satin cloak and was presented with a splendidly arousing view of her breasts in the low cut blue gown he had objected to at the Marlboroughs' party. His control snapped. "Where the hell have you been?"

Her chin tilted stubbornly. "Would you care, my lord?"

"Aye, damn it, I would."

"Why?"

"You are my wife, and my responsibility. It is my duty to protect you. God's oath, you do not make it easy for me to do so."

"Perhaps you take your duty too seriously, my lord."

Was she mocking him? He cast her a sharp suspicious

look, but she had already turned away and was heading for the staircase. "If you will excuse me, my lord, I am very tired."

He fell into step beside her. It was the first time he had walked with her to her bedchamber since their quarrel over her visit to Wrexham. "You have not answered my question, Angel. Where were you?"

"At the Duke and Duchess of Carlyle's party with Selina. On our way home, the axle cracked on her coach. Do not look so alarmed, my lord. We were never in any danger. Lord Brompton insists armed grooms accompany her wherever she goes at night."

They had reached the door to Angel's room. He held his breath, hoping that she would issue her customary invitation to join him. He was aching to make love to her.

"Good night, my lord," she said as she opened her door.

He concealed his disappointment behind a hard glare. He would never let her know how much he wanted her. "My name is Lucian," he growled. "I want to hear you say it." He was behaving like an autocratic prick, but he could not help himself.

"Good night, my lord Lucian."

He had no choice but to continue down the hall. As he opened his own door, she called softly, "Lucian."

He turned toward her, hoping against hope that she was about to relent and issue a belated invitation to join her.

"Please, talk to your father." There was a pleading note in her voice. "You yearned for fourteen years to force him to admit that he misjudged you. Now he has done so, yet you refuse to have anything to do with him. At least listen to his reason for rejecting you. It is all I ask. If after hearing him you cannot forgive him, so be it."

With that she stepped into her chamber and closed the door.

Would she never give up? Lucian would be damned if he would call on his father. Much as he wanted to know what reason Wrexham could have had for what he had done to him, he would not go to his father. The old man thought that after all these years he had only to snap his fingers and his son whom he had so cruelly and cavalierly rejected would come running to him.

Lucian remembered all the times as a boy that he had tried to win his father's attention and approval and had been denied it.

He had driven himself mercilessly to be the best at everything he tried in the vain hope that his father would notice him. Lucian had been the finest swordsman, the most accurate shot, the most accomplished rider. He'd excelled at mathematics and natural philosophy, and had even mastered subjects like Greek and rhetoric that held no interest for him. All to impress his father. But it had been wasted effort. His father had ignored him. He had cared only for Fritz.

What the hell did Wrexham's reason for hating his younger son matter now anyhow. Nothing on earth could justify what his father had done to him.

But as Lucian lay in his lonely bed, aching for his wife in his arms, Angel's soft plea echoed in his mind. He wished he could fathom why it was so important to her.

His wife had grown increasingly precious to him. He had told himself—and told her—it was because he had given her his name, and she was his responsibility, but he at last conceded that he was fooling himself. She was far more dear to him than he had been willing to admit.

He would do damn near anything to be back in her bed and her good graces—except see his father.

Chapter 26

Two days later, the elderly butler answering Lord Wrexham's door inquired, "Whom shall I say is calling?"

"Lord Vayle," Lucian said curtly. He did not recognize the butler, but then he had never been familiar with the servants at his father's London house.

The butler's jaw dropped, then, recovering himself, he hastened to welcome Lucian into the house so effusively that it was the visitor's turn to be astonished. Despite what Angel had told Lucian, he had half expected to have his father's door slammed in his face.

As the retainer left Lucian in the drawing room, he assured him that Lord Wrexham would be with him momentarily.

The warmth of the butler's welcome notwithstanding, it still galled Lucian to come to his father's house like this. He had been determined never to do so, but it seemed to be the only way to win his wife back to his bed.

He wondered how long his father would keep him cooling his heels before he deigned to see him: fifteen minutes, a half hour. What glee Wrexham must be in now, knowing that he was keeping his son waiting downstairs.

As Lucian looked around the drawing room, he was astonished to see that his own childhood portrait was hanging there with his mother's and brother's. He remembered when it had been painted. It had been such torment for an energetic nine-year-old to sit for it. He had wanted to be outside riding his new pony.

Lucian, contemptuously certain that his father must have had the portrait hung after Angel's visit, lifted the heavy frame to check the condition of the wall behind it.

The brightness of the green flocked wallpaper told him that the painting had been hanging in this spot for years.

As he stepped away from it, Wrexham hurried into the room. It was the first time in fourteen years that Lucian had seen him. He was shocked by the changes that time had wrought in his father and by the sudden rush of emotion that suddenly assailed him.

Wrexham had not taken the time to don his wig, and his once thick, sandy brown hair was white and sparse. He was thinner, too, not nearly so robust, and perhaps even a little shorter than Lucian remembered him, scarcely coming up to his son's jaw. Pain had etched deep lines in his round face.

But now, at the sight of Lucian, he broke into a smile of such joy that the son was momentarily speechless. Wrexham would have embraced Lucian had he not stepped back with a frown that brought the older man up short. His smile dimmed.

"Please, be seated," Wrexham urged. He waited politely until Lucian sat down on a settee covered in green brocade, then he chose a carved oak chair opposite him, pulling it closer to his visitor.

There was a moment of awkward silence until Lucian said dryly, "The prodigal son returns."

"No, the worthy son returns to the prodigal father," Wrexham corrected in a broken voice. "The wrong I did you borders on the unforgivable, but I pray that you are a bigger man than I was and can find it in your heart to forgive me."

"I am not *that* big a man."

To Lucian's shock, tears glistened in the viscount's faded blue eyes. He had never seen his father cry before, and the sight brought a fierce pain to his own heart.

"I caused you enormous misery, my son, but know that I caused myself even greater agony for the wrong I did you."

My son. Lucian could not remember hearing his father call him that before. Fritz had always been "son," spoken with love and patience. Lucian had been "you," spoken with an edge of undisguised dislike.

Lucian could not keep the acid from his voice. "Why should disowning me have bothered you? After all, you had *'the best reason in the world for doing so'*, did you not?"

His father flinched at having his long-ago words sarcastically recalled to him. "I thought I did at the time, but I was wrong. Oh, God, how wrong I was!"

It was a cry of grief wrenched from a tormented soul, and Lucian was moved, despite himself, by the despair and self-loathing it revealed.

"You cannot know how bitterly I have regretted that day nor how often I have cursed myself for it. When I learned I was wrong, I wrote you time and again, begging your forgiveness. I offered you anything that was within my power to give you—a colonel's commission, an estate of your own, anything—to try to atone for what I had done, but the letters were all returned to me unopened. I continued to write you when you were in Holland, but I heard nothing."

Lucian had no intention of letting his father bribe his way back into his affections. "I burned those letters, unopened," he said coldly.

"I feared that," Wrexham said with a sigh.

"Furthermore, I had—and have—no interest in anything you can give me."

"I know that, too. You have done astonishing well for yourself, my son. I am very proud of you."

"I am very proud of you." An involuntary thrill coursed through Lucian. Those were the words that he had once desperately yearned to hear, that he had worked unstintingly to earn in his boyhood. Now, all these years later, he was hearing them when they no longer meant anything to him.

But if that were true, why was he so pleased by them. Lucian could feel a tug at the walls he had built around his heart. Then he remembered the agony of having his love rejected. This man before him had hurt him as no other person ever had. The memory strengthened his resolve against his father. "I have no interest in anything you could say to me—except what 'the best reason in the world' was."

Wrexham nodded. "I will tell you, but first I must clear up a misconception. Your wife tells me that you thought Fritz was always my favorite son. That was not true. You were my favorite."

Lucian did not for a moment believe him, and he observed dryly, "You had a peculiar way of showing it."

"I was trying not to show it at all! Fritz was slower, not nearly so quick or bright or talented as you were. He was never your match in anything. You were something else. So brave and smart. There was nothing you could not do well. I was so damned proud of you. When you were small, I could not help wishing that you had been my first-born. You were far more fit to inherit my title and responsibilities. I felt so guilty about feeling that way that I tried to make it up to Fritz by spending more time with him." Wrexham sighed wearily. "And your brother needed more help, so much more."

Lucian was dumbfounded by this explanation of his father's attention to Fritz. He thought of all his boyhood efforts to secure his father's approval, and his acute distress at failing. But he had not failed. The realization was bitter as bile to him. If only he had known.

But it was too late now. Too late by a score of years.

He said icily, "I am still waiting to hear 'the best reason in the world.' "

His father nodded. "You know that I adored your mother."

That had been clear to anyone who had ever seen them together. And her love for him had equaled his for her. "Aye," Lucian said impatiently, "but I fail to see what that has to do with me."

"Everything. You see I was excessively jealous of her."

Lucian frowned. "Are you saying you were jealous of her love for me?"

"No. Dear God, I am making a mull of this."

"You are," Lucian snapped. "She gave you no reason to be jealous of her. She would never have cuckolded you."

"You are right on both counts, my son, but when she

was young, I fear I had not so much faith in her. About a year before you were born, one of our neighbors, Geoffrey Ames, Lord Chelms's second son and as handsome and strapping a devil as there ever was, began lavishing his attention on your mother. She did not reciprocate his interest, but I was too jealous to discern that."

"I do not recall a neighbor named Ames."

"No, he emigrated to the American colonies seven months before you were born."

Lucian's face hardened. "I gather that timing bears on your story."

"Aye, I tried very hard to believe that your mother had been as faithful to me as she professed to be, but it was hard. It became harder as the son conceived during that period—my black-haired, silver-eyed son so unlike anyone else in a family of short, compact, blue-eyed blonds—grew older. Not only did you not resemble your mother or me or any of my relatives, but you were so much larger than anyone else in the family. My doubts grew apace with you."

"Do I look like Ames?" Lucian asked, his voice suddenly hoarse. He himself had often noted how different he looked from the rest of his family.

"Very much in coloring and build. Not in the face, although his eyes were gray. They were not, however, the unique silver shade of yours."

"So that is why you said I was unworthy. You did not believe I was your son." Despite his lack of resemblance to the rest of his family, nothing would ever make Lucian believe that his gentle, loving mother had been unfaithful to his father.

"God forgive me, that is what I thought. The suspicion was particularly devastating to me because you were so much brighter and more promising than Fritz, who I had no doubt was my own flesh and blood."

"Do you still doubt that I am?"

"No." Wrexham stared with wistful eyes at the portrait of his late wife. "Your mama swore to me repeatedly that you were my son, that she had never been unfaithful to me, and that you looked just like her black-sheep brother, the one who had been shipped off to India before I met her. But, God forgive me, I could not believe her."

His voice broke, and it was a moment before he could continue. "Every time I looked at your face that last year or two, I saw Ames in it and I saw myself the cuckold. I would have sent you away earlier, but your mama insisted that she would go, too. And she meant it. It was the only time in our marriage that she defied me. I loved her too much to lose her, and so I let you stay."

"At least until she died." At last, Lucian knew why his father had acted as he had, but it made him feel no better. He gave Wrexham an inquiring look. "Why do you believe my mother now when you would not before she died?"

His father's blue eyes, tears glistening in them, met his son's hard silver gaze. "Five years after she died and I sent you away, her brother returned from India. When I first saw him, I thought for a moment that it was you, prematurely aged. Your mama was right. You are the image of him in size, coloring, and face. Even the silver eyes." His voice faltered. "I was overjoyed to know the truth, and sick with horror and disgust for what I had done to you. I have prayed every day of my life since then for your forgiveness."

"It is my mother's forgiveness you should be praying for," Lucian snapped, standing up abruptly, ready to take his leave. He was outraged that his father could have suspected his gentle, faithful mother of cuckolding him. "She loved you so. How could you think she would ever be unfaithful to you?"

"Jealousy makes you blind to the truth that is so obvious to others," his father said sadly.

"Not that blind! No man could be that blind."

Wrexham looked as though he wanted to say something in his own defense, even opened his mouth, then shut it resolutely.

Lucian said bitterly, "Even if I could forgive you for

what you did to me, I cannot forgive you for thinking that of my mother. Good day, Lord Wrexham."

Angel had just left her bedchamber to go downstairs when her husband come home. To her surprise, she heard him ask Reeves, "Where is Lady Vayle?" She had thought her whereabouts of absolutely no interest to him.

"In her bedchamber."

Angel, hearing him bound up the stairs two at a time, stepped hastily back into her room. Lucian was at her door before she had time to close it. He stepped into her room and shut the door behind him.

He had dressed for wherever he had gone in one of his handsomest suits, a rich burgundy velvet trimmed with gold buttons and braid, that accentuated his dark good looks and the silver of his eyes.

Lucian acted as though nothing had been amiss between them the past week, giving her that devilish grin, which she found irresistible. He looked so achingly handsome that her body grew hot and moist in its yearning for his. She clenched her jaw against the temptation. Until he agreed to see his father, she could not weaken. She forced herself to ask coolly, "My lord?"

"You have won, my lady," he said quietly. "I have been to see Wrexham."

Surprised and overjoyed as Angel was to hear that, she was appalled that he would view the visit as a victory for her. The victory was his if the knowledge he had gained would free him to trust and love again.

"I hope it is you who have won, Lucian. Did you learn his reason for disowning you?"

"Aye."

"What was it?"

"Wrexham was right. It is for my ears alone."

Angel's heart dropped. "Why won't you tell me?" she cried in frustration. "Why must you always shut me out like this?"

He looked genuinely surprised. "I am not shutting you out, but the truth is he had no valid reason at all for disowning me." Lucian's face twisted in anger. "What he thought was so disgusting that I will not repeat it to anyone, even you."

"Will you forgive him?" Unless Lucian could do that, Angel feared that his heart would remain frozen.

"Never! He made his decision fourteen years ago that I was no longer his son, and I intend to live by it."

"But he is suffering, Lucian," she pleaded.

"I suffered, too, Angel. Have you any idea how painful it is to have the father whose love and approval you craved tell you, *for no valid reason,* that you are unworthy of being his son and he will have nothing more to do with you."

"I am sorry, Lucian." Angel instinctively reached out to him, wanting to offer him comfort. Her heart ached for both men. But unless one or the other of them would tell her the reason for father rejecting son, there was nothing more that she could do.

Lucian squeezed her hands tightly, then released them as his mouth came down on hers in a kiss that left her quite unable to think of anything else, including that his fingers were busily undoing the lacings of her gown.

It was not until he slid the fabric of her gown and chemise from her shoulders and they fell about her waist that she realized what he was about. She tried to break the kiss, but he would not let her. His hand, its fingers splayed behind her head, gently but firmly held her so that her mouth could not escape his. His tongue grew bolder in its exploration.

His hand captured the weight of her breast, and his thumb began caressing the nipple with a seductive slowness that sent ripples of desire arching through her.

His lips suddenly deserted hers and moved down her throat with nibbling kisses. His mouth replaced his thumb on her taut nipple, teasing it with his teeth and tongue in a way that made her moan. His hands fumbled at her waist, and then her clothes lay in a heap at her feet.

Lucian lifted his mouth from her breast. He looked at

her as though she were some delicious delicacy just served up for him. She was naked before him except for her pink slippers and pink silk hose fastened above her knees with satin garters. She felt herself blushing and growing rosy all over beneath his intense scrutiny.

"You are beautiful, little one, and I cannot wait to have you."

He swung her into his arms, lifting her out of the pool of her clothes, and carried her to the bed.

"But it is the middle of the day," she protested as he pulled back the covers and laid her on the crisp, white sheet.

"I would not care if it were high noon on Judgment Day; I have been too long without you."

He began shedding his own clothes with such urgency that a still-fastened button on his vest was torn off and rolled away across the floor.

He came down on the bed beside her, his mouth fastening on her breast as his hand moved lower to seek her moist hot depths, already aching for him.

"Good, you are ready for me," he whispered in satisfaction, "and I cannot wait for you." He lifted himself above her and they came together, moving in unison. She had missed him every bit as much as he professed to have missed her.

She opened her eyes and looked up at him. His silver eyes were closed, his face mirrored the strain of delaying his own pleasure until she could scale the heights of passion with him. It was enough to make her convulse around him. He groaned, stiffened, and his essence flowed into her.

"Do you love me?" he whispered with hoarse urgency in her ear. "Tell me."

She started to ask why it would matter to him when he did not believe in it, but sensing from his tone how desperately he needed this reassurance, she told him, "I love you, Lucian. I love you so very much."

He let out a long explosive breath, as though he had been holding it a long time, and relaxed against her.

Angel held her own breath, wondering whether he would reciprocate. But he did not. She was terribly disappointed but consoled herself with the knowledge that she must be making inroads into his heart.

He would not have gone to see his father if she were not.

Chapter 27

Lord Randolf Oldfield, another guest at the Duchess of Stratford's garden party, strolled up to Angel in the rose arbor. "Are you looking for your shadow, my lady?"

Angel, wishing to be alone for a few minutes, had chosen the arbor because it was deserted and it partially shielded her from the other guests while offering an excellent view of the door that led from Stratford House into the garden.

She was watching the door in the hope her husband would appear. He had gone off this morning, as he had the two before it, on some mysterious business. He had refused to tell her what it was—he was still shutting her out—but he had said he thought he would be finished in time today to join her at the duchess's party.

Angel had had such high hopes that if only she could get Lucian to meet with his father and learn the reason for his rejection, he might break free of the past and be able to give her his trust and affection.

But it had been a week since his visit to Wrexham and, although he wanted reassurances of her love for him, he did not reciprocate. Nor had he forgiven his father. He refused even to see him again.

Angel found herself trying to comfort Wrexham. Distraught as the older man was, he would not tell her the reason he had rejected Lucian either. How could she hope to bring the two men together when she did not know that?

She had begun to despair that she would ever be able to thaw her husband's frozen heart. Angel wondered gloomily whether after years of ruthlessly stifling his softer emotions, they were dead beyond resurrection. It was becoming increasingly hurtful to her that her candid confessions of love for him were not reciprocated by so much as a declaration of modest affection.

Angel dragged her attention away from the door and focused on rotund Lord Oldfield. She did not like the man. He was a meddling, mean-tongued gossip.

"Looking for my shadow, my lord? I do not understand."

"Roger Peck is not beside you," Oldfield said with an insinuating smile. "He is so attentive to you that we have taken to referring to him as the Angel's shadow." He gave a sour little chuckle. "Until now, it was always the ladies who were besotted by him, but you have turned the tables on him."

Angel had heard that Lord Oldfield's young wife had been one of those infatuated ladies. Knowing he would distort whatever comment she might make about Roger, she said coolly, "The only man I have any interest in is my husband."

"How boring."

She gave a little flutter of her silk fan. "Not when one's husband is Lord Vayle." Then she deliberately changed the subject. "It is a beautiful day for a garden party, is it not."

"Clouds would not dare to mar nor rain to fall upon the Duchess of Stratford's party," Oldfield said sarcastically. "She would not permit it."

To Angel's relief, he wandered away in search of less boring topics of gossip than herself, and she turned her attention back to the door in time to see Roger Peck there, scanning the garden.

She shrank back, hoping that he would not notice her, but apparently he already had, for he was threading his way through the crowd toward her.

Angel was surprised to see Kitty, a brilliant smile on her face, step into Roger's path, catching hold of his braid-trimmed sleeve and greeting him warmly.

He looked annoyed as he responded to her greeting. He pulled his sleeve from her grasp and within thirty seconds was edging away from her.

Kitty stared after him with a hurt, mortified expression.

Roger came up to Angel. Looking every bit as besotted as Lord Oldfield claimed he was, he kissed her hand, lingering too long over it. She hardly noticed him for her eyes were still on Kitty.

When Kitty saw whom Roger had been in such a hurry to reach, she glared at her childhood friend with such naked hatred that Angel shivered.

She escaped from Roger as quickly as she could and made her way into the house to use the retiring room set aside for female guests. It was empty when she went in, but within a minute the door opened. Angel, checking herself in the looking glass, saw Kitty come into the room.

Her angry, determined expression told Angel that her arrival was not accidental and that their meeting was likely to be unpleasant. Nevertheless, Angel greeted her warmly.

Her former friend did not respond but came up to stand beside her. The two regarded each other's reflection in the looking glass. Angel's expression was quizzical, Kitty's malevolent.

Kitty hissed, "So now that you are Lady Vayle, the men flock to you. Enjoy your brief moment of success while you can! You will not be Lady Vayle for long."

Angel stared at Kitty's reflection, full of malice and hate. "What?" she faltered.

Kitty's mouth twisted in scorn. "So Vayle has not told you? No, I can see why he would not want to do so until he obtains the annulment. He would want no trouble from you in the interim."

Angel's mouth was suddenly as dry as dust. "Annulment?"

"As soon as Vayle can find your maid Maude and wring the truth of how she tricked and drugged him into appearing to have slept with you, he will use her testimony to prove your marriage was based on fraud and to secure an annulment of it. He says Maude is the key to winning his freedom from you."

"You are making that up," Angel said flatly.

"I am not," Kitty cried vehemently, her angry gaze meeting Angel's squarely. "It is what Vayle told David

Inge, and David told me. I swear to you before God that it is the truth."

Angel knew Kitty well enough to be certain she would never dare give such an oath if she were lying. Nor would David, a man of impeccable integrity, tell Kitty such a thing unless Lucian had told him. And David was the one man in whom Lucian confided.

For a moment Angel was too stricken and horrified to speak. She had not for an instant believed the excuse Lucian had given her for why he wanted to find Maude, but Angel had not been able to fathom what his real reason could be. Now she knew. He wanted an annulment. If he intended to have their marriage set aside on grounds of fraud, as Kitty claimed, he would need the testimony of a witness to it.

Angel was staggered. For a moment she could not believe that was Lucian's intention, but it was the only reason she could think of that could explain his continued search for Maude.

How could any man make love to her with the aching tenderness and shattering passion that Lucian did while he was intending to abandon her? Then she remembered what he had said about a man wildly lusting for a woman's body without loving her.

With hemorrhaging heart, Angel recalled other words of Lucian's: *"If you get nothing else from this marriage, you will get Belle Haven."*

"If you get nothing else from this marriage . . ." The words reverberated in Angel's reeling mind. Lucian planned to have their marriage annulled and leave her with Belle Haven as her consolation and, perhaps, a sop to his conscience. She had told him once that her former home was what she most wanted. It had even been true then.

It no longer was.

Her husband was what she most wanted now.

She would love him to the end of her days, but he could not reciprocate. *"I cannot force myself to love you—that is beyond my control."*

He wanted her in bed "for the usual reason," but he had

made it very clear to her that it had nothing to do with love. And she knew now that was how many men felt. She was not nearly so naive as she had been when she had arrived in London, and she was well aware that the rakes thought nothing of bedding every woman they could coax beneath the covers.

Kitty said triumphantly, "Enjoy being Lady Vayle while you can. You will not be much longer. Then no one will have anything to do with you." She turned away from the looking glass and marched out of the room.

Angel felt as though her heart had been trampled. She could not face the gay throng in the garden. Nor would she be able to suppress her tears much longer. Her pride rebelled at having other women guests discover her crying in the retiring room.

Angel had noticed a small sitting room beyond the retiring room. She went into it, closed the door, and threw herself down on a settee covered in needlepoint.

She felt like such an incredible fool. All the while she had been trying so hard to win her husband's love, he had simply been biding his time until he could find Maude and be rid of her.

Well, Angel would try no more. She would play the fool no longer. Her tears came then in torrents and continued for some minutes before she could control them.

She was wiping them away when she heard the door to the sitting room open. Roger Peck rushed to her side, his handsome face a study in concern for her.

"What is it, my sweet Angel? When you did not come back to the garden, I was worried."

She should have known that her "shadow" would have kept an eye on her.

Roger dropped down on the sofa beside her and put his arms around her in an effort to offer her solace. "Tell me what has hurt you so," he pleaded.

"No," Angel said on a gulp. She hated for anyone to see her crying. "Please go away."

"No, let me help you," he begged.

At a less vulnerable moment, Angel would have briskly

rebuffed him, but now she let him continue to hold her, accepting the comfort he offered her.

But even as she did so, she knew that neither Roger nor any other man would ever replace Lucian in her heart. The thought of her marriage ending filled her with bleak despair. But she had too much pride to beg a man who did not want her to change his mind. Better to accept her rejection with fortitude and dignity.

Nor would she mortify herself by confronting Lucian with what Kitty had told her. She knew that she would not be able to do so without crying.

Roger pulled out his handkerchief and wiped away the tears that still stained her cheeks. He bent his head to kiss her, but she pulled away from him and jumped up.

He rose from the settee and would have put his arms around her again had she not stepped back in evasion.

"I cannot bear to see you so unhappy." Roger's voice rose on an emotional note. "I love you so much, Angel."

It was nice to know that someone did.

Lucian, unable to find his wife in the Duchess of Stratford's garden, caught sight of Roger Peck, whom people had started calling Angel's shadow, going into the house and went after him. Seeing Peck disappear through a door, Lucian went toward it, thinking his wife might be there.

As he reached it, he heard Peck declare, "I love you so much, Angel."

"Do not say that!" Angel said sharply. "I am married, and so long as I am, I shall be faithful to my husband."

"So long as I am." What the hell did she mean by that?

Lucian flung open the door. Fortunately for Peck's longevity, he was not touching Angel. They were standing, facing one another.

Lucian roared, "What the hell is going on."

Angel looked as though she wanted to burst into tears. Was that because Lucian was interrupting her tête-à-tête with Peck?

She said wearily, "Nothing is going on, absolutely nothing."

"I am relieved to hear, my dear, that you consider Peck's protestation of his love 'absolutely nothing.' "

Lucian took her arm, noting her red, swollen eyes. She might be determined to be a faithful wife, but she did not look a damned bit happy about it.

That rasped his already raw temper, and he said in a tone that prohibited argument, "I am taking you home."

She went with him, rather like an automaton.

When they were in Lucian's carriage, he said, "I have good news for you, Angel. I sued to have your father's old will set aside. The court ruled today in my favor and removed control of your inheritance, including Belle Haven, from Rupert Crowe. He has been ordered to vacate Belle Haven immediately, and we have been granted permission to go there to search for the missing will. We will leave immediately." That would frustrate Peck's attentions to his wife. Perhaps Lucian would leave her at Belle Haven to keep her away from her eager swain.

Angel's face brightened, and she asked eagerly, "You mean this very afternoon?"

"If you wish," he said, pleased that she did not seem in the least reluctant to leave London and Roger.

"Can we go on horseback?" she asked. "It will be quicker."

He frowned. "It would be a difficult ride for you."

"Oh fie, I shall enjoy it, especially if this lovely weather holds. Please, Lucian."

He gave in, as anxious to get her away from London and Roger Peck as she was to see Belle Haven.

"Lucian, why did you not tell me about the suit? Could you not even trust me enough to tell me what you were doing on my behalf."

It had nothing to do with trust. He had not told Angel about the suit because he feared that it would fail. "I did not want to build up your hopes, only to have them dashed if the court ruled against us." Surely she could understand that he was only trying to protect her.

"Is Belle Haven mine now?"

"Not yet." Lucian explained that while he had wrested control of her inheritance from Crowe, the court had ruled it could not be awarded to her until the missing will was found. Instead control would rest with a trustee appointed by the court.

Angel asked, "What if we do not find the will?"

He took her small hand in his. "Do not worry, little one, I swore to you that I would recover Belle Haven for you, and I will."

To his surprise, this pledge seemed to have the opposite effect from what he had intended. Instead of looking reassured, she suddenly appeared on the verge of tears again.

"Aye," she said, her voice cracking. "You promised me that if I got nothing else from this marriage, I would get Belle Haven."

"And so you will. I swear it." Her reaction to this nonplussed him. Why the devil did his promising her what she most wanted make her look so unhappy? Women, he thought in bewilderment, there was no understanding them.

"If your suit had failed, Lucian, what would you have done?"

"Tried another strategy. Never fear, I will get Belle Haven back for you."

She gave him an inexplicable look of distrust and betrayal. "Have you found Maude yet?"

Lucian was startled by Angel's sudden change of topic, but he said, "No, but I will." He was determined the Crowes would hang for Ashcott's murder.

"Why do you want to find her?"

"I told you why." Anxious to forestall more questions he did not want to answer, he said curtly, "Stop bedeviling me about it."

Angel, a suspicious sheen to her eyes, turned her face away from him and stared silently through the chariot window.

Lucian studied his wife's profile. Her chin was trembling, and he realized that she was fighting back tears. Never had Lucian seen her so distressed and dispirited.

Bloody hell, was it because she was falling in love with Peck? The thought made Lucian's blood run cold. Much as he might mock love, he suddenly realized how desperately he wanted Angel's.

Chapter 28

Angel's depressed spirits lifted at the sight of Belle Haven. As she and Lucian rode up the gravel drive, she examined the familiar grounds and facade of the mansion with loving eyes.

When they reached the front portico, she was so eager to see the interior of her home (she still thought of it as that even though it no longer was) that she did not wait for her husband to help her dismount. She jumped down and rushed up the steps.

In her impatience, she tried to fling open the great oak door. But it was locked, and she was forced to bang the knocker.

Lucian came up behind her and put his hands on her arms. His touch, as it always did, sent a frisson through her that died painfully at the thought of the annulment he planned to get.

"Patience, little one," he whispered, his warm breath an erotic breeze against her ear. She longed to turn into his embrace and seek the comforting enclosure of his arms, but she could not when she knew that he would soon abandon her. The thought that then she would never again enjoy his touch or his company cast a black shroud over her happiness at being back at Belle Haven.

Belle Haven's butler, Jepson, always insisted upon answering the door himself, and Angel was surprised to see a young footman performing the task. She was even more disconcerted when, at the sight of her, he began to weep and tried to block the door to her entrance.

"Oh, milady," he said dolefully, "you cannot come in."

Lucian said sharply, "The court has ruled that Lady

Vayle has every right to enter and that the Crowes have no authority here, so you will no longer heed their orders. You will step aside and allow us to enter."

Looking miserable, the footman did as Lucian bade, mumbling, " 'Tis not their orders, but . . ." He broke off, so choked up he could not continue.

"But what?" Angel asked as she and her husband stepped inside the entry hall.

Before the footman could answer, she gasped in shock as she saw that the imposing walnut chest in the entry had been attacked by someone who had been intent on reducing it to kindling. She rushed over to the wreckage.

"What happened to it?" she cried.

Tears welled up again in the footman's eyes. "I fear, milady, that is only a small part of the damage the Crowes have done. His gaze darted unhappily toward her father's library.

Thoroughly alarmed, Angel ran into it, and a low moan escaped her lips. The library was devastated. The rich walnut paneling had been ripped from the walls and holes punched in them.

All the books, including those rare volumes that had been among her father's most prized possessions, had been dumped from the shelves. They lay scattered about the floor like driftwood after a storm.

More ugly holes had been gouged behind where the books had once resided.

But most shocking of all was her father's desk. That massive piece had been destroyed by someone who appeared to have taken an ax to it in a frenzy.

Angel had never seen such wanton destruction. Not even Ardmore had suffered as much at the soldiers' hands.

"What happened?" she asked in a choked voice, unable to stop the tears from trickling down her cheeks.

Lucian sighed. "Is it not obvious?"

The footman said, "The Crowes tore the house apart looking for something."

"Did they find it?" Lucian inquired tersely.

"I do not know, milord."

Angel stifled a groan. Were she and Lucian too late? Had the Crowes found the will?

"They acted like madmen," the footman related. "They attacked the walls and the furniture with axes and picks. The library and his late lordship's apartment suffered the worst damage, although the rest of the house did not escape. When Jepson tried to prevent them from destroying his lordship's desk, they broke his arm."

Angel gasped in shock. Jepson was one of her favorite servants at Belle Haven. "Is that why he did not answer the door?"

"Aye, his arm is giving him considerable pain this morning."

Lucian said grimly, "We had better go up to your father's rooms and see the worst."

"Oh, milady, I am so sorry," the footman burst out, "but there was nothing we could do to stop them."

"No," Angel agreed, through her tears.

Lucian took his wife's arm, dismissed the footman with a nod, and led Angel up the narrow staircase that Ashcott had built to connect his library to his bedchamber.

When she beheld the damage in her father's room, she thought she would be sick. The destruction seemed total. The wardrobes, chest of drawers, and the massive tester bed had been chopped into pieces. Even the bed's posts had not escaped the ax. The crimson brocade hangings and coverlet were torn to shreds.

The late earl's clothes had been tossed on the floor after the linings and pockets had been ripped from them.

Angel picked up her father's favorite coat, a blue velvet, that had suffered this fate.

"Why even his clothes?" she asked brokenly.

"They obviously thought he might have sewn the will into the lining of one of his garments or in the bed curtains," Lucian said. "Or hidden it in a secret compartment in the furniture."

He picked up a carved oak cylinder that had once been part of a bed post. "It does not appear they discovered such a compartment in the posts."

"Do you think they found Papa's will?"

Lucian looked grim. "If they did not, little one, then I would say your father could not have hidden it at Belle Haven. The Crowes do not appear to have overlooked any possible hiding place."

"But he had to have hidden it here!"

Which meant that the Crowes must have found it.

Angel's frail hope of recovering the estate crumbled. Belle Haven would never be hers, and when Lucian found Maude and obtained his annulment, he, too, would vanish from her life. She would soon be all alone without a home, without a husband. The two things she had most loved were lost to her forever.

She could not help herself. She began to cry.

When her husband tried to take her into his arms, she pushed him away. He was no comfort to her when she knew that he would soon abandon her. "Leave . . . me . . . alone," she gulped between sobs.

He drew back as though she had stung him. She moved away, tripped over a pile of ruined clothing, and sank to the floor, burying her head in the fabric.

Lucian watched his weeping wife. He wanted to comfort her, but she had pushed him away, and he did not know what to do to help her. Not since the day his father had disowned him had he felt as miserable and helpless and inadequate as he did at this moment.

His wife was slipping away from him. He had known it since last night, when he had tried to make love to her in the inn where they had stopped for the night. She had not rebuffed him but for the first time in their marriage she had not responded to him with that sweet, hot passion he loved. Its absence had deflated his own ardor—along with a crucial part of his anatomy—and he had turned away, pretending to fall asleep.

He looked at her now, thinking how much he wanted her. More than he had ever wanted anything in his life. Even more than he had once wanted his father's admission that he had misjudged his younger son.

And now Lucian was losing her to a man who professed to love her. At first, Lucian had scoffed at the idea that

Roger Peck could have any affection for Angel, but he was less certain now. He had seen the way Roger looked at his wife yesterday.

The memory sent white-hot jealousy streaking through Lucian. Adding to his pain was the knowledge that he was not the kind of husband she wanted. She wanted a man who loved her and who, like Roger, would tell her so over and over. She wanted a man who regarded his wife as his partner in life.

And Angel deserved that. She was wise beyond her years. Lucian was coming grudgingly to respect her ideas and advice. She had been right to insist that he talk to his father, for it had given him a measure of peace. Even though Lucian could not forgive Wrexham, he was no longer buffeted by the secret fear that some unspeakable flaw in himself, which he had never detected, was to blame for his father's rejecting him.

He looked down helplessly at his weeping wife, longing to console her, but she had made it clear she did not want solace from him. She had pushed him away, refused to let him help her when he wanted so desperately to do so.

She had shut him out.

Just as she had accused him of doing to her.

So this was what it felt like!

He didn't like it one damned bit.

Lucian's mouth tightened in determination. Nothing and no one would take his wife away from him. He could not imagine his life without her. Who else would tell him when he was wrong, challenge him to duels, and make such sweet, wild passionate love to him? He swooped down on Angel, picked her up from the pile of ruined clothing, and placed her on her feet.

Before she could push him away, he wrapped his arms around her and held her tightly to him. His hands stroked her hair and face comfortingly, and he murmured soft, consoling words in her ear. Slowly, she relaxed against him, and her sobs subsided.

When her storm had spent itself, he told her. "It'll be all right, little one. The Crowes may have made a shambles here, but any woman who can perform the miracle you did at Ardmore will soon have Belle Haven looking good as new. You do not have to go back to London with me."

Although he hated the thought of being separated from her, it would keep Peck away from her, and Lucian would contrive to spend as much time as he could at Belle Haven with her. King William was expected to return soon from Ireland. Once Lucian's duties with the Council of Nine ended, he would not leave Angel's side.

He told her gently, "You may stay here at Belle Haven for as long as you want, to see the damage repaired."

Angel stiffened. She raised her tear-flooded eyes to meet his gaze, and he saw anger in them. "I am not crying because of the damage the Crowes did."

Baffled, Lucian asked, "Then why?"

"For one thing, I know the Crowes must have found and destroyed Papa's will, and Belle Haven is lost to me."

Somehow, even if the Crowes had destroyed her father's will, Lucian would restore this house she loved so much to her permanently. He did not know how, but he would find a way. It was what she wanted and, by God, she would have it. He would not rest until he did.

He tilted Angel's face up toward his and said reproachfully, "Have you no faith in your husband, little one. I promised you I would get Belle Haven back for you, and I will. You will live here again, and you will be very happy."

Aye, she would. Lucian intended to devote himself to making her ecstatically happy here and everywhere else that they lived.

She flinched as though he had struck her. For a moment, he saw heartrending pain in her brilliant blue eyes. Then they blazed with anger.

She jerked away from him, demanding in a seething voice, "Is that a sop to your conscience to promise me that?"

He was so dumbfounded by her reaction he could not speak.

"You intend to recover Belle Haven as a consolation to me for ending our marriage and banishing me from your life!"

Lucian stared at her in shock. God's oath, she was clearly hysterical. She made no sense.

Angel glared at him. "So you think I will be very happy living here alone?"

Alone? "What the hell are you talking about?" he roared.

"I am talking about your determination to have our marriage annulled."

Lucian could scarcely credit what he was hearing. It was the last thing on earth he wanted. He would never give her up. The mere thought of losing her filled him with despair. Angel had become more precious to him than life itself.

"Bloody hell, I have no such intention."

"Do not lie to me, Lucian. I know that is the real reason you are looking for Maude."

He gaped at her. "Whatever gave you that ridiculous notion?"

"You told David Inge that once you could find Maude and prove that you had been tricked into our marriage, you would have it annulled."

Lucian scowled. "David did not tell you that, did he?"

"No, he told Kitty, and she told me."

"When?" he asked tersely.

"Yesterday, at the garden party."

With dawning horror, Lucian realized the reason for Angel's suddenly altered behavior toward him. He tried to take her in his arms, but she pushed him away.

"Angel, I swear to you before God that I will never have our marriage annulled."

She did not look convinced. "But you told David. Do you deny that?"

"No, I told him that less than an hour after that scene in my bedroom at Fernhill. I was in a fury because I thought you had willingly participated in the Crowes' plot, but once I learned the truth, I knew that I would never seek an annulment."

"I do not believe you!"

He searched for a way to convince her. "I also told David that I would dump you at Ardmore and never set eyes on you again until the marriage was annulled. I did not do that, did I?"

"No," she admitted.

"And I will never, upon my oath, seek an annulment either."

"Then why are you still looking for Maude?" she asked plaintively. "I do not, cannot believe the reason you gave me."

"I think that in addition to what the Crowes did to us, they are guilty of very serious crimes," Lucian said carefully. "I want to see them punished for them. Maude's testimony against them will help convict them."

Angel looked dubious. "Do you think that she would testify?"

"She was deeply involved in the schemes, and she can be persuaded to testify to save her own skin."

"What serious crimes has Rupert committed?"

"Among others, extortion and even piracy." Lucian did not mention murder.

"Piracy?" she echoed.

"Aye, you must have heard of the notorious One-eyed Jake. Crowe financed him."

Eager to cut short this conversation, Lucian's mouth descended on his wife's. This time when he pulled her into his arms, she did not resist him.

"Angel, my darling," he whispered, holding her hard against him, his mouth so close to hers that his breath was warm against her lips, "You are my wife and you will remain my wife until death do us part. I will never let you go."

"Why not?" Hope and skepticism warring in her voice.

His answer came instantly, without conscious thought. "Because I love you more than I can ever tell you."

Even he was shocked by what he had said.

But after the unbidden words had left his mouth, he realized they were the truth. His sweet, passionate wife had melted his frozen heart and claimed it as her own.

Angel tilted her head back to look at his face. He saw that her eyes, filled with happiness, were as brilliant as blue diamonds.

He swept her up into his powerful arms and carried her out of the ruined bedchamber and down the hall until he found a room that had escaped damage. He carried her in, kicking the door shut with his foot, and laid her upon a bed with yellow brocade coverlet and curtains.

It did not take long for Angel to grasp that Lucian was trying to prove to her just how much he did love her. His mouth bathed her face with soft, tantalizing kisses while his hands gently opened her clothing so that he could caress her body first with his hands, then with his lips. He did so slowly, with infinite care, as though she were a rare and precious work of art to be treasured.

Lucian, his voice husky with passion, whispered to her that she was beautiful and sweet and enticing. The hot appreciation in his silver eyes told her that he meant it.

He kissed and stroked, nuzzled and caressed her until her body cried out to be joined with his, but still he held himself back, prolonging his sweet, sensual torture until she was begging him to take her.

As he did, he whispered over and over, "I love you. I love you." It was as though once he had said it, he could not stop.

She thrilled at hearing at last the words she had so longed for.

Then his mouth closed over hers, and his tongue moved slowly at first, then in quickening rhythm with his body as they scaled the heights of passion together until they reached a peak so glorious and shattering that it left them awed and weak and infinitely contented.

Angel hugged him to her, unwilling to surrender him.

"I love you," he whispered again.

Later, surveying the room, he asked, "Was this your bedchamber?"

"Aye. How did you guess?"

"You told me once that it was yellow. If I paint my bedchamber in London yellow, would you share it with me?"

"So you have decided you no longer wish us to have separate rooms?"

"I never wanted anything of the sort," he protested indignantly. "I neglected to tell Mrs. McNally to put you with me. Then you seemed so happy with your yellow room that I had not the heart to insist you give it up to share mine."

Angel laughed. "And I pretended to love it so you would not know how hurt I was that you had me put in a separate room. Although I confess I began to wonder why you had bothered when you spent every night in my bed."

He groaned. "You will move into mine as soon as we return to London. I love you too much to be separated from you even by a door."

Smiling, Angel ran her hands caressingly over the hard, powerful muscles of his shoulders and back. "Was it so hard to admit to yourself that you loved me?"

"Harder than you'll ever know," he said ruefully, lifting his head a little so that he could gaze into her eyes. "I swore after my father disowned me that I would never let anyone hurt me again as he had, but you slipped beneath my defenses and stole my heart away before I realized it was gone. You say I do not trust you, but that is not true. I do trust you. That is one of many reasons why I love you."

She felt him swallow hard, and his eyes, liquid silver rimmed with a thick sweep of jet black lashes, beseeched her. "Do not, whatever you do, little love, betray my trust in you." The poignant vulnerability in his voice clawed at her heart. "I do not think I could bear it if you did."

Angel ran her finger lovingly over his lips. "I swear that I never will."

Chapter 29

The crush of people in the gallery of Lord and Lady Kingsley's London mansion had separated Angel from Lucian. The night was hot and the packed room even hotter. The heat had sapped Angel's energy, leaving her tired and thirsty, and she wished that she could find Lucian so that they could go home.

She smiled to herself as she thought of what they would do when they reached home. In the week since Lucian had finally admitted his love for her, he had seemed intent on proving it to her in every way he could.

Angel's smile grew dreamy. Their visit to Belle Haven, which had started out so unhappily, had turned into one of the happiest interludes of her life. Even the terrible damage the Crowes had inflicted on it and the knowledge that they must have found and destroyed her father's will could not dim her joy at Lucian's admission that he wanted her, loved her, and would keep her beside him always.

When, after four days at Belle Haven, he could postpone his return to London no longer, they had come back together. Instead of leaving her at Belle Haven as he had suggested, he confessed that he hated being separated from her. They had spent their first two nights back in London at home, wanting no other company but each other. Tonight, however, they were committed to attend the Kingsley party.

"You look radiant," Lord Wrexham complimented her. The pride in his pale blue eyes as he regarded her left no doubt that he was sincere. "Your trip to the country surely agreed with you."

Angel smiled at her father-in-law. She still had not been able to persuade Lucian to forgive his father and reconcile with him, and she felt very badly for Wrexham, knowing how desperately he wanted that.

Smiling at her, he said, "You enhance the pearls, my dear."

She was glad that she was wearing his late wife's necklace. He took such pleasure in seeing it on her.

"Your gown is lovely, too," he said with an appreciative smile for her midnight blue satin overdress, looped up at the sides and trained at the back, over an azure blue lustring undergown, which was trimmed with rows of Mechlin lace. "A Madame de la Roche creation?"

"Aye," Angel said, "delivered only today."

A crony of Wrexham's came up to them, and as the two men talked, she slipped away to resume her search for Lucian.

A stocky footman carrying a tray of glasses filled with punch came up to her. He was not much taller than Angel, and his face was marred by an ugly scar across his chin beneath his mouth. He plucked a glass from the center of the tray and offered it to her.

The room was so hot and she was so thirsty that she gratefully took the glass from him and drank the fruity liquid down quickly. Although the drink was very sweet, it left an odd, bitter aftertaste in her mouth.

Roger Peck, in a turquoise brocade coat with huge cuffs over an embroidered white satin waistcoat, appeared in the door, his eyes searching the room.

Angel knew that he was looking for her.

Before she and Lucian had returned to London from Belle Haven, he had told her that he wanted her to cut Peck whenever she saw him, but Angel had refused.

"Not because I care for him," she had explained, "but because he does not deserve such treatment and, more importantly, because it means you still do not trust me enough to believe that I will always be faithful to you. I find that very hurtful, Lucian. If you truly trust me as you say, you will not insist I cut him."

Her husband had reluctantly bowed to her argument.

But now Angel found herself wanting to avoid Roger. Everything was going so well between her and her husband that she did not want to do anything that might upset the happy, still delicate balance.

She knew how difficult it had been for Lucian to trust her with his love. She knew, too, that his trust was still tenuous and would have to be nurtured carefully to robust maturity.

Angel stepped behind a large man as broad as he was tall to conceal herself from Roger's questing eyes.

Suddenly she felt so woozy and light-headed that she swayed and had to catch the back of a chair with her hand to steady herself.

A strange lethargy seized her, and she wanted nothing so much as to sit—or better yet lie down—for a few minutes. Unfortunately, she could see no empty chairs in the gallery, but she remembered a small sitting room adjacent to it.

Angel made her way along the edge of the ballroom to the hall. Only a few steps from it, she suddenly felt as though a brake had been applied to the train of her gown. An instant later, she felt—and heard—the satin rip.

Looking around, Angel saw that not only the skirt of her overdress but the undergown, too, had been torn away from the bodice at the waist, leaving a gaping hole that exposed her under garments. Reaching behind her, she grabbed the torn skirt and clutched it to her waist.

"Oh, I am so sorry," a high-pitched female voice exclaimed.

A statuesque blonde in an elaborate gown of pearl gray satin was wringing her hands in dismay.

"I cannot conceive how I could have been so clumsy," she apologized. "You must let me help you repair the damage I have done."

Angel could not recall ever seeing the woman before, and she wondered who she was.

As if reading her mind, the stranger said, "I am Lady Kingsley's sister, Irene. Here, come with me."

She took Angel's arm and led her to a handsomely furnished bedroom at the back of the house.

Once there, she closed the door and told Angel, "Quickly, let me help you out of your torn gown, and I will have Jane, my sister's maid, repair it for you. She is an excellent sempstress, and she will have it as good as new in ten or fifteen minutes."

The wit-dulling lethargy that had gripped Angel was even more pronounced now, and she was glad to let Lady Kingsley's sister deal with the torn gown. Obediently, she allowed Irene to remove her overdress and then the undergown.

"Oh dear, I am afraid that I have torn the ruffle on your underpetticoat, too."

As Irene spoke, she hurriedly unfastened the tapes holding that garment and let it fall about Angel's feet, leaving her clad only in her thin lawn shift. "I shall have Jane mend that, too, so that it will not hang down below your skirt. She is so quick with the needle that it will only take her a minute."

As Angel stepped out of the underpetticoat, she hid a yawn behind her hand, and Irene said, "Poor child, you look exhausted."

Before Angel could stop the kindly woman, she pulled back the covers of the bed and said, "Here, lie down and take a wee nap while your gown is being repaired. It will do you good."

The bed looked so enticing to Angel that she could not resist doing as Lady Kingsley's sister suggested.

"I will be gone only a few minutes," Irene said as she left the room carrying Angel's torn garments, and leaving her with only the shift that she was wearing.

Angel's head seemed too heavy to hold up any longer. She sank back upon the pillow and dozed off.

She came awake to a man's voice assuring her in a low, seductive tone, "My darling Angel, you have made me the happiest man on earth."

It was not her husband's voice.

Alarmed, Angel opened her eyes to the sight of Roger Peck. He had already shed his turquoise brocade coat, white satin waistcoat, and lace cravat and was now divesting himself of his white lawn shirt, revealing his bare chest beneath.

"Dear God," she cried in shock, "what are you doing here?"

His brow knit in puzzlement, "Obeying your command, my beautiful Angel. Did you think I would not come after your note to me?"

"What note?" she demanded. Shock and fear proved a powerful antidote to the strange lethargy and cobwebs that clouded her mind. She sat bolt upright in bed.

The situation was too similar to the one with Lucian at Fernhill to believe it could be a coincidence. Angel had been too naive then to realize what was happening, but now she knew how Lucian must have felt when he had awakened and known instantly what had been done to him.

Angel should have guessed the Crowes would not accept the loss of Belle Haven and the rest of her inheritance without seeking revenge.

"What note?" she demanded again, but Peck did not answer her. His gaze was fixed hungrily on her breasts. Looking down, she saw that the thin, nearly transparent lawn of her shift was molded to them. Blushing with embarrassment, Angel hastily pulled the sheet up about her.

Certain that she had again fallen into a cruel trap, Angel cried in despair, "I sent you no note!"

He gave her an indulgent smile. "So you are losing your courage, are you? It is only to be expected, but never fear, my love, I shall give you such bliss that you will never forget this night."

"No!" Angel cried, frantic now. She was certain that Lucian would burst through the door at any moment. "Can you not see? This is a trap. Quick, put on your clothes and get out of here before my husband finds us."

She might as well have been speaking to a deaf man for all the heed Roger paid her warning.

"I do not fear Vayle." He settled on the bed beside her, he said soothingly, "Pray do not be frightened, darling Angel." He seized her in his arms and began showering kisses on her face. "I shall make you the happiest woman alive."

As if he could after Lucian, she thought scornfully, furious at his unwarranted presumption.

Angel jerked her face about trying to avoid Roger's mouth. Forgetting the sheet she had been holding about her, she struggled with all her strength against his embrace, but he was too strong for her to escape him.

She cried in outrage and desperation. "Let go of me, you fool! Can you not see I do not want you!"

The door flew open with such force it bounced against wall and Lucian stormed into the room.

When he saw his wife and Roger on the bed, his expression turned murderous. He shouted, "You bastard, release my wife!"

At the sight of Lucian's face, Peck did so with celerity, jumping away from her as though he had suddenly discovered she was a venomous snake. His earlier assurance to Angel that he did not fear her husband was obviously untrue.

Lucian's furious gaze swept across Roger's shirtless torso, then suddenly froze as it reached Angel.

Looking down, she saw to her horror that during her struggle with Roger the left side of her shift had been pulled down, exposing a rosy-tipped breast.

She would never forget as long as she lived the terrible, searing look that her husband gave her. It was fury and loss and betrayal; it was dying trust and dawning hatred.

"You seem to have misplaced your clothes, madam." His voice was as frigid as the Arctic.

"Lady Kingsley's sister took them. She . . ."

"You damned liar," Lucian exploded. "Lady Kingsley has no sister!"

He spun around toward the door.

"No, Lucian, it is not what you think," Angel cried. She scrambled from the bed and grabbed at his arm, but he shook her off as though she were a reprehensible insect clinging to him.

"Don't touch me again, madam, or I swear I will not be responsible for the consequences."

"Lucian, you must listen to me. It was another trap. I am certain the Crowes are behind it."

He gave her a look of such contemptuous disbelief that the blood seemed to freeze in her veins.

Then he turned to Peck.

"Do you mean to call me out?" Peck stammered.

"Why? To defend the honor of a slut who has none?" he snarled. "You are welcome to her!"

He stormed from the room. Angel would have followed him had she had any clothes.

But she did not. She snatched up the velvet cover from the bed and wrapped it around her. She thought wildly of trying to follow Lucian draped in it, but instantly realized she would only make the situation—and the certain scandal—even worse.

If that were possible.

In helpless frustration, she wheeled on Peck, who was still sitting dazed on the bed. "How could you do this to me?"

"But you invited me to come to you," Peck stammered. He grabbed for his discarded coat and pulled a note from its pocket. "You sent me this."

Angel looked at the neat, carefully formed handwriting of the note signed with her name and protested, "This is nothing like my handwriting! I told you it was a trap, but you would not listen."

An ashen Peck began scrambling into his clothes.

Lord Wrexham strode through the door that Lucian had left open. His eyes widened in shock as he saw Angel wrapped in the velvet coverlet and Peck pulling on his shirt. "What the blazes?" he exclaimed.

Then his eyes narrowed in disillusionment and disgust, and he began backing out of the room.

"Please, Lord Wrexham, do not leave," Angel begged, her voice cracking. "I swear to you this is not what it looks like."

Her father-in-law hesitated, clearly skeptical of her claim.

"Please, you must believe me," Angel pleaded.

For an instant, she had the feeling that he was seeing another scene from the past. Then, after a long moment, he reached for the door and, stepping back into the room, closed it carefully behind him. "Tell me what happened."

Angel related the incident with Lady Kingsley's sister—"except," she noted, "Lucian says Lady Kingsley does not have a sister."

"Nay, she does not," Wrexham confirmed. "Was this fraudulent sister the tall blond woman I saw leading you to this room."

"Aye! You saw her?"

He nodded. "I wondered at the time who she could be. I thought I recognized everyone in society but I have never seen her before. Later, when I saw my son rush out of this room and out of the house looking as though he had just been tortured with rack and thumbscrews, I thought I ought to investigate."

"How could Lucian think that I would betray him with Roger when I swore to him I would always be faithful to him?"

Her father-in-law looked pointedly at her wrapped in the coverlet, then at Roger, who was tying his cravat with shaking hands. "I fear that under the circumstances, it would be a quite easy and very rational assumption."

He was right, and Angel had to admit it. Her head drooped, and she fought back tears.

Wrexham asked Roger, "How did you come to be in this room?"

Angel handed the viscount the note as Roger explained, "I received that note from Angel, but she says it is not her handwriting."

Her father-in-law examined the note. "Did a blond woman deliver it to you?"

"Nay, it was a footman."

"Could you pick him out again?" Wrexham asked.

Roger nodded. "Aye, he had a nasty scar on his chin."

Angel gasped. "Was he short and stocky?"

"Aye, not at all the sort of fellow you would expect the

Kingsleys to hire as a footman," Roger said with distaste. "Did you notice him too?"

"He offered me a glass of punch, and after I drank it, I felt very strange—groggy and lethargic." It had left the same strange aftertaste in her mouth that Maude's elixir had, but this time Angel must have been given only enough to daze her.

"We must find the footman," Roger exclaimed, heading for the door.

"I suspect you are wasting your time," Wrexham warned, "but I will come with you. I want to get Angel's cloak for her. We must all act discreetly in the hope of averting a scandal."

It was ten minutes before Lord Wrexham returned, carrying Angel's midnight blue velvet cloak. Concealed beneath it were the clothes that the imposter had taken from Angel.

He handed them to her. "Unfortunately, your clothes were all we found. The footman and the blond woman have vanished. They no doubt left through the servants' entrance, which is where your clothes were discarded. I have asked Lady Brompton to come to you. You will leave with her, and she will take you to my house. You will stay with me tonight."

"But I must go home. I must make Lucian understand . . ."

"You will not succeed in doing that tonight. I have never seen such a look on a man's face as I saw on my son's when he came out of this room. He is a man ready to commit mayhem, if not murder. Lucian will not be reasoned with tonight. I know, for he has inherited my temper. You must let it cool first."

"I am certain that the Crowes are behind this trick. It is so very like what they did to Lucian and me at Fernhill." A small flame of hope flared with Angel. "Surely Lucian will be able to see that."

"I would not count on it," Wrexham said sadly. "You must admit it is a highly improbable story you tell, especially since Peck was nearly naked, too."

Angel turned as white as the linen on the bed. "Do you not believe me either, my lord?"

"I do, but I fear Lucian will not."

Despite her father-in-law's warning, Angel insisted that Selina take her home. When they reached it, Selina said anxiously, "Perhaps it would be better if I came in with you."

"No." Although Angel was more than a little nervous about facing her husband's rage, she would not shrink from it. If she were to have any hope of recovering his trust—and the bliss they had shared the past week—she had to make him understand and accept the truth.

It would not be easy, though.

"I will at least accompany you to the door," Selina said, getting out of the coach after her.

As they reached the door, it opened a scant six inches, then stopped. Reeves faced her through the small opening. The usually emotionless butler looked as though he wanted to burst into tears.

"I am sorry, my lady, but Lord Vayle has ordered that the door be barred to you from now on. I am forbidden to allow you to enter." His voice caught. "Lord Vayle said to send a note to what address you wish your clothes sent."

Angel reeled back as though the butler had physically struck her. She had known Lucian would be in a fury at her, but it had never occurred to her that he would refuse even to see her.

He was rejecting her even more cruelly than his father had rejected him all those years ago.

"Do not whatever you do, little love, betray my trust in you. I do not think I could bear it if you did."

"I am very, very sorry, my lady." Reeves paused, then added in a whisper. "If you will permit me to say so, perhaps it is for the best that you do not come in tonight. I am not certain that you would be safe. I have never seen his lordship in such a temper."

Selina tugged at her arm. "Come, Angel, Reeves is right."

Angel, feeling as though her heart had been ground into dust, let Selina lead her away.

How would Angel ever be able to convince her husband of the truth if he would not even see her?

Chapter 30

Lucian awoke with a muddled, throbbing head and automatically reached for Angel but she was not in the bed beside him.

Then his aching head remembered why she was not there.

And why she would never be there again.

How could he have been such a damned fool as to trust anyone with his heart again. Would he never learn?

He despised his treacherous, unfaithful wife.

He ached for her.

It had been three nights since he had discovered her and her lover, three nights since he had barred his door to her.

She had come home that first night. He had not thought that she would have the effrontery to do so, but he had taken the precaution of prohibiting her from entering his house. After she had been turned away, she had not come back again.

He had half expected her to return the next day with more honeyed lies about how that scene at the Kingsleys had not been what he thought.

As if it could have been anything else. His fury rose at the memory of Peck, half-naked, and Angel, her shift about her thighs and her breast bare, on that bed.

The lying, cuckolding witch!

He never wanted to see her again!

Where the hell was she now?

With her lover, of course, Lucian told himself furiously.

But why had she not sent for her clothes to be delivered there?

Because for what they were doing together, she needed no clothes.

The thought made him murderous.

He would kill them both.

He would not give Angel the satisfaction of knowing that he cared in the slightest.

Lucian opened his eyes. From the brightness of the light seeping through the curtains, he knew that it must be late in the morning.

He touched his throbbing temples gingerly. His head felt as though one of Dutch William's regiments was marching through it.

At first, Lucian had been consumed by rage and an overwhelming sense of betrayal, but by last night the loneliness of his house and his life without Angel had begun to set in.

Knowing that he could not sleep, he had sat up until dawn, drinking himself into a stupor, before he had finally stumbled to bed.

Lucian went to the washstand, poured cold water from the pitcher, and splashed it on his face. As he dried it, he glanced into the looking glass above the stand, and grimaced at the sorry reflection he saw there.

His jet hair was tangled and unkempt. His eyes were bloodshot, and a thick black stubble of whiskers darkened his face. He truly looked like his nickname this morning.

The door to his bedroom opened, and for an instant an irrational hope flared within him. Only Angel would dare enter his room without knocking first.

He turned eagerly. It was not his wife, however, but his father, carrying a large mug.

"What the devil are you doing here?" Lucian asked irritably. He ought to throw the interloper out, but his head ached too badly to attempt any exertion. He settled for glaring at him.

"You look like hell, Lucian." Wrexham thrust the mug at his son. "Here, drink this. It will make you feel better."

"I doubt it," Lucian said, looking dubiously at the brown liquid in the mug.

"Take my word for it, it will," his father said cheerfully. "Been there myself, my boy. Now, drink it down."

Lucian did and discovered the liquid did not taste quite as bad as it looked. He closed his eyes wearily and was suddenly ambushed by a long-suppressed memory of a day when he had been eight years old. He had sneaked out and tried to ride a half-wild stallion that had thrown him hard, knocking him unconscious.

When he had come to, his father had been kneeling over him, carefully examining him for broken bones. It had taken a moment for Lucian's eyes to focus. When they had, his breath had caught at the relief and love on his father's face as he saw that his son had regained consciousness.

His father had picked him up gently and carried him into the house and up to his room, where he had sat beside him holding his hand. For the rest of the day, he had basked in his father's concern and full attention. Even though he had felt as though he had been pounded all over with a sledgehammer, it had been one of the happiest days of his childhood.

"You will be feeling more the thing shortly," Wrexham said. "I suggest you make yourself presentable so you can come with me and apologize to your wife."

Lucian stared at his father. "God's oath, are you out of your mind? I apologize? For what? Interrupting her while she was going to bed with her lover? Bloody hell, it is she who should be at my feet, begging my forgiveness. Not that I would ever forgive her."

"Don't be a damned fool, Lucian. You are behaving exactly as the Crowes want you to."

"What the hell are you talking about?"

"That incident at the Kingsleys was set up, just as surely as the scene at Fernhill in which you were found in bed with Angel. I think we can be quite certain that the Crowes were again responsible."

"You do not know what I saw."

"I know precisely what you saw. You are very much my son. Your reaction is identical to my own nearly thirty-one years ago when I discovered your mama in very similar circumstances with Geoffrey Ames."

"What?" Lucian exclaimed in outraged disbelief.

"It was the reason Ames left the country so hastily. When I told you why I had rejected you, I left out that part of the story because I thought no purpose would be served by telling you the sordid details. I did not want to chance you might think ill of your mother for she was blameless in that affair"—Wrexham's lips twisted in a bitter half smile—"nonaffair actually."

"Of course she was blameless," Lucian snapped. "My mother would never have—"

"Aye," his father said sharply, "she would not have, no more than Angel would have sought out Roger Peck."

Lucian absently ran his hands through his tangled hair. "Mother loved you. Everyone could see that she had eyes only for you."

"Everyone could see it but me. Just as everyone can see that Angel has eyes only for you. Once again, you are proving to me that you are my son by acting as foolishly as I did. Angel is no more deserving of your suspicion than your mama was of mine."

"How did my mother convince you that you were wrong."

"She could not, but I loved her so much. After a few days I came to realize how miserable and empty my life would be if I put her out of it."

As miserable as Lucian's would be if he did that to Angel. He ran his hand through his thick hair in frustration.

"In the end," Wrexham was saying, "I forgave her for myself, not for her. I vowed that I would accept her word for what had happened, and that the subject would never come up between us again."

"And?" Lucian asked tersely.

"And it did not for years." Wrexham's voice faltered. "But then as you grew up, you more and more resembled Ames, and I began to doubt. That doubt grew in me like a cancer. Sometimes, my son, I think that hell is of our own making."

He turned hastily away, and Lucian knew that he was

trying to control his tears. After a moment, he continued in a choked voice. "The worst of it is I was not the only one who suffered. So did your mama and, worst of all, you."

The aching in Lucian's head was subsiding. Wrexham's remedy clearly worked. "You seem not to have the slightest doubt now that my mother was blameless."

"If seeing your uncle had not been enough to convince me of that, Ames returned home two years after that. He had not long to live, and he told me he wanted to clear his conscience. He confessed to me that your mother would have nothing to do with him, but he was so obsessed with her that he had staged that scene with her for my benefit in the hope that I would be so enraged that I would cast her off. Then, he reasoned, because she would have nowhere else to go, she would give herself to him."

Lucian swore viciously. "You should have killed him!"

"I thought about it. He had cost me not only my happiness but the son I had been so proud of. By then, though, I was wiser. I realized that was exactly what he wanted me to do. He was suffering terribly, and he hoped that I would end it for him. I did not."

Wrexham fell silent, lost for the moment in a past he could not change. Then his eyes refocused on his son, and he asked briskly, "How did you happen to discover Angel in that bedroom at the Kingsleys'?"

"A footman told me she was there."

"A short, stocky fellow with a wicked scar on his chin?"

"Yes," Lucian admitted.

"Odd-looking sort for the Kingsleys to hire, don't you think?"

In fact, that was exactly what Lucian had thought when the man had come up to him. He frowned. "What are you saying?"

His father responded with another question. "Do you know your wife's handwriting?"

"Aye," Lucian replied, thinking of her untidy scrawl. It was as impetuous as she was.

"Then look at this." Wrexham thrust a sheet before him. "Is this it?"

Lucian glanced impatiently down at the neat, round letters that had clearly been formed with care. It bore no resemblance to Angel's hand.

"No," he said, then frowned as he began to read the words formed by those tidy letters and the signature.

His father explained, "This is the note that Angel allegedly sent Roger Peck, asking him to come to her in that bedroom. It was delivered to him by a footman with an ugly scar on his chin. Peck, too, wondered why the Kingsleys would employ such a rough-looking character as a footman." Wrexham paused. "I checked and, in fact, they have never employed such a man."

Lucian stared at his father skeptically, but within him, hope was bursting into pure, bright flame.

"It was that footman, by the way, who gave Angel a glass of punch that left her so lethargic and dull-witted that she did not question the woman who passed herself off as Lady Kingsley's sister. The woman 'accidentally' ripped Angel's gown half-off her, hurried her into that bedroom, and took her torn clothes, ostensibly to be repaired."

"Bloody hell!" Lucian exclaimed.

"Ah, yes, the scenario sounds familiar, does it not?"

"But if Angel is so innocent, why the hell has she not made any attempt to see me since the night it happened."

"Blame me for that. I counseled her to stay away until your temper cooled."

"I would not have hurt her," Lucian protested hoarsely.

"But neither would you have listened to her. You would have behaved as I behaved toward your poor mother, and it would only have exacerbated the tension between you and your wife. She is not the docile creature your mama was."

Lucian smiled wryly. His father was a wise man.

"I knew, too, that after a day or two your rage would recede, and the loneliness and the wanting would set in. Do not look so surprised, son. Remember, I have been there."

At last, Lucian could understand how his father had felt when he had been faced with strong evidence that his wife had been unfaithful to him. Lucian had reacted much the same way, and with perhaps less justification, for he had known that the Crowes would be eager to exact revenge after he had taken the Ashcott fortune away from them.

Lucian thought of how painful it must have been for his father to watch a son he loved growing up to resemble more and more the man he suspected of cuckolding him. After experiencing himself the jealousy and the terrible sense of betrayal and loss that had assailed him when he thought Angel had been unfaithful to him, Lucian could not say with certainty that he would have acted any differently than his father had.

Wrexham's mouth twisted in a grim, downward-slanting curve. "I beg you, son, not to make the same mistake with Angel that I made with your mama. Believe me, in the end, it will be you who will be hurt the most. I know because I have been there, too."

Lucian looked at the deep lines of sorrow etched in his father's face, and his heart went out to him for what he had suffered. It was clear he desperately wanted to prevent the son he loved from making the same mistake he had.

All the years of bafflement and anger, of bitterness and hatred toward his father dissolved in that moment of insight, and Lucian embraced the old man, hugging him to him.

And forgiving him at last.

Chapter 31

When Lucian noiselessly slipped into his father's drawing room, his wife was standing with her back to him, staring up at the portrait of him as a child.

"Angel," he said quietly.

She whirled around. Joy leapt in her eyes, replaced in an instant with wariness. She did not rush forward to greet him, but remained where she was, her usually expressive face cautious and unreadable.

Angel was not making it easy for him. He had hoped that she would throw herself into his arms the moment she saw him. As he crossed the room to her, he was uncertain of how best to proceed with her in her present mood. He tried teasing. "You hardly look the repentant wife."

Her eyes narrowed angrily. "I have nothing to be repentant about."

God's oath, but he was making a hash of it. "No, you do not, and I ask your pardon for thinking you did," he agreed gently. "But given the scene that met my eyes when I walked into that bedroom, should I not be forgiven for drawing the wrong conclusion?"

"Oh, Lucian," she cried in an agonized voice, "how could you possibly think that I would betray your trust like that after I swore to you that I would never do so? You have sorely impugned my honor."

He asked gravely, "Does this mean that you are going to challenge me to another duel?"

The thought clearly appealed to her.

It appealed to him, too, if only to see her charming derriere in those breeches. The thought had a pronounced effect on his own breeches.

"Perhaps I should, but you would win," Angel conceded. "You were right when you said that it is not at all a just way to settle one's disputes."

He smiled. "I will let you win this time."

"Why?"

"Because you are in the right. I should have known better than to doubt you."

He opened his arms to her. "Won't you come here, little love, where you belong."

With a strangled sob, she rushed into them, and he kissed her as though he might never have the chance again and must make the most of this one. His hands moved over her, soothing her, caressing her, molding her sweet body to his.

For a full minute, he reveled at having her safe in his arms again, but then a disquieting thought struck him. Would she ever be truly safe so long as the Crowes were free?

They had very nearly torn them apart three nights ago with one of their insidious schemes. They would concoct others.

Until they were imprisoned or, better yet, hanged for Ashcott's murder, they would remain a threat to him and his wife and to their happiness. Lucian held her more tightly to him as though to ward off the danger.

He lifted his mouth from hers and coaxed, "Come home with me. Let me show you how sorry I am that I doubted you."

He led her into the hall, his arm about her shoulders, holding her possessively.

His father was waiting there. He grinned broadly at them.

Lucian told him, "I am taking my wife home."

Wrexham nodded approvingly.

At the door, Lucian smiled at his father and said softly, *"Merci beaucoup, mon père."*

Angel waited until they were in the privacy of the coach before exclaiming in high excitement, "You have forgiven your father?"

"Aye."

She threw her arms around him, hugging him exuberantly.

When Angel entered the house on Lucian's arm, a spontaneous cheer went up from the inordinate number of servants who were gathered in the vicinity of the entrance.

She felt her face grow warm and rosy. Anxious about her husband's reaction to such impertinence, she cast a sidelong glance at him.

He grinned at her and whispered, "They are *almost* as happy to have you home as I am." Then he said quietly to Reeves, "See that we are not disturbed for the rest of the day. Not for *any* reason."

"Aye, my lord," the butler said with a twinkle in his eye.

Lucian led Angel directly upstairs to their bedchamber. The door had not shut behind them before he was hastily divesting her of her clothes.

Suddenly shy, Angel protested, "Everyone will know what we are doing."

"Aye." He gave her a wicked grin. "And only think how it will relieve their minds to have this added proof that all is now well between us."

As darkness enveloped the city, Angel lay happily in Lucian's arms. She had never seen him as he had been with her this afternoon, as playful as a young boy, full of glee and mischief and of new and inventive ways to pleasure her.

He nuzzled her temple. "Did you enjoy yourself, little love?"

"As if you need to ask!" She smiled and said dreamily, "Papa used to tell me to look to the stars and I would find my earthly due, but he was wrong. It is in your arms that—"

She felt her husband's body stiffen beside her. "What did your papa mean by finding your earthly due in the stars?" he asked in an urgent tone.

"I never thought much about it," she confessed, startled

by his reaction. "I assumed he meant that if I set lofty enough goals for myself, I would have a successful life."

"Bloody hell!" Lucian exclaimed, leaping out of bed.

"What is it?" she asked in bewilderment.

He grabbed her father's telescope from the table where she kept it and began examining it closely. It was a simple design: two veneer cylinders—the narrower partially enclosed in the wider—with a reflecting mirror at the base of the larger cylinder, and an eyepiece near the top of the smaller.

Lucian removed the metal clip and two pins that held a metal ring in place around the base of the outer cylinder. The mirror dropped into his hand, and he stared into the telescope's circular interior.

Peering over his shoulder, Angel could see there, carefully and neatly rolled around the wall of the smaller cylinder, a paper.

Lucian slid it out.

Angel stared at it, hope flowering within her. "Is it? Could it be?" she asked breathlessly.

Lucian grinned at her. "I will wager every pence I own that it is."

He carefully unfolded the document and read aloud, "The last will and testament of Hadrian Winter, the sixth Earl of Ashcott."

Lucian silently skimmed the rest of the short document, then grabbed Angel. He lifted her off the floor and whirled her around in sheer joy. "Belle Haven is indisputably yours now, my love!"

"I think you are as happy about it as I am," she observed.

"Aye, I am. I swore to you that you would get it back, and I was beginning to fear I would not be able to keep my vow. I could not have lived with that." He tenderly soothed back a lock of hair from her forehead. "My honor is as important to me as yours is to you. Besides I know that Belle Haven is the most important thing on earth to you."

She smiled. "Not quite. That was true when I met you,

but now I would trade Belle Haven and all the rest of my inheritance for you."

He groaned and hugged her to him, laying her head against his shoulder and stroking her hair gently. "Don't ever change your mind, little love. I thought that nothing could ever hurt me as much as when my father rejected me, but when I saw you in that bedroom with Peck . . ."

His voice failed him, but the pain in his silver eyes was so intense that it nearly brought tears to Angel's own eyes.

"You must have patience with me, and try to understand how hard it is for me to trust even you, little love."

In silent answer, she pulled his head down so that she could kiss him hard upon the mouth.

When the kiss ended, he lifted his head a little. "I do not think I would be responsible for my actions if I found my trust in you was misplaced."

Angel stroked his bronzed face lovingly. "I swear to you upon my honor that it never will be."

Lucian summoned Mr. Kennicott and gave him Lord Ashcott's will.

The solicitor examined it. "This is it, no doubt about it. Your wife's inheritance will be entirely hers without challenge now. This will end forever any claim by her mother or anyone else to a share of it."

Lucian wished that he could see Rupert Crowe's face when he heard the missing will had been found.

Kennicott asked, "Where did you find it?"

"In this." Lucian showed him the telescope.

Kennicott shook his head in amazement. "So that is why he wanted it short and written on the thinnest paper I could find."

After the solicitor's departure, Angel and Lucian did not go out and accepted no callers for three days. They wanted no company but their own.

They talked of many things. Now that Lucian had opened his heart to her, he opened his mind as well. Until Angel had come into his life, he had been absorbed in the injustice of the past instead of the promise of the future.

Now he looked forward to the life they would build and the children they would make together.

But one shadow darkened Lucian's happiness. So long as the Crowes were free, they were a threat to him and his wife.

On the fourth day, Lucian's father called and informed them that he was taking them to Sir Percival Mather's musical entertainment that night.

Lucian groaned. "Why the devil would you think I want to attend that?"

His father's eyes twinkled. "I know very well that you do not *want* to. It is necessary, however, that you and Angel appear there to prove that all is well between you. Lady Selina and I have been able to keep the talk down by putting it about that Angel was taken ill at the Kingsleys and that is why neither of you has been seen publicly. But the longer you go without being seen together, the louder the talk will get."

"You are right," Lucian agreed with a sigh. "We will see you tonight."

After Wrexham left, Angel told her husband, "I do not care to go to the musical either."

"You will care even less when we get there. The music is always good, but Sir Percival invites too many people for the size of the room, which is hot and stuffy. It faces on an overgrown jungle behind his house that he calls his garden. I suspect one would need a hatchet to chop his way through it."

And Angel suspected her husband of grossly exaggerating. "I believe you are trying to persuade me that we should stay home."

He sighed. "I wish we could, but my father is right."

Angel noted happily that Lucian now referred to Wrexham as his father.

That night as Lucian guided Angel downstairs to join his father who was waiting for them in the hall, the knocker banged.

Reeves opened the door, revealing Joseph Pardy standing there. Ignoring the butler, Pardy called to Lucian, "Must see you at once, m'lord. It cannot wait."

Lucian could think of only one reason for Pardy's insistence upon seeing him immediately. He had found Maude.

"This is urgent," Lucian said, turning to his father, "Will you take Angel to Sir Percival's? I will join you there as soon as I can."

"It would be better if you and Angel arrived together."

"I know, but I cannot help it."

Angel said, "I would rather remain here with you."

"No," Lucian said, "go with my father. I promise you that I will be no more than an hour behind you."

He turned to Reeves. "Order up my carriage and have it waiting for me."

Lucian escorted his wife and father to the door, then led Pardy into his library. "Have you located Maude?"

"Aye."

Lucian gestured for Pardy to take a seat, then took a large upholstered chair opposite him. "What were you able to learn from her?"

"She was an easy one to crack," Pardy said gleefully, displaying his crooked teeth, "thanks to Rupert Crowe—and me excellent timing."

Lucian frowned. "I don't understand."

"Crowe's wot finally led me to 'er. 'Ad 'er 'idden in a cottage at Blackheath. Paid 'er a visit there today, 'e did." Pardy grinned. "Nothing quiet about their meetin'. Maude likes to toss the crockery when she's angry, and 'er was in a rage today. Can't blame her. Seems Crowe 'ad come to bid 'er farewell. " 'Im and 'is son's leaving the country tonight—"

"Tonight?" Lucian exclaimed.

"Aye, but 'e'll not be taking 'is faithful Maude, and so 'e told 'er today. A right fierce row they 'ad. As a partin' gift to remember 'im by, Crowe blacked 'er eye. When I comes in a minute after 'e leaves, she's more 'an 'appy to tell me most everything."

"Including about Ashcott's murder?"

"She weren't so talkative 'bout that at first. 'Ad to twist 'er arm, so to speak, afore she'd sing on that one. The

Crowes murdered Ashcott just as you thought. Lured 'im to that isolated path with the fake note and clubbed 'im from behind."

"They'll hang for it," Lucian said with satisfaction.

"If they don't escape the country first. Got a vessel at Gravesend waiting to carry them cross the sea. *The Golden Goose,* 'tis called.

"Named after Crowe's wife, no doubt," Lucian said dryly. He was still puzzling over why the Crowes should suddenly be so anxious to flee the country. "Speaking of his wife, is he taking her with him, do you know?"

"Nay. 'E only married 'er for 'er late husband's fortune."

"What I do not understand is why she married him," Lucian said.

"According to Maude, when Lady Helen—that's the wife's name—came back to England after 'er lover died, no one would 'ave anything to do with 'er. Both 'er beauty and 'er money were gone, and she was desperate. Rupert befriended 'er, thinking there might be some gain in it for 'im. She boasted to 'im how when 'er husband died, she'd be rich because Ashcott's solicitor would do anything she wanted. That's when Rupert got the idea of killing Ashcott and marrying 'is widow."

"They deserve each other," Lucian muttered.

"Be that as it may, Rupert 'as no use for 'er now. Maude says 'e's kept 'er in a drugged stupor at 'is London house since 'e married 'er so she can't cause 'im no trouble."

"He is very good at drugging people," Lucian observed. "I want him stopped from leaving the country."

"Don't know, m'lord, if that's possible now. Likely as not 'e was agoing to Gravesend when 'e left Maude's. Wouldn't surprise me none if 'e slipped away already. Might be best if 'e 'as. Be no scandal that way."

Pardy had a point, and Lucian considered it for a moment. But his desire to see the Crowes pay for their murder of Angel's father overrode his desire to be rid of the matter. "No, I want him and his son brought to justice."

"Me'll see what can be done, but . . ." Pardy shrugged

his shoulders expressively. "Me'll need some lads. Even if me's luck's in and me finds them at the Black Knight Tavern, it'll take time to get to Gravesend. Methinks 'tis hopeless."

"Try!" Lucian ordered curtly. "I will drop you at the Black Knight on my way to join my wife."

Lucian would have preferred to go to Gravesend with Pardy, but he had promised his wife that he would join her at Mather's within the hour, and he intended to keep every promise he made her.

"There will be a handsome bonus for you if you succeed in capturing them," Lucian told Pardy.

But he knew that it was highly unlikely that he would be called upon to pay it.

The musical had not yet started when Angel arrived with her father-in-law, but most of the seats were already taken. The back row, however, was empty, and they sat there.

In the corner, an open door led out to the garden. Looking at it, Angel saw that Lucian had been right. It was an overgrown jungle, desperately in need of taming.

He had also been right about the room. It was already very hot and stuffy. Most of the women in the audience were making good use of their fans, and a number of people had drinks in their hands.

As she sat down, Wrexham whispered, "Let me see if I can find us something to drink."

A moment later, Angel saw Kitty, looking lovely as always in a turquoise brocade overgown and a white silk petticoat trimmed with Dresden lace, pass the door with her married half sister Anne. Anger rippled through Angel at the memory of the grief her last, unhappy meeting with Kitty had caused her.

The musicians had taken their places at the front of the room and begun tuning their instruments.

When the music started a few minutes later, Wrexham still had not returned. Angel looked around for him and saw that he had been waylaid just outside the door by an elderly gentleman in a flowing white wig.

As she looked away, she caught sight of Kitty crossing the rear of the room with a short, stocky footman in ill-fitting livery.

The servant, his back toward Angel, led Kitty through the door in the corner to the overgrown garden.

How odd, Angel thought. The garden was not lit, and it was clearly not intended for the guests' use. And something about the footman was vaguely familiar.

He guided Kitty down a narrow path. As she disappeared into the vegetation with the footman behind her, it dawned on Angel that he was the same size and build as the man who had caused so much trouble for her at the Kingsleys. Surely it could not be, could it?

A shiver of alarm and fear ran up Angel's spine. Was Kitty in danger? She remembered Horace's obsession with her. In her concern for Kitty's safety, Angel forgot the girl's cruel, malicious behavior at their last meeting.

If only Angel had seen the footman's face. Most likely he was not the man with the scar, but Angel had to find out. Impulsively, without any thought of the danger she might be placing herself in, Angel jumped up and slipped out of the door after the pair.

The garden was unlit except for the weak illumination coming through the windows of the house and the wan light of a sliver moon. Kitty and the footman had disappeared into the darkness that engulfed most of the garden.

Angel followed the same narrow, winding path that they had taken. The going was difficult in the dark for the way was winding and uneven.

With each step, Angel's concern for Kitty intensified. Finally, she called softly, "Kitty, Kitty."

Ahead of her, Angel heard what sounded like a smothered cry.

In the dark, she failed to see a thick root protruding into the path. She tripped over it and fell hard to the ground with a thud that sounded as loud as a cannon shot to her ears.

She heard a muffled exclamation ahead of her.

As Angel tried to scramble to her feet, a burly silhouette twice her size burst upon her, grabbing her roughly.

One arm went round her waist, pinning her arms helplessly to her sides while a ham-sized hand closed over her mouth, sealing off her scream.

Chapter 32

Angel struggled against her captor with all the strength she possessed, even though he was twice her size. Deprived of the use of both her arms and her voice, she had to settle for trying to squirm from his iron grasp and kicking him as hard as she could in the shins.

He grunted in pain but did not let her go. Instead, he yanked her off her feet. Careful to keep his hand over her mouth, he tucked her under his arm as though she were a parcel of negligible weight and carried her toward the back wall of the garden.

Angel tried to shove his hamlike hand away from her mouth and continued to kick at him furiously, but her efforts were of no avail.

Her captor suddenly hauled her upright. Another shadow, this one considerably shorter, stepped in front of her. From his stature, she suspected that it must be the fraudulent footman with the scarred chin.

The huge hand came away from her mouth. She got only the first half-note of a shriek out before the second shadow stuffed a loathsome rag into her mouth and tied it, silencing her again.

A second later, the big man released her so unexpectedly that she stumbled forward. Before she could recover her balance, a thick blanket of scratchy, stinking wool engulfed her.

Even though she knew it was hopeless, she fought against the confines of the blanket until a rope was tightened with cruel force around her waist, pinning her arms helplessly at her side. A second rope bound her ankles, effectively stifling her struggles. She was trapped in the smothering blanket, which smelled of horses, dirt, and sweat.

"This 'un's a 'ellcat," a man's gravelly voice observed.

"Too bad 'er didn't faint like the other one and make it easy," a second voice, also male but not as deep, observed.

" 'Ave to take this 'un with us, too," gravel voice muttered.

"The man won't like it, Sam," his companion warned nervously. "Ye know 'e won't."

"Can't leave 'er 'ere to spread the alarm," Sam answered tersely. "Get the other one in the carriage."

Grabbing the trussed-up Angel, he slung her over his shoulder as though she were a sack of flour. He moved briskly forward in an unrhythmic gait, and she bounced helplessly against his shoulder. The stench of the blanket made her want to gag.

Angel heard a soft grating like the sound of a gate opening. A horse neighed. She heard a soft thud ahead of her. A minute later she was tossed onto a hard surface that she gathered from its narrowness and height from the ground was the floor of a carriage. Her thigh landed on a pair of boots.

A minute later, the carriage rocked from the sudden addition of weight, and she felt a second, larger pair of boots—Sam's, no doubt—take their place by her own bound feet.

Angel longed to throw herself about on the floor and strike out at her captors, but she knew it would be a foolish waste of her strength. Better to save herself for a moment when she had a chance of succeeding.

The carriage door slammed shut, and wheels clattered against the cobbles as they rolled forward.

It was stifling inside the rough, reeking blanket. Between it and the gag in her mouth, Angel felt as though she had to battle for each breath she took.

The coach rattled along at a fast pace. When it careened around a corner, Angel's head slammed into the vehicle's door. She fought down her panic. She had to remain calm if she were to save Kitty and herself.

Surreptitiously, she tested the rope tied around the blanket at her ankles. It had no slack in it.

Angel heard a low, feminine moan from above her.

" 'Er comin' round?" Sam asked.

"Nay. Still out cold."

" 'Ope 'er stays that way."

It was some time—Angel could not guess how long—before the carriage rattled to a stop, and its door was flung open.

One of the men—Sam, Angel surmised from his size and strength—hauled her up, tossed her over his shoulder like a sack of turnips, and carried her from the coach.

She thought she heard the sound of the river, then the scrape of a door opening. She surmised she was being carried into a building. Then she was unceremoniously dumped on a hard floor. The man who had carried her propped her up in a corner, and left her, still gagged and bound in her blanket. His heavy tread receded, and she heard a key turning in a lock. As nearly as she could tell, she was alone.

Angel wondered in despair whether her abductors meant to leave her bound, gagged, and muffled in the scratchy, stinking, suffocating blanket all night—or longer. She fought down the panic that threatened to engulf her.

Several minutes later, the door squeaked open, and she heard two sets of footsteps coming toward her. They stopped in front of her, and someone fumbled with the rope around her feet.

A man growled, "Hurry up, you flea-brained whoreson. I want to see what you have snagged here."

Angel froze at the sound of the familiar voice. Surely it could not be. "Please God, not him," she prayed, but even as she offered it up, she knew that this plea was in vain.

"Damn you, Sam, you should have left her in the garden."

"Couldn't," Sam protested as he pulled away the rope that bound her feet. "If 'er was found, 'er woulda giv' alarm."

"I hope for your sake as well as mine that she proves to be a lush beauty who will be worth the trouble she is causing me."

Angel felt the rope around her arms and waist loosen

and drop away. The foul blanket was yanked off her. Its smell was replaced by one almost as unpleasant, a fetid odor of mildew, refuse, and rotting fish.

In the meager illumination of a rushlight, Angel looked up at Sir Rupert Crowe's hard, dissipated face, glowering above her.

Her stepfather's mouth parted in surprise as he recognized her. Then he threw back his head and emitted an exultant burst of laughter.

Sam was still hovering over Angel, but his small, close-set eyes were watching Crowe uneasily. Perceiving that his employer was pleased by the identity of his captive, he visibly relaxed, and his mouth twisted in an ugly grin that revealed a jumble of crooked, yellow teeth.

Angel grabbed at the filthy rag tied around her mouth and began unknotting it.

Sam seized her wrists to stop her.

"Let her go," Crowe ordered. "She can scream her lungs out here, and it will do her no good. There is no one about who would care." He nodded at Sam. "Wait for me outside the door."

The burly giant let go of Angel and obediently withdrew.

She finished unknotting the horrid rag and yanked it from her mouth. Then she put her hands on the floor, touching damp, rough stone, and pushed herself up into a more comfortable sitting position in the corner.

Angel was in a small room with a cot along one of the high walls that were of the same gray stone as the floor. The only other furnishings were a small wooden table and stool in the middle of the room.

The sole window was set high in the wall, at least eight feet up, and was no more than a foot square. It was so small that Angel could not wiggle through it, even if she could reach it. Oiled paper rather than glass covered it.

She suspected that she was in a watchman's room in one of those grimy warehouses on the docks of the Thames.

Crowe was eyeing Angel with such a mixture of triumph, enmity, and malevolence that she shivered despite herself.

"You cannot know how much I wished that you as well as Kitty could accompany Horace and me on our little voyage that your husband's persecution is forcing us to undertake." Rupert smirked and gave her an ironic little bow. "How very kind of you to accommodate me like this."

Angel managed to keep her countenance impassive. She would not let Crowe know how much his words frightened her.

"Voyage to where?" she inquired with feigned nonchalance.

"The Americas," he answered vaguely.

It was all Angel could do to keep from gasping aloud in dismay. When Crowe had mentioned a voyage, she had thought they must be going to the Continent. She would never have dreamed that they intended to sail for the wild lands on the other side of the ocean.

His smirk widened. "Once we are at sea, you may stand witness to the marriage of Horace to Kitty."

"She despises him," Angel cried. "She will not have him."

"Her feelings are of no interest to me. Horace wants her as his wife, and he will have her. She was a fool to think she could escape him."

"She will fight him."

He gave Angel a smile so cruel that it seemed to freeze her blood. "I hope so. It will make it all the more exciting for him. And she'll come round quick enough. His whip will see to that."

Angel felt sick. She could not let this happen to Kitty.

"What of me? Why would you want to take me to the Americas with you?"

"I don't."

Angel frowned, "But you said—"

"I said that I wanted you to sail with us for the Americas. I did not say that you would arrive there. Once you have witnessed Kitty's marriage to my son, I fear that you shall be washed overboard in an unfortunate accident."

Angel was so shocked that she blurted out before she could stop her tongue, "You mean to murder me!"

He gave her a smile so awful in its baleful cruelty that she shivered.

"You meddling little bitch, you and that devil husband of yours managed to ruin all my plans. I assure you that nothing will give me greater pleasure than to feed you to the sharks."

It took every ounce of self-control that Angel possessed not to betray the terror that his threat generated in her, but she would not give him that satisfaction.

Instead she spit out defiantly, "I would prefer sharks to your company."

Anger glinted in his eyes, then he said mockingly, "You will not be so brave when the time comes."

Angel had to find a way for her and Kitty to escape, and she must do so before they were taken on Crowe's ship. Once they were aboard it, there would be no hope of rescue.

Behind Crowe, the battered door, black with age and grime, was open a crack. Angel thought of trying to catch him off guard and lunging for the door now while it was unlocked. But even if she succeeded in getting past him, Sam would be lurking beyond the door.

She glanced back at her stepfather, and alarm prickled along her spine her as she saw the evil glee on his face. He was hatching some new, despicable scheme. She was certain of it.

"I think," he said at last, "that it is time for Roger Peck to receive a message that will have him rushing immediately to Northumberland to see his father, who is unexpectedly dying."

Angel smothered a groan. Another forged note, but what was the point of sending Roger north?

"Then your husband will receive a note from Peck that he has eloped with you."

Angel bit her lips together to smother the moan that rose up in her. Wrexham had managed to persuade Lucian that she had been tricked into that apparently compromising situation at the Kingsleys. But if she and Roger were to disappear simultaneously and Lucian received a note that they had run off together, what would he think?

"Try to understand how hard it is for me to trust even you, little love."

Crowe rubbed his hands together in delight. "Ah, 'tis a beautiful scheme. When Vayle finds Peck, he will say he went to Northumberland to see his sick father—but Vayle, being as thorough as he is, will quickly ascertain that Lord Peck has never been ill. He will think that Peck has hidden you away. Likely as not, he will call Peck out. Young Roger will be no match for your husband with a sword. Vayle will kill him."

Angel's stomach was roiling. An innocent man would die, and Lucian would forever be convinced that she had deceived and cuckolded him.

He would never forgive her.

What was even more horrifying was that he would never have the opportunity to learn the truth. She would be dead, and there would be no one to tell him what had actually happened, no one to defend her to him.

Lucian would shut her out of his memory as he had shut her out of his house after the Kingsley incident.

Crowe gave an ugly little laugh. "Vayle will never guess that you made a fine meal for the sharks."

In the light of the flambeaux lighting the entrance to Sir Percival Mather's house, Lucian checked his gold watch to make certain that he had kept his promise to Angel. He had four more minutes before his hour would be up.

The swell of euphonious music greeted Lucian's ears as the butler opened the door to him.

Since the program was well under way, he was surprised to see David Inge standing in the hall.

As Lucian came up to him, he said, "You are even later than I am. I only just got here myself. The wheel on my chariot came off as I was pulling away from my rooms. Fortunately, no one, including me, was hurt, but I had to see that it was cleared away."

"How did you get here?" Lucian asked.

"Tried to find a hackney—not an easy thing to do at this

time of night. Had to walk five-sixths of the way. I was so desperate that when I passed Roger Peck's, I stopped in the hope he would give me a ride here. But as my luck would have it, he'd left no more than two or three minutes earlier for Northumberland. His butler said he had received word that his father is dying, and he set out immediately."

"This late and in the dark?" Lucian scowled. "He must be mad. Everyone knows how treacherous the roads north are."

"He is very devoted to his father."

Lucian headed toward the music room to find his wife and father. At the door, he noticed Wrexham, Selina, and their host, a nervous little man in a luxurious wig of flowing auburn curls, whispering at the back of the room.

Lucian's breath caught at the sight of his father's expression. He had seen that look on his father's face only one other time—the day his mother had died.

He hurried over to the trio. "What is it?" he demanded.

His father nodded toward the door into the garden. "Come outside with me."

As they crossed to the door, Lucian looked around for his wife but saw no sign of her. Alarm prickled along his spine. When they stepped outside, Selina and their host followed them. Mather shut the door quietly.

"Where is Angel?" Lucian demanded.

His father shook his head helplessly. "She has vanished."

"*What?* Where? When?"

Wrexham said, "We took those empty chairs in the back row. I left Angel there while I went to get us something to drink. I was stopped by Lord Brixton. You know what a windbag he is. When I finally got back to our chairs with the drinks, the music had started, and Angel was gone. She was nowhere in the music room. When she did not come back after several minutes, I got Lady Selina to check the lady's retiring room, but she was not there either."

Their host, wringing his hands anxiously, said, "I saw Lady Vayle leave her chair and come out here. I confess I was surprised to see her walk toward the back of the garden as though she knew exactly where she was going."

Lucian gestured toward the tangled jungle behind them. "Back there?"

"Aye."

"But it is black as pitch," Lucian pointed out. "Why would she be going there?"

In the pale light falling through the door, Sir Percival flushed. "I . . . I thought she was meeting a gentleman. It is a perfect spot for a tryst."

Lucian thought of Peck's sudden trip north and an ugly suspicion gnawed at his mind.

Mather, misunderstanding Lucian's suddenly murderous look, nervously hastened to make bad worse by saying defensively. "You see I had heard rumors about Roger Peck and Lady . . ."

Selina cut him off. "I assure you such rumors are vicious, malicious lies. I am shocked, Sir Percival, that a man of your integrity would spread them about."

He started to protest, but Wrexham silenced him, saying, "The important thing is to find Lady Vayle. Bring us lanterns, and do it quietly. No point in disturbing the audience."

Sir Percival hurried back into the house. His other guests were listening raptly to the music, their backs to the scene in the garden.

Lucian did not wait for a lantern but plunged down a narrow path that wound through foliage as thick as some of the jungles in the New World were reputed to be. He followed it toward the back of the property and was soon swallowed in darkness as black as the bowels of hell.

He called Angel's name softly, but only the cry of a night bird answered him.

Finally, he turned back toward the house. By the time he reached Selina and his father, Mather had returned with two lanterns. He handed them to Wrexham and his son.

The two men, with Lucian in the lead, worked their way down the winding, overgrown path, pushing aside branches.

Wrexham tripped on a protruding root and cursed aloud. "I do not see how Angel could have made it down this path without a light."

Nor did Lucian, and he said bitterly, "Perhaps she had a guide."

He stopped abruptly as he spotted the crushed and broken vegetation just ahead of him. The damage was newly done. Lucian raised the lantern and examined the area carefully. He caught sight of a torn piece of turquoise brocade caught on the broken branch of a tree.

"What did you find," his father asked.

Lucian held up the torn fabric. His father looked stunned.

"Clearly, you remembered the same thing I did," Lucian said brusquely. The coat Roger Peck wore to the Kingsleys had been turquoise brocade. Angel had been wearing scarlet tonight.

The path took one more turn, and then Lucian found himself at an open gate to a narrow, unpaved street. There had been a shower earlier in the evening, and it was clear from the tracks through the mud and the fresh horse dung that a coach had been parked beside the gate recently.

A white hot wave of molten rage washed over Lucian.

Without a word, he turned and made his way back to the house. Both Selina and their host had disappeared inside.

As Lucian reentered the house, the musicians were still playing, and the engrossed audience was unaware of the small drama that had been played out in the garden.

David and Kitty's married half sister, Anne, were standing at the door of the music room, anxiously surveying the room. As Lucian passed by, David plucked at his arm. "We cannot find Kitty. Anne has not seen her for some time now, and she is very worried."

Lucian was too disturbed about Angel for his friend's words to register immediately. Just then, Selina rushed up to him.

"A messenger just delivered this for you, Lucian. He said it was urgent that you read it at once." Selina's face was frightened. "Do you think Angel could have been abducted by ruffians who are holding her for ransom."

Lucian broke the wax seal and hastily read the note's contents:

LORD VAYLE,

Your wife and I are wildly in love. We cannot bear to be apart any longer, and we have run away together. My servants believe that I am going to Northumberland to see my father but this was a lie to calm suspicions about my hasty trip.

By the time you read this, we shall be on our way to Dover, where we will board my yacht and sail out of England and your life forever.

ROGER PECK

Lucian, cursing viciously, dropped the note as though it had burned him.

Selina, seeing the terrible look on his face, snatched it up and gasped aloud as she read its contents.

Lucian turned toward the door. "Bloody hell, I will kill them both with my own hands."

As he ran out the door, he heard Selina cry, "David, Lord Wrexham, go after him. For the love of God, stop him."

Chapter 33

Angel, pacing the floor of her dank, gray prison, stiffened as she heard the metal bolt on the outside of her door being lifted. Had Rupert Crowe written yet another poisonous note that he had come to read her?

His first had been to Roger Peck, telling him that his father was dying in Northumberland and that he must go there at once. Rupert had labored much longer over his second note, directed to Lucian. When it was done, he had insisted upon reading it to Angel with great glee. She had been so infuriated at its contents that she had flown at Rupert, grabbing the paper from his hands and ripping it up.

He had struck her then so hard that she had staggered back and fell sprawled on the cot.

"Damn little bitch," he had snarled, gathering up the pieces of the note. "Now I will have to rewrite it."

By the time he finished it a second time, the messenger who had delivered his note to Roger Peck returned with word that Roger had taken the bait and rushed off to Northumberland.

"Wonderful," Rupert chortled. "Now, Abe, deliver this to Lord Vayle at the same house where you snatched the two women."

Once Lucian read that note, he would think what her evil stepfather intended him to think, and he would be devastated, believing that Angel had betrayed his trust and his love.

Her head drooped in despair.

The grimy, battered door of her cell creaked open on

rusty hinges. She lifted her head defiantly and braced herself for another confrontation with Rupert.

Instead, it was Sam, carrying an unconscious Kitty. He deposited her on the cot.

"What have you done to her?" Angel cried, hurrying to her.

"Nothing, damn it!" cried Horace Crowe, who had followed Sam into the room. "Every time I touch her, she faints."

The frustration in his voice was so intense that it almost made Angel smile. So Kitty had found a way to foil, at least for now, Horace's attentions to her. Angel would have tried to scratch his eyes out, but perhaps Kitty's method was more effective.

Horace stalked from the room, followed by Sam. Angel heard the metal bar on the outside of the door drop into place.

The turquoise satin bows had been torn from Kitty's eschelle, the ribbons holding the stomacher in place untied, and the fabric pushed down to expose her small breasts, firm and rosy-tipped. No wonder poor Kitty, timid and easily frightened, had fainted.

Angel hastily pulled the bodice together and retied the ribbons. She had nothing with which to revive Kitty so she settled for rubbing her icy hands and whispering her name softly.

When Kitty's eyes fluttered open and focused on Angel, she gave a small, relieved moan. "Thank God, it is you, and not that horrible . . ." Her voice failed her and she shuddered violently. "He is not here, is he?" she asked in alarm.

"We are alone for now."

Kitty looked around her. "Where are we?"

"Locked in a what I believe is a warehouse on the Thames."

"Are you the other woman they abducted? Rupert Crowe was very angry that they brought you, too. Why did they?"

"To prevent me from raising a hue and cry that you had been abducted, which was what I would have done."

"How did you know?"

"I was concerned when I saw you go into the garden with that footman. I followed you, thinking to help you if you needed it. Some help was I." Angel's voice was edged with scorn for herself.

"I heard you calling me, but when I tried to answer, that awful footman grabbed me and put his hand over my mouth."

"Why did you go with him into the garden?"

"He told me that David Inge was waiting there, that he wanted to talk to me."

Angel frowned. "Did it not seem strange to you that—"

"I know it should have, but I was so eager to see David that I did not think about anything else. I am astonished that you would try to help me after . . ."—Kitty's voice faltered—". . . after what I told you at the Stratford garden party. It was a dreadful thing for me to do. What I told you was not even true, although I believed that it was when I said it."

Kitty pushed herself into a sitting position on the cot. "You see, when David was trying to comfort me after that dreadful scene at Fernhill, he told me what Vayle had said." Kitty's mouth trembled. "When David learned from Vayle that I had told you, he was furious at me. He said that while Lucian might have felt that way about you that morning at Fernhill, he very soon changed his mind."

She looked at Angel almost in awe. "Indeed, David says that Vayle loves you. I cannot conceive of him loving anyone."

It had not been easy for him, Angel thought.

"David said that even if what I told you was the truth, which it was not, I should never have said anything to you. He said that it was a spiteful, mean thing to do. And he is right." Tears welled up in Kitty's eyes. "But I was so miserable and mortified over what happened at Fernhill and so jealous of you that I could not help myself. I am truly sorry. Please, forgive me."

Angel did not doubt that Kitty's remorse was genuine and deeply felt. This was the Kitty she had once known, the Kitty of her childhood, and she was delighted to have her back. "Of course I will forgive you."

"You are kinder than I deserve. I hurt you, but I hurt myself even worse. David is so angry at me over it that he no longer wants to marry me—not that Papa would ever let him." The tears were pouring down Kitty's cheeks now. "I did not realize how much I loved him until I lost him. When that awful footman told me tonight that David was waiting in the garden for me, I was so anxious to see him I never thought of anything else."

Kitty dissolved in tears. "Now I will never see David again!" she sobbed.

Angel held her and comforted her until her crying subsided. Then they sat quietly on the cot, clinging to each other.

Beyond the door, Rupert Crowe shouted an unintelligible command to one of his minions.

Kitty shuddered at the sound of his voice. "What does he plan to do with you now?"

"Feed me to the sharks?"

Kitty turned green and moaned.

"Do not worry—that is not to be your fate."

"What is?"

"He intends for you to marry Horace."

Kitty shuddered. "I want to die."

"Well, I want to live!" Angel was not going to quietly let Rupert Crowe make her shark bait. "We must find some way to get away before they take us aboard the ship."

"But how?" Kitty asked helplessly.

Angel wished she could answer. She would have to pick the moment carefully, for she was unlikely to get more than one chance to escape. "Our best hope is to catch our captors unawares as they transport us to the ship. Perhaps we can make a break for it as we are getting in or out of the coach, or failing that, jump out of it as it is moving."

"While it is moving," Kitty echoed in a faint, frightened voice. "We would be killed! I could not."

"You just said you wanted to die," Angel reminded her.

"But not that way."

Angel sighed. She could see that it would be up to her to save both of them. "I shall attempt something, and if I succeed, I will try to get help for you before the ship sails." They would have a better chance of one of them escaping if they both tried to get away simultaneously and ran in different directions, but she had no hope of persuading Kitty of that.

Nor would Angel herself, hampered by her full skirts, be able to run very fast. Looking down at her gown, she devoutly wished she had worn black or some other dull color tonight instead of bright scarlet that would make her easier to spot in the dark.

Angel jumped up from the cot and began shedding her long petticoats, one by one, until she was down to the skirt of her chemise, which reached only to her calf.

"Why are you undressing?" Kitty asked.

"So I can run faster. Now step on the train of my overgown with both your feet. Hurry."

Rising from the cot, Kitty did as she was bid. Angel thrust herself forward until she heard a very satisfying ripping sound.

"You have ruined your beautiful gown," Kitty wailed.

"That was my intent," Angel said, pulling the puffed and trained overskirt away from the bodice. Hastily, she rolled the torn scarlet skirt and her discarded petticoats into a tight ball. "I can run much more easily without these," she explained as she stuffed the skirts under the cot.

She picked up the smelly blanket in which she had been brought to this cell. Wrinkling her nose at its foul odor, she folded it in half so that she could wrap it around her quickly when she heard the bolt on the door lifting. She hoped that, wrapped in it, the men would not notice in the murky light that much of her clothing had disappeared.

"What if you do not succeed in getting help for me?" Kitty asked. "I cannot bear to be alone with Horace."

"Pretend to faint whenever he touches you," Angel advised. "It is your best defense."

"I do not have to pretend," Kitty said with revulsion. "I cannot bear his hands upon me."

Angel, who had never fainted in her life, begin to think that she had been wrong to hold this female weakness in contempt. She was discovering that it could be an effective weapon.

"I wish I were brave like you," Kitty said, sinking back on the cot. "I am so afraid." She was trembling uncontrollably now.

Angel sat down beside her and gathered the shaking girl to her, trying to comfort her.

After awhile Kitty's shivering subsided, and she said in a choked voice, "After the way I acted toward you, I am astonished that you tried to help me tonight. You have always been such a good friend to me. Vayle told me once that I was no friend of yours, and I am afraid he was right. I think I was always a little jealous of you."

"Dear heaven, why?" Angel could not conceive how a girl as lovely as Kitty could possibly be jealous of her.

"You were always so good at everything you did, and you were *Lady* Angela while I was plain Miss Kitty."

"Not plain at all," Angel said with an affectionate smile. "I was the one who was that."

"Perhaps, but you were always so vibrant with that wonderful smile that no one noticed."

The two girls clung to each other on the cot for a long time.

Then, through the closed door of their prison, Angel heard Abe, the messenger Rupert had sent with the forged note to Vayle, reporting back: "Me waited outside like you said, and 'e come flying outta the 'ouse, ashoutin' 'e'd kill 'em both. Looked like the devil 'imself, 'e did."

Angel felt as though her heart was sinking to the bottom of the Thames. Even now Lucian would be riding hellbent for Dover in a futile search for her and Roger Peck. Her husband would never believe that she had not deliberately betrayed and cuckolded him.

More time elapsed. Perhaps another hour. At last, she heard the bolt on the door lifting.

Angel jumped up from the cot. As the door swung open on its creaking hinges, she wrapped the blanket around her.

Rupert, Horace, Sam, and another man Angel had not seen before came into the room. The stranger and Sam each carried a large handkerchief and a length of rope.

"Abe, Sam, tie their hands and gag them," Rupert ordered.

Angel had not bargained on that. As the man named Abe reached for her hands, she hastily tucked the blanket under her elbows to hold it around her.

"Please," she said, making her teeth chatter as she spoke, "I am freezing. Let me keep the blanket."

Abe looked to Rupert for instructions. He shrugged, and she was allowed to have the blanket.

Abe fastened the handkerchief across her mouth first. As he knotted the rope around her wrists, Angel managed to keep the blanket about her with her elbows.

She had never tried to run with her hands tied. It would make it more difficult, but not impossible.

Abe tugged on the rope to lead her from the building. She followed him, desperately anchoring the blanket with her elbows.

As Angel stepped into the moonlight, she saw that she was on a wharf. The Thames, murky in the moonlight, swirled no more than a foot or two beneath its boards. She had been right about the building's location.

Instead of leading her to the coach as she had expected, Abe pulled her along the wharf to the edge, where two short burly men stood. Below them in the water, a wherry with two thickset men in it was tied to the pier.

Angel stared down in consternation at the long, light boat curved sharply at bow and stern. Clearly the sleek vessel had been designed for speed. It had not occurred to her that they would go to Gravesend by water instead of using the coach that had brought her here. How could she escape now?

She thought of trying to throw herself into the black water of the Thames. Thank God Papa had insisted upon teaching both her and Charlie to swim.

But how far would she get with her hands tied? Especially when Abe, who held the other end of the rope, kept her on such a tight leash. He allowed her so little slack that she could not raise her hands above her waist. If she tried to jump, he would merely yank her back, and she would have accomplished nothing except to alert them that she was capable of taking desperate risks to escape.

The brawny oarsmen seated on the wherry's two center thwarts slid to the far side of the boat. Sam scrambled awkwardly down into it, his weight causing it to rock wildly. One of the oarsmen muttered a curse.

When the wherry was stable once more, Sam helped Rupert into it. Crowe went forward, seating himself in the narrow bow.

Kitty, her eyes huge with terror above her gag, balked at going aboard the boat. One of the men on the dock unceremoniously lifted her off her feet and handed her down to Sam, who dumped her on the thwart behind Sir Rupert. Horace jumped down after her, settling beside her. Kitty instinctively shrank as far away from him as the narrow confines of the boat would allow.

Angel, knowing any resistance from her would be met in the same way Kitty's had, allowed herself to be handed aboard. She was seated aft of the center thwarts. Sam retreated to the narrow stern while Abe boarded. He sat next to Angel, still holding the rope that bound her hands so closely that she could not raise them more than a few inches.

The oarsmen on the pier were the last to get in the wherry, joining their companions on the two center thwarts. Each of the four seized an oar and began to row in rhythmic unison. From the impressive size of their arms and shoulders, they had had much practice in their work.

The boat glided toward the center of the channel, where the current ran swifter.

Angel looked up at the sky. From the position of the moon, she knew that it was past midnight. During the day, the river was a teeming highway full of boats and barges, wherries and lighters, ferrying people and cargo, but now it was quiet. Rupert must have been waiting until no one was about to observe his voyage down river and departure from Gravesend.

They had reached the faster current now, and the

wherry, moving with it and propelled by the oars, fairly flew over the water. It was not long before the lights of London along the shore began to recede.

Horace pulled Kitty roughly to him and began to fondle her.

She promptly fainted—whether in pretense or for real Angel could not tell. She instinctively leaned forward to help Kitty but the rope tether that Abe held jerked her up short.

Horace's father growled at him, "Leave the chit alone until you have her aboard *The Golden Goose*. Then you can rut the rest of the night away on her."

Horace apparently took this order to leave Kitty alone most seriously, for he made no effort to revive her.

Neither did Rupert, but he kept a watchful eye on his captives even though they were both tied and gagged and one was unconscious.

Angel shuddered in sympathy for poor Kitty. Being fed to the sharks might be an easier fate than being forced to spend the rest of one's life with her horrid stepbrother.

At least two minutes went by before Kitty revived, and Angel decided the faint had been a real one.

As the wherry sped over the water, Angel wondered where Lucian was. On the road to Dover, no doubt, with murder in his mind and undying hatred of her in his heart. He would go all the way to Dover in search of his quarry, thinking it had somehow eluded him on the road.

And what of poor Roger, rushing to Northumberland in the false belief that his beloved father was dying.

When he returned to London, he would be confronted by her husband at his most deadly, accusing him of running off with her. Lucian would never believe Roger's protestations of innocence.

Angel had no doubt that the drama would play itself out exactly as her stepfather had intended, with Lucian calling Roger out and killing him.

"I do not think I would be responsible for my actions if I found my trust in you was misplaced."

Her husband would curse her and her memory all the rest of his days.

The night had grown damp and cloudy. It was so cold now that Angel was glad to have the blanket around her for warmth. No one spoke, and the only sounds were the rush of the current and the slap of the oars hitting with metrical precision as the wherry carried her farther and farther from all that she loved.

More lights came into view along the shore ahead of them, but as they drew closer tendrils of fog drifted low across the water, obscuring them.

Then a large ship, partially hidden by the mist, suddenly loomed a hundred yards beyond them.

Rupert said, "There's *The Golden Goose*, dead ahead of us."

The oarsmen skillfully maneuvered the wherry alongside the ship.

Rupert shouted up, "Jake, drop the ladder to us. As soon as we are aboard, weigh anchor and unfurl the sails."

"Aye, aye," came a guttural response from high above them.

A moment later, a rope ladder was flung down from the ship's deck, dancing tantalizingly just beyond the reach of the wherry's occupants as it bobbed about in the water. Finally, one of the forward oarsmen managed to grab the ladder and used it to keep the small, light boat at the side of the ship.

Kitty's eyes bulged with terror at the sight of the flimsy, swaying ladder and the gunwale so far above. She slumped forward in a faint.

Sam swore. So did Rupert. Then he called up to the ship. "Quick, Jake, drop us a cargo net. We have a piece or two of troublesome baggage we need hauled up."

As they waited for the net, the fog, hanging low on the water, increased in density until Sir Rupert, only a few feet away in the bow, became no more than a vague shadow to Angel.

Finally, the net was lowered. The two forward oarsmen placed the unconscious Kitty in it. Abe was so engrossed in watching this operation that his grip on Angel's rope tether unconsciously loosened.

Rupert gave a shout, and the net began its slow ascent

with its human cargo. It disappeared almost immediately in the fog.

One of the oarsmen turned and jabbed a finger toward Angel. "Wot about 'er? Wanta lower it ag'in for 'er?"

Seeing one final possibility of escape, she jerked her bound hands up and pulled the gag away from her mouth before Abe could stop her.

"I prefer to climb the ladder," she said regally. "Untie my hands, and I will do so."

" 'Twill be easier," Abe told her stepfather, who acquiesced.

Hers was a truly insane scheme, but it was her only hope. She would climb part way up the ladder, then jump from it into the water. Angel ran the risk of hitting the wherry instead, but she had noted how its stern was turned at an angle from the ship. If she jumped in that direction, she just might make it.

The fog was so thick now that she could barely see the waves lapping at the boat. She counted on it to hide her from the men in the boat after she jumped.

Instead of taking the time to untie the knots that bound Angel's wrists, Abe whipped out his dagger and sliced through the rope.

"She will go up first," Rupert instructed. "I will follow. Then Horace will come last. As soon as he starts up, the rest of you head back for land."

One of the oarsmen helped Angel to the ladder. Horace was only a couple of feet from her, and he was staring up at it in terror. For a moment, she wondered whether he would join Kitty in a dead faint.

Angel let her protective blanket drop as the oarsman lifted her on to the wherry's gunwale. She grabbed the ladder's rope sides and clung to them as the wherry bobbed up and down beneath her. The hemp cut cruelly into her hands as she struggled to retain her balance while trying vainly to place a foot on the lowest of the dancing wooden rungs.

A guttural voice from above called loudly, " 'Urry, damn ye 'ides. Ain't got all night!"

The oarsman planted her foot on the rung, and she began her dizzying climb up the swaying ropes.

She tried not to think about how far away land was.

It would be a long, cold—perhaps hopeless—swim.

But it was her only chance.

Chapter 34

The ghostly fog enveloped Angel like a suffocating gray cloak. The wherry and the rest of the world around her had vanished into it as though they no longer existed.

It took every inch of willpower she possessed to force herself to continue upward through the cloying cloud.

Suddenly, when she was about twenty feet above the water, she climbed out of the dense murk into a night that was bright with stars and moon. She was so astonished by this sudden change that for a moment she could only pause and stare.

A few light fingers of mist still drifted around her, but above her the air was clear. When she looked down, however, the water and the wherry were hidden by a blanket of thick, fluffy cotton.

Glancing toward land, she saw far in the distance a few blurry lights. Her heart fell at the distance. Could she possibly make it?

Angel looked up toward the ship's deck, and a shiver of fear went through her at the sight of a muscular giant of a man, dressed all in black, leaning over the gunwale, watching her. His face was shadowed by a hat pulled low on his forehead, but she saw that a black eye patch covered his left eye.

One-eyed Jake, Angel thought as she forced herself to resume climbing toward him.

With his swarthy complexion and hair as black as his eye patch, he looked the perfect pirate. He wore no coat and his shirt was half-unbuttoned. Angel could see swirls of ebony hair curling on his broad chest.

She was nearing the deck. If she were going to jump, it would have to be now.

She looked down but could see nothing except the fog, and she froze at how far beneath her even that seemed.

With the wherry on the water below her, she would not be able to drop straight down but would have to swing to the side from the ladder and push herself toward its stern as she let go.

Angel's courage failed her.

She was paralyzed, unable to force herself to open her hand, let go of the rope, and drop into that gray miasma beneath her.

She tried to tell herself that the fog was her friend. It would keep the men in the boat from seeing her in the water.

But it also prevented her from seeing the stern of the wherry below. What if it had swung back toward the ship again, and she hit the boat instead of the water?

You must do it, she told herself.

Stepping aboard *The Golden Goose* would sign her death warrant. At least if she jumped now, she would have a slim chance of surviving.

And there were no sharks in the Thames.

She had to do it.

Still she could not.

Then she thought of Lucian. She could not stand to think of him spending the rest of his life despising her. If she survived, she might be able to convince him that she had not betrayed his trust. That remote possibility fired her determination and her courage. She had to try.

Angel grasped the right side of the ladder with both her hands. As she slipped her feet from the rung, her left hand released its grip, and she twisted her body sideways away from the ladder in the direction of the wherry's stern. For a moment, she was hanging only by her right hand.

As she forced herself to open her fist and drop into the fog beneath, her wrist was clamped in an iron grip. Instead of falling, she was dangling by her arm over the water.

Her head snapped up in shock. The big, one-eyed pirate,

apparently divining her intentions, had leaned far down over the gunwale and grabbed her wrist in his powerful fist.

Slowly, inexorably he hauled her up as though he were reeling in a troublesome fish he had hooked. Dear heaven, the brute was strong as a team of oxen.

The pirate pulled Angel none too gently over the gunwale. Then, to her shock, he crushed her so hard against his iron body that she could scarcely breathe.

She lifted her face to look at his. His uncovered silver eye gleamed at her from beneath a black, flaring brow. His head dipped, and he kissed her as she had never thought she would be kissed again.

Kissed her as only her husband could.

When he set her back on her feet and released her, he tossed the pirate hat aside and ripped off the eye patch, revealing a second gleaming silver eye framed by jet lashes.

Angel was speechless with joyous shock, unable to comprehend how Lucian could possibly be here.

"Did the bastards hurt you, little love?"

Her husband's endearment brought tears to her eyes. She had thought that he would hate her. She shook her head negatively, still too stunned to speak.

A feminine moan from a nearby bench drew her attention. It was Kitty coming out of her faint.

Angel would have gone to her had she not recognized that the shadowy figure hovering over her friend was David Inge. Kitty's eyes fluttered, opened, and focused on David.

She promptly fainted again.

David swept her up in his arms and carried her toward a nearby companionway.

Looking about, Angel saw several other men in the shadows.

"What the hell!" Sir Rupert exclaimed as he climbed over the gunwale onto the deck.

Angel had been so flabbergasted at the sight of her husband she had forgotten that her stepfather would be coming up the rope after her.

Crowe's face contorted in hatred and rage at the sight of his enemy. His sword was out of its scabbard in a flash.

Lucian thrust Angel away from him into another pair of arms. "Guard her for me," he ordered, drawing his own sword.

The arms tugged Angel back. Looking up, she saw that they belonged to the man who had come to see her husband as they were leaving for Mather's.

"Joseph Pardy at your service, m'lady."

His words were nearly lost in the clang of steel against steel as Lucian's and Rupert's swords engaged.

Their loathing for each other was clear on their faces. They began with a flurry of thrusts, parries, and feints as each man seemed bent on annihilating the other.

They were both big men, and strong. Angel's arm ached in sympathy at the force with which, time after time, blade met blade.

She belatedly appreciated that had Lucian unleashed his full strength against her that day at Fernhill, he would have defeated her in a moment.

Angel was surprised and dismayed at how quick on his feet her stepfather was. And how cunning his hand. He was well-trained, too. There did not appear to be a move that he did not know how to counter.

Lucian fought with more dash and daring than Rupert, taking risks that made Angel cringe.

The battle raged back and forth across the deck, and neither man was able to drive home his advantage. The other men Angel had noticed earlier watched the fight silently from the shadows, taking care to stay out of the opponents' way.

Lucian's sudden feint followed by a thrust at Rupert's chest took the older man by surprise. Parrying weakly, Crowe caught the forte of Lucian's blade against the foible of his own, which nearly spun from his hand. As he attempted to recover, Lucian pressed his attack.

Rupert, retreating before Lucian's offensive, was backing directly toward Angel. She moved quickly sideways toward a large winch to get out of the men's path and give them more room.

Her foot became entangled in something on the deck. She tripped and might have fallen had not Joseph Pardy caught and steadied her. Looking down, she saw the offending object was a sword that had slid against the winch and now lay wedged there, abandoned and forgotten. Her foot had caught in its hilt.

Pardy smiled grimly. "The weapon of m'lord's last opponent," he explained. "May he dispatch this one as successfully."

So Rupert was not the first man her husband had dueled this night. She offered up a prayer of thanks that Lucian had won. "To whom did the sword belong?" she inquired.

"One-eyed Jake." Pardy grinned broadly. "Put an end to the miserable cur's pirate career, 'e did."

Angel stifled a cry of alarm as Lucian slipped and nearly lost his balance. As he fought to recover it, Rupert instantly seized this opportunity. He dived forward, aiming his sword at Lucian's heart.

Angel thought that her husband was a dead man, but somehow he managed to deflect the blade slightly with his own.

The steel penetrated the side of Lucian's shirt, and blood blossomed around the hole.

Angel felt as though the sword had gone through her own heart.

"A mere scratch," Lucian scoffed, and she dared to breath again.

Rupert growled. "Damn you, you have the devil's own luck!"

"I make my own luck," Lucian snapped, taking the offensive again with a thrust below the heart that had Rupert leaping sideways.

There was another spate of feints, thrusts, and parries as the two men tacked across the deck.

Out of the corner of her eye, Angel, still standing by the winch, caught sight of a figure hunched in the shadow of the gunwale. It was Horace.

She had forgotten about him, and she had been so absorbed in the duel between his father and her husband that she had not noticed him come aboard. She wondered how long he had been crouching there unobserved. His devious, calculating expression as he watched his father and Lucian fight sent a shiver of fear through Angel.

Suddenly, with a determined gleam in his eye, he pulled his own sword. Glancing in the direction that he was staring, Angel saw her husband's back, broad and unprotected.

With a smothered cry, she bent down and grabbed the sword still lodged against the winch. She ran at Horace as he moved toward Lucian's back, his sword raised.

Angel leapt forward. With all her strength, she brought her own weapon down on Horace's blade as he was about to plunge it into her unsuspecting husband.

The point missed Lucian's back by no more than an inch, but it missed.

He was concentrating so intently on his duel with Rupert that he was unaware of what had happened behind him. Lucian suddenly lunged forward, driving Rupert back across the deck.

"On guard, you little worm," Angel cried at Horace, incensed by his sneak attack on her husband.

Horace looked incredulous. "You cannot mean—"

"Fight or die!"

He decided to fight.

Angel thrust at his belly, he parried, and she counterparried, then riposted.

Horace had neither his father's ability nor training with a sword. He was no match for his stepsister, and she ended it quickly with a shrewd blow that sent his sword spinning from his hand.

Disarmed and panicked, he backed frantically away from her and fell over the winch behind him, landing on his back amid the rigging.

The point of Angel's sword was instantly at his throat, lest he try to get up.

"Don't kill me," he pleaded in terror.

Joseph Pardy came up beside her, a new respect for her

shining in his eyes. "Me'll tie 'im up, m'lady, and put 'im with the other flotsam."

She nodded and turned to see how her husband was faring.

Rupert was panting hard now. It was clear he was spent, and the end was near.

Apparently recognizing that himself, he made a wild, desperate lunge that nearly slipped below his opponent's guard, but Lucian quickly parried, then followed with a lightning riposte in quinte that caught her stepfather completely off guard.

Lucian's sword plunged deep into Rupert's shoulder.

As the earl withdrew his blade, blood spurted from Crowe's wound. He swayed, his expression one of dazed disbelief; then he crumpled to the deck.

Lucian pulled out a handkerchief, cleaned the blood from his sword, and started to sheathe it.

"Damn you, don't do that," Crowe growled. "Finish what you have started."

"Nay," Lucian said bluntly, "I prefer to see you hang."

"Hang! I have committed no crime."

Lucian laughed aloud at this protestation. "To the contrary, there are damned few you have not committed, including murder. You know what I am talking about."

From the shock in Crowe's eyes, he did.

"Don't bother to try to deny it. Maude has told us all we need to know."

Rupert's already white face turned ashen.

"Bind his wound and take good care of him," Lucian instructed Joseph Pardy and the other men who had gathered round. "He will not cheat the gallows if I can help it."

Lucian returned his sword to its scabbard.

Angel ran up to him. "You are wounded." She pointed in concern to the blood on the side of his shirt.

"A mere scratch."

She did not try to hide her skepticism.

He smiled. "Come with me to the captain's cabin and you can minister to me." He took her hand and led her down the companionway that she had seen David use earlier.

Below deck, they made their way down a narrow passageway. Soft sobbing could be heard through an open door. Angel stopped and peered inside.

David was sitting on a bunk in the small cabin holding Kitty, who was weeping in his arms.

"Don't cry, my sweet," he murmured reassuringly. "You are safe now."

"I cannot believe it is you," she cried. "Oh, David, I was so afraid that I would never see you again. It made me realize how much I love you. Tell me that you still love me, too."

"I do," he said softly.

Kitty gave a little sob, and hugged him to her.

Then she said with more determination in her voice than Angel had ever heard before, "I do not care what my father says, David. I am going to marry you if you will still have me."

Lucian tugged on Angel's hand and guided her down the passageway. "Let us give the lovebirds a little privacy."

"I hope Bloomfield gives his permission for Kitty and David to marry."

"If he does not, Kitty, her mother, and I will convince him." Lucian turned and drew his wife into the circle of his arms. Burying his face in her hair, he whispered, "Thank God, little love, you are not given to fainting and hysterics like Kitty. Though at times, I wish you were not quite so brave. God's oath, I aged at least a decade when I realized you intended to jump into the water." His arms tightened around her. "I was terrified that I would not be able to reach you."

"Thank God, you could, although that was not my sentiment when you grabbed my wrist. I thought you were One-eyed Jake."

He grinned at her. "He and I are much alike in coloring and build, which was fortunate, for his clothes fit me very well. I did not want Rupert to suspect he was climbing into a trap." Lucian held her a little away from him and frowned. "Speaking of clothes, love, your skirts seem to be missing."

"Oh-h-h," she gasped, feeling hot color flooding her cheeks. "I had to get rid of them so they would not hamper me when I tried to escape. To hide that they were missing, I kept myself wrapped in a blanket until I began climbing the ladder."

"My clever wife," Lucian said with a chuckle. "Let me see if I can find you something to wear."

He escorted Angel into the great cabin. She stared in surprise at its luxurious appointments including a gilt-framed looking glass attached to the bulkhead and an oversized bunk covered with a fur rug. A coat that Angel recognized as one of Lucian's had been tossed carelessly onto the bunk.

He went over to a cupboard built into the bulkhead. As he opened it, Angel tugged his shirt from his breeches, saying, "First, I must check your wound."

"I was hoping it was something else you were after," he complained with a wickedly seductive smile that turned her bones to water. "My wound is nothing, I assure you. It was another kind of ministration I had in mind when I brought you down here."

"After I examine your wound," she said stubbornly.

With a sigh, he pulled up his shirt to reveal that his assessment of it was right. It was no more than a very deep scratch across his side that had already stopped bleeding.

Looking up from it, Angel gasped as she noticed for the first time the array of women's gowns in satins, brocades, and velvets in the open cupboard behind her husband. "What did One-eyed Jake want with those?"

"Nothing. This cabin was to be Horace's honeymoon chamber with Kitty. He intended to dress her in style."

Angel shuddered at what this night would have held for both her and Kitty had Lucian not come. She wrapped her arms around him.

"How is it that you are here?" she asked. "I thought you were riding to Dover intent on murdering poor Roger and me. The messenger who delivered Rupert's forged note said you ran from Sir Percival's house, shouting that you intended to kill us both."

"He misunderstood. The pair I intended to kill was Rupert and Horace. Rupert outsmarted himself with that note. I knew as soon as I saw it that he had written it, and it confirmed my suspicions that he and Horace were responsible for you and Kitty vanishing."

"Why did you suspect them?"

"Pardy told me that the Crowes were fleeing England on *The Golden Goose* this very night. I could not understand why they were in such a hurry to get away until you and Kitty disappeared. Then it made sense. I knew how determined Horace was to have Kitty and that both Crowes were thirsting for revenge against me."

Lucian stroked Angel's hair lovingly. "I already had Pardy collecting men to try to stop the Crowes from sailing. David Inge and I linked up with them. Fortunately, Rupert planned to wait until the tide went out shortly before dawn. So the crew, including One-eyed Jake, went off to a Gravesend brothel to celebrate their last night on land. When we reached the ship, there were only two lookouts aboard, and they had been doing some celebrating of their own. We quickly disposed of them."

"But Pardy said that you dueled One-eyed Jake."

"Aye, when he and the others returned to the ship. They no more suspected a trap than Rupert did. Most of them surrendered without a fight, but not Jake."

"How could you know that Rupert wrote the note you received at Mather's?"

"Rupert did not realize I already had a sample of his handwriting."

Lucian went over to his coat lying on the bunk. From the inside pocket he extracted two folded sheets of paper and opened them, laying them side by side on the bunk. It was clear from the slanting hand and the curling flourishes of the letters that both had been written by the same hand.

Angel frowned as she began reading the second note: "Lord Ashcott: We have your precious Angel . . ."

Her head jerked up in shock. "Where did you get this?"

"I found it balled up under your father's desk the night we were married."

Angel stared at him in dawning, horrified comprehension. "That was the murder you accused Rupert of committing."

Lucian held her tightly to him. "You were quite right, little love, to be disturbed by what happened that day. I was certain that Maude was the woman who delivered the fatal note to your father. That is the reason I was searching for her. I wanted to see the Crowes hang for his murder. And now they will. Pardy found Maude, and her confession has sealed their fate."

"Why did you not tell me the truth?" Angel asked brokenly.

"Because I was afraid, my impetuous wife, that you would do something rash. It was another one of my attempts, misguided perhaps, to protect you."

As Angel grasped the awful enormity of what the Crowes had done, she began to sob. She could not help it. She wept for the tragedy and horrible waste of a man as brilliant and good as her father, cut down in mid-life by greedy, worthless scoundrels.

Lucian, still holding her to him, stroked her hair consolingly and murmured words of love and comfort.

When she regained control of herself, she looked up into his silver eyes. "I thought you would never hold me like this again. Even if I somehow managed to escape the Crowes, I feared I would never be able to convince you that I had not betrayed your trust.

Lucian said, "I did not for an instant think you had, little love. When I first heard that Roger had left London in a rush, I feared that he might have abducted you."

"You did not think that I had willingly run away with him?"

"I knew that you had not done that. You had sworn to me on your honor that you would never betray my trust, and I knew nothing on earth would make you do so."

His mouth descended on hers in a long, tender kiss, then he lifted his head and smiled down at her, his silver eyes filled with so much love that it took her breath away.

"It took me longer than it should have to do so, but I trust you, my dearest Angel, as much as I love you—absolutely and unconditionally."

Epilogue

The coach carrying Lucian's brother and his family had scarcely rolled to a stop in front of Belle Haven when Fritz jumped down and ran up the steps toward Angel and Lucian, who had come out on the portico to greet them.

Angel suspected that the short, round-faced Fritz, so unlike her husband, was a copy of his father when he was young.

Lucian held out his hands. "Welcome, big brother."

Fritz gripped Lucian's hands. "Bigger brother, I have prayed for this day for years." He grinned, but there was a sheen to his eyes. He let go of Lucian's hands, and the two men hugged fiercely.

Angel went down the stairs to greet Fritz's wife, Fanny, as she emerged from the coach. She was a pretty little blonde with soft hazel eyes. Angel suppressed a gasp of surprise as she saw how big with child her sister-in-law was.

After welcoming her warmly, Angel murmured, with a significant glance at her swollen body, "We did not know. How very brave of you to make the journey."

"I would not have missed this reunion for anything. My husband has yearned for it for years, and I want my children to know their uncle."

Fanny looked around at a boy of four and a girl of two, who were tumbling out of the coach. Both had pale blue eyes, round faces, and hair the color of ripe wheat. They rushed up the stairs to meet Lucian.

The boy did not wait for an introduction. Staring up at

his uncle in awe, he exclaimed, "You are even bigger than Papa said."

Lucian laughed and hoisted the boy up in his arms. When their eyes were level with each other's, he said, "Now you are as tall as I am, Freddie."

The little girl, who did not even reach Lucian's breeches, tugged frantically at his silk hose, crying, "Me, too! Me, too!"

He dropped down and picked her up in his other arm.

Reaching the portico with Fanny, Angel looked beyond her husband to his father, watching his sons and grandchildren from the door of Belle Haven. A lump rose in her throat at the joy in the old man's face.

Fritz embraced Angel. "How happy I am to meet the woman who has made our family whole again."

Angel's gaze returned to her husband. After King William had returned from Ireland, ending Lucian's duties with the Council of Nine, he had suggested inviting his family for this autumn holiday in the country. Angel had been surprised that Lucian wanted it at Belle Haven instead of his own estate, Ardmore.

"I prefer Belle Haven," he had confessed. "From the moment I saw it, I wanted it to be my home. And we will be going there anyway for David and Kitty's wedding."

Lucian, still carrying his niece and nephew in his arms, shepherded his family into Belle Haven. Angel looked with pride at her home. Lucian had spared no expense to obliterate the scars the Crowes had inflicted upon it.

Although as Angel's husband, he legally controlled all that she owned, he had insisted that Belle Haven was hers alone. Nothing was done on the estate until she was consulted and gave her approval. And it was not just Belle Haven that Lucian discussed with her. Their marriage was becoming the partnership that she had wanted.

The Crowes would never again disturb her and Lucian's happiness. They had been tried, convicted, and would soon be hanged for her father's murder.

After Rupert's arrest, Angel's mother had been found dead in his London town house from an overdose of laudanum that he was strongly suspected of having administered to her. But that could not be proved.

Later that afternoon, Fritz's children were put down for naps and their mama, who was feeling unwell after their journey, opted to take one too. Lucian asked his father, wife, and brother to go riding with him. Fritz, who was worried about his wife, elected to remain with her, but the other three rode out.

As they neared the top of a hill near Belle Haven's boundary, Lucian reined in his horse. "We will stop here."

As they dismounted, his father asked, "Why here?"

Smiling, Lucian took the older man's arm. "Because I have a present for you," he said as he guided Wrexham the final few steps to the crest of the hill.

Lucian held out a large ring of keys to him.

His puzzled father asked, "What are they for?"

"That," Lucian said with a sweep of his hand toward the house in the dale below them. "It is yours now."

Wrexham was clearly flabbergasted as he recognized his boyhood home. "Sommerstone," he whispered. "I never thought I would see this day. How did you manage it?"

"Lord Bloomfield was so grateful for Kitty's rescue from the Crowes that I persuaded him to sell it to me."

Wrexham smiled proudly up at his son.

"I am overjoyed to have the estate back in our family, and I thank you a thousand times over for it," he said in a quavering voice. "But you had already given me the gift that I craved above all else—your love and forgiveness."

That night after Lucian had made love to her with aching tenderness and soaring passion, Angel lay in his arms, remembering how enthusiastically he had played with his niece and nephew. He would be a good father.

She turned her head on the pillow and lightly stroked the strong line of his jaw with her fingertips.

"Lucian, I have a gift for you, although it will be a few months before I can actually present it to you."

He blinked uncomprehendingly at her, a sweep of jet lashes over silver, then his mouth curved up in a delighted smile.

"Are you telling me you are giving me a little angel?"

"Or perhaps a little devil," she said wryly.

Lucian hugged her to him, kissing her exuberantly. "How long?" he asked in a voice husky with emotion.

"Six months."

He touched her belly reverently. "You have already given me so much—my father and brother back, peace, love, happiness, now this."

"But I will never be the obedient wife you wanted."

"No, I thank God every day that a little hoyden flew into my life and promptly turned it and all my stupid notions about love and marriage and the kind of wife I wanted upside down."

His hand stroked the curve of her hip. "Your father was right as usual. Marriage should be based on mutual love and respect. That is what makes ours so satisfying."

She said softly, "I did not think I would ever be able to thaw your frozen heart."

Lucian grinned at her. "When an angel falls in love with a devil, nothing is impossible."